Rocks & Gravel

Peri Jean Mace Ghost Thrillers #3

Copyright © 2016 Catie Rhodes.

All rights reserved.

Published by: Long Roads and Dark Ends Press

This is a work of fiction. Names, characters, businesses, places, events, and incidents are either the products of the author's imagination or used in a fictitious manner. Any resemblance to actual persons, living or dead, or actual events is purely coincidental.

Cover artwork by Book Cover Corner Content Editing by Word Webber Press Copy Editing by The Independent Pen Proofreading by Julie Glover

First Printing, 2016

ISBN Ebook: 978-1-947462-06-9

ISBN Print: 978-1-947462-07-6

Rhodes, Catie.

Rocks & Gravel/ Catie Rhodes. — 1st ed.

Visit the author website: www.catierhodes.com

SERIES LIST

Forever Road (Book #1)

Black Opal (Book #2)

Rocks & Gravel (Book #3)

Rest Stop (Book #4)

Forbidden Highway (Book #5)

Rear View: Prequel (Book #6)

Crossroads (Book #7)

Dead End (Book #8)

Dark Traveler (Book #9)

Wrong Turn (Book #10)

Last Exit (Book #11)

ROCKS & GRAVEL

PERI JEAN MACE GHOST THRILLERS #3

CATIE RHODES

For Mamaw. Love you to the moon.

1

I RAN up the museum steps, breathing hard, sweat running down the back of my neck. The August humidity pushed at me like a wet, invisible wall. Every step was an effort. My heart pounded both from the strain on my cigarette-singed lungs and the shock of Hannah's phone call. *Get here, now. I need you.* I stopped to stare at the poster mounted in the museum's plate glass window. It featured a picture of a guy who could have been a movie star and read:

DEPUTY DEAN FOR SHERIFF
NEW BLOOD
NEW IDEAS
THE RIGHT MAN FOR THE JOB

I'd bet my last pair of clean undies this poster and the guy in the picture—who happened to be my boyfriend— were the problem. If someone in Hannah's family just saw it, they probably got all butt hurt she wasn't supporting her uncle, the incumbent sheriff. I took a deep breath and raised my hand to knock on the door. It swung open before my fist made contact.

"Peri Jean Mace, what are you doing out there? Playing with yourself? Get on in here." Tear tracks striped Hannah's freckled cheeks, and her wildly patterned kimono hung limp around her legs. I couldn't believe she wasn't even dressed yet.

She grabbed my arm and jerked me into the museum's foyer. Then she leaned out the door and peered up and down the misty streets, empty at this early hour. Satisfied nobody was there, she closed the door and locked it. She grabbed her oversized coffee mug from the reception desk and lifted it to her lips, hand trembling so badly she almost spilled coffee on herself. She set it back down and closed her eyes.

I dug for my cigarettes but stopped when I remembered she wouldn't let me smoke inside. The clock at the Catholic church a block away chimed seven times, reminding me I got less than three hours sleep the night before. Caring for my terminally ill grandmother was a twenty-four-hour job with no sick days. Adrenaline would keep me moving for a little while longer but not much.

"Take the poster down if they're upset over it. Dean'll understand." Acknowledging how tired I felt had been a mistake. I wanted nothing more than to crash on Hannah's couch for a half hour. If I wrapped up her problem right away, I could grab a half hour of sleep before my first job of the day started.

"Huh?" The upset drained off her face, replaced by

confusion. "What are you talking about? The campaign sign? Oh, they're mad, but they weren't speaking to me anyway, so they can pound sand."

"Then what on earth has you calling me over here at the ass crack of dawn?" I pushed past her, followed the scent of coffee to her office, and poured myself a cup, still holding onto the hope this problem could be solved with a few wise words. Maybe she'd figured out one of her silly, interchangeable boyfriends had a wife stowed somewhere.

"Someone broke into my safe last night and stole some..." She glanced around her office as though the thief might have left a listening device and delivered the last part of her announcement in a loud whisper. "Some really important stuff belonging to the Bruce family."

I nearly dropped my coffee. Once I got over my surprise, the disappointment set in. There was no way I'd get a nap. Hooty's family heirlooms getting stolen, especially while Hannah had possession of them, constituted tears, tantrums, and anything else Hannah could think of to do. I groaned and sat down in my usual chair next to the window and fought against the fatigue gumming up my brain.

"What got stolen?"

"Some old journals. A book on folk medicine." Hannah sat behind her desk and began twisting her fingers. I wanted to tell her if she didn't quit pulling on them they'd get as long as octopus tentacles. "Irreplaceable. There aren't even copies."

"Who'd care enough about those to steal them?"

"Both were connected to the Mace Treasure."

I closed my eyes and rubbed the bridge of my nose. She didn't need to say more. Damn it all to hell and back. I hated the Mace Treasure. I hated the people who ran around like jackasses hunting for it. I bit my lower lip, wishing I could tell Hannah I had to leave, any excuse would do. *Suck it up, Peri Jean Mace*, said my inner adult. I sat up straight, still thinking maybe there was a way I could extract myself from the craziness.

"I saw Rainey's car in front of her law office when I passed through town. Want me to call her?" I knew Rainey Bruce would shout at me. She'd been doing it since we were in kindergarten. Her father might act nicer, but I hated to call him this early. "Hooty's probably still at home. I didn't see his car in front of the funeral home."

"Hell, no. I don't want you to call them. Do you know how this is going to look? They're important people here in town. Everybody at Hooty's church is going to know, and—and—and..." Hannah's face crumpled, and she lowered her head.

I let her cry for a few seconds. "Okay. Enough boo-hooing. We have to get on top of this. Have you called in the theft? Let the sheriff's office do their thing?"

"Uncle Joey's not speaking to me. I can't talk to him." She said it with such finality I knew there had to be a long, juicy story. Another time.

"Call Dean directly. He can get the wheels rolling." Truth was, if Dean figured out Hannah called me instead of reporting the theft, he'd be hurt and angry. Probably at both of us for not trusting his ability to do his job.

She stared at me, face long and sad, still tugging on her

fingers. My Something-Is-Wrong detector went on red alert.

"I'm not sure Dean can help." She sounded like a little girl asking an adult if she could use the restroom. "But I think you can."

Oh, no. If Dean couldn't help, but I could, it could only be one thing.

Ghosts.

It was too damn early in the morning for ghosts. What's more, I didn't want the trouble they brought into my life. Things were stressful enough between caring for my sick memaw and my boyfriend running for sheriff. I sat back in my chair, fighting against the stress headache starting in the back of my neck.

"What haven't you told me?"

"Maybe I'd better show you."

Some days, hiding in a hole would be preferable to facing the world. This was turning out to be one of those days. I sucked down the last of my coffee and set my cup aside.

Hannah clicked some keys on her laptop and motioned to me. "Come over here so you can see too." I obeyed but not happily. She tapped a key, and a grainy picture of her empty office popped onto the screen. A shadow crossed the room, and my heart jittered. I leaned closer to the screen, not wanting to see but unable to help myself. The shadow moved to a picture on the wall and hovered there for several moments. A stack of books drifted from the wall and floated across the room.

"Holy stinking socks." I'd never seen a ghost move

items, especially substantial ones, very far. "But how did the books get in the wall behind the painting?"

"New safe. Installed last month at the insistence of the museum board. Apparently, this one isn't secure." Hannah gestured at the huge, cast iron safe behind her desk.

"Those clever little tricksters. Gonna tell them the theft probably wouldn't have happened if the items had been in the iron safe?"

She shook her head and stared at me, waiting for me to say something, but I was too full of fatigue to pick up on what she wanted. "So was the shadow on the video a ghost?"

"I guess." I stared longingly at the coffeemaker. I wanted another cup, but the acid in my stomach wouldn't allow it.

"You don't know? You've seen ghosts your whole life and don't know?" Her voice rose with each word. "I want you to wear your black opal necklace and watch it again."

She spun around in her chair and fiddled with the door to the cast iron safe.

"I don't know." I put one hand on my churning stomach. "I sort of promised Dean to keep the woo-woo stuff on the down low until the sheriff's election ended."

"You won't help me?" Angry red, which matched Hannah's hair color, bloomed on her cheekbones. "Because your boyfriend's scared of what you can do?"

My cheeks grew warm, and I fought to keep my calm. I did not want to start the day fighting with my best friend.

Hannah glared at me across the desk. The glare itself didn't bother me. Her hissy fits changed as often as the

East Texas weather. The pure hurt behind her anger, however, chipped at my heart. *Maybe I should help.*

"I'll do it on one condition."

"What's the condition?"

"The black opal goes back in your cast iron safe when I'm done."

"Agreed." She opened the safe, took out a velvet pouch, and set it on the desk between us. The pouch's contents formed a small lump. As we watched, the lump moved and then disappeared altogether. I felt the weight of the black opal around my neck. Hannah gasped.

"It truly does freak me out when it does that," she said.

"Yeah. Imagine how I feel." My nervous system felt like it was lined with ground glass. "Play the video again."

She did. The black opal lent me a little extra ghost vision, giving the shadow a more human form. Between the lighting and the video's low quality, I couldn't make out much detail. Broad shoulders and narrow hips tipped me to the ghost's sex.

"I think it's a man, but I can't see his face yet." The books floated out of the safe, only this time, I could see two ghostly hands holding them. The ghost turned to leave the room and faced the camera. His face was fuzzy with dark hollows for eyes and a blur where the nose and mouth were, but I saw nothing identifying. I was ready to give up, but I heard something.

"Stop the video."

Hannah scrambled to do what I asked.

"Do you have headphones? Loud ones?"

She dug in her desk and got out a set of bright green

headphones and plugged them into the laptop. She rewound the video, and I turned up the volume as loud as it would go, wincing at the hiss bombarding my eardrums.

"Don't want to do this," said a garbled, tiny voice.

The hair on the back of my neck stood up. I leaned closer to the screen as though it would help me hear better.

"My friends. Can't do this." The books came out of the wall. The shadow turned to face the camera. "Please make it stop."

I jerked away from the computer, knocked into Hannah, and pulled the headphones off my head. My skin stung as every nerve ending in my body tried to short circuit and burn out. I tossed the headphones into Hannah's lap.

"What was it?"

I shook my head and took out my cigarettes, lighting one with shaking hands and turning my back on Hannah's protests. She restarted the video and put on the headphones. When it finished she took them off and shook her head. "Your face is green. You look ready to spew puke all over my office. And you're stinking this place up with your awful cigarettes. Please tell me what you heard."

The pleading in the ghost's voice bothered me, but something else did too. Something deep in my brain where I couldn't quite access it. I squashed out my cigarette in my empty coffee cup.

"What is it?" Hannah grabbed my arm and gave it a shake. "Please."

"Whatever we saw on the video didn't want to be there. It was forced. Someone, somewhere, is controlling it."

Hannah and I stared at each other, both of us breathing hard.

"So if I find who's controlling the ghost—"

"You find your thief." I might have said more, but I heard running footsteps on the street outside. I got up and peered out the window. "There's Dean on his morning run. Let's tell him what's happened. He can at least alert local antique dealers and pawn shops to be on the lookout. If someone stole the items to sell, you might get them back." I tapped on the window to get his attention. My muscles tensed while I waited for him to turn around. These days, I never knew which Dean I'd get. The sweet, reasonable one or the one this election changed into a crotchety old grouch who could turn petty and mean over a popcorn fart.

Dean turned and smiled at me. I smiled back and motioned him inside. Shoulders relaxing, I went to the door and let him inside. This election couldn't be over soon enough. Dean's moodiness wore me out worse than a hard day's work. I wanted us to start having fun together again.

"Hey, gorgeous." His kiss almost made me forget the weird feeling I had about all this. "Missed you last night. Your memaw okay?"

"Sleeping when I left." She was dying of cancer, and I was overwhelmed. Not much help for either problem. "Got something job related for you. Hannah's had a theft."

A few minutes later, Dean sat in Hannah's office chair

—which she'd insisted on covering with a towel so his sweat wouldn't get on it—watching the video.

"Somebody tampered with your system, but I don't understand how." He restarted the video and watched with his face close to the screen. "I know an expert in Houston, but who knows how long it'll take him or if he can figure out who did it. I'm not even completely sure Burns County can afford him."

Hannah and I exchanged a glance. Frustration brewed in her caramel eyes, taking them from warm to hot. Dean's reaction didn't surprise me either. Hannah needed to understand we were at a dead end.

"My first job of the day starts in less than ten minutes," I said. Dean rose to kiss me but sat right back down to replay the video for the umpteenth time.

"I'll walk you out." Hannah followed close at my heels, not speaking until we reached my car. I opened the door, pretending I thought we'd said all we had to say to each other.

"Dean can't help, and you know it." She leaned into my face. "If you think I'm going to let you walk away from this because you're afraid—"

"I'm not afraid." I took off the black opal necklace and held it out to her. "Don't let Dean see this, please."

She took it, dropped it into her pocket, and fixed me with a dirty look. "Soon as I said the stolen items had to do with the Mace Treasure, you got this tightassed expression on your face and started doing the pee-pee dance. But okay. You're not afraid."

I opened my mouth to argue, but the sound of several

loud motorcycles drowned me out. Hannah and I stopped talking to watch them come.

"What are the Six Gun Revolutionaries doing here?" Hannah yelled at me. I shrugged. She stepped back from the curb and glanced toward the museum, probably looking for Dean. I hoped he didn't hear the ruckus but knew there was no way he could miss it.

The convoy of motorcycles slowed and pulled up next to the curb, surrounding my car. It was then I saw who they had with them. King Tolliver, the president of the motorcycle club, had attached a matching sidecar to his bright blue Harley Davidson. Sitting in it, goggles on her face and a bandana covering her hair was Memaw. *Oh, hell no.* I marched over to her.

"What on earth are you doing?" I had to yell to hear over the motorcycles. She shook her head. Furious, I screamed, "Shut these loud-assed road mongers off."

Nobody did anything until King cut off his motorcycle. He gave me a lizard-eyed stare.

"What are you doing?" I studied Memaw for signs the cancer had spread to her brain. I could think of no other reason for her to be associating with these outlaws.

"Calm down." Like magic, Wade Hill appeared at my side to tower over me. He draped one heavy arm over my shoulders. I shrugged him off. We worked together at least once a week for my odd jobs business. I knew his ways, and I wouldn't let him soft shoe me.

"This is on my bucket list." Memaw grinned wider than I'd seen on a long time. "I wanted to ride with a real badass biker gang. Just like on TV."

"This isn't TV. It's going to be a hundred degrees by noon. It's already hellish out here." To prove my point, I pulled my already damp T-shirt off my skin.

"That's why we started early," Memaw said. "I'm gonna have a fried chicken lunch for them as thanks."

"See?" Wade tried putting his arm over my shoulders again. I tried to shrug him off, but he didn't budge. He tugged me away from Memaw and walked me a short distance away. He spoke in a low voice. "She's running out of time. Let her enjoy herself without giving her shit."

My first impulse was to tell him Memaw wasn't running out of time, but I knew she was, which infuriated me. I wanted to argue, to tell him she needed to take care of herself, but I knew it didn't matter. The end would be the same. I nodded to let Wade know I understood and squeezed his huge arm in thanks. He gave me a rough back pat, nearly knocking me off my feet. I walked to Memaw and gave her a hug.

"Enjoy," I told her. To King, I said, "Make her drink water." He gave me the same lizard stare but winked to let me know he understood. He started up his motorcycle, and the rest of his club followed suit. I waved as they drove away, feeling as though I'd lost something, but I didn't know what.

I turned to find Hannah and Dean whispering together on the museum steps and glancing at me. I got into my car and hightailed it out of there before they decided to include me in their conversation.

———

I CHAIN-SMOKED my way to the first job of the day, trying every trick I knew to forget the creepy figure in the surveillance video. I needed to forget the theft and go about my business. Nothing concerning the Mace Treasure had any place in my life, ghosts or no ghosts.

Those awful, pleading words wouldn't leave me. *Don't want to do this. My friends. Can't do this.* Then the most awful part, when the ghost faced the camera as though he somehow knew I'd watch this video. *Please make it stop.*

The same sense of déjà vu I had at the museum crept over me. Somehow I should know this voice, but I didn't. A familiar weight settled around my neck, and I almost dropped my cigarette in my lap trying to feel what it was. *The black opal. Could this day possibly get worse?* I wondered how the piece of jewelry got away from Hannah before she had time to put it up.

Dean's mother gave me the black opal because of what I am. It originally belonged to Dean's great-grandmother, who had what some folks call the Sight. The black opal had serious power. Aside from following me around like an overzealous dog, the gem's magical properties increased my ability to see ghosts and communicate with them. If I spent all day every day farting around with woo-woo, the black opal would have helped me immensely. But I did my best to stay away from magical stuff.

Amanda's Hair Flair, my first job of the day, came up on the right. I turned into the parking lot but stayed in my car to finish my cigarette. Time to put on my game face. Running a business required me to act competent. Business aside, I didn't want to revive the town rumor about my lack of sanity. A spring in the backseat creaked. The car shifted. I glanced into the rearview mirror and screamed.

A shadowy figure sat in my backseat. The voice came to me again, the black opal vibrating with the words. *Please make it stop.*

I grabbed for the door handle, fingers slipping off in my eagerness to get away from this thing. It had power, power enough to take a pile of books out of the library. What could it do to me? I swung open the door and found myself face to face with my mother. I screamed again.

"What do you think, honey?" She finger-fluffed her hair. Her grin would have put a shit-eating possum's to shame.

Didn't she hear me scream? It expressed exactly what I thought about her and her hair. Seeing her reactivated the acidic coffee in my stomach, and I clutched my middle. *What on earth was she doing in town?*

"Amanda told me you were scheduled to help her today, and I just had to see my baby girl." She made a shrill sound likely meant as a combination giggle and squeal and grabbed me in a hug I didn't want. The little girl who lived deep in my psyche, the one who still ached for her mother's love, forced me to half-assedly return the hug. It was enough for Barbie. She dropped her arms immediately. "Last time I saw you, your hair was in one of those sleek, short styles. Looked good. You've got your daddy's hair, you know."

"I saw some old pictures of myself. Thought it was time for a change." I picked at my nails, which looked awful, so I wouldn't have to make eye contact with Barbie and waited for her to say something so I could formulate a response. I wanted to run away from her, get in my car, and leave, but Memaw raised me to act better. She raised me to treat people with respect, even the ones who deserved to have roach doo doo rubbed on their faces.

"Might look good if you can get past the stage it's at now." She snorted. "I cut mine short when I was about ten years older than you. Tried to grow it out a dozen times and never made it."

The back of my neck began to throb from me clenching my shoulder muscles. I had no idea how to communicate with the woman who gave me life, nor any desire to learn. Amanda joined us with a bottle of one of her homemade beauty potions in hand.

"I am so glad you are back in town to stay." She drew Barbie into a one-armed hug and gave her a loud kiss on the cheek. She turned to me and pulled me into the hug. I stiffened, but Amanda was stronger than I could have imagined. Resisting her would have been noticeable, and I never aired dirty family laundry in public. "Ain't you glad your momma's gonna be living near you again?"

"You can't imagine," I mumbled. A buzz filled my head. *Back in town to stay?* It made no sense. "W-w-w-" *Pull it together, Peri Jean,* I instructed myself and started again. "What made you decide to move back here?"

"You mean back to a one-horse town?" Barbie threw back her head and laughed. "Back to everything I couldn't wait to get away from when I was twenty-five?" She stared at me for too long and pressed her lips together. "Mostly you. I missed you." She threw her arms around me again.

The reek of her perfume cloaked me, and I felt my gorge rising. The buzz in my head got so loud it made me dizzy. I willed my knees not to buckle. Barbie released me so she could stare into my face. I couldn't meet her gaze.

"Amanda said you're dating the guy who's running for sheriff. I saw his campaign poster. What a hottie." She rubbed my arms as though trying to warm me. I noticed the tremors jerking through my body. The twit thought I was cold. Unreal. Her smile grew so wide I hoped her head would split, spilling what passed for her brains onto the asphalt of the parking lot. "He's from Louisiana money, I heard. You hit the lotto, kid. She's a chip off the old block, all right." She pecked my cheek and exchanged a grin with Amanda. I fought to keep from wiping the dampness from her kiss off my face.

"Where's...Ron?" It took me a moment to remember her current husband's name.

"Who cares?" She exhaled a world-weary sigh. "The jerk traded me in for a newer model. His new lady is probably younger than you, Peri Jean. Of course, she's not nearly as pretty." She and Amanda laughed, reminding me of those cartoon crows Memaw thought were so funny. Barbie's phone buzzed, and she took it out of her handbag to glance at it. "I've got to get moving. That's the realtor. She's going to show me a cute little house."

Amanda quickly told Barbie about the natural anti-aging ingredients of the homemade lotion she was selling her, conveniently leaving out the way all her homegrown miracle cures smelled. Then she told her the price.

"Well, I sure hope it works." Barbie handed her two

twenties.

"Oh, all my formulas do exactly what they're supposed to. Right, Peri Jean?" Amanda winked at me.

"They do." I didn't care to continue the conversation with Barbie, but Amanda wanted an endorsement. I had no choice but to give it. "I burned this hand last month at work. It blistered, puss ran out of it, the whole song and dance. Bought some of Amanda's herbal healing salve. Look here. Not even a red mark." I held out the hand for her to inspect. The way the wound healed really had impressed me. Amanda might act a little loopy, but she knew her stuff.

Barbie inspected my hand. "I'll take your word for it, but only because you're my baby girl." She walked toward her car but turned back before she reached it. "My cell number's still the same," she said. "Set up a time I can meet your honey. I am absolutely bursting with excitement. *Louisiana money,*" she muttered under her breath and walked to her car, actually throwing me a big wink before she got inside.

Once a gold digger, always a gold digger. I'd have laid down the twenty-dollar bill in my back pocket to bet Barbie's real interest in me had to do with Dean's family money. She probably thought she could worm her way back into my life instead of finding a new husband, which might be hard with her no longer being young. My foot itched to kick her departing behind, but she was gone, and I needed to act as professional as I could.

"The new washer won't be here until this afternoon," Amanda said. "I need you to get these towels over to the laundromat and wash them." She took a closer look at me. "Are you all right, hon?"

I was, and I wasn't. For the life of me, I couldn't remember what I'd been so upset about when I drove over here. I remembered being at the museum with Hannah, making her angry because I didn't want to get crazy from the Mace Treasure on my shoes. But what had I been so upset about when I pulled into the beauty shop parking lot?

"Peri Jean, honey, you all right?" Amanda stepped closer and closed one of her strong hands around my arm. My knees weakened, and I listed to the side, black spots in my vision. Amanda got one arm around my waist and had me in the beauty shop before I could recover enough to protest.

Every face turned to me, eyes alight with curiosity. A few women tried to feign pity, but not very hard. I tried to pull myself together and fast. The gossip grapevine in Gaslight City could have competed in NASCAR. I didn't want to give any of these people an evening's entertainment. I fought to rein myself in, but my feelings welled up, flooding and overflowing the shallow reserves of my emotions. *How dare my awful mother act as though I'd let her swing back into my life?* I let the outrage the thought generated cancel out some of the hurt and immediately felt more stable.

Barbie acted as though she'd been on a long trip and we were picking up where we left off. Then the core of it hit me like a bucket of ice cold piss. In the depths of Barbie's artfully made up eyes had been nothing but confidence in her ability to win me over. She either had no idea how she'd made me feel all my life or didn't give a rat's ass.

I could get as mad as I wanted. I could act as much of a horse's ass as I wanted. It wouldn't touch Barbie. I could buy into her act whole hog and eat until I popped. No matter how nice I was, no matter how hard I tried, Barbie would dump me when it suited her. Inside, I sagged, the hurt pounding like a bad injury. Outside, I used every trick I'd learned to push a smile onto my face. I turned to Amanda.

"Sorry about that. Memaw had a bad night last night, and I'm tired."

I waited while all the woman in the shop clucked in sympathy. Hazel Siegler pushed the hair drying apparatus off her head and turned it off, leaning forward in the dryer chair to catch all the action.

"Sugar, I'll spend the night with Miss Leticia if you ever need a break," she said. "We worked together over at the high school all our adult lives. It'd be just like a slumber party."

"Thank you, Miss Hazel. I'll sure keep it in mind." Problem was, Hazel lived at a nursing home because she couldn't care for herself. I turned to Amanda. "You still got a job for me?"

"I do." She patted my back. If I hadn't known better, I'd have said it was congratulations for pulling myself together. She led me into a side room, which held a washer and dryer. Piles of towels littered the floor. "You can do this however you want, but I need them out of here ASAP and washed today."

I knelt on the floor and began gathering towels, pushing them into a canvas bag I'd spotted hanging on the wall. Amanda leaned against the door frame and watched me.

"I never realized you and Barbie had issues."

"I didn't realize you and Barbie were such close friends." I finished loading the towels and slung the bag over my shoulder.

"We aren't." The lines around Amanda's eyes deepened into what would have been a smile had her mouth not remained still. "When she lived here, she came to me for haircuts. Came in here for a perm the day she left town. Never said a word about moving away." She moved away from the door. "Come on. I'll open the door for you and help you get them into your car."

I waddled through the shop, mulling over what Amanda said. It rang true in my ears. Maybe Barbie didn't really make friends. Too self-absorbed? Too conniving?

"What's she doing in here?" The raspy, squeaky voice jabbed into my thoughts like sharp ice.

I dropped the towels on the floor and turned to face its source, even though I knew exactly who'd spoken.

Felicia Brent Fischer Holze smirked at me from underneath her red-streaked mousy hair. She'd smeared oddly colored makeup over her angular features, and her gut had grown considerably since I'd last seen her. Either she'd made good friends with after-work beer drinking or she was pregnant again. I didn't care which it was. All I cared about was not doubling up my fist and hitting her with it. I got away with beating up my childhood tormentor once. It wouldn't happen again. She was married to a sheriff's deputy, and her father-in-law was the sheriff of Burns County. I had a feeling I wouldn't escape prosecution if I hit her.

"What's around your neck?" She took a few steps toward me and plucked the black opal from my shirt.

"Don't touch me, Felicia." I tightened my grip on the canvas bag holding the towels.

"Is it a substitute for an engagement ring on your finger?"

I turned my back to her and stood in front of the door. Amanda appeared next to me and held it open. She held my elbow as I took the step down onto the stoop.

"He's gonna lose, Peri Jean," Felicia sang after me. "Are y'all going to live out there in your Memaw's house and be jobless together?"

"That's enough, Felicia. We have customers." Amanda's voice brooked no argument. She followed me out of the shop.

"Thanks for ignoring her," she said when we reached my old Nova. "She's a good stylist, brings in a lot of clientele, but sometimes I could wring her neck."

"I'm glad I'm not the one who has to work with her." I handed Amanda the keys and let her pop the trunk.

"Sometimes you have to work with people you don't like because of who they're related to." Amanda stared at the Nova and ran her hand over the flank. I hefted the canvas bag into the trunk and closed it.

"I ever tell you how cool I think it is for you to drive your daddy's car?" Amanda stared at the street, eyes unfocused and misty. She didn't seem to expect an answer, so I didn't bother thinking of one. "Paul Mace. Your daddy was the best looking guy in town. He'd rev up the engine on this baby, and you could hear him a mile away." The corners of her mouth turned down. "Too bad he died so young."

Yep, too fucking bad. I kept the comment to myself and walked around to the driver's side door and waited for Amanda to dismiss me.

"Look...I hate it when people tell me what I ought to do, but right now I'm about to do it. Try to make friends with your mom. My situation growing up was a lot like yours. My mom left me for my grandmother to raise while she went off and got remarried."

I would rather bathe in hot garbage than open the door for Barbie to crucify my emotions.

"Did you make up with her?" I couldn't help asking. Amanda never, ever discussed her past, and it remained a mystery because she didn't grow up here.

"Nope. Last time I spoke to her, when I was about nine, I told her I hated her guts." Amanda took a breath and let it out. "She died two years later in a house fire. She, her new husband, and my half-brother."

Would I regret it if Barbie turned up dead? I didn't think so. I barely knew her, and what I did know was negative. But I could never be sure until the situation presented itself.

"Sometimes we forgive people, not to give them a pass for whatever wrong they committed against us or to get them to do a certain thing, but to be kinder to ourselves."

Amanda watched my face and then nodded. She patted my arm. "Think about it. Okay?"

"I will." I opened the door climbed into the car. "I gotta get on this if I want to finish. Thanks for the talk."

"You bet." A car pulled into the parking lot, and Amanda walked over and talked to the person, following them inside her business, still chattering.

I started the car, a little fear tingling at me. I tried to remember why I'd been scared again, hoping it would come with Barbie gone, but I couldn't access it. It was gone, as though it had never been. Just as well. If it had to do with the Mace Treasure, I was better off forgetting it. I put the car in gear, and my cellphone rang. I checked the caller ID. Eddie Kennedy. *Uh oh.* "Hi, Eddie."

"What do you mean telling Hannah you can't help her? Don't you know what this is about?"

"Something I don't want any part in." I cringed as I said the words. Back talking Eddie felt wrong no matter how old I got.

"I want you to meet me at Hooty's."

"I have a job. I'll spend the day at the laundromat doing Amanda's towels from her beauty shop."

Eddie slapped his hand over the phone, nearly deafening me, and said a few things. I heard Hooty Bruce's deep voice answer.

"Hooty says bring the towels here. And, Peri Jean? Darlin'?"

"Yes?"

"Move your skinny ass."

2

———

Hooty's graceful two-story house on Spence Street usually made me smile. I helped paint the gingerbread trim white and the house its lovely wisteria color when Hooty and his wife Esther restored the 1920s home. Today, the sight of Eddie's beat-up old truck in the house's driveway settled a heavy weight onto my shoulders. Much as I didn't want to argue my duty to help find Hooty's lost family heirlooms, I knew the only way to extract myself from the drama was to listen to what they had to say.

Gaslight City residents called Hooty's neighborhood Bed and Breakfast Row. True to its namesake, and despite the hellish late summer weather, tourists determined to get in one last vacation before school started swarmed the street. I had to drive five miles per hour to keep from hitting any of the nitwits wandering around holding up their cameras and cellphones, totally unaware of the world around them. I caught a mini SUV vacating a parking spot right in front of Hooty's house and slipped into the space, slick as mayonnaise.

"Hey!" A guy wearing a golf visor leaned out of his huge diesel truck. "We've been waiting for that spot for five minutes."

"There's a public lot a block over." I locked my car and started up Hooty's stone walkway.

"Ma'am? Ma'am?"

Groaning, I turned back to them. A woman with perfectly straight, perfectly tinted blond hair, and super white teeth leaned over her husband, her coral tank top sliding to reveal a matching bra strap.

"Are you Peri Jean Mace? Of the Mace Treasure?"

"No." I spun around and jogged up the walk. I got to the door and realized I'd forgotten Amanda's towels. I sure as hell didn't want to go back for them. I knocked on the door, and Esther Bruce opened it.

"What's going on out there?"

"Tourists. Mace Treasure." I pulled out my cigarettes, took in Esther's ick face, and put them away.

"It's like a TV show to them. We aren't even real people. My advice? Ignore it." She motioned me inside, closing the door behind me, and pulled me into a gentle hug, which I returned just as gently to make sure I didn't make her injuries flare up.

"How are things?" I gestured at her hip, which seemed to give her the most trouble.

"Quite well. I'm trying a new therapy. It's given me some relief." Her smile seemed less forced than when I saw her last. I hoped the treatment continued to help.

"What's the therapy?" I knew nothing about medicine but thought it polite to ask.

Her eyes widened and her mouth dropped open, but she recovered quickly and smiled again. "One of those new age type things. Your grandmother's the one who told me about it." Her shoulders cranked up nearly to her ears, and her jaw clenched. She obviously didn't want me to ask any more about her therapy.

"Hooty's expecting me."

"Oh, he sure is. They're back in his study." She led me through the antique-filled foyer and living room. The ugly limp she'd picked up with her injury was absent, and she moved faster, even kneeling to pick up a piece of paper from the floor. *What is this mystery treatment?* We walked down a short hallway off the living room, and she tapped on a closed door.

"I saw her drive up." Hooty's deep voice floated through the door. "Peri Jean, come on in."

Esther patted me on the shoulder and got away from me before I could ask her more about her miracle healing. I made a mental note to ask Memaw what treatment she was taking and hoped it wasn't a regimen of expensive vitamins. I opened the door to a roomful of people. *Should have known Eddie would bring out the heavy artillery.*

Hannah sat in a leather chair leafing through a huge book. Rainey Bruce, Hooty and Esther's daughter, sat in a stiff, carved wooden chair next to the bay window. Eddie, head lowered and scribbling in one of his many notebooks, took up most of the loveseat. Hooty half rose from behind a paper-piled desk.

"Do you want coffee? Or a cool drink?" He gestured at a restored Art Deco bar, which held a coffee maker with a full pot of coffee.

"Don't do it," Eddie said. "He buys the cheap shit. Apparently, his congregants and his customers from the funeral home don't rate the good coffee."

Hooty doubled up one fist and shook it at Eddie, but he wore a smile. I went to the mini-fridge and took out a bottle of water. Hooty motioned me toward a Victorian-style, high-backed chair upholstered in lilac velvet, roses carved into its rosewood trim.

"Let's get down to business." Rainey checked the slim watch on her wrist. "I've got paperwork to finish before Dean's campaign barbecue tonight."

A sharp reminder I had to get my poop together before the barbecue kicked me in the chest. Sour acid oozed into my stomach and burned. I dug into my pocket, found a roll of antacids, and crunched one.

"Pressure getting to you, short stuff?" Rainey's steel gaze flicked over me, and amusement lit her face. "Get used to it. When he wins, you'll be in the public eye all the time."

I ate another antacid.

"Rainey." Hooty stared down his daughter who turned her gaze to her expensive, high-heeled shoes. He turned to speak to me. "Hannah said you have some inside knowledge about the loss of our family heirlooms."

"Nice way of saying I saw a ghost steal them." I glanced at the roll of gut soother, considered it, and slipped them back into my pocket without taking another one.

"Hannah also said you don't want to help find the journals or the book of folk medicine." Eddie glared at me the same way Hooty had glared at his own daughter. Though Eddie and I weren't related by blood, he was the only father I remembered having.

"Hannah knows everything I know," I said.

"There's no chance you could do more?" Eddie set aside his notebook. "I see you got your black opal necklace back on. Don't it make your powers stronger?"

I retrieved my antacids from my pocket and ate three.

"Peri Jean used the black opal to enhance what she could see." Hannah gave me an apologetic glance, looking away when I bared my teeth at her. "But she couldn't identify the ghost."

"Even if I could," I said, "I have no idea who's controlling it." The tortured voice and the shadowed figure in the backseat of my car popped back into my mind, almost like it had never been gone. *How did such spooky shit slip away from me? Am I so stressed out I can't remember stuff from an hour ago?* I rubbed my aching shoulders.

"Do you think you could contact the ghost itself?" Leave it to Rainey Bruce to cut to the heart of the matter. A barracuda in the courtroom and in life, she didn't care who she offended. She set her course and never stopped.

"Maybe, but I don't want to." I played it Rainey's way, subtle as a jackhammer at dawn.

Eddie pressed his lips together and narrowed his eyes at me.

"If somebody were dead over this, I'd try, but contacting ghosts ain't my business. Matter of fact, it's gotten me thrown in the loony bin before. I don't think it's a fun way to pass the time."

"This isn't for fun." Hannah's voice tightened. "This is justice. Someone stole from the museum, which is the same as stealing from this town."

I thought back to the curious stares in Amanda's Hair Flairs and assessed my give-a-shit level. It wasn't too high. Rainey rolled her eyes.

"Forget about the people in this mud hole who can't stand you because they're afraid. What about your friends?" She gestured around the room, silver bracelets jangling on her dark arm to punctuate her point.

I lowered my head, face flaming. "Dean's on it."

"Oh, come on. Don't play stupid," Hannah said. "He's doing all he knows to do—contacting pawn shops, encouraging us to make the theft as public as possible so people will know to be on the lookout, but he can't do what you can. And you know it."

"Listen." Rainey pointed one sharp, red fingernail at me. "I will not let my family's heirlooms disappear and not fight to get them back. Just because you don't care about your family, doesn't mean I don't care about mine. I'm proud of my family's heritage in this county."

"Would you be so proud of it if people treated you like an attraction at a carnival?" My voice raised. All the fatigue and hurt of the last few months bubbled, its steam becoming anger.

"Enough. Both of you." Hooty stood behind his desk. "I know you like to stay away from the Mace Treasure. I respect your reasoning, though I don't necessarily agree with it. I'll ask you to try to understand the reason we want our heirlooms back so badly. It isn't so much the connection to the Mace Treasure but their historical value we care about."

"Hooty, I brought the video from last night's museum board meeting." Hannah dug in her bag and came up with a DVD in a plastic jewel case. "Maybe we could let Peri Jean see the part where you read from the journal."

"I'm willing if she's willing." Hooty stared at my face, waiting for my answer.

I wanted to say no so badly it hurt. Getting embroiled in the Mace Treasure nonsense and communicating with the spirit world did not appeal to me at all. Rainey's reminder this room was filled with my friends stopped me. I needed to at least hear them out.

"All right," I said. "I'll watch." I ate the last two antacids from my roll and washed them down with water, mindful of Eddie's worried gaze lingering on me.

Hooty took the DVD from Hannah and plugged it into a combo DVD player/TV sitting on a converted antique sewing table. The video began to play, and I sat back in my chair, wondering how I'd gone from wanting to step away from the crazy to sitting here watching its tendrils sneaking into my life.

———

THE SCENE SHOWED the long oval table in the museum's main classroom, each chair taken by a museum board member.

Felicia Holze and her father-in-law Sheriff Joey Holze both wore sour expressions. It probably rubbed their asses raw to attend the meeting, but I bet they'd allow their fingernails to be yanked out before they gave up their spots on the museum board. They got their jollies making other folks miserable.

Amanda King sat at the table, ignoring everyone else and tapping on her cellphone. It surprised me not to see her animated and socializing. Maybe she got enough of it at the salon.

Eddie Kennedy and Julie Woodson sat huddled together, smiling and whispering. The two dated on and off but wouldn't commit to each other. It made me feel sorry for Eddie because I thought having someone to come home to would do him good.

Hooty sat with a battered book in front of him. Its cloth cover had worn away in spots, revealing the cardboard underneath, the page edges faded to yellowish tan. The book reminded me of the picture-book sized ledgers I sometimes saw in antique stores, and I could almost imagine the dry, musty smell coming off it.

Rainey sat next to Hooty, staring at something she held out of sight in her lap. I assumed it was a cellphone until she raised it to table level, and I saw it was a card-sized photograph. I couldn't make out any details. She leaned over to Hooty, and the two had a whispered discussion. Rainey shook her head and slipped the photograph into a padded envelope and put it in her purse.

"Okay, Hooty, we're ready," Hannah said from somewhere off screen.

Hooty nodded and opened the journal to a marked place and began to speak. The door opened before he could, and Benny Longstreet rushed in.

"Sorry y'all. Had an emergency at the plant. Almost thought I wouldn't make it." He glanced around the room, embarrassment dawning slowly on his long, homely face. "Oh. Y'all done started, ain't you? Lemme just set down." He pulled a rolling chair away from the wall and sat next to Amanda who scooted away from him. I didn't blame her. Benny turned my stomach too.

"Okay, then," Hannah said. "Hooty, please continue."

"All right. First I'd like to introduce what I'm about to read." He held up the journal. "This journal belonged to Hezekiah Bruce, the first of my family to settle in Burns County. His parents were slaves freed by the Emancipation Proclamation. They instilled a sense of entrepreneurship in him. He saved his money, came here, and opened a general store. He was the first black business owner in Burns County. He used these ledgers to record the goings-on he saw." The barrel-chested man's voice boomed through the room, and it sounded like he was getting ready to deliver a sermon at church. Hooty took a deep breath and began to read from the journal.

When I settled in Burns County to raise my family, I knew I would run into some of the same problems my parents suffered in Mississippi. But I never expected to see the horror I saw last night.

Around dark time, men came on horses and rode past our store and home. Usually nobody rides past because the last house on this road is that of Priscilla Herrera and she is thought to be a witch. My children ran out to see the commotion, but my wife shooed them back inside. I told her to hide them. Everything about these men and their horses scared me. As a boy, I saw a mob come take a man away who they decided had abused a white woman. This had the same feeling.

After I made sure my wife understood to keep the children and herself out of sight, I sneaked through the woods, going as quiet as I could, and found the men crowded in front of Priscilla Herrera's, just where I expected.

One man said to her, "You made Reginald Mace lose his mind and fall ill with your sorcery."

She said, "I did no such thing. Reggie and I were friends. I helped him, and he helped me."

Another man said, "The Bible says to never suffer a witch to live."

She said, "You didn't care about that when you and your wife wanted a child."

He slapped her, and she fell down.

It was then I heard footsteps sneaking up behind me. I spun around, ready to fight for my life, only to find the children of Priscilla, a boy named Samuel and a girl named Samantha. Twins, but the ones who don't look the same. Tears streaked those two little faces. I knew right away their momma sent them away to keep them from harm. I sent the two to hide with my wife and children. I didn't know what I'd do with them, but helping others is the way of a Christian.

The men dragged Priscilla from the house, kicking and screaming. They tied her to a horse and left with her. I went back home, saddled my mare, and rode the short distance to town. They had her over to the jail. A crowd had gathered.

I motioned Hooty to pause the video and spoke to Eddie.

"This is the witch you told me cursed the treasure?" My vague memories of the conversation didn't render much detail. At the time, I'd been solving my cousin Rae's murder and didn't pay close attention.

He nodded.

"The old newspaper article you showed me only mentioned Priscilla Herrera having a son."

"I showed you all the information I had at the time." He shrugged and spread out his hands. "The article also mentioned the boy was deaf, but Hezekiah's account says nothing of it. Lots of information gets lost or mixed up."

"As long as we are clearing up facts, Reginald Mace was Peri Jean's great-great grandfather?" Rainey asked.

"More like four greats." Eddie counted on his fingers. "Peri Jean ought to make the effort to know all this herself." He shot me a stinky glare.

Hooty started the video again.

They already had her on the gallows with a noose around her neck.

Old Bertram Holze said to her, "There is one way to save yourself. Tell us where Reginald Mace's fortune is hid. That way, we'll know you mean only good to this community."

Well, Priscilla snorted at him and said, "You done made up your mind what to do with me, no matter what I tell you. But I'll tell you something you did not expect. None of you, save one who has the blood, will have the treasure. Trespassers will come to a bad end."

"What kinda bad end?" That was from old Theo Franklin who never had any sense to begin with.

"Those who don't die will wish they had."

Bert Holze threw the trap door, and Priscilla hanged right there. It was a bad sight, one I'll remember all my days. I came home to more confusion. My wife said the children ran off as soon as her back was turned. I pray for their safety but feel powerless to do more. My wife and children need me.

Those men came back and tore apart Priscilla's house. Don't know if they found nothing useful, but one of them rode away from the house on his horse like the hounds of hell chased after him. Old Doc came the next morning to ask after my family. Said he was checking in as he does about once a month, but I saw the fear in his eyes. I told him the events I witnessed. Old Doc allowed the man I saw fleeing on his horse didn't survive the night. He died foaming at the mouth and snapping at his family like an animal. Another of the men developed whelps all over his body and was in a bad way. Maybe what Priscilla said about trespassers seeking the treasure had some truth. Old Doc advised me to lay low for a while. Some of the town folks wondered if my involvement with Priscilla included hiding her children. But I have no idea where those children ended up. My sole hint of their continued existence is a rumor poor Priscilla Herrera's body was stolen.

For me and my family, I keep my eyes and ears open. If the tide is about to turn for us here, we may have to run.

Hooty stopped reading and turned to another marked page in the book. "This entry's shorter, but it might interest the board to hear it too."

Last week, Luther Palmore's house burned in the night. All inside perished. Nothing is left but the brick chimney, and it is charred black. It does not escape my attention that Luther Palmore and Reginald Mace were great friends. Did the same mob who hanged Priscilla Herrera pay Luther Palmore a deadly visit?

I gasped. Everyone stopped listening to the video to stare at me, and I flinched, sorry I'd interrupted. The Palmore property sat behind Memaw's land. It was as haunted as a cheesy B-rated horror movie. I waved my hand at them to let them know I would live.

Business at my store has been the same as usual, mostly colored. But Bertram Holze came by today. He asked if I knew the whereabouts of the Herrera children. Holze said they were looking for them. I asked if it had to do with the tragedy that befell their momma. He told me to mind my own business if I wanted to keep my store. I said no more.

All I own is in this store. People in these parts have little coin. My family eats well, but we do so on trade. If I leave here, I leave with nothing.

Hooty stopped reading, but the video kept running. The members of the museum board sat in silence. I took notice of the reactions of the members.

Eddie and Julie didn't look surprised. Hooty must have read it to them beforehand. Sheriff Joey's face had gone the color of red dirt, and his breath came out in puffs. Felicia wore her usual resting bitch face. I knew her well enough to see the anger and indignation brewing behind her flat eyes.

Amanda still tapped on her cellphone, oblivious to it all. I wondered if she'd heard a word. I liked Amanda well enough but thought she was doing the Burns County Museum a disservice by not giving up her husband's chair on the board after his passing last summer. Benny leaned forward in his seat, eyes wide with shock, mouth curled with distaste.

"That was some ugly stuff," he breathed.

Sheriff Joey turned to face the camera. "Hannah, turn off this camera right now. And I mean it."

The screen went blank.

For a moment, silence reigned in Hooty's study. Nobody moved or made a sound. I guessed we were all busy trying to get over the window of ugliness Hooty's ancestor's words had opened. The lynching felt immediate, not like events dating back a century. The horrible images had jumped right from the crumbled page and into my mind, vivid in their horror and cruelty. My chest tight, muscles hot with rushing blood, my breath came in shallow pants. Sweat dampened the back of my neck. I couldn't stop picturing the old gallows behind the museum. I saw them at a distance at least once a week. I could have been Priscilla Herrera a century ago, hanged because I could see ghosts.

A huge, black bird landed on the windowsill, watching us like some sort of spy. It tapped the glass with its beak, breaking the spell in the room. Everyone seemed to let out the collective breath we'd all be holding.

"You all right?" Hooty asked me and exchanged a glance with Rainey. She grabbed a box of tissues from the small table next to her chair and brought them to me.

"You're sweating," she said. I mopped my damp face,

trying to get hold of myself. The stuff I'd heard on the video happened a long time ago. It had nothing to do with me.

"I'm guessing Sheriff Joey argued against adding the journal to the museum's collection after he made you shut off the video?" I asked Hannah.

"And how," she said. "Felicia threatened to sue the museum for libel."

"After the meeting, she followed me out to my car to talk about it." Rainey snorted and shook her head. "She's about as smart as a jar of peanut butter, but her outrage is still loud enough to cause problems."

"I've got the minutes of the meeting," Eddie said. "I'll be happy to show 'em to you if you want to know what-all got said."

I didn't, not really. My imagination filled in the blanks pretty well by itself. Every gaze in the room rested on me, waiting for my answer. Would I help or not? I still wanted to say no. Hearing what happened to Priscilla Herrera for being different made refusal seem an even more attractive option.

"Someone stole the journals for a reason," I said. "If we can figure it out, it might go a ways toward finding who did it. I bet Sheriff Joey wanted the journals burned, right?"

Hannah shifted in her chair and nodded, her eyes on the carpet.

"Any other idea on why someone would want them?" I glanced at each person in the room in turn. If there was a way to get this done without using magic, I wanted to figure it out.

"The journals have the exact wording of the curse in them." Eddie scribbled something in his notebook. "Someone might think they can use the journals to get the curse off the treasure."

"If we're going to call the motive for the theft magical," Rainey said, "I have a theory the book on folk medicine actually belonged to Priscilla Herrera. Some of the stuff in it went further than herbs and roots."

I hunched my shoulders. *More mumbo jumbo. Groovy.*

"These ledgers are an amazing representation of the darker side of Gaslight City's history," I said. "I am more sorry than any of you know they've been stolen, but I'm not sure—"

"I see the no all over your face. Might as well be a flashing neon sign." Rainey stood, smoothing down her skirt and making a face at the wrinkles sitting down had carved into it. "I've got to go back to the office."

"I've got Amanda's laundry to do." I pushed myself out of the chair.

"I told you to bring it here," Hooty said.

"There's too much. I couldn't impose on you and Esther. I'll take it to the laundromat."

"Watch out for the tweakers—I mean my clients," Rainey said. To my surprise, she pulled me into a hard, fast hug. "Thank you for listening to us. Will you promise to give it some thought?"

"I will." My promise was really to figure out a way to resolve this without contacting the spirit world.

Hannah and Eddie hugged me too, and Hooty walked me to the door, planting a firm kiss on my cheek as I left.

I hurried to my car, not wanting any more close encounters with tourists today, but I took my time lighting a cigarette and getting back into traffic as thoughts cluttered my mind. I kept coming back to the way Sheriff Joey and Felicia acted at the museum board meeting. Did either of them have enough larceny in them to steal the journals to keep people from seeing what a jerk their ancestor was? Yep. Absolutely. Would they take the risk? Much harder question. There was one person who might be able to give me some insight into them.

Hannah Kessler.

3
____

GASLIGHT CITY'S nicest laundromat was located in a newish shopping center on Highway 59, nearly out of town. It catered to the folks who had houses on Piney Lake and featured top-of-the-line washers and dryers, an on-site attendant, and air conditioning. I didn't go there.

I went to the cheapest and least nice laundromat in Gaslight City, partially because it was less than two blocks from the Burns County Museum and partially because the less I spent washing the towels, the more money I'd make. The facility featured dirty floors, one broken dryer, and no air conditioning. Sweat pouring down my face and dripping off my jawbone, I divided Amanda's towels between the two largest washing machines in the place and went outside to sit on the curb and smoke.

I hated to call Hannah and voice my thoughts about her uncle and cousin-in-law. Even though she told me they were no longer on speaking terms—and I was dying to know why—it somehow felt wrong to butt into other people's family business. I sure hated when people did it to me.

It wasn't like Joey or Felicia would tell Hannah they'd stolen the journals. Talking to her might result in no more than hard feelings between us. Despite my refusal to play paranormal investigator when Hannah demanded it, I loved our friendship and would do just about anything to keep it.

If I didn't figure out someone who might be behind the theft, my next course of action was to conduct an informal séance to contact the ghost who did the stealing. That settled it. I decided to send Hannah a text instead of putting her on the spot with a voice-to-voice phone call.

I'd like to talk some more about how Joey and Felicia reacted to Hooty's reading at the board meeting. I pressed send and went inside to put the towels in the dryer. My cellphone buzzed, signaling the arrival of a text message, as I put the last quarter in the dryer's coin slot. I hurried back outside before viewing the message.

I think we do need to talk.

I quickly tapped in a reply. *I'm at the laundromat on San Jacinto Street.*

Be there in 10, came her answer.

Seven minutes later, Hannah marched up the sidewalk. I couldn't believe she'd opt to walk even two blocks in the dog days of summer. Invisible waves of fiery heat rose from the asphalt, rippling over Hannah's approaching form, her face turning redder by the second. I met her with a bottle of cold water I took from the cooler I kept in the backseat of my car. She guzzled the water and held the bottle to her face.

"Why walk?"

"The little high-schooler I hired for summer help is nosy as all get out. Her mother and Felicia are big buds. I didn't want her to know I was meeting you." She sat down on the curb next to me, still gasping from her trek and holding the sweating water bottle to her cheek.

"I guess the big question is whether you think, from what they said at the meeting, Joey or Felicia would steal the journals."

"And I guess my big question is why you won't contact the ghost we saw in the video. How hard could it be?"

"This why you agreed to come down here?"

"Okay, okay. I think they were pissed enough to do something stupid." Hannah drank the rest of her water, staring out at the hellish landscape.

"My one problem with this theory is the surveillance video," I said. "It shows a *ghost* breaking into the museum. I know how the Holze family, especially Felicia, feels about anything they consider satanic."

Hannah snorted. Her snort turned into laugher, which rang over the empty street and bounced off the brick buildings. At first, I worried she might be suffering heat stroke. I pushed myself to my feet, the combination of the extreme heat and the sudden movement making me unsteady, and hurried to my car, where I dipped a paper towel in the icy water in my cooler and took it back to Hannah. She held it to her face and closed her eyes.

"You ever hear of those people who protest in front of

abortion clinics all the time but go in the back door to get abortions?" She glanced at me. "Then the next day they're right back out front protesting again?"

I shrugged, wondering where this was going.

"The Holze family—my uncle's family—would do that."

I squinted at her, trying to reconcile the abortion clinic to our current conversation.

"What it means is they'll do whatever they need to do so things'll go their way, which brings me to why we're no longer speaking." She stood from the curb, went to my car, and helped herself to another bottle of cold water. "I'm embarrassed to tell you this stuff about my family. Are you sure there's no way I can convince you to contact the ghost? I'll provide whatever you need."

I dropped my gaze. Embarrassing Hannah made me feel like a second-rate person. I knew from experience the receiving end of embarrassment hurt and demeaned like nothing else. I pressed my lips together, trying to reconcile myself to dropping the subject, offering an olive branch, when I felt her hand on my arm.

"Forget what I said. I know this is hard for you too, and I know my family's behavior has made your life harder than it has to be. I can take one for the team." She flashed me a weak smile, and I nodded in thanks.

"You know I bought the Mace House from the bank, right?"

"Yes. Still planning to turn it into a bed and breakfast and event venue?"

She nodded. "And I plan to generate a little income

giving tours of the place. But this is more about what you found in there the night you solved your cousin Rae's murder. Remember?"

"Those books. Luther Palmore's books." An icy shudder climbed up my spine as I remembered the night I found those books.

"Gone."

"Maybe the bank auctioned them off to recoup some of their expenses."

"No. They sold the house and contents as a single package. I saw the box of books when I toured the house with the bank's realtor. They were in there as late as three weeks before we closed. Someone came, literally like a thief in the night, and took them." She pulled up her knees almost to her chest and draped her arms over them. "I was disappointed but accepted it, until I was at Uncle Joey's house last Memorial Day."

The direction this was going sounded really, monumentally bad. My shoulders tensed in sympathy for Hannah.

"You ever been in Uncle Joey and Aunt Carly's house?"

"You kidding? They'd probably have to burn the place to purify it after I left." I nudged her with my elbow, and some of the tension broke. We shared a brittle laugh. "I do know they had a new house built on Piney Lake last year."

"The house has all these nooks and crannies and closets for storage. One of them is a little room off the laundry. One of Felicia's kids helped me spill wine all over myself, and I went in there to look for some stain remover. I opened the door thinking it was the logical place for

Aunt Carly to have laundry supplies, but what I found sure wasn't stain remover."

My imagination supplied several different things she could have found in the room. Drugs. Sex toys. An electric chair wired for home use.

"This closet was full of old stuff. Most of it didn't mean anything to me, but Luther Palmore's trunk of books was sitting right in the middle of it."

"What? Did you look through any of it? Was it all Mace Treasure stuff?" My pulse kickstarted and sped up. I never knew Joey Holze had an interest in the Mace Treasure.

"Regretfully, no. Aunt Carly came up behind me and berated me for snooping in her home."

"What'd you say?"

"I let my temper get the best of me. Told Aunt Carly I knew exactly what I'd seen in there and went outside, interrupted the barbecue, and accused Uncle Joey of stealing from a former crime scene."

I kept my mouth shut, already seeing the writing on the wall.

"Uncle Joey went bananas. I mean, I really thought he was going to hit me, and Scott was right there behind him, waiting for his turn. In one instant, the whole family turned on me, calling me a traitor, telling me to get off their property."

"And you left." Though I loathed Hannah's family with the intensity of a flaming case of herpes, her falling out with them made me feel bad for her. Finding out people aren't who they pretend to be is never fun. Especially when they're loved ones.

"Nothing else to do but leave. Thing is, I'm wondering now if the Bruce journals and Priscilla Herrera's book of folk medicine are sitting in the storage closet at Uncle Joey's and Aunt Carly's."

"One way to find out." I said the words jokingly, knowing Hannah would never break into anybody's house.

"Yep." She checked her watch. "Aunt Carly's weekly hair appointment and manicure starts in twenty minutes. She's usually at Amanda's Hair Flair for an hour, longer if she gets to gossiping, but lets depend on an hour. I've still got my key. Want to go see for ourselves?"

She didn't have to ask me twice.

———

WE HURRIED to fold towels in the stifling laundromat, both of us shining with sweat. Whoever decided to call it a glow needed his or her head examined with an ice pick. By the time we loaded the towels into the car, I was soaked and exhausted and ended up letting the hot metal burn the undersides of my arms. I jumped away from the car with a yelp. Using a bandana to protect my hand, I opened the driver's door, started the car, and turned the air conditioner on high to push out some of the pent up heat.

"We'll take the towels by Amanda's," I said. "See if Carly's there." I leveled my gaze on Hannah. "You sure you want to do this?"

Hannah bit her lip and twisted her fingers.

"We don't have to do this." I didn't know how else we'd see if Joey had the Bruce journals and the folk medicine book with the rest of his treasure trove, but I didn't want to force Hannah into doing something she didn't want to do.

"Yes, we do," Hannah said. "I won't stop wondering until I know for sure."

I took Amanda's towels into the salon and saw Carly Holze's sour, lemon face for myself. Her gaze, glowing with hate, followed me as I took the towels into the laundry room and put them away in the cabinets Amanda had set aside for them. She sneered as Amanda paid me, jabbering nonstop about how happy she was to have her new washer. I gave Carly a wave on my way out, and she turned her face away, pretending not to have seen.

Did I feel guilty about breaking into her house? Not as much as I should have.

The drive out to Piney Lake took us a good twenty minutes, during which we said little. Hannah took a key off her keyring and fumbled it through her fingers until she dropped it and had to dig on the floorboard for it. I turned into Joey and Carly's subdivision.

"No," Hannah said. "Their house backs up to some woods over by Billy Ray's Marina. Let's park there, and we'll sneak through the woods."

I did as she suggested, adrenaline pumping jangly tension through my body, and pulled into a parking place between two super-sized trucks with empty boat trailers hitched to them. The subdivision's houses peeked through a screen of skinny pine trees and overgrown brush. People loitered everywhere. There was no way we'd be able to walk into the woods without someone seeing. Hannah gazed out the window, probably realizing the same thing I did.

"The thing to do," I said, "is act like we belong in those woods. Walk into them like we do it every day." I glanced at Hannah. "We can call this off if you're too scared. No shame."

She got out of the car without answering. I followed. Together, we strode toward the woods, both of us keeping our eyes straight ahead.

"Hey. What y'all gonna do in those woods?" A male voice yelled.

"Can I watch?" Hollered another.

I half-turned, ready to tell them they could all go masturbate and use sand for lubricant. Hannah grabbed my arm and squeezed hard.

"Ignore 'em. They'll remember us better if you answer them."

I grumbled but obeyed, and we stepped into the woods. About twenty feet from us rose a wall of seven-foot wooden privacy fences, the second stories of the houses visible behind them.

"Uncle Joey's is the third one from the left." Hannah started pushing her way through the brush, her face stony. I picked my way after her, wishing I had a machete to cut the thick brush, but knowing it was best I didn't. The people in the marina parking lot would have remembered a woman carrying a machete.

Hannah stood in front of the house she'd pointed out, hands on her hips. The problem was obvious. No footholds to use to climb over. The surrounding trees were not thick enough to hold either of our weight.

"Shit," Hannah whispered. "I'd hoped we could go in the back, lessen the risk of one of the neighbors seeing."

"How about I give you a boost over?"

Hannah nodded. "On the other side of the fence is the frame work. I'll climb onto it and help you over."

Boosting Hannah over presented little difficulty. She hooked one long leg over the top of the fence and pulled herself into the yard. The fence rattled, and Hannah's head appeared over the top. She held out her hand. I craned my neck to study the distance between me and the fence's top. A good two feet. I got ready to tell Hannah I couldn't do it, but one look at her face stopped me. Arguing would do nothing more than waste precious minutes before Carly came home.

I jumped up and grabbed her hand, using my feet to walk up the fence. As soon as I could, I used my free hand to grab the top of the fence and used it for leverage instead of pulling Hannah's arms from her sockets. My shoulders twitched and shuddered by the time I dropped into the yard. I caught Hannah studying where the rough fence boards had scratched her arms and found similar spots on mine. We crept to the back door, both of us looking over our shoulders like the criminals we were. Hannah unlocked the white French door and slipped inside, quickly punching in the alarm code.

"I can't believe they didn't change the locks and the alarm code after they disowned you," I said.

"Maybe they figure I won't come back, and I wasn't going to. Come on."

The huge kitchen Hannah led me through had every possible frill I could imagine. I wondered how Joey and Carly afforded it on a teacher's and a sheriff's salary. The laundry room was right off the kitchen. Hannah turned on the light and held the door wide enough for me to follow her inside. To the right was another door. Hannah opened it and darkness faced us.

"Oh, the light," she said and flipped the switch.

I held my breath, ready to see the Bruce family journals, the book of folk medicine, and a bunch of other contraband Sheriff Joey shouldn't have. We both stared in shocked silence for several long moments. The storage room was empty except for an electric tile floor cleaner.

From across the house, we heard the front door open and a gruff voice say, "Damnit. Don't know why I bought this alarm system if she can't set it."

Sheriff Joey Holze was home. My thoughts scrambled into a meaningless roar. I stood paralyzed beside my friend. Joey's heavy steps thumped up the stairs, his angry grumbles drifting back to us.

"Let's go. Right now." I turned to Hannah and almost lost hope. My buoyant friend stood with her eyes squeezed shut, her hands raised in trembling fists. Was she just going freeze up and let us get caught? I nudged her.

"He'll be able to see us from the bedroom window."

"Does it look out on the front or the back?"

"The back," she hissed as though I should have known.

"We'll go out the front then. Hope nobody sees us."

"Somebody will, though."

"It's either stay here and wait for him to find us or try to get away." I doubted our ability to get out undetected, too, but I'd be damned if I stood in this utility room like a lump of shit on a log waiting to get stepped in. I tiptoed out of the room, towing Hannah behind me.

We crept through the other side of the kitchen and came out in a dining room, which opened onto a massive living room. The front door stood on the other side of it, right by the stairs. I tugged Hannah, motioning at the door. The squeaking sound my sneakers made on the tile seemed to fill the room—hell, the whole house. I tried to take my steps differently, but nothing helped. If we could make it to the thick, cream colored carpet in the living room, we'd be home free.

I held my breath, gritting my teeth against the desire pounding in me to run, banging off walls and knocking over furniture if that's what it took, anything to get me out of there. Sheriff Joey hated me, had since I was a kid. No telling what he'd do if he found me here. Maybe shoot me. Definitely arrest me.

I took the first step onto the carpet, relief flooding my body. Ten more steps to the front door. *We got this.* I glanced at Hannah, giving her an encouraging nod. Her face had turned the color of old socks, neither white nor gray, and her lips trembled. Seven more steps. Just seven little steps.

Joey's cellphone began ringing. It was too loud to be upstairs. I spotted it on a catch-all table next to the front door. Joey's heavy footsteps thumped across the upper floor. Hannah and I made a run for it. I grabbed the door-knob, and it slipped right through my sweaty hand. The inside of my mouth went arid. I couldn't move. Hannah reached around me and twisted. Still nothing. We both saw the deadbolt was engaged at the same time. Our hands collided. Hannah brushed mine aside and flipped the thumb turn, opening the door.

"Carly? That you? Answer my phone, would you?"

His footsteps stumped closer, his grunts of effort drifting down the stairs.

"Hey," he yelled. "Who's down there?"

We ran through the front door, leaving it standing open, and sprinted down the street. Hannah pulled ahead of me, leading the way to a vacant lot at the street's end and cutting through it. We lunged into the woods, ignoring the branches tearing at us, and didn't stop running until we dove into my car.

"Go, go, go," Hannah yelled, slapping her thighs for emphasis.

"I can't. They'll notice us for sure if I go screeching out of here." Trying to ignore Hannah bouncing in the seat next to me, I crept out of the lot and stayed with the speed limit all the way back out to the main road. Once I assured myself I heard no sirens and saw no flashing lights, I turned to Hannah to make a joke about our close call. My words died a quick death. She sat with her elbow wedged against the passenger window and her forehead resting on the palm of her hand. I asked, "You all right?"

"The books were there, Peri Jean. I swear to you." She squinted her eyes and shook her head.

"I don't doubt your word," I said.

"Those sons of bitches moved them. That's why they didn't bother to change the locks." Hannah's jaw moved like she was chewing on a big wad of gum.

"We'll figure something else out." I pulled to the curb a block from the museum so Hannah could sneak back in without her gossipy helper seeing me.

"I'll call you if I have any new ideas." Hannah got out and walked down the block, head swiveling around as though she still feared getting caught red-handed.

I could have kicked myself for the whole fracas. We didn't find a damn thing and could have ended up in jail over it. The likelihood of me having to contact the thieving ghost had just grown exponentially.

I dragged the recesses of my mind for ideas on how to connect a living person to the crime without resorting to what Dean called my woo-woo talents. Half the town and hundreds of treasure hunters would have given their left nipple for the stolen items. Which brought me back to Joey Holze and his fancy house.

The house Hannah and I illegally entered earlier was a year old and on a tiny subdivision lot. There hadn't even been a storage building in the backyard. Where else could Joey have hidden the stuff Hannah saw on Memorial Day? The possibilities were limitless. He'd had nearly three months since Hannah stumbled upon his stash to pick the perfect hiding place. My first guess was public storage, but I saw no way to locate his rental.

Gaslight City had a population of two thousand or so, plenty of residents to justify the three storage facilities dotted around the city. Burns County, with an overall population of twenty thousand, had even more rent-by-the-month storage businesses. No way could I check them all. Even if I could, how would I get the owners to admit Joey rented a unit there?

I needed someone who had better resources to investigate this stuff. Rainey Bruce. She went through assistants faster than shit through a goose, and I worked for her at least a couple of days a month so she wouldn't drown in mundane tasks. I'd heard her talk to a private investigator several times for help on a case.

I took out my cellphone and called her. She answered on the first ring.

"I've had an idea about who may have stolen your family's property. Can you meet me to talk about it?"

"I'm closing the office for the day. Fifteen minutes at my house?"

4

I TOLD Rainey about the day's events in her huge living room, trying not to stain her pristine white couch. At points in my monologue she closed her eyes and clenched her jaw. Mostly she shook her head.

"I hate to leave you and Hannah Kessler alone together. The two of you are like a pair of dumb, teenage girls." She pushed herself off the couch and glided across to her open air dining room and picked up a brown leather messenger bag probably worth more than anything I owned.

I curled my toes into the chocolate colored carpet, Rainey having insisted I leave my nasty shoes outside. She glanced at my sock encased feet, shook her head again, and set the messenger bag on her coffee table. The scratches and drink rings on the expensive surface suggested she worked here often.

"What you want me to look into is illegal without a search warrant, and one of those would require probable cause. Of which we have none." She tapped her long fingers on the closed laptop. "Plus, if we do learn he has a storage unit, who goes in?"

I opened my mouth to speak.

"Don't say anything. Forget I asked." She took her cellphone out of the messenger bag and placed it on the coffee table where she could see it. "I think the legal risk involved is not worth the possible gain."

"But—"

"Let me finish. I think you are stalling, trying to keep from facing who and what you are."

"You're right," I said. "So what?"

Rainey stared at me for too long. Then she leaned forward and pointed one of her blood red, inch-long fingernails at me, her gaze never leaving mine. "Those journals belong to my family, and I intend to have them back. You, as my friend, could help me. There's your 'so what.'"

"I'm trying to help. There's a good chance Joey might have the journals."

"Wouldn't it be easier for you to contact the ghost we saw on the video and find out?"

I sighed and considered asking if it would be easier for me to wring her neck. "It's not like those mediums you see on TV solving crimes. I get flashes, images, sometimes a short vision. It's not like the ghost is going to *say* anything to me." I left out the part where the ghost appeared in the backseat of my car, begging for my help.

"What about the thing around your neck? Eddie mentioned it had powerful magic." She pointed at the black opal. I took it off and handed it to her. She hesitated before she took it but smiled as soon as it touched her hand. "This reminds me of a tour I took once in New Orleans, an occult tour. We went to this museum right in the Quarter and looked at voodoo artifacts. Some of them emanated power. This is the same. Why don't you wear it more often?"

I squirmed a little. "Dean asked me not to because when I wear it, I see more stuff, and more of it tries to interact with me."

"Is this resistance to helping us coming from Dean? Like an issue between the two of you?" Rainey crooked an eyebrow.

"I don't want this either." I gestured at my head, where I guessed the power came from. I could tell by the way Rainey mashed her full lips together she disagreed, but she simply handed the black opal back to me without saying anything. We sat in silence for several long moments. Rainey's forehead crinkled, a line appearing between her perfectly plucked, maybe even waxed or threaded, brows. Finally, she turned to me.

"May I tell you why this is such a big deal to me?"

I thought I knew, but refusing to listen might cause her to have an outburst, and I didn't want any part of one of Rainey's fits. Aliens in outer space feared Rainey Bruce's temper.

"I think we can talk from the perspective of two women who share an understanding of what it is to be the odd woman out. Me because of the color of my skin. You because you have this quirky gift." She raised her eyebrows at me in question. I nodded to show I agreed.

"These journals represent what my family overcame in this county, what we achieved in spite of racism and lack of opportunity."

A calico cat slunk into the room and bounded onto the couch. Rainey petted it with the back of her fingers. I wondered how she kept her couches so clean, why she bothered to buy furniture so receptive to showing dirt, if she had this cat. For the first time ever, I saw the complexities Rainey faced in being Rainey.

"My ancestor Hezekiah Bruce, who wrote the journals, came here with nothing, yet managed to build a solvent business and gain respect in the community. His son, Isaiah, worked his way up at Longstreet Lumber to become the first black foreman. Isaiah's son, who was my grandfather, became the first black judge in Burns County. We march forward, no matter what, no matter how badly it hurts."

I didn't understand where this was going or how I was supposed to respond.

"Letting those journals go, writing them off without fighting to get them back, seems like I'm saying I don't respect the sacrifices my family made or the road they fought to pave for me."

"I can see what you mean, but—"

"Still not finished." She held up one hand. "It would be bad enough to let go of my family history, but losing the history of what happened to Priscilla Herrera, poor woman, rankles even more. She deserves for people to know her story, the persecution she faced, as much as my ancestors do. It surprises me how much your story parallels hers, and how it doesn't seem to matter to you." She settled her intense gaze on me, and it took a while before I realized she expected me to speak, to explain.

"People think because I'm a Mace, I'm treasure crazy. They think because I can see ghosts, I'm a freak of nature. Both together is like being an attraction in a carnival. People pointing all the time, laughing, jeering. I've dealt with it all my life, and I'm sick of it. I want to pretend to be normal."

She barked a short, bitter laugh. "At least you can pretend to be something you're not. I don't have that luxury."

My cheeks flamed. Of course she didn't. The prejudices she faced wouldn't go away, no matter what she did.

She gave me a tight smile as though she knew the thoughts in my mind better than I did. "Here's what I see: a thirty-one-year-old woman who wants to hide from who and what she is when she *could* use it to better both herself and the world around her."

I shook my head. "Not when people think I'm a Satanist. Don't you remember when Felicia told everyone I was a Satanist? Back in eighth grade?"

"So what? Who cares what assholes think?" Rainey yelled the words at the ceiling. The calico cat raised its head and regarded its crazy mistress. "Let me tell you something, Peri Jean Mace. You're going to face prejudiced, bigoted assholes for the rest of your life. This woman whose book of folk medicine was stolen along with the journals, paid the ultimate price for standing up against mean, hateful bullies."

Her words stung, but they didn't change how I felt. The journals and the folk medicine book belonged to the Mace treasure and all the crazies who got their jollies hunting for it. I blamed Priscilla Herrera's horrible death on the Mace Treasure as much as I did the ignorance of a bunch of greedy jerks. Rainey might have her point, but I had mine too, dammit.

"Whoever has the journals and the folk medicine book wants them because of the Mace Treasure. I know first-hand about the havoc the Mace Treasure can cause." I clenched my hands in my lap. "I've lost family and friends to it, and I don't want to lose myself in it."

Rainey started to speak.

"No. I listened to you. Now it's your turn to listen to me." I took a deep, fortifying breath. "There is a lot of risk involved. If things get out of hand, I face both Priscilla Herrera's fate and the curse of the Mace Treasure."

"And you face whatever's going on with you and Dean." Rainey's lips curved, and it wasn't the smile she used to win the title of Miss Texas.

I jumped. "Why do you keep bringing Dean up? Who's been talking to you?"

Rainey held up both hands. "Before you get too upset, remember I read people for a living—juries, law enforcement, clients, you name it. I've seen the tension between the two of you and wondered what it was about. Now I know for sure." She sat back on the couch and crossed one long leg over the other. "I'll rephrase what I said earlier. Do not, under any circumstances, let other people tell you what to be. Embrace what you are and let the rest follow."

"But aren't you trying to tell me what to be?" I leaned forward and met her gaze as steadily as I could. "Don't you want the services of a medium?"

"Okay." She shrugged. The expression on her face suggested I was lucky to get even that. "You got me. Only you can decide what matters to you, and what you need to do to matter to yourself." She unzipped the messenger bag and took out the padded envelope I saw her fiddling with in the video from the museum board meeting. "I'd like to show you something we found with the folk medicine book. Aside from the book's contents, this picture backs up my theory Priscilla Herrera penned the book." From the envelope, she pulled the rectangular card I'd glimpsed and set it in front of me.

What I saw stunned the arguments I wanted to present to Rainey right out of my head. I looked at a very old picture printed on what amounted to card stock. It featured a full-length shot of a woman wearing a dress I thought looked like a wedding cake. Blazing, defiant dark eyes topped by eyebrows Joan Crawford would have envied dominated the woman's oval face. Full lips compressed into not quite a pout and not quite a scowl, she thrust out her chin as though to say, "Here I am." The picture would have been the same as every other cabinet card I've ever seen except for one thing: every visible area of this body was tattooed.

"I think this might have been Priscilla Herrera." Rainey's voice lost its courtroom force, and I raised my head to look at her. A wistful sadness replaced the determination and near anger from a few minutes earlier. "She was a woman just like us, maybe more like you than me, but she knew all the fears and pressures we face."

I returned my gaze to the picture, staring into the tattooed woman's determined eyes. Something about her drew me in. I felt a pull every time I looked at her. The black opal zinged to life on my chest, the way it often did when ghosts were near, and I felt a little breeze from nowhere pass over my skin. Time seemed to grind to a halt as I lost myself in the picture. One of her tattoos caught my attention. I glanced up at Rainey.

"Do you own a magnifying glass?"

She went into the kitchen, came back with a cheap plastic one, and gave it to me. I held the glass over the picture and squinted at the tattoo. I couldn't see all of it, but it looked like a bird, not dissimilar to the one tattooed on my bicep, which I got under decidedly weird circumstances. I set the magnifying glass aside and stared at the picture again. For some reason, it seemed different than it had the first time I'd viewed it as a whole. From outside, the caw of a large bird reached my ears, and it hit me. There was a big, black bird in the background of the picture. It was perched on some sort of stand. While I watched, it flared out its wings and slowly moved them. Then it flew away. I jerked in my seat.

"What happened?" Rainey's voice, for all her trying to convince me I should get more in touch with my supernatural side, sounded panicked. "Did you see something?

"Probably not." The pulse of energy coming out of the black opal and soaking into my skin said different. Rainey's narrowed eyes suggested she heard my lie. I waited for her to call me on it, but she didn't. Instead she reached for the picture.

"Do you mind if I take a picture with my phone?" I couldn't explain why I wanted to so badly, but I did.

"If you'll promise to keep thinking about contacting the spirit on the video and if you'll think about what I've said here today."

"If I figure out where Joey stored the stuff Hannah saw, I'm breaking in to see if the journals are there."

Rainey made a face. "But you'll also consider contacting the ghost?"

Agreeing to think about contacting the ghost felt like a commitment I didn't want to make, but I nodded anyway. I wanted my copy of the picture of Priscilla Herrera enough to do it. She set the photo back on the coffee table, and I snapped my picture.

Rainey saw me to the door and followed me onto the stoop.

"See you in a couple of hours at Dean's barbecue." She took one look at my face and assumed the expression she seemed to reserve especially for me—half-lowered eyelids, lips pressed flat with one corner quirked under. "You forgot, didn't you?"

I ran for my car, not bothering to answer.

———

I HURRIED out to my car and drove away from Rainey's house, through her upscale subdivision, and past the guard shack. How could I forget Dean's campaign barbecue? He told me at least once a day that voters needed to see us together in social settings.

My mind raced with all the getting ready I needed to do. Dean would want me wearing tasteful makeup and the delicate jewelry he bought for my birthday. My dress needed a last-minute touch-up with the iron.

My cellphone buzzed with the tone I selected for text messages. I took my eyes off the road to steal a glance at it, fully expecting a message from Hannah about what she planned to wear tonight. Instead, I saw a picture, sent from a blocked number. I drove a few more seconds, but curiosity got the best of me. I pulled my car onto the shoulder and opened the message.

"Weird," I muttered. The text consisted of nothing more than the picture of Priscilla Herrera I snapped at Rainey's. I could even see the edges of the coffee table around the picture. *Why would a picture I took come to me as a blocked text message?* I hoped my smartphone wasn't malfunctioning.

I tried switching to the smartphone's main menu. Nothing happened. The picture stayed there on the screen, Priscilla Herrera's dark eyes boring into me. I sensed, rather than saw, a movement in the picture. The raven perched behind Priscilla moved its head ever so slightly. Underneath the hum of my car's engine, I heard other sounds. Muffled voices talking. Horse's hoofs clopping on a hard surface. I smelled something frying. Priscilla Herrera's image blinked, and she tilted her head in my direction. The car faded away as I slipped fully into the vision.

"Come with me, Peri Jean Mace." She stepped toward me. I cringed because there was no way to get away from her. I saw the tattoo on her shoulder without the filter of a hundred-year-old photograph. It was a black bird—a raven or a crow—same as mine. A light, dizzy feeling spread through me, and black spots appeared in my vision. Why did we have the same tattoo? Before I could ask, the tattooed lady grabbed my hand, and the room we were in faded, leaving us to float in darkness so black and complete and soundless, I wondered if I had died.

Fear closed my throat, choking me. Coughing, gasping, and gagging, I twisted in the darkness, hoping to break free but found I couldn't move. This wasn't so bad, even if I was dying. It was sort of soothing.

Whispers of a million voices saying no words arose around me. I forgot about returning to where I came from and focused on where I was. This place felt wrong, heavy and suffocating, as though if I spent too much time here I could get lost. I needed to hurry. I searched my senses, trying to find something I could focus on, something I could use to ground myself. I smelled the faintest scent of spearmint and clung to it. The sound of wind whispering through pine trees filled my ears, and the blackness faded.

The woman who'd shanghaied me was no longer young. She'd thickened with age and wore a frumpy calico dress which covered all her wonderful tattoos. Her hair had grayed and was pulled into a plain bun. The image before me faded in and out like a radio station does on a long drive. Black holes where her eyes should have been made me want to scream and recoil. Teeth clenched, I held in my emotions and focused instead on my hostess. "What do you want?" The words wouldn't come out of my mouth. It was as though I'd lost the ability to speak, but I could hear my thoughts clearly.

A rush of arctic wind blew back my hair and cooled my face. My heart couldn't beat fast enough to keep up with the adrenaline coursing through my veins. The black opal sent painful shocks into my skin, maybe magnifying my power so I could see more of this vision, maybe protecting me. I regretted my shamefully limited knowledge of it.

"Why am I here?" Again the words formed perfectly in my head, but my hostess said nothing.

Anger and hurt rolled off her with violence, whipping at me, throbbing in the deepest parts of my soul. In addition to the spirit's emotions, I picked up her intent. She wanted something from me.

My body experienced the same weightless feeling going downhill on a roller coaster gave me. Doing favors for ghosts never ended well. I had to get out of here. I concentrated on moving my hand. It was like lifting an anvil, but I managed to pull the black opal from my shirt and squeeze it in one fist. Back in Louisiana, when I first became acquainted with the black opal, it enabled me to hear snatches of words from the ghosts. Maybe it would open my senses further this time as well.

Instead of speaking, the ghost floated toward me. I became aware of a clacking sound in the room and realized it was my teeth chattering. She closed one hand over mine, the cold burning my skin. The room came into stark, painful focus.

"You can't leave yet." Her voice, soft and clear as the song of angels, was not what I expected. Her grip on me tightened. "Pay careful attention. I did a great evil in cursing the treasure. For my sins, I've been unable to find rest in the spirit realm. The one who stole my book will unleash destruction on Gaslight City. Watch and learn because only you can help me stop this evil and find peace."

Time jumped again, and it was late afternoon, heading toward dusk. I was in a cabin surrounded by pine trees. The whisper of wind caressing the pine needles came through the windows along with the croak of ravens. One of the huge, dark birds lighted on the windowsill, cocking its head at me and staring at me with one black eye. It let out another deep call. Sharp smoke from the open fireplace burned my eyes and dried out my throat, but the chilly wind coming through the open windows made me want to move closer.

Priscilla Herrera knelt before a long bench, her hands working at something. She hummed words to a song I didn't recognize in a language unfamiliar to my ears. Her purpose came to me, almost as if it had been implanted in my mind. Someone was coming, and when they got here, they'd kill her. She couldn't keep from dying, but she could keep her killers from winning in the end. She'd make them hurt.

Priscilla took out a worn book, hand bound in some sort of leather, opened it, and read, her finger moving along with her progress. She set the book aside and leaned back her head, her eyes drifting closed, and took slow deep breaths. The air in the room charged with some sort of power I couldn't see. The fillings in my teeth ached, and my earrings thrummed with it.

She turned to make sure I saw her place flat stones, polished and carved into geometric shapes, in a circle on the bench before her. She rummaged around on the plank floor at her knees and raised a small object concealed in one trembling hand. She fumbled and it fell to the floor, rolling away from her and landing ass end up. Best I could tell, it was a tiny chest, no bigger across than my smartphone. On the bottom was a bird like the one I had tattooed on my arm. Just like the one she had tattooed on her body. The hairs on the back of my neck, already standing at attention, stiffened. Priscilla retrieved the box and set it on the table. She gave me a sly smile. A glowing nimbus appeared around the box, its edges vibrating and dancing. Priscilla spoke, still in the sing-song language I could only identify as not Spanish, but I understood every word and felt the power she wielded as though it belonged to me.

"Entity trapped within these stones, go to live in this box and in the thing it represents, keeping it from the eyes of he who does not see and does not hear and does not have the Blood. Find your new home in this box and seek revenge on he who comes to steal that which is not his. Recognize my Blood and remember it from now until the end of time, for you belong to me and do my bidding."

She picked up a knife and slashed her thumb pad. I flinched, imagining the pain, and reached out to stop her, but it was like grabbing for something underwater. Some force weighed me down and held me away from my hostess. Priscilla squeezed the wound, dribbling blood onto the toy-sized chest. Then she opened it. She pulled her hair out of the bun and used her knife to cut off a lock. She placed the hair inside the chest and closed it. She lifted a glass vial and held it to the spare light filtering into the windows. Though clear, I could see particles swimming sluggishly in the liquid. She swirled the vial and upended its contents onto the chest.

She took several deep breaths and began to speak, her words guttural, her voice shaking with the force of them.

"One of mine, one with power, will return some day to reward you for a job well done and allow you to return to the dark outposts from which you came. You will know it is me from the Blood and from these stones in which you have lived and to which you must return to receive your reward. If one who separates you from this box does not have these stones, you will be forced to wander this plane for eternity. Level this town and destroy all who live within for your revenge."

Finished speaking, she struck a match and set it on the tiny chest. Blue flame engulfed it, burning so bright my eyes stung and watered. The odor was one of sulfur and spice. As quickly as it started, the fire burned out. The box survived the fire undamaged. Priscilla Herrera palmed the tiny box and made it disappear into the folds of her dress. Then she picked up the stones one by one and performed the same trick with them.

She leaned over the open book and traced a pattern on the open page, whispering words in the same odd language, but this time I did not understand the words. As I watched, the words wiggled and shifted, changing into other words. She closed the book, performing the same ritual, and the book lengthened and flattened, resembling a store-bought ledger like the ones I'd seen in the video of the museum board's meeting.

Realization slammed into me, squeezing my already abused muscles into even more painful contortions. The book Hannah and the others thought to be a book of folk medicine was actually Priscilla's spell book, disguised by magic.

The door opened, and an adolescent boy with black hair and dark skin rushed inside. He communicated with the woman in gestures. I began to shake as I caught the gist. Whoever was coming was close. The woman yelled, in English, "Samantha!" and a teenage girl appeared.

"Take this book and go hide in the woods. Mr. Bruce will be along shortly, and he'll want to take you to his home. You go and give this book to Mrs. Bruce and tell her it's full of remedies to help with her children's maladies, and it's my gift to her for her friendship."

"But, Mama," the girl whined.

"Shush and listen. Thank both Mr. and Mrs. Bruce the way I taught you. Tonight, once it gets dark, you slip away from the Bruce place and walk south all night, never stopping. Sleep through the days and walk at night. Keep walking until you reach Nacogdoches. If someone asks your family name, say it's Goyo, not Herrera. Bad people may be looking for you. In Nacogdoches, find a man named Bob Skanes. Ask him to help you get work."

The boy shook his head, ran to the corner, and grabbed an axe.

"No," Priscilla said. "It's too late. I trusted the wrong people, overstayed my welcome."

"It's not too late," Samantha yelled.

"It is." Priscilla rushed to her, grabbed her hand, traced something on the palm and said a few words. She repeated the same ritual on the boy. Then she gathered both children close and hugged them tight, all of them rocking and crying. She pushed them away, ignoring their protests, and shooed them out the door. She followed them outside.

"Remember what you see here on this day. Never forget it. Never come back to this godforsaken gathering of ignorant, greedy fools." She hugged both children again. "Now go. Forget who you are. Never come back." She stood outside her house, tears running down her face, until she could see her children no more. Then she went back inside.

In the distance, I heard hoof beats, and the first horse came into view within seconds. The man astride it swung off its back and came to the door and knocked. Priscilla sighed deeply. Ignoring the knock, she returned to the bench and sat to wait.

"Open this door, witch," an ugly, harsh voice shouted. Many birds returned the man's shout, the sound of their flapping wings filling the small cabin, the noise of them so loud my eardrums rattled.

I woke from the vision gagging and gasping, trying to scream at Priscilla to run, and found myself still sitting in the front seat of my car. My muscles ached as though I'd taken a beating. The smell of smoke from Priscilla Herrera's hearth fire lingered on my clothes. Had she somehow taken my physical form there? The thought of so much power scared me worse than any ghost ever had.

The words from her incantations replayed in my mind, especially the part about her ordering whatever spiritual baddie she'd assigned to protect the treasure to level Gaslight City and kill all the residents.

What if Eddie was right, and the person who stole the Bruce Journals and the book of folk medicine intended to try to remove the curse? Then I remembered seeing Priscilla turn her spell book into the book of folk medicine and what she told me about stopping her evil from being made worse. The thief already had the spell book used to create the curse. *One step closer to destruction.*

Priscilla's words returned to me, as clear as if she sat in the car with me, whispering them in my ear. I almost felt her breath tickling my skin. *Only you can help me stop this evil.*

I did a slow burn. Why did this whole thing have to come along and dump garbage all over the life I was working so hard to normalize? I picked up my phone again and took in Priscilla Herrera's picture.

A wild hope occurred to me. Priscilla may not have possessed the power or skill to unleash Hell to destroy Gaslight City and its inhabitants. I shook my head. I didn't even believe it myself. Of course she had power, more than I could imagine. Whatever she intended would happen. Scratch the idea.

I rummaged through my brain for another way out and

found one. All the people who hurt Priscilla died years and years ago. Surely she wouldn't annihilate a bunch of innocents, no matter how much wrong their ancestors did to her. Or not. Facing death, Priscilla Herrera may not have cared who she stomped and squished.

I needed to talk this whole thing over with somebody, and I knew one person who would selflessly help me without considering his own agenda. Eddie had spent his entire life researching the Mace Treasure and all the people connected to it, and I trusted him with my life. I did a U-turn and drove toward his house, using my free hand to call him on my cellphone.

Maybe I could get back to pretending to be just an everyday gal after this whole mess blew over.

5

———————

PICTURES of me growing up nearly hid the cheap, yellowed paneling in Eddie's living room. He'd committed to helping raise me because he'd been my daddy's best friend. His judgment wasn't always the greatest, he did the best he knew how to do. The contrast between his loyalty to me and my foot-dragging over using my natural ability to help find the stolen items burned at my conscience.

The sweltering living room smelled like the devil's butthole after six months without any washing, even with all the box fans Eddie had running. He entered the living room bearing a paper plate piled with smoked sausage, cheese, and saltine crackers. He gave half to his dog, Ugly, who'd been lying on top of one of the mobile home's floor vents. The dog scooted where he could eat the food, a big grin on his face. I took a good look at Ugly and realized where the smell must have come from. The dog's patchy coat was covered in black smudges. *Gross.*

"So what's up?" Eddie made himself a sausage, cheese, and cracker sandwich and ate it in one bite.

"We've got to find the stolen journals and folk medicine book as quickly as possible." I contemplated Eddie's hors d'oeuvres and decided against them. "I'll help all I can with the finding, but I don't think I can get them back by myself."

"I feel like I've walked into the middle of a movie." Eddie shoved another cracker sandwich into his mouth whole and chewed as he talked. "Why don't you tell me what's got you so upset you changed your mind?"

Shivering, I told Eddie about the vision in as much detail as I could remember. His face lit up as soon as he realized what I'd seen. He set his paper plate on the floor for Ugly. The dog raised his head, waited a beat to make sure Eddie didn't intend to take it to him, and lazily rose to check it out. He ate the paper plate, too. This close, the smell coming off the dog nearly choked me. Eddie got out a yellow legal pad, scribbling while I talked.

When he finished eating, the dog raised his misshapen head and grinned at me, tongue lolling out of his mouth. I smiled but couldn't make myself touch his nasty fur. Ugly's resilience touched my heart. Eddie and I found the dog wandering on the side of the road near death a few years ago. The vet who helped us save him speculated Ugly'd been a bait dog for dog fighters.

"Aw, he's okay. You can pet him," Eddie said.

"What'd he get into?"

"Neighbor's septic tank is overflowing. Ugly found it a

few days ago. Figured I'd wait 'til he got it fixed to give old Ug a bath."

I swallowed my rising gorge and gave Ugly a perfunctory pat. He trotted back to his air vent and flopped down on it. I tried to sit on the couch while touching as little of the ratty floral printed fabric as possible.

"That all you seen in your vision?" Eddie spoke without taking his eyes off the pad.

"Pretty much."

"Well, ain't blackbirds you seen. It's ravens." Eddie turned his notepad so I could see where he'd sketched a raven while I talked. "I know because I researched 'em once after seeing 'em out on Priscilla Herrera's old place. Only place I've ever seen ravens 'round here."

I thought of my tattoo, how it matched the picture on the bottom of the box. No need to mention it to Eddie. This whole thing was too big for me as it was.

"I'll go back in my notes on Priscilla Herrera. See if I can learn anything about her connection to ravens. I ain't got much information though." He made a note on his pad.

"What really matters is what she said when she cursed the treasure." I worried Eddie would get lost in details and miss the part where removing the curse could unleash hell on earth.

"Right. I was fooling with the dog and almost missed it." He leaned forward, his gaze fixed on my face. "Tell me again."

I took a deep breath. "Way I understood, if anybody tries

to remove the curse and doesn't put those demons, or whatever they were, back into the stones or send them back to the dark outposts, Gaslight City's going to get mashed flat. She said, 'Level this town and destroy all who live within.'"

Eddie's mouth went slack, but his eyes didn't. In their muddy depths, I saw his mind spinning ninety to nothing. "Oh, hell. You seen them things guarding the treasure, ain't you?"

"Two times, yes." My body tightened, remembering the experience. "Neither meeting was any fun."

"You think these...guardians? Ain't that what she called 'em? You think they got enough power to do what she says? Level the city? Destroy all who live within?" He chewed on his upper lip.

"Let me put it this way. It'll be like when you step on one of these roaches I keep seeing run across the floor." I paused to let Eddie think about it for a few seconds, then continued. "So if you're right about the thief planning to undo the curse, the shit is about to hit the fan and splatter. But there's no way I can fight someone so powerful." I stared at Eddie, waiting for him to tell me how it could all be fixed.

"What you mean? You faster'n a two-dollar pistol when you set your mind to something."

"This person's way ahead of anything I can learn in time to help." I barely resisted the urge to scream the words. There was no way I could do this. It wasn't like some miracle was going to come along and transform me into someone who knew about this kind of crap. "Whoever this is can control ghosts. If we're right, they know enough magic to think they can undo Priscilla Herrera's curse. It's beyond me."

"Tell me the vision again from the beginning," he said.

"How many times do I have to repeat it?"

"When'd you get to be such a smart ass?" He furrowed his bushy gray brows. "You used to have better manners."

"Gee, I wonder where I learned bad ones." I went through the vision again, this time stopping to answer Eddie's questions and repeating bits and pieces until he had them straight.

"Now I don't know much about magic, so I might be wrong." He caressed the stubble on his cheeks as he thought. "But you said Priscilla Herrera put the demons into the little box with the raven on the bottom."

I nodded.

"My thinking is if someone wanted to undo the curse, they'd need the little box." A smile grew across his grizzled face. "So what you got to do is find the box, Peri Jean Mace, before they get to it. You don't need to be no ace magic practitioner to do it either."

I snorted. "The box is gone. Got lost a hundred years ago when those assholes hanged Priscilla Herrera."

"You saw her put it in the pocket of her dress, did you not?"

Frustrated, I nodded.

"Either it's with her dead body or whoever buried her took it." He patted the loveseat next to him, and Ugly ran over and jumped on it. The smell hit me again. It was all I could do to stay still. Eddie patted the dog's head, either used to the smell or not caring. "Thing is, the little box sounds so familiar to me. For the life of me, I can't remember where I heard about it. The mind is like a rubber band, munchkin." He tapped his temple. "It loses its snap as you age. Give me some time to think about it. I got another plan we can try first."

I hated to ask what.

"I want you to contact the ghost we seen on Miss Hannah's surveillance video."

I actually groaned. For all the wiggling and dancing I'd done on this awful, long day, I was right back where I started. Forgetting where I was, I sat back on the couch and stared at the ceiling. What I saw there gave me an idea what to get Eddie for his birthday—a house cleaning.

I tried to picture the ghost I'd seen on the video and sorted through everything I knew, which wasn't much at all, about contacting the dead. The black opal sent a little tingle of magic into my skin, as though telling me it would help. I drew in a deep breath of the foul air and called up the ghost's voice begging for help.

"My friends. Can't do this. Please make it stop."

I recalled the desperation and sadness I'd felt when I heard the voice, trying to pull those emotions to me, in hopes they'd make the ghost come.

The humid air in the trailer cooled, chilling my sweat-dampened skin. I shivered and pulled my arms tight around myself for warmth. The black opal warmed on my chest and waves of its power radiated through me.

Don't let her come. Don't let her get hurt.

The ghost's voice. Was it talking about me? I might not like visiting with ghosts, but they rarely did me any lasting harm. I pushed harder and reached out my mind to latch on to the spirit connected with the voice. It was like chasing myself through a maze. Down one row and up against a dead end. Around another corner, but the shadow stayed ahead by a fraction of a second. This ghost asked for help. Why wouldn't it let me help?

The black opal, which had become my only source of heat as the room grew frigid, suddenly stilled, growing cold as a block of ice against my chest. I gasped, my eyes flying open, and pulled the awful thing out of my shirt. I looked around for Eddie but found myself back in the dark place where I'd gone before I had the vision. Priscilla Herrera stood watching me, hands on her hips.

This time the dark wasn't as dark, and I looked around. I was in a room with a wood floor and no windows, bare of furniture except for a rough table and chair. A few toys lay scattered on the floor. I could see two doors, one on each side of the room. *Where am I?*

I recognized some of the toys as ones I'd played with as a kid but hadn't seen in years. The table was cluttered with a tangle of junk. I made out a pack of cigarettes, the extremely strong ones I'd smoked during a dark time in my life. My wedding ring, the one I'd thrown in the Trinity River after my divorce was final, sat beside the cigarettes. My heart thudded dully. *What is this place? How can I leave?*

I walked toward the door closest to me, but a cold hand grabbed my arm. Priscilla Herrera shook her head no and gave me a light push toward the other door. I hesitated, wondering if she meant me harm since I knew her secrets.

She smiled as though I'd asked the question out loud, shook her head again, and shooed me toward the door.

I took halting steps to the closed door, hand reaching for the worn brass knob. It felt warm under my hand as though heated by a hot summer day. Maybe it would take me back to Eddie. I turned the knob and opened the door and took a step into the blackness. I fell fast and came down on something soft, sucking in air and half screaming.

"Peri Jean, you all right?" Eddie's hands gripped my arms. His face was so close I saw the veins threading their way under the skin of his nose. Ugly barked in the background. Eddie gave me a hard shake. "You okay? Want me to call the ambulance?"

I forced myself to come to life. "No. No. Don't want the ambulance or a doctor."

"Hush, Ugly, and come here." Eddie held out his hand, and the dog came to him. His horrid odor hit me like smelling salts. I woke up in a flash.

"Didn't see anything useful. Sorry."

"I'm the one ought to apologize. Your eyes rolled back in your head, and it scared the shit out of me. Never realized you'd roll up your eyes like that. Won't never stop seeing it, don't imagine."

I stood, wanting to get away from Ugly's stench even though I usually loved him.

"We'll just focus on getting the box," Eddie said.

I nodded, my head swimming and my knees weak.

"Give me long enough, and I'll remember where I saw it or heard about it." Eddie kept petting Ugly. I noticed his big hand shook. I had scared him, and I owed him an apology.

"I'm sorry I scared you, Eddie." My voice sounded sluggish like I'd been asleep.

"Never apologize for doing what I asked you to do, Munchkin. You caught me off guard is all." He tried to laugh. It came out flat and insincere.

My cellphone buzzed, indicating I had a text message. It was from Hannah.

Where the blazes are you? Dean is frantic you aren't here yet.

The campaign barbecue. People'd been reminding me all day. It was scheduled to start in ten minutes, and I looked and smelled like hell.

"The barbecue," I said to Eddie. "I'm going to be late."

He ushered me to the door and said something nobody but Eddie would have said or thought. "Just go like you are, baby. You look all right." We hugged, and I gave Ugly a goodbye pat. "Tell Dean I'm feeling a little under the weather but I'll make the debate, I promise. I'll stay here and research and think on this box, see what I can remember."

We said our I love yous, and I went to my car and looked down at myself. There was no way I could show up at Dean's barbecue in dirty jeans and a T-shirt. I started my car and headed toward Memaw's.

———

I HADN'T GONE a mile before my cellphone dinged again.

Couldn't Hannah give me a few minutes to get it together? I'd have to wait to look at it. I pushed the button on the side of the phone so it wouldn't keep alerting me.

A sound came out of the phone's speaker, a low hiss. Had I somehow turned on video or music? The message bell dinged again. Then again. And again. I whipped off the road, the car leaning on the gravel shoulder, and grabbed my phone. If this was Hannah Kessler acting a fool, I'd get her good.

The hiss played again over the phone before I could get it up to eye level, so I went into my messages, automatically tapping Hannah's name to get her message thread up. To my surprise, there was nothing since she'd asked where the hell I was. The messages button at the upper left of the screen indicated I had ten messages. 10? I clicked the button. All the messages were from an unknown number, and all of them were videos. I tapped one of them.

The video started, and it looked like nothing more than static on a TV screen. I was getting ready to shut it off because I really did need to get to Memaw's and get fixed up for the barbecue. Then movement in the static caught my eye, and I held the phone's small screen close to my face, trying to figure out what I was seeing.

The shadow moved toward me fast, its face coming into view and then too close for me to really see.

"What the—" I yelled and flinched back from the phone, tossing it into the passenger seat.

A wisp of shadow came from the phone, gaining in substance as it grew in length. The top of a head covered in some sort of shroud became visible.

"No, no, no, no." My voice sounded like a sick car alarm, blaring the same stupid sound over and over. I stopped shouting and got hold of myself. I had to get out of this car and away from this thing at once.

I reached for my door handle, pulling hard on it several times. The door handle moved, but the door didn't open. I whined like a little animal about to get gobbled up by a bigger, meaner animal, yanking the door handle as hard as I could. The door stayed closed. My bladder turned into a heavy, hot rock, and I just knew I was going to wet my pants.

A scratching, crawly sound came from behind me. Gasping, unable to get enough oxygen to breathe, I twisted in my seat. The vapor birthing itself from my phone had expanded to nearly touch me. I went still. *If I stay here much longer, it'll be able to touch me. What then?*

I turned to the door and reared back my fist to hit the window. Then I looked at the little silver knob that locked the door. It was pushed all the way down, flush with the door. The relief felt as sweet as sunshine on a cold day. I used my thumb and forefinger to pull on the old-fashioned lock, almost giddy. It wouldn't move.

A light breeze caressed the back of my neck. My stomach clenched into a tight, hard ball. It was too late. I'd failed. I twisted in my seat, muscles nearly slack, thinking I didn't have any fear left in me to invest in this horror. I stared at what shared the car with me and opened my mouth to scream. A little hiss was all that came out. The mist formed into a cracked and scarred forehead, and black soulless eyes appeared below it.

The black opal came to life on my chest, heating to a burning temperature in seconds, and searing the skin underneath. I writhed in my seat and made animal sounds. The door lock popped up on its own. Moaning, I grabbed the handle and pushed open the door, letting myself slide out head first and cracking my forehead on the pavement. I glanced back into the car. The thing's misty, wavering face showed a hole where the nose should have been and a gaping mouth full of matchstick teeth.

"Help me," My plea echoed in the darkness, and I knew deep down nobody was there to hear me. I got my hands underneath me, preparing to scoot backward.

The thing whipped out a hand wrapped in dirty cloth and grabbed my ankle, clamping down. I heard and felt something inside me snap. A bolt of pain shot up my leg. I screamed like a prissy little girl and moaned, "Please, don't," through my sobs. Blood from my ruined ankle pattered onto the pavement and ran up my leg.

I looked around at the empty night. I was going to die out here alone, and nobody would ever really understand what happened to me.

The thing yanked on my leg. Pain flared through my body, and I screamed again, reflexively grabbing the black opal in hopes it would come back to life. The gemstone had gone cold on my chest. Exhausted? I cursed myself for not knowing but kept trying to crawl, not really sure how I'd go anywhere with some monstrosity hanging on to my leg. Nothing mattered except getting away from whatever it was trying to hurt me.

"Peri Jean Mace." The thing's voice sounded brittle and

dry, so quiet it was hard to hear. "Look at me, Peri Jean Mace."

I flopped over on my back and stared at the awful thing. It had grown shoulders and a torso, the lower half of its body still fading into the mist coming from my phone.

"If you fail in your duty, I will be the last thing you and your loved ones see." Its hand clamped down on my leg again.

I clawed at the pavement, kicking my legs, a terrified groan coming from my mouth. The thing's black eyes locked on mine. The sound of a thousand voices screamed inside my head. I grayed out.

The roar of a motorcycle snapped me out of my fear fit. It bore down on me in seconds, its lone headlight blinding me. I put my arms over my head and waited for impact. It never came.

"Peri Jean?" Huge hands spread out on my back, hands I knew. Wade Hill. I leaned into him, scooting as far as possible away from my car and pulling my injured leg to me. He stroked my hair. "What is it? What's wrong?"

Unable to do more than gibber, I raised one arm and pointed at my leg. Wade leaned over and looked at the wound and hissed through his teeth.

"What did this to you?" He didn't wait for me to answer. "Never mind. I'll fix it." He shrugged off his leather jacket and set it aside. I watched, expecting him to take off his T-shirt and rip it into a bandage. Instead he got so close to me I thought he was going to kiss me or something. He took my hand, using his fingers to push open my closed fist, and twined his fingers in mine like a lover. The warmth radiating off his body and the smells of gasoline and open road, scents I'd forever associate with Wade, enveloped me in a comforting cocoon.

Wade closed his eyes and took a deep breath, his lips moving. At first I thought he was doing a spell, but then I heard the words "Heavenly Father" and realized he was saying a prayer. Then he began to speak aloud. I didn't recognize the words, but I knew the cadence, knew where they must have come from.

The first electric pinpricks of magic passed from Wade's hand and into mine, radiating through my body and settling in both the wound on my head and the one on my leg. The feeling intensified, and my body jerked with each prickle. The magic found the black opal, and my skin went numb, singing with power. I felt whatever bone the horror in my car had broken slide back together and fuse.

Next to me, Wade stiffened, his head thrown back and cords standing out on his neck. The heat radiating from him grew uncomfortable, and beads of sweat formed on his forehead and ran into his hair, slimy dampness growing between our joined hands. I heard my own breathing coming in pants, Wade's words punctuating them. It took me to a place, an old place, somewhere in my mind where my subconscious and body knew what to do even if the conscious part of my mind didn't.

The world clouded, my heart thundering in my chest. The pain from the wounds ebbed away into an awful itch. The black opal heated to an unbearable level, and a hum filled my ears as even the itch went away. Wade let go of me and sagged forward, putting his hands down on the pavement. We sat panting in silence until I heard a car coming and struggled to my feet, forgetting the injury until I put weight on my bad leg. It held without a twitch or a tingle. Wade hurried to his feet and got his motorcycle out of the road before the car reached us. Both of us waved as it passed. I turned to Wade, seeing not the jokester thug I'd grown to love as a friend over the months but, instead, someone whose weirdness surpassed even mine.

"What did you do?" Speaking hurt my throat. *Had I screamed that much?*

"Healed you." Even though I couldn't see his eyes, I heard the uncertainty in his voice. He knew I didn't like seeing ghosts and wished I could be normal.

"How though?"

"By the power of the divine." He took a deep breath. "I've been working with your memaw and Esther Bruce, too. Your memaw was the one who figured out what I am, though."

"What are you?"

He turned his face away from me and then spoke. "The seventh son of a seventh son. There's a lot of folklore, but the only parts true for me are the ones about being a healer and always getting in a bunch of trouble."

"Thank you." I gripped his arm, barely able to get my hand around it. "Thank you so much. I think my foot was broken."

"Broken?" He snorted. "Looked like someone took a pair of pincers and nearly sheared it off. What the hell got after you?"

"It came out of my phone. It's still in my car, I guess."

But I wondered why the sharp-toothed monster hadn't come after both of us. Had it considered its message delivered and gone on its way?

Wade let go of me and marched over to the vehicle, bending double to lean in. He came back almost immediately, shaking his head.

"I don't understand. What happened?"

"A, uh, monster came out of my phone." I described the thing to Wade as best as I could, but ended up talking more about its hands and teeth than anything.

Wade retrieved my phone from the car, his brow knitted. "It's dead. Got a charger?"

I didn't want to get back into the car, so Wade found my charger and hooked it up to a rig he had in his saddlebag. I tried to calm myself, but the thing I'd seen had been real. It hurt me badly, and I might have died out here had Wade not come along. A few minutes later, the cellphone powered up.

"It's in the messages. Look for some from unknown." I didn't want to go near the thing, even though I knew I needed it for work and life. I told Wade my passcode, and he tapped the phone's screen to access the messages. He stared at the phone for a long time, his face expressionless. Finally, he turned it where I could see it.

The screen was filled with the picture of Priscilla Herrera.

"Tell me everything again. Slow this time."

I explained what happened again, going as slowly as I could. My voice sped up at parts, and Wade simply shook his head at me, motioned for me to calm down. I conveniently left out the part about the curse, needing to think it over by myself before I let others know what I'd seen. Other than that, I didn't leave out one scream. He listened stoically.

"My great-aunt, the one who taught me to use my gift, would'a said somebody sent a booger after you." He glanced at the blood still pooled on the road. "Like to've got you from what I can tell."

My cellphone dinged with a message. Wade held out my phone to me, but I shook my head. He read the message.

"It's Hannah Kessler. She says to get your ass to the barbecue now. You're late."

"No. I can't."

"What are you going to tell them happened? Think Mr. Dean Do-Right'll like it?"

I went to my car and held out my hand for the cellphone.

"You want me to follow, I can."

I rubbed my arms against the chills ripping through my body, despite the pent-up feel of the day's heat still hanging in the night air.

"I can give you a ride."

His words hit me like a blast from a sink sprayer. Dean would have a fit if Wade came roaring up at the barbecue and dropped me off.

"Will you follow me to town?" I took one more look at my clothes but knew it was too late to do anything about them.

"Flash your signals left and right like you're crazy if you run into trouble."

I nodded and held my hand out for my phone again, flinching when it touched my skin. This whole thing was no joke. I could have gotten run over cowering in the highway like a teenager at a horror movie. Either Priscilla Herrera's order to the dark guardians was no joke or she was a great bluffer. Didn't matter which. She had my attention. I wished with all my heart she'd picked somebody else to save Gaslight City. I didn't even like most of the people here.

———

THE TREMORS ROCKING my body ceased after the first mile, and I put one of my father's ZZ Top cassettes in the ancient player set into the dashboard and turned it up loud to drown out any thoughts of what I just experienced. It was too much for my brain to comprehend. All I knew to do was move forward, keep surviving. The hum of Wade's motorcycle blatting behind me made the task seem possible. What if he hadn't happened along to save me?

Dean's campaign had rented an establishment named the Hoedown Party Barn for the barbecue. The ten-year-old corrugated metal building, new by Gaslight City standards, squatted a quarter mile from downtown on Textile Road. It occupied the site of the old Fountain Textile Mill, where both my uncle and father worked before tragedy took away their lives. I knew I was in trouble as soon as I got close enough to see the parking lot.

Cars and trucks jammed the prairie of asphalt, spilling over into an overgrown grassy area next door. I parked on the edge of the herd of vehicles and shut off my Chevy Nova. Wade pulled in behind me and cut his engine. I met him at my bumper.

"You want to come in for a plate of barbecue? It's free."

"Nah. You were right earlier. Little man might split the seams of his boy's extra medium dress shirt."

I didn't bother defending Dean to Wade. Their different paths in life ensured they'd never be friends. "Thanks for following me."

"Never any need to thank me. Just doing what I need to do." He started his motorcycle before I could offer him supper again and did a U-turn on the narrow road, raising his hand to wave goodbye. I watched him until the noise of his ride faded into the night.

"Where the hell have you been?" Hannah stormed across the parking lot, Rainey Bruce right behind her. Both their arms pumped like people I'd seen walking in a mall. I realized I didn't have the emotional energy to deal with them about the time they reached me.

"Dean's waiting on you," Hannah said. "He wants you to stand onstage with him when he gives his welcome speech. Come on."

"She isn't going in there looking like she's been bar crawling for a week," Rainey said. "Not as long as I'm Dean's campaign manager. Eddie said you left his house forty-five minutes ago. I figured you'd gone to change. What did you do? Go partying with Wade Hill?"

My throat ached with the buildup of what I'd seen.

The thing came out of my phone, reached for me. It could have killed me. The whispers I'd heard all my life filled my head. *Schizophrenic. Hallucinations.* I shook my head to clear it.

"It came out of the phone and chased me into the road." Even as I said the words, I knew they were out of context and wouldn't make sense. Sure enough, both Hannah and Rainey shook their heads. I explained what happened, leaving out the stuff about how the boogie man would kill me and everybody I loved unless I kept the curse attached to the treasure. No need to cause a panic. What little I told them must have been enough. Both women drew away from me, their eyes widening.

"Oh no." Hannah put her hand over her mouth. "No wonder you're filthy."

Rainey took out her cellphone. "Dean. Stall them ten minutes, okay?" She paused while he said something. "Just do it, you hear me?" She hung up and spoke to Hannah. "You got anything to fix her up?"

Hannah studied me, raising one eyebrow. "I've got my makeup box in the car. But it's the one I travel with. Not much in there."

"It'll have to do. Let's get her over there."

They dragged me to Hannah's BMW sedan and forced me inside. Hannah took out a plastic case bigger than some of the toolboxes I'd seen and opened it. Inside lay an array of tubes and tins, all filled with mystery substances. I reached for a black eye liner pencil and Hannah slapped my hand.

"Clean some of the dirt off your face. Get your neck

too." Rainey handed me a damp disposable wipe. I started scrubbing. Rainey grabbed a hairbrush out of the toolkit and started dragging it through my hair. I moaned once to let her know it hurt. The look she gave me dried up any more complaints. Hannah dabbed at my face with creams and powders, the brushes she used tickling my face. Three minutes of tickling, tugging torture later, both women leaned back to scrutinize me.

"Her shirt's still filthy," Rainey said. "You got anything else?"

To my amazement, Hannah went to her trunk and pulled out a pile of clothes. "None of this is going to fit her. She's smaller than me."

Rainey picked through the clothes and came out with a sleeveless spandex shirt and tossed it at me. I wanted to argue. The color was a pastel blue, and the straps looked like bra straps. One glance at Rainey's face convinced me to keep my mouth shut and do as they said. Hannah took one look at me and dug through the pile of clothes again, this time pulling out a short black jacket. I slipped it on over the tank top and waited for their judgment.

"A dress would have been better, but this'll work in a pinch. She doesn't look as awful as she did." Rainey gripped my arm and tugged me toward the party barn, lecturing me in her courtroom voice as we went. "Sheriff Joey Holze posted to some online social media sites today about Dean's problems back in Louisiana."

"How bad?" My throat ached again, and I knew I'd end up crying if I didn't get myself under control. The day had taken its toll on me. What Sheriff Joey did made sense.

The poisonous son of a bitch hated Dean and me whole-heartedly. Me for being a ghost-seeing, devil-worshiping freak and Dean for having the temerity to run against him in the sheriff's election. Using underhanded methods to get ahead in the election fit the nasty SOB to a tee.

"Bad enough," Rainey said. "He posted links to newspaper articles about Dean's partner getting killed and about him resigning in a cloud of drunken disgrace. The article he linked to mentioned Dean and his wife-at-the-time were getting divorced and did all kinds of creative speculating about the reasons." She puckered her lips as though she tasted something sour. "Of course, Sheriff Joey made comments like 'Is this who you want for your sheriff?' in his postings online."

"This is so embarrassing," Hannah moaned. "I can't believe my uncle acts like this."

Teeth clenched together so hard it hurt, I imagined how satisfying it would be to put signs with stuff like "gorilla cock sucker" and "dookey breath" in Joey's yard right alongside his "Joseph Holze for Sheriff" signs.

"You've got to get in there and make Dean look good." Rainey gave my arm a shake to emphasize her point.

"What if we leak what you found in Joey's house?" I spoke to Hannah.

"There's no proof either of you found anything." Rainey, many inches taller than me, stooped to lean into my face. I'd known her since we were six. She was the most competitive person I'd ever met. She signed on as Dean's campaign manager with one conclusion in mind: winning.

She wouldn't tell me to keep Joey's likely theft of the Mace House to myself to be nice.

"She's right," Hannah said. "We've got nothing."

A rivulet of sweat tickled its way down my side. The day's upheaval had pushed the election to the back of my mind. All my worries came roaring back wearing streamers and waving. *How you doing, Peri Jean? Let's partay.* Dean's chances of winning looked dire, and I had no idea how to help. Me showing up to a public appearance looking like a dirty possum would actually crap things up worse.

Dean came out of the big metal building, turning his head left and right, obviously looking for me. Rainey inspected me once again, grimaced, and pushed me towards Dean.

"What the hell happened to her?" He spoke to Rainey.

"She was visiting Eddie." Rainey put her hands on her hips. "Time got away from her, I think."

Dean took several steps closer to me and put his arms around my waist. I leaned against him, and his lips brushed mine, casually at first, then more seriously. "You're beautiful no matter what," he mumbled against my lips, his breath mingling with mine. I drank in the scent of soap coming off his clean skin and thought, as I always did when he touched me, we'd figure out a way to make everything work.

"Come on in." He threaded his fingers through mine. "I want to you to stand with me onstage. Your memaw has her camera ready."

Dean opened the building's door. Both of us winced as a blast of country music greeted us.

A loose crowd had congregated on the far side of the room. Nobody paid much attention to either Dean or me until we took the small stage. There was no microphone, so Dean raised his voice. He knew how to holler from his job in law enforcement.

"Folks?"

People slowly turned our way. Someone began clapping, and a short burst of applause swept through the room.

"First, thank you all for coming out tonight. Hope the weather's been warm enough for you all." He waited while the polite laughter died down. "Peri Jean and I want to welcome you all to the barbecue." He tightened his arm around me as they applauded. "Thank you all for coming out, and I hope you enjoy—"

"Deputy Dean?" The voice came from the dimly lit area where some tables had been set up, so we couldn't see the speaker, but I recognized the voice right away. Myrtle Gaudet was a harmless busybody by herself, but she became a formidable biddy when she joined forces with Loretta Brent, who happened to be the mother of Felicia Brent Fischer Holze. The two of them sat at a table near the bandstand. The tension I'd almost let go of came roaring back with its friends migraine and backache. Dean stiffened next to me as he made the same connection I had. We could do nothing but wait to see what horror she was about to shit upon all of us.

"What's the necklace around Peri Jean's neck?"

My legs went soft as cooked noodles, and I struggled to keep my face impassive and stand as tall as someone my height could. Dean glanced over, saw the necklace, and his shoulders relaxed a little.

"My mother gifted it to Peri Jean. It goes back several generations in my family."

"Didn't it used to belong to a witch?" Myrtle stood from her table and picked her way toward the stage. People hurried out of her way. They probably hoped she'd keep talking. No matter how much people like other people, they love seeing them suffer even more.

Several gasps came from around the room. I searched for Memaw, looking for support. Her face was stiff with rage. When our eyes met, she gave me a small nod of encouragement. I stood a little straighter.

"My great-grandmother was absolutely, positively not a witch." Dean probably didn't sound angry to anybody else in the room, but I knew him well enough to know that tone of voice. "She might have been an eccentric old lady who visited local *traiteurs*, but that does not make her a witch."

Myrtle stood in front of the stage by then. She held up an electronic tablet of some sort. "But it says right here online that the necklace is magical, and you're descended from witches. Burns County don't want no hocus pocus happening behind the scenes."

Dean took the tablet with a trembling hand. On its screen was a post by Felicia Brent Fischer Holze on a popular social networking site. It said pretty much everything Myrtle had told the room. Dean gaped at it, his normally golden tan turning yucky green.

"Myrtle?" Julie Woodson, owner of Silver Dreams Antiques, appeared at Myrtle's side.

Myrtle slowly turned, the triumph on her face souring. The two women exchanged sneers. Earlier in the year, Julie outbid Myrtle at an estate auction. The war started then, each woman searching for ways to make the other one look stupid.

"Who cares if the necklace belonged to one of *the* Salem witches? The design of the chain and setting indicate they're at least two-hundred-fifty years old." Julie stared down her thin nose at Myrtle. "It's a wonderful antique piece of jewelry with a great family history. Any real antiques person should be able to appreciate it."

I shot Julie a grateful smile. She nodded in acknowledgment. Her on-again-off-again romance with Eddie probably fueled her desire to defend my honor, but every little bit helped.

Myrtle's mouth opened and closed several times, then her face lit with glee. "But Peri Jean Mace is a—"

My cellphone picked right then to start ringing. I dug it out of my jeans pocket and saw Eddie's face on the screen. Had it been anybody else, I'd have ignored it, but I needed to talk to Eddie no matter what. I pressed the answer button, and Dean's mouth dropped open in shock. Everything was going wrong for him, and I was making it worse.

"Eddie?"

"Peri Jean, baby, you gotta help me. It's here, and I can't

stop it." He took a rattling breath. "My chest. I think I'm having a heart attack."

The stress of the day pressed down on me, suffocating me. I turned to Dean, took in his angry face, and croaked one word, "Eddie."

He shook his head. He probably meant he didn't understand what I wanted, but I took it to mean "not right now."

"Eddie's having a heart attack," I screamed. "You have to go help him."

Everybody spun into action. Dean shouted for someone to call an ambulance to meet us out there and jumped off the stage and ran for the door. Somehow I kept my phone in my hand throughout all my acrobatics.

"Eddie, we're coming. Hold on, okay?"

Gasps and coughs came over the phone's speaker and served as Eddie's answer. I reached Dean's car and slammed my hand against the passenger window for him to unlock it and let me in. He glared at me but did as I wanted. I slid into the car next to him.

"Eddie? Eddie?"

"Oh, honey, I think I'm gonna die." He coughed again and moaned in pain.

"Eddie?" I screamed into the phone.

He didn't answer. I heard a ground-shaking thump, and the phone went dead.

6

———

EDDIE'S mobile home was about two miles out of town. The speedometer on Dean's '80s era Trans Am hovered between seventy and eighty miles per hour.

"Go faster," I said. "We're not going to get there in time to help Eddie."

Dean, both hands fisted on the wheel, gave no indication he heard me. I nudged him with the heel of my hand.

"Stop it," he said. "I can't concentrate, and we're going too fast on this curvy road."

"Eddie needs me," I yelled. "I don't care about the damn road."

Dean didn't bother to respond.

"Where's the ambulance?" I twisted in my seat to peer out into the impenetrable darkness and saw nothing but shadows and gloom. The county didn't mount streetlights outside the city limits.

Dean shook his head.

"They're so unprofessional. It's a wonder anybody in this town ever makes it to the hospital alive." Urgency choked down any and all rational thoughts. The reflectors marking Eddie's driveway flashed in Dean's headlights.

"Here, here," I yelled.

He slammed on the brakes, throwing me forward in my seat, the seatbelt digging painfully into my collarbone. Dean sped down the potholed driveway like a madman unleashed and skidded to a stop ten feet from the mobile home.

All the lights blazed. Usually, Eddie only kept a reading lamp burning in the living room, where he either watched TV, researched, or read. We clambered out of Dean's Trans Am and bounded up the rickety wooden steps. Dean pounded on Eddie's door. A muffled moan came through the thin aluminum. He tried the knob and found it locked.

"Your keys," he yelled. "Use them. It'll be easier than busting it in." I fumbled my keys out of my pocket. Dean snatched them out of my hand, unlocked the door, and barreled into the house.

Eddie lay curled on his side, writhing in pain. My head swam. Floating on panic and adrenaline, I had to hold onto the wall and the backs of furniture to stagger toward him. Dean crashed to his knees and leaned his head close to Eddie's. I crowded in, ignoring Dean's sharp elbow in my way.

"Mahoney." Eddie grabbed at my arm, his usual iron grip weak and clammy. "Ask Julie." His gaze, cloudy with pain and fear, flickered to mine. "Ask her about Mahoney."

"Mahoney? Who is Mahoney?" I yelled the words because I couldn't hear anything over the freight train roaring between my ears.

Eddie swallowed and closed his eyes.

"Shit. He quit breathing." Dean pushed Eddie onto his back and began chest compressions. "Come on, come on." Dean blew into Eddie's mouth.

I knelt frozen on the floor, tears burning my eyes and leaving hot streaks down my cheeks, mind unable to process the scene before me. I was losing Memaw. I couldn't lose Eddie too.

Dean continued working on Eddie until we heard the sirens. I leapt to my feet and ran to the door, throwing it open.

"He's not breathing." I jumped up and down on the wooden stoop, making it groan and shake. "Get your sorry asses in here."

They pushed past me and surrounded Eddie. One of them, a guy who was in junior high when I was a senior, shook his head at Dean.

"Noooo," I shouted before giving in to huge, gulping sobs. I should have called Wade Hill to save Eddie the way he helped me. But it was too late. I wailed louder.

The paramedics barely gave me a glance. They made notes on charts. One of them took out his cellphone and made a call. Dean put his arm around me and pulled me out of the house. I tried to wiggle away from him, but he held me fast.

Throbbing, unbearable pain blossomed in my chest,

aching like a real wound. Eddie wasn't dead. He couldn't be. I never saw his spirit leave his body, and I would have. I'd known Eddie all my life.

The pain in my chest grew too big to hold inside. I let it out in the form of screams and yowls, clawing at Dean when he tried to hold me. I'd never considered losing Eddie. He was my rock, my mentor, the only daddy I really remembered having. He couldn't be dead.

Dean closed his arms around me so I couldn't move and rocked me. I drew back to look at him and was surprised to see his cheeks wet with tears too. I clutched at him, and we mourned together. Ugly, shaking from the confusion and excitement, nudged my hand. I knelt and wept into his stinky fur.

I raised my head and spoke to Dean. "Julie. I've got to call her. She can't hear this from one of the gossip mongers."

"Let me do it." Dean took out his cellphone and walked away before I could argue.

Other people began arriving. Dr. Longstreet, Hannah and Rainey, a Burns County Sheriff's cruiser containing Deputy Brittany Watson and a middle-aged deputy named Fitzgerald I'd met in passing.

I found a leash for Ugly. The dog, Hannah, and I stood off to the side, staring at the activity. Rainey sat in her car staring out in to the darkness both hands on the wheel. She got out of her car and picked her way toward us, the former Miss Texas and most graceful, poised woman I knew wobbling on her high heels.

"I'll take the dog." She took the leash from my hand without waiting for my response.

Hannah turned. "I want Ugly. Eddie would have wanted me to have him. I played with him every time I came out here to talk history with him."

"Ugly's mine." Dean jogged over. He actually had the brass balls to reach for the leash. One scowl from Rainey, and he withdrew his hand.

Nobody asked me if I wanted the dog. Truth was, he'd create too much stress for Memaw, but I resented not being asked. I cleared my throat. "Why can't I have him? Eddie practically raised me."

Hannah, Dean, and Rainey glanced at me and went back to glaring at each other.

"I'm taking the dog," Rainey said through clenched teeth. "I need him. He reminds me how awful people are and how good they are at the same time. I have to remember that to keep my sanity."

I knew winning words when I heard them and knelt in front of Ugly, kissing his face and patting his scarred hide. He licked my nose.

"Love you," I whispered. "Enjoy your new life."

"So the story is Eddie had a heart attack?" Hannah's voice trembled.

"I'm not so sure some outside force didn't cause Eddie's heart attack." I swallowed back another flood of weeping. "Eddie said 'It's here,' when he called me. I can't help but think he meant the ghost we saw on the museum surveillance video."

Rainey nodded her understanding, and Hannah squeezed my hand. Dean took a step away from us.

"There was no ghost on the video." He crossed his arms over his chest, bunching his muscles. "Someone tampered with it. I've called an expert in Houston to examine the footage. We'll figure out who stole from the museum."

Hannah, Rainey, and I stared at each other, ignoring him. We said nothing. We didn't need to. Each of us knew the plan. Find out who was behind this thieving, murdering ghost, and put the beat-down on them. Eddie's death ached all the way into the deepest part of my soul. I'd do everything in my power, risk everything, to avenge his death. He deserved no less.

Dean snorted like an angry animal and marched away, his posture stiff.

"Peri Jean, would you go in Eddie's house and get a towel or something for my car seat?" Rainey asked.

I cast a glance at the other woman's sporty Mercedes. The dog would trash it and every beautiful thing she had. Maybe she needed the chaos in her life. I nodded and walked toward the trailer.

Hannah caught up to me and stopped me. "Where's Eddie's ghost? You need to communicate with him—whatever you do—and find out what happened."

Her words jolted into my mind. This was the first time where the ghost of a recently deceased person I knew didn't come see me right away. I lit a cigarette and hoofed it toward the trailer.

Dr. Nathan Longstreet stood near the rickety wooden

deck off Eddie's front door talking to Deputy Brittany Watson about what happened. The sole female law enforcement officer working for the Burns County Sheriff's Office, she was eager to learn the job, and Dean wanted to help her. Sometimes too much, I thought. They stopped talking as we approached.

"I need to go inside and get Rainey a towel for her car. She's taking the dog."

"Deputy Watson can go get it," Dean said. "You don't need to."

"I want to," I said. "Plus, I know where everything is."

"Darlin', you might ought to go on home, maybe check on your memaw. Take Hannah and Rainey with you." Dean tried to pull me against him, but I resisted.

"Dean's right," Dr. Longstreet said. "There's no more you can do for Eddie. I'm sure he was grateful to have you with him in his last moments. He loved you like you were his." Tears glossed the old doctor's eyes. "I warned Eddie at his last three checkups to quit drinking and smoking so much, to eat healthier foods, to exercise. He ignored me. His heart kept getting weaker and weaker. I knew this was going to happen…" He pulled me into his arms, and I breathed in the familiar odors of rubbing alcohol and spearmint. Dr. Longstreet let go of a sob. He'd loved Eddie too. I returned his hug.

"Tell Brittany where the towels are, honey. Then I want you to be on your way." Dean put his arm around my waist as soon as Dr. Longstreet released me. "I'll wait here until Hooty brings the hearse, and Deputy Watson will help me close up. No reason for you to have to…" His mouth worked. "See Hooty take Eddie away." The pain in his eyes suggested he didn't want to see it either. It made me hate what I had to say next, but I pushed myself to do what I needed to.

"I need to be the one who goes inside."

"Oh, honey, you don't either." Deputy Brittany Watson stepped in front of the door. "Eddie wouldn't want you to."

"I need to see..." I wasn't quite sure how to tell someone I was going looking for a ghost.

"There's nothing in there you need to see." Brittany moved toward me, so confident and sure of herself I barely recognized the little girl I used to babysit.

"I need to see his ghost." I jerked away from her and grabbed the doorknob, my words echoing in the quiet country night. The frogs and crickets stopped their opera to watch the show.

Brittany, who knew the rumors about me even if she'd never seen me do anything weird, widened her eyes and took a step away from me. Dean squeezed his eyes shut and rubbed one hand over his stomach. Dr. Longstreet nodded tiredly, possibly expecting no less, and stepped away from the door. He'd seen a lot over his years doctoring Burns County. He knew good and well what I could do. If he understood why I wanted to go in, maybe he could get Dean off my case. Before I could think of a discreet way to tip Dr. Longstreet to what I wanted, Dean started motormouthing again.

"Baby, listen to me," Dean said. "I don't want you going in there. It's upsetting to see a dead person when they haven't been prepared for viewing. It's not like going to a funeral."

He glanced at Dr. Longstreet for confirmation. The doctor shrugged and leaned against the deck's railing, crossing his arms over his chest. He knew there was no use arguing with me.

I ignored Dean and opened the trailer's front door. He grabbed my arm and tugged me away from it.

"You can't go in there." He said the words in a gruff, near shout. His cop voice. It brooked no argument. If I hadn't seen him naked, it might have scared me into obeying, but it just made me mad.

"Actually, she can go in there." Rainey's voice came from behind me. "Eddie left his estate to her. I have the will at my office. It's not probated yet, but all this belongs to Peri Jean."

Dean's mouth worked, and I took the opportunity to slip inside the trailer.

———

I STOPPED RIGHT inside the door and took a good look at the room. Eddie lay where he'd died, more motionless and silent than I imagined possible. Living people make noise just by being alive. They add a presence to the room. Once the heart stops beating and the brain stops creating, it's over. What's left behind is like a creepy kind of furniture. I knew the part of Eddie I wanted to talk to—his spirit—still had to be here. He had something to tell me on the phone, and I needed to hear what it was to help me find whoever did this to him.

"Eddie?" I said to the empty room. My voice sounded flat and muted. "Eddie? Come on. I want to talk to you." Nothing happened. The black opal hanging around my neck didn't even give me a little shock of magic. I walked through the living room and kitchen to the master bedroom. Maybe Eddie'd gotten confused in death and went in there.

I swung the door open. The odor of stale cigarettes, beer, and beer farts assailed me. I took a step backward, viewing the unmade bed and clothes strewn on the floor from the doorway. A plate of greasy chicken bones, the remainder of a fried chicken dinner, sat on the dresser. Steeling my gag reflex, I crept through the room and took baby steps to the bathroom. If the bedroom was this bad, I wasn't sure I wanted to see what waited for me in there.

I stepped into the room and put the back of my hand over my mouth. How did Eddie stand using this room? The sink, once white, was caked with dark colored splotches and sprinkled with hair. The counter had a layer of dust so thick I could have written in it if I'd been willing to touch it. The tub and the toilet looked like they could have been used in biological warfare. Empty.

I'd try his office. He spent a great deal of time in there researching local history and the Mace Treasure. He'd been doing treasure research on my behalf when he realized he needed help. Maybe his ghost went back to finish his task.

I walked back through the kitchen frustrated enough to holler. The irony infuriated me. All the damn times I'd seen ghosts and wished I didn't, but the one time I really wanted to see a ghost, I couldn't do it. I bit my lip, trying not to see Eddie sprawled out on the living room floor. I did okay at keeping my eyes averted until I got right alongside his sad remains.

Eddie always seemed huge to me, strong and sure, full of wisdom and good fart jokes. Death took all that way from him. Lying on the living room floor, robbed of his dignity, he seemed small and old. Just a middle-aged guy on his way down the hill of life. I noticed for the first time how age and bad health had changed him from the man I had once seen lift and throw a refrigerator several feet while searching for a lost child in the aftermath of a tornado.

Eddie's big heart had kept him big in my eyes. It made me not notice the way his body shrank and became less vibrant. No matter what happened, Eddie waded in without a thought for his own safety to help those in need. I sank to my knees next to the man who'd treated me like his own when he didn't have to, put my face in my hands, and let the ache well up in me.

Tears seeped out of my eyes and burned the back of my throat. Eddie deserved better than a death like this. Maybe I could have prevented it had I not been so stubborn about helping. This morning, instead of turning Hannah over to Dean, I could have gone to see Hooty and started planning. Instead, I'd dragged ass. It cost Eddie his life.

Get up, you sorry piece of shit. I pushed myself to my feet and marched through the living room and down the hall to the other two bedrooms, sobs still hitching out of me. I pushed open the door to the one I knew Eddie used as his office and groaned. I'd never find anything in this jumble. Books on Burns County history lay open all over the desk. The small, flat-screen TV was paused on a frame I recognized from the TV documentary on the Mace Treasure. Maps hung on the walls, red pushpins marking spots I knew nothing about. Eddie'd been researching, all right, but this mess gave no indication to any conclusions he'd reached.

I thought back to Eddie's words when he called me in distress. *It's here, and I can't stop it.* Couldn't stop what? Whatever it was, Eddie tried. The effort he made cost him his life.

For all the stuff strewn about Eddie's office, Eddie's ghost was nowhere to be found. He could have already moved on. I'd seen ghosts pass out of this existence and into another, and I never saw them again. What if Eddie was gone for good? I couldn't believe he'd left without trying to let me know what his research turned up or at least to say goodbye.

I gently grasped the black opal pendant in one hand. It was time to bring out the heavy weaponry. Closing my eyes, I pulled up an image of Eddie the way he'd been in life. The husk of Eddie, the one on the living room floor, tried to creep into my mind, but I closed it out. I thought of Eddie's special smell of Old Spice aftershave and cigarettes. The cadence of his voice, the way he'd let his words paint him as an ignorant redneck, played in my mind. A thump came from the hallway. I turned, searching for the noise, and noticed the mirror for the first time.

Behind the old, black-spotted glass stood Eddie, his hands splayed on either side of his face. I ran to the mirror, letting go of the black opal in my hurry. Eddie vanished. Nerves jangling, I grabbed for the stone, fumbled it, and finally grasped it in one sweaty hand.

"Eddie." I focused my concentration again, tension building in my neck and shoulders, sweat popping out all over my body. "Come back, please."

A faded image of Eddie came into focus behind the glass. Tears stung my eyes, and I put my hand on the glass over his.

"Oh, Eddie, I'm so sorry. I should have agreed to help sooner."

He shook his head, and his lips moved. I'd never been able to read people's lips when they mouthed words at me. This time was no exception.

"I'm sorry. I don't..."

Eddie mouthed the word again. I frowned, thinking hard about the way his lips moved. Eddie glanced upward and leaned over, examining the edges of the glass. The realization he was looking for a way out hit me. I nodded so hard it rocked my whole body.

"Yes," I said. "Come out here. I think I can understand you better."

Eddie ran his transparent fingers around the edge of the glass and shook his head. Bracing himself with both hands, he pushed at the glass. A frown grew on his face, and he slapped the glass, his anger radiating from the mirror. He shook his head. It was no use. He was trapped. He mouthed the words again. This time I caught one.

Paul.

"My daddy?"

Eddie nodded and mouthed the whole sentence for the fifth or sixth time, saying each word slowly. I still had no idea what he meant.

"My daddy what?" I asked again.

A shriek came from Eddie's side of the mirror. Eyes widening, he turned toward the source of the noise. The world behind him, the reflected image of the trailer's shabby walls and the open office behind me, shook. A rumbling, grinding sound issued from the mirror. Eddie tried to run from whatever he saw coming and simply disappeared. The mirror went solid black, the kind of black too dark to reflect, and cracked down the middle. A bolt of force came from it and threw me backward into Eddie's office. I came down wrong on an old injury and screamed in pain, holding my lower back. The front door opened.

"Peri Jean?" Hooty's deep voice came from the living room. "You all right, girl? What happened?"

"Back here."

Heavy footsteps shook the flimsy walls as he ran toward me. I rolled onto my knees and tried to push myself to a standing position, but the old injury spasmed. I sucked in air, unwilling to let Hooty hear me call out in pain again. He rushed toward me and grabbed my arm, pulling me upright. I kept my hand on my back as the old injury wailed.

"What happened?" he asked.

"I saw Eddie in the mirror. He tried to tell me something, but I can't read lips. The only word I got was 'Paul.'" I stopped talking and leaned over with my hands on my knees, trying to catch my breath. Bolts of agony still flared in my lower back.

"Dr. Longstreet's still here. Let's get you out there so he can look at you."

"No," I said. "This happened a year ago, back when Rae was murdered. He's looked at it before and wants me to go to a bigger city, see a specialist."

"And you don't want to." He narrowed his eyes at me.

"It can wait until later." I forced myself to stand straight. "Look. It doesn't even hurt anymore. Figuring who did this to Eddie is what's important." I stood with my hands on my hips, making a show of surveying the mess. Something felt off about the room. I didn't come back here often and didn't know what should be back here.

My gaze fell on the empty spot near the window. The trunk, Eddie's crown jewel of treasure research, usually sat there. It contained a few actual artifacts but also old newspaper clippings and some handwritten diaries.

"Trunk's gone," I pointed to the spot where it usually sat. "When Eddie called me he said 'It's here, and I can't stop it.' I think the ghost who stole from the museum also stole his trunk."

Hooty sagged into the rolling desk chair. "Somebody sent the ghost to get Eddie's treasure notes. They won't stop until they find what they want, will they?"

I shook my head.

Hooty picked up the book Eddie had laying open and scanned the page. I glanced at the words over his shoulder. Nothing I recognized. I glanced at the other items on the desk and saw the yellow legal pad with words scrawled in Eddie's nearly illegible handwriting. I reached over Hooty and picked up the pad. I frowned. Eddie, not the most verbose of men, wrote even more terse notes.

Mahoney...see Julie. I handed the notepad to Hooty. He read the note and returned his gaze to my face.

"Eddie said the name Mahoney to me right before he st-stopped breathing." I brushed away a tear. "I'll go see her tomorrow, once her shop opens."

"Fine," Hooty said. "Tell Hannah and Rainey what-all happened in here. Get them brainstorming about what the thief thought they'd find. Especially Hannah. This was her and Eddie's favorite topic." He stood and ushered me out of the room. "I have a job to do, and I don't want you seeing me do it. Understand?" He kept a firm hold on my arm as he towed me through the living room, keeping his body between me and any view I might have had of Eddie. Hooty opened the front door and gestured for me to go ahead of him. I did but turned back to him and leaned forward to whisper in his ear.

"Maybe the murderer is looking for the same thing we are—the box I saw in the vision."

Hooty nodded, his face still and impassive, giving away no information to anybody who might have been watching.

"You all right?" Dean grabbed my arm and pulled me away from Hooty. "I heard you yell, but Hooty said he could help you." He glanced down at where I had my hand pressed against my back. "That place where Veronica Spinelli kicked you hurting again? You have to be more careful. You're not taking good enough care of yourself."

In too much pain to argue, I nodded and let him convince me to get a ride home with Rainey and stinky Ugly.

7

———

RAINEY TURNED into Memaw's driveway, and I saw right away the house was dark.

"Let me out here. Memaw's already gone to bed." I had more reasons for wanting out of Rainey's car than not wanting to disturb Memaw. Ugly had the whole car smelling like sewer. I hoped Rainey didn't want to hire me to clean her car. Getting the smell out would be a bitch.

Rainey, bless her, didn't argue or bargain. She slammed on the brakes long enough for me to get out. She said, "Call me tomorrow," and left without waiting for my answer.

I took careful steps on the gravel drive, hurting inside and out. Part of me wanted to talk to Memaw, to seek comfort in her strength, while the other part knew I had to learn how to find my own strength. I stopped at the front gate, staring at a newly familiar shadow standing at the window.

Memaw lost her husband, George Mace, before I was

born, but I recognized the ghost of the middle-aged man from family photos when he first showed up a month or so ago. I guessed he came to escort Memaw into the afterlife. My time with Memaw was coming to an end. Each time I saw him, I wondered if today was the day and how it would go down.

I opened the front gate, mindful not to let the metal latch make too much noise, and walked up the brick path, breathing deeply the scent of the gardenias. Shadows of bugs circling the porch light skated over a small area of sun-scalded St. Augustine grass and the concrete steps leading onto the wood floored porch. I held onto the metal rail to mount the steps, my back screaming with every movement, and stood facing the window where the ghost stared out. We exchanged wary nods. He disappeared into the house, probably to hang out near Memaw's bedroom, which was where I usually saw him.

I sat down on the front porch, my back to the house, and lit a cigarette, unable to even think about bed and sleep. Before I knew it, I'd smoked most of a pack. A pile of dead butts littered the concrete steps, and my mouth tasted like dirty feet. Dean's *Smokey and the Bandit* era Trans Am came up the drive and parked by the carport. He got out and walked toward me, his shoulders slumped with fatigue. I stood and met him at the bottom of the porch steps. He held open his arms, and I went to him, laying my head on his shoulder, throat burning with tears. I was too tired to cry anymore.

"I can't believe Eddie's dead." His chest vibrated with his voice.

"I wasn't ready." I sniffed hard. "I didn't even know to expect it."

Dean's arms tightened around my waist. "I'm sorry you lost him. I know he meant the world to you."

"Thank you," I whispered.

Dean broke our embrace and brushed at his arms, probably knocking away mosquitoes. Blasted things followed him like a fan club.

"Can we go inside to talk?" he asked in a soft voice.

I put one finger to my lips, and he nodded his understanding. Inside, Memaw's snores drifted out of her room. We tiptoed through the living room and into my bedroom. I shut the door.

"What happened tonight can't happen again." Dean kept his voice pitched so low it was barely a whisper. "At least not until after the election."

I puzzled over his words, thinking at first he meant Eddie dying. I shook my head at him. "Huh?"

"You announcing you were going in Eddie's trailer to talk to his ghost. Stuff like that." He waited to see understanding on my face and then continued. "Deputy Fitzgerald lit up like a Christmas tree. You know he's good friends with Scott and Felicia Holze. I'm sure he went straight over there and told them."

I stared at him, too stunned to think of anything to say. He had to know I would never do anything to intentionally damage his chances of winning the sheriff's election. I knew how important it was to him and wanted him to win.

"I wasn't thinking," I managed to choke out. The

dismay at losing Eddie so suddenly had let my mouth get ahead of my brain.

"I know, but you saw Myrtle Gaudet and Loretta Brent tonight."

I moved away from Dean and bent to straighten the bedspread, relieved to escape his disappointed pout. I pulled the fabric tight and smoothed my hands over it. The activity did nothing to comfort my spiking nerves, but it slowed things down enough for me to think. Something new occurred to me. "Myrtle wouldn't have known about the black opal necklace if Felicia hadn't posted it on Facebook. How did she know? I sure didn't tell anybody."

"I've been thinking about it all night." Dean's cheeks darkened, and the tips of his ears reddened. "Lisette could have given her the information."

"How would Felicia know your ex-wife?" Sharp-edged fury jabbed at me and hit all the tender spots.

Dean shifted from foot to foot. "I-I-I don't know how they met, but they're friends on social media." He held his hands out to me. "We're skirting the real point here."

"All right. Tell me the real point." I had to fight to keep the sarcasm out of my voice.

"They planned the whole little scene with the necklace to do exactly what it did. Make people think I'm hiding something."

Oh, for all the cat poop in the world. "Dean, everybody in this rinky-dink town knows what I am. There's no hiding from it."

"You don't have to be so obvious about it. You can use

discretion." Dean came to stand right behind me, so close I could hear him breathing.

"How dare you—" I caught myself as my voice raised and stopped speaking. I had to calm down to keep from waking Memaw, if for no other reason. "Do you honestly think I don't know about discretion? What do you think I've spent my whole life doing?" I expected Dean to back down, to apologize, but he just shrugged.

Fuming, I turned my back on him, got out my cigarettes, lit one, and sat down at my desk, running my hands over the slick wood and trying to calm down. I bought the desk at a garage sale for twenty-five dollars. Dean spent a weekend helping me refinish it. This was the side of him I loved, the one who'd roll up his sleeves and work right alongside me, the one who rubbed the kinks out of my shoulders at the end of the day, the one who had sage advice when I asked. I had to try to see things from Dean's perspective. *Part of a grownup relationship is working things out, not stomping off in a rage.*

I tapped my ashes into a plastic ashtray and twisted in my seat to face Dean, to tell him I'd do my best. But when I saw what he was up to, the words shriveled in my mouth. Dread pulsed into my bloodstream with every thud of my heart. The argument about me flaunting what made me different was one thing. What I saw Dean doing was a whole other monkey dance.

He had removed one of the pictures stuck into my mirror's wood frame and had it pinched between his thumb and forefinger. From the expression on his face, he could have been unclogging a toilet.

"I thought we worked past this." He held out the picture so I could see which one he had. I didn't need to see it because I could see the empty space right near the middle of the mirror's frame, but I looked anyway. The picture showed me with Chase Fischer standing in front of a tall face of sheared off white stones, both of us wearing cutoff jeans, him shirtless and me wearing a bikini top.

The Guadalupe River three years ago. Benny Longstreet hired Chase and me to clean up a vacation property he owned out in the Texas Hill Country after some so-called friends shit it up. We stayed a month and vacationed about as much as we worked. The lazy day we spent floating down the Guadalupe remained one of my fondest memories of Chase.

"Worked past what?" My fingers itched with the urge to snatch the picture away. Those days with Chase had no bearing on Dean and me. He had no right to confront me with it.

"Your unhealthy relationship with Chase Fischer." His voice took on a didactic cadence I'd gotten real familiar with lately. "Chase was an addict and...well, I hate to say it, but he was a loser." Dean raised his eyebrows at me. I wanted to knock the know-it-all look off his face. "I thought we agreed he was no good for you and your decision to maintain the friendship was low self-esteem. It was self-destructive behavior. I don't like to see you selling yourself short."

"I remember you saying a bunch of stuff you thought sounded good. Was that us working through it?" I stood from the desk, strode over to Dean, and calmly took the picture from him. I stuck it in back in the mirror's frame and turned to stand face to face with the man I loved. We didn't have a lot in common. We didn't even think the same way. Most times, I thought we complimented each other well enough. This was not one of those times.

"You admitted he wasn't good for you. If you believe that, why do you have this picture of him on your mirror like some teenage girl with a crush?"

Teenage girl with a crush? You've got to be kidding me. I wrestled with my anger, holding back the venom I wanted to spew at him, and counted to ten. When I spoke, my voice barely shook. "I knew Chase a long time. He was—"

"The great romance of your life, the one you can't leave behind," Dean finished.

Indignation flared in me, righteous and hot. Dean knew more than he should about my long history with Chase. My choice to enable my old friend one last time got him killed. Dean held me together while I grieved. He let me express my guilt over Chase's murder, holding me while I cried myself into a stupor, telling me Chase bought a one-way ticket to his fate long ago and nothing I said or did could have changed it. He asked sensitive questions, and I took comfort in his insight, thinking we were bonding over similar life experiences since Dean's bad judgment cost a life once upon a time.

This conversation shed new light on all those talks. I saw something different. Dean thought those talks meant I put Chase out of my mind permanently, deleting both the good and the bad memories, like tapping the "cut" button on my smartphone. How could he think I'd be shallow enough to simply forget the longest running friendship I ever had? How dare he reduce me to a hormonal teenager, sad over a silly broken romance, because I wouldn't delete my relationship with Chase like an unwanted email? The insult hurt, and the hurt pissed me off.

If we'd been anywhere other than in Memaw's house, with her a couple of rooms away, I'd have chewed Dean up one end and down the other, but I had enough snap to know this was neither the time nor the place. Maybe it wasn't even the right argument to have.

"I will not apologize for or justify having a picture of a man I knew and loved from when I was six-years-old until he died when I was thirty. Do we understand each other?"

Dean stuck out his jaw, his blue eyes chilling with anger.

"I will do the best I can not to embarrass you with the election so close, but I can't make any promises." I paused to get a firmer hold on my temper. "I am what I am. Just like Chase was what he was."

Dean shook his, head, shrugged, and rolled his eyes all at the same time. I wanted to kick him in the gnards.

"Whatever," he said.

"No." I bristled. "Don't say whatever to me. Make some indication you understand what I'm telling you." I knew he wouldn't. Once he labeled something or somebody, the subject was closed tighter than a dick's hatband. Dean stuck to whatever he'd said as though reconsidering made him somehow unfit to walk the earth. His snap judgment of me burned. I put my arms over my chest to keep my fist from striking out on its own. I did not want to shit up our relationship further by adding physical violence to it. We stood glaring at each other, both of us breathing hard.

"Okay. I won't say whatever. You want to discuss this, we will." He flared his nostrils. "Your friendship with Chase is part of a lifelong pattern with you, and what happened this morning is a perfect example of it."

This morning. It seemed so long ago. Then it hit me. "Are you talking about the Six Guns coming by the museum?"

"I can't believe you let them take Miss Leticia riding. No telling what could have happened to her."

"What did you expect me to do? Forcibly drag her out?"

"I expected you not to stand out there chit-chatting with them like y'all are buddies while Wade Hill put his hands all over you."

"Wade Hill is my friend. He helps me with my business." I could barely believe my ears. It was not the damn time for Dean to get his undies in a bunch over Wade. If not for him, I might not have survived the night.

"Yeah. He's done a real good job of stepping into Chase's shoes, hasn't he? You traded one loser for another." He clenched his fists. "It's bad enough you hang out with him, but it's even worse when you do it right in the middle of downtown Gaslight City for all the world to see."

"And we're back to me keeping you from getting elected."

"The truth is the truth, no matter how much it hurts."

Angry tears burned my eyes, and I felt furious sobs clawing to get out. I didn't want to cry in front of Dean. I didn't want to give him the satisfaction of seeing me break, but I felt the tears brimming, and one of them slid down my cheek.

"Oh, sweetie, don't cry. I hate to see you doing this to yourself." Dean tried to brush away my tear, and I almost fell over backward flinching away from him. "The look in your eyes is killing my heart. I let this get out of hand, let a lot of things I've been stewing over for a while come out. I handled it wrong."

In other words, he meant every word he said but hated to see me crying over it. He took a step toward me and put his hands on my arms.

"You're so mad, you're shaking." He leaned in to kiss me, and I turned my face away. "We will work it out. I promise."

"Please go home." I pushed his hands off my arms. "I need to sleep." I did not need to sleep, but I needed Dean as far away from me as I could get him.

"Okay." He nodded too quickly. "I've got to work in a few hours too. I'll go."

I walked him out on the front porch where he immediately began brushing mosquitos off his arms and neck.

"Don't spend all night fuming about this." He smiled. I didn't bother to try to smile back. I went inside, shut the door, and locked it.

I stayed up most of the night smoking and fuming. Dean was a good man, but he had an arrogant side to him, and it brought out the worst in me. He had good points about everything he said. My ability to see ghosts could kill him at the polls. Chase Fischer had been a loser, no matter how much I loved him. Memaw hanging out with the Six Guns and me hanging out with Wade Hill looked bad for Dean. The right person could question whether it meant Dean would tolerate illegal activity in our town, maybe even help it happen. I understood, damn it, but the way he acted about it still made me mad as hell, and I didn't know the solution. I loved our relationship. I loved Dean when he was relaxed and having fun. I didn't love this side of him, though. At all. If I could stick it out through the election, things would get better. I hoped.

Around daybreak, I took the house phone off the hook, made coffee and waited for Memaw to get out of bed. I didn't want her hearing about Eddie's death from anybody but me.

———

MEMAW'S WAKING cry brought me running. I slammed into her bedroom and leaned over her bed, wiping sweat off her face. Her gaze, wide and wild, darted around the room, finally settling on my face.

"You hurting?" My words came out in a breathless rush. "You want your medicine? Or I can call Dr. Longstreet."

She took a deep breath, then another. I sat on the edge of the bed, holding her hand and waiting.

"Thank God it was just a dream. Oh, thank God." She pulled her hand out of mine and reached for the glass of water on her nightstand. She took a long drink. "You're right here and safe."

"Yep. I'm right here." I took the nearly empty glass from her and set it back on the nightstand.

"I dreamed you were on the roadside, fighting somebody in your car. They were hurting your leg." She rubbed her temple and frowned. "You were crying and screaming and so scared."

My scalp tightened and began to tingle as sweat broke out on it. *She couldn't know what happened last night. Could she?* I leapt off her bed and walked to her closet, keeping my back to her so she couldn't see my face and got out her robe. I forced a smile onto my face.

"Dreams are weird, aren't they?" I held out her robe and set her house shoes right by the bed so she could slide her feet into them. "They seem so real when you're in the middle of them."

"This one scared me so bad." Grunting with effort, she pushed herself to a sitting position. "Your grandfather, George, was there with me. He held me back, wouldn't let me go help you."

Cold fingers walked down my spine.

"You know what George said, Peri Jean?" Memaw slid her arms into her robe.

"No, ma'am. I don't." I shoved my hands in my pants pockets because I didn't want Memaw to see them trembling and hoped she couldn't see all the places I felt sweat forming on my body.

"He said I couldn't save you. It was your turn to do the right thing." Her dark eyes bored into me, as though looking for an answer. I avoided her gaze.

"It's over now. Let's go out to the kitchen. I've already got your coffee ready. We need to talk."

Ten minutes later, Memaw and I sat in the kitchen drinking coffee. She'd taken the news of Eddie's murder—because if the ghost who came to museum caused his death, it was murder— better than I thought she would. Her worsening sickness sometimes had her emotions on edge, ready to jump off the nearest cliff screaming. I then told her about the items stolen from the museum, the vision, and how I thought it connected to Eddie's death. Memaw put one hand over her mouth and stared at the wall for several seconds.

"So this curse...Priscilla Herrera put it on the treasure to get back at the townspeople?" She put a spoonful of sugar in her coffee, stirring deliberately while not looking at me. "Not because Reginald Mace, the rightful owner of the treasure, asked her to?"

"Not from what I could see. She was angry about what was about to happen to her and wanted to get even." I took a sip of my coffee and winced as the acid burned my belly. "Specifically, she wanted to put the hurt on those greedy enough to mount their own treasure hunt."

"Now another greedy so-and-so is about to try to take off the curse, and you think finding this box will stop them." Memaw's shoulders rounded. "What's your plan to stop them?"

"Last night, I found this in Eddie's office." I slid the piece of yellow note paper across the table to Memaw.

She picked it up and squinted at it. "Nothing in his

office to give you a hint what this means? Julie might not know either."

"I have to ask anyway. Otherwise, I'm at a dead end."

"And you're determined to do this?" She watched me over the rim of her coffee mug.

"I'm not sure I have much choice." I couldn't tell her how true her dream was. She would worry too much. "Priscilla Herrera won't leave me alone until I do." *And she'll send a nightmare to kill us all if I don't.*

Memaw frowned and sipped her coffee. "She feels bad for what she did."

"I think it's more than that." I arranged and rearranged the items on the table until Memaw put her hand over mine.

"What is it then, baby?"

"She said something about not being able to move on." I tried to think of a way to explain to Memaw what I meant.

She pointed at me. "Oh, like she's caught in some kind of punishment place?"

"Maybe. I think maybe." I folded my napkin and unfolded it.

"My mama always said you have to be careful. If you set out to harm, all you get is harm in return. Makes sense Priscilla got sent to prison for ghosts." She settled her gaze on me. The corners of her mouth turned down. "But, baby, what if you end up dead too?"

The idea of dying disappointed me. I wanted to see how things turned out for Dean and me. I wanted to get past the stress of the sheriff's election and start enjoying life with him. Then I thought of Hannah. What if she got killed because of this current round of bullshit? My fingers tightened around my coffee cup, and I reached for my cigarettes with my other hand.

"I can't refuse to help because I couldn't live with it if someone else I love died."

Memaw's eyes moistened. "You can't go against your loyal nature. I want to knock you over the head. You know it? But I'm so proud of you at the same time."

"Rest assured I ain't in this for the long haul. I'll stop whoever's behind this, but I'm out after I finish." I lit a cigarette and blew out a cloud of bluish smoke. "I'm tempted to burn the witch's spell book, and you're the last person I plan to tell about the vision I had."

"Over the years of living here, I heard a lot of stories about the treasure curse." She took a sip of her coffee and grimaced. "Most of the rumors are useless. It's almost like a superstition—step on a crack, the curse'll get you." Memaw's gaze flickered from mine to the window. Her eyes widened, and her mouth dropped open. "No," she muttered.

I half stood in my chair to see what she saw. A huge raven perched on our chain-link fence, facing the window. Goosebumps raised on my arms. Why were they after me? The black opal heated on my chest, and I flinched, trying to get away from the discomfort. I glanced back to Memaw to find her trembling.

"What is it?"

She jumped as though she'd forgotten I was with her and hearing my voice surprised her. As I watched, she pulled herself ramrod straight in her chair and fixed her face into a phony smile.

"Oh, nothing, darling. You know I hate those damn crows." She barked out a fake laugh. "Must be those old legends about them being an omen of death."

"Are you sure it's not a raven?" I couldn't quit thinking about what Eddie said about the ravens. "It's an awfully big bird to be a crow. Next time, look at the shape of the tail feathers. If it's a spade shape when the bird flies, it's a raven, not a crow."

"I ain't a backyard bird watcher, so I've never paid much attention." Memaw took her coffee cup to the sink and pitched the bitter brew down the drain.

I turned back to the window to find the bird still watching us. His stare was like no other animal's I'd seen. An intelligence I didn't like lurked behind the raven's black eyes. It was almost like he knew we were discussing him. Memaw hurried to the window, swatted the glass, and hollered, "Get on out of here."

The bird watched us a few more seconds and flew off. I let go of a breath I didn't know I was holding.

I DROVE to downtown Gaslight City and parked in front of Silver Dreams antiques. Inside Julie Woodson, the shop's owner, talked to a customer. *Damn.* I'd hoped to catch her alone. Everybody and their dogs would know I'd been to see Julie and would be wondering why. I dragged myself out of my car, shuffled the twenty or so steps to the shop, and opened the door. A bell announced my arrival. Every head in the store swiveled in my direction. I saw Julie right away and realized she was talking to my mother. The fun never stopped.

Julie glanced at me and smiled. I gave her a brief wave and pointed to the back of the store. She held up a finger to indicate she'd join me as quickly as she could. Barbie turned to see who wanted Julie. Something flickered behind her gaze, but she recovered quickly and broke into a huge smile. She motioned me over. I started not to go, but Julie joined in. I dragged myself across the store to them.

"Guess who's gonna be working here?" Barbie pulled me into an unwanted hug. I felt a tension headache starting in the back of my neck.

"You?" I didn't even try to smile. Why couldn't Barbie stay away? She'd hated me all my life. There was no reason to start over.

"Yep. Julie's part-time help quit this very morning. Can you believe the coincidence?"

"What happened to Stella?" I turned to Julie, doing my best to resist the urge to kick my mother in her shin.

"You know Donny retired last year. Well, he's now decided he wants to travel, and Stella's job is getting in the way."

I was too surprised to say anything. Donny Dotson never hit me as the traveling kind, but I supposed we all changed as we passed through life.

"Oh, honey, I was sorry to hear about Eddie." Barbie put her cold hand on my bare arm. I moved away from her and caught Julie staring at me with a puzzled expression on her face.

"Thanks. His heart was bad, and he didn't want to change his lifestyle." I had no intention of telling anybody what I really thought happened to Eddie.

"I heard," Barbie said. She glanced between Julie and me, her smile dimming to a vague grimace. "I guess the two of you have some things to talk over. I'll watch the front."

Julie held open the door marked "Employees Only" and led me up two flights of creaking stairs to a loft housing her extra stock. Julie walked to the kitchenette tucked in one corner of the loft and directed me to sit at the table with her.

"Oh, Peri Jean, I'm gonna miss him so much." Tears swam in her eyes. She obviously thought I'd come to her so we could mourn together. I took her hand and squeezed, feeling not a little guilty for being so self-absorbed.

"I can't imagine life without him." That was sure the truth. "How are you doing?"

"Shocked." Her voice wavered, and she stopped speaking and took a tissue out of her pocket and dabbed at her eyes. "Of course, me and Eddie haven't been anything more than pals for years. But we had a good, lifelong friendship."

"Eddie's the only father I remember having."

"He loved you so much." Tears overflowed her eyes and tracked down her cheeks, leaving shining trails. My throat tightened, and I pinched my lips together, straining against the sobs trying to force their way into the world. Julie said, "He was so proud of you making a living for yourself and was glad you'd found someone to love."

I replayed my memories of Eddie. Him teaching me how to drive his awful old truck. The two of us rushing Ugly to the vet after we found him in the woods starving and sick, the pity and anger at how cruel people could be sharp in Eddie's eyes. I'd planned for Eddie to walk me down the aisle if Dean and I got married and for him to play Papaw to my children. He'd do none of that. To add insult to injury, some greedy shithead looking to cash in on the Mace treasure was responsible for his death. I'd get whoever did this. I'd get them no matter what.

"I came for more than one reason." I pulled the piece of notepaper from my pocket and handed it to her. She read it, her lips moving, and frowned. I slumped. Memaw had been right. "You don't know what he meant either, do you?"

"Well, my great-grandmother on my mother's side was a Mahoney. Her people were one of the first ten families to settle here in Burns County." She set the paper down on the table and stared at it, muttering to herself. "What did you mean, Eds?" She took her eyes from the paper and shook her head. "You know, our love of history drew us together. He'd come in here and start talking about something like we'd been discussing it several hours already. I'd have to tell him 'Okay. Stop and go back to the beginning of all this.'" She tried to smile, but her lips trembled.

I thought about what I could tell her. I didn't want to

relay the creepy vision about the creation of the curse to anybody else.

"Come on, honey. You can tell me anything. I won't think it's weird." She meant it too.

"Eddie was looking for a little box about this big." I held out the palm of my hand for reference. "It was a mini chest, sort of like something you'd associate with pirates and treasure."

"It had silver bands over it and a silver closure? And a bird just like your tattoo on the bottom?" She gestured at my bare arm.

Her words sent my stomach rolling. "You know about it?" I could think of no reason anybody else would know about the mini treasure chest. I seriously doubted Priscilla Herrera would have gone around showing the thing to people.

"Well, not really. I had a young woman in here asking about something like it a month or so ago. At first, I thought she was looking for wedding favors and told her about a few online stores she could try, but she was emphatic about having an antique. I took her phone number and told her I'd get back to her if one came in the shop."

"Did it? And may I get her number?"

"No, one didn't come in. And yes, I'll give you her number." Julie stood and went to a huge antique roll top desk. The lid stood open, revealing at least a dozen cubby holes. She reached into one of them, withdrew a stack of papers, and shuffled through them. She separated a business card from the jumble and laid on the table in front of me.

I glanced down at it. *Mysti Whitebyrd.* I rolled my eyes. *Sounds like a kook.* The card listed a phone number with a Tyler area code. I took a picture of it with my cellphone and handed it back to Julie.

"One thing puzzles me." She took the business card and tapped it on the table. "I don't understand why Eddie would have wanted you to ask me about the Mahoney side of my family. Actually, they're so far removed, I don't even know any of them. The one great-aunt I knew died when I was in my twenties. If they ever had a box like the one you mentioned, I don't know about it." She shook her head. "Drives me crazy. I know he had something in mind, and now it's lost."

"If you think of anything…"

"You bet, hon." She opened the door to the loft. Barbie stood there with her hand raised as though she was about to knock.

"What is it, Barbara?" Julie pushed around my mother and descended the stairs. She hated the store to be left unattended. It was one of her cardinal rules. I bit back a nasty smile at my mother's mistake.

Barbie trailed after her. "Those people looking at the old Coke machine are ready to buy, but they have some questions."

"Oh, goodness. That thing's sat in here almost a year." Julie took off at a near run, leaving me with Barbie.

I took the last couple of steps as quickly as I could and strode toward the exit.

"Where'd you get your tattoo, sweetie?" Barbie called after me.

"Roadside carnival." I kept walking.

"But why'd you choose that design?" She grabbed my arm and pulled me to a stop.

I faced her but couldn't make myself return her smile. "Young and stupid, I guess. How come?"

"Ron hated them, but now I'm thinking of getting one. Maybe we can go together?" She broadened her grin. "Like a mother-daughter thing."

You've got to be kidding. I forced myself to nod. "Give me a call." I'd be sure not to answer.

I hurried outside and got into my car. After several deep breaths, I was ready to call Mysti Whitebyrd. I got out my cellphone and punched in the number. The call connected, and one ring, then two, then three buzzed in my ear. I took the cellphone away from my ear to hang up, and a breathless male voice answered. He mumbled what sounded like the name of a business and said, "Can I help you?"

"May I speak to Mysti Whitebyrd?"

"Ms. Whitebyrd has taken ill and is currently not seeing clients. May I ask who's calling?"

"My name's Peri Jean Mace."

"What's the nature of your business? Maybe I can help."

"Ms. Whitebyrd inquired about a mini treasure chest at an antique store in Gaslight City, Texas—"

"Aw, hell no. No more of that crazy town or the fucked

up people who live there. Y'all are what made my sister sick in the first place."

The call disconnected.

Really? I redialed.

"Don't call here a—"

"I won't if you answer me one question."

Silence. At least he didn't hang up right away.

"What did you say the name of your business is?"

"Whitebyrd Potions and Notions. Not that I'll do business with y—"

I hung up. *See how he likes it when somebody does it to him.* I grinned despite my grinding nerves. Potions and Notions. The name of the business sounded like something new age-y. Maybe even something supernatural. Perhaps good old Mysti was a witch.

If the guy on the phone told me the truth, Mysti was sick. Dealing with the Mace Treasure tended to be bad for people's health. Sick didn't mean Mysti wasn't behind the ghost who'd stolen the Bruce family's journals and Eddie's treasure chest. *And murdered Eddie.* I needed to have a chat with Mysti.

I used my smartphone to access the internet and typed in *Whitebyrd Potions and Notions Tyler*. The address popped up like magic.

8

———

To be safe, I sent Hannah a message telling her where I was headed, why, and the address. She replied almost immediately.

Need company?

No.

Get your skinny ass over here and pick me up.

Hannah insisted on taking her BMW to Tyler because my ride stank like cigarettes. She chattered part of the hour's drive but, when I provided monosyllabic answers, quit talking and drove. About a mile away from our destination, when traffic picked up to the point I felt trapped in a video game, she couldn't stand it anymore.

"What's up your ass?"

"My mother is working at the antique store. My grandmother is dying. My boyfriend is going to lose the sheriff's election. The man who helped raise me is dead. Take your pick."

"Boy, talk about glass half empty."

"Eat my shorts."

Hannah's GPS navigator began talking then, and we said nothing else until we reached Mysti Whitebyrd's house, which turned out to be no more exotic than an '80s era brick ranch style house on a street of jammed-together houses, identical except for the color of their shutters.

"She must run her business out of her house." Hannah pulled up to the curb in front of Mysti's house and put the car in park.

"Maybe she does house calls." I unbuckled my seatbelt and opened my door. "You wait out here."

"I don't believe you." She turned in the seat to shake her finger at me. Her cheeks darkened to match her hair. "You can't leave me out."

"Can too." I got out of the car. The shrill cries of children playing or killing each other drilled into my eardrums. Hannah jumped out of the car and huffed around it to join me.

"Wait a damn minute. I'm going, too."

I stared at the closed mini-blinds in Mysti's window. A finger snaked between the slats and pulled one down enough to see through. Great. Whoever was inside knew we were here. So much for the element of surprise.

"If we both go, then I have you to worry about," I said.

"But then I have to sit out here and worry about what's happening to you inside," she said.

The front door opened a crack, and I took off walking toward the house, sick of arguing with her. The crowded street was like a whole other world to me. My senses struggled to keep up with the deluge of competing information.

Cars whizzed by, trailing stereo noise and the stench of exhaust. The smell of food frying wafted from a nearby house and made my stomach growl. The feeling of eyes watching from every direction set me on edge. I did a slow turn, trying to see who was watching. The curtains in the house across the way twitched, but I saw no other signs of life other than the kids, who were all gathered in the largest yard on the street. I stepped up onto the sidewalk and walked toward the house.

Mysti's yard may have once been the nicest on the street, but weeds had invaded the flowerbed and her annuals were dying from neglect. An empty hummingbird feeder swung from the eaves of the tiny front porch. I closed in, and the door opened wider. A guy stepped out onto the porch.

"I'm not letting you in the house." His deeply tanned skin suggested regular tanning bed use while his unlined eyes pegged him at mid-twenties or younger. The barely disguised tremble beneath his gruff words suggested I had his age pegged. "I don't want to talk to anybody from Gaslight City ever again."

His words snapped me to attention. How'd he know where we came from? Nothing about Hannah's vehicle or either of us said we were from Gaslight City. The black opal on my chest heated, as though it recognized something otherworldly, and I took a closer look at the guy.

Nothing about his clean-shaven, sideburn-free face screamed magic or witch. His khaki shorts and tucked-in button-down linen shirt came closer to screaming "nerd" than anything else. Hannah stomped up next to me, muttering about me not even waiting for her. The guy's demeanor did a one-eighty. He put his hand to his mouth and practically made a "squee" sound.

"You're Hannah Kessler." He pointed at her and actually bounced on his heels. "I saw your swimsuit spread. Pardon my boldness, ma'am, but you're hot."

Hannah flushed but stood a little straighter and held out her hand for him to shake.

"What's your name?"

"Brad W-W-Whitebyrd." The guy glanced behind him, then back at me.

"I'm Peri Jean Mace." I held out my hand. He shook it but the look on his face said he'd rather have touched Hannah again.

"Let us in, Brad." I said. "We're as scared of you as you are of us." I didn't know why he was scared of people from Gaslight City, but I was ready to find out.

"We can talk out here."

I twisted to glance behind me. Across the street, a woman with an enormous potbelly stepped out onto her front porch and stood smoking and watching us, a bottle of beer at her feet. Two cars pulled up at the house next door, spilling out a family with two kids, all talking at top volume. I turned back to Brad.

"Come on, dude. You'll get to tell all your buddies Hannah Kessler was in your house." I leaned closer. "Beat off material for *months*."

He flushed and opened the door, motioning us inside. The house smelled like unwashed clothes and TV dinners. Scattered papers and magazines littered the living room, and a game show flashed on the muted TV. Brad hurried to clean the junk off the furniture, piling it all on the brick fireplace hearth. He sat down on the papers and motioned Hannah and me to sit. We chose the couch.

"First thing. How'd you know we're from Gaslight City?" I leaned forward, bracing my elbows on my knees.

Brad frowned, shifting around his nest of newspapers and magazines. "Why are you here?"

"We could do this all day," Hannah said. "Sooner or later, somebody's going to have to give up some information. We'll start." She nudged me with her elbow.

I felt like elbowing her back but started talking instead. "You said on the phone Mysti is sick, right?"

Brad nodded.

"I got Mysti's name from Julie Woodson, who owns Silver Dreams Antiques in Gaslight City. She said Mysti came in looking for a box about this size." I demonstrated with my hands. "It looks like a treasure chest."

"I knew it." He waved one hand in the air. "More crazies looking for the Mace Treasure. I told Mysti not to take the job, no matter how much it paid."

"So someone hired her?" Hannah asked.

Brad's gaze ping-ponged between Hannah and me, his dilemma clear to me. He wanted to please Hannah, but he didn't want to say too much. I needed to build some trust with him or I'd never find out if Mysti was behind sending the ghost to steal the treasure.

"Let's start with something easy," I said. "Where is Mysti now? Maybe we could talk to her."

Brad wiggled some more. He was either about to wet his pants or start scratching like a dog.

"Which one of you is doing magic?" He stood and practically ran across the room to tower over us, some of the papers he'd been holding down sticking to his bare legs, others fluttering in his wake.

Hannah cringed away from him, clutching her purse to her chest. I stood and knocked him back, then crowded in chest-to-chest with him.

"Nobody's doing magic, and don't ever get in my face. Understand?" Despite being several inches shorter than him, I expected him to back down.

"Liar," he shouted in my face. I flinched at the sweet smell of energy drink on his breath. No wonder he was so fidgety. "Get out of this house. Everything Mysti learned about that dumb-assed treasure is in her head, and nobody—not even you—can get it out. I might not be as good as Mysti, but I can hurt you."

"Don't threaten me, you little goon head." I shoved Brad out of my face. "I'll beat you into next year." I reared back a fist, but Hannah shot up off the couch and grabbed my arm.

"Stop it, both of you," she yelled. "We're not here to hurt you, Brad." She gave my arm a hard yank. "You calm down. This isn't a barroom brawl."

I snatched my arm away from Hannah and stooped to pick up one of the papers. The letterhead read Pineywoods Hospital for Mental Health. I held the paper out to Brad.

"This where Mysti's at?"

"I'm not answering any more questions." Brad backed

away from us, his face twisted and red and his eyes wild. "I can feel one of you doing magic. If whoever hired Mysti sent you..."

"Who hired her?" The black opal sent a sharp shock of magic into my skin. Without thinking, I reached to grab it and pull it away from me.

"There!" He pointed, white spittle forming in the corners of his mouth. "See? You've got something in there. Spelling stones, a crystal."

I pulled the black opal out of my shirt. Brad scrambled backward and tripped over a leather ottoman. I grabbed his shirt to keep him from falling on his ass.

"Settle down." I kept my voice low and calm. "Let's you and me calm down."

Brad regained his balance, breathing hard. He and I stared at each other while we took deep breaths.

"Listen to me," I said. "I ain't doing magic, okay? This thing is magic, but I barely know how to use it."

"You a witch, too?"

"No. I can see ghosts. The black opal makes it so I can sort of hear them too."

"Her ability to see ghosts helped her solve her cousin's murder last year," Hannah said.

"I actually used the gemstone to solve my boyfriend's sister's murder." I held the black opal between my fingers so Brad could get a good look at it. "Someone in Gaslight City is using a ghost to steal stuff related to the Mace Treasure. My—" I tried to think of a way to describe Eddie. "This guy who's always been like my father is dead because of it. I came here to find out if Mysti was behind it. I came here on my own. Nobody sent me."

Brad turned away from me and began pacing, muttering under his breath. He got louder as he walked, and I began to pick out a few words. "Wish Mysti could help...driving me crazy..."

"Okay, Brad. It's your turn. This hospital where Mysti's at? What happened to her?"

"She's in the hospital because of that shitty treasure." He spun to face me. "She's lost her mind. They have to keep her in restraints so she won't hurt herself." He shoved past Hannah and me and stormed down the hallway toward the bedrooms.

Hannah and I exchanged a glance. *Are we supposed to see ourselves out?* Sounds of Brad rummaging around in the back drifted out to the living room. Something slammed, and he came running back into the living room and threw an object at me. I raised my arms to protect my face. The object hit my forearm with a bone-jarring clang and dropped to the floor.

"That was completely unnecessary." Hannah knelt in front of me to pick up the item Brad had thrown.

It was a keyring, the old-fashioned kind with an oval leather fob on which sat a metal circle with a logo protected by a layer of clear plastic. A long-dead memory wiggled in my subconscious. My muscles ached as my body shot adrenaline into them, and my stomach turned into a cold, hard ball. A little girl's voice screamed in the deep recesses of my mind, *"Daddy! Daddy! Daddy!"* I reached for the keyring, my hand jerking uncontrollably.

Hannah took one look at my face, and her mouth dropped open. She handed me the keyring. The world around me took on a too-bright-yet-blurry dream quality, and I turned over the keyring, knowing what I'd see on the back but not believing. Burned into the leather were two words:

Paul Mace

My knees went loose, and I swayed against Hannah. She righted me, and I closed my hand over the keyring and shoved it into my jeans pocket. Still feeling lightheaded and dreamy, I turned to Brad Whitebyrd and said, "This ain't no game no more. You'd best tell me where you got the keyring, else I'm gonna call some bikers I know and let them beat the living Jesus out of you."

Brad backed away from me, his hands up. "Get out. I talked to you—I let you in here—when I didn't have to, and—and—and..."

"Tell me where you got the keyring. Last chance."

"Mysti got it as part of the job. The guy who hired her gave it to her."

"What was the job?"

He didn't answer right away, and I took two huge steps toward him, letting our chests press together. I stood on my tiptoes and whispered, "What was the job?"

"Peri Jean..." Hannah said from behind me. I ignored her.

"She was supposed to contact two spirits. One was a lady who was hanged, like, a hundred years ago. The other was this guy, Paul Mace." Brad gulped and tried to go backward but hit the wall. "My sister went to Gaslight City for the day. She came home feeling out of sorts and went to bed. She slept for a couple of hours but then...she snapped, started talking about monsters in mirrors coming to get her, started trying to peel off her own skin so the monsters couldn't find her." Brad's voice cracked on the last word, and his lips trembled. I took a couple of steps away from him, and he twisted away from me and covered his face, wiping hard at his eyes.

"You don't understand," he said in the wobbly voice of someone trying not to cry in front of strangers. "Mysti does everything. She keeps the books, cleans the house, and she's a more powerful witch. I can do the chakra cleansing and the tarot reading, but Mysti has the real talent. She was dead longer than me."

Dead longer? What did he mean? I tried to wrap my mind around his words and couldn't. Brad put his face in his hands and began to bray these ugly, body-wracking sobs. All I could do was stand and stare at this dude who I'd shat upon the same way I'd been shat upon my whole life.

"How about I fix you a drink?" I took off toward the kitchen, found a bottle of tequila with a glass next to it, poured two fingers, and took it back to Brad. He snatched it from me and gulped it down.

"I know you're wondering what I meant," he said. "Now I guess I have to tell you."

"Nope. No explanation necessary. It's your business," I said. "I owe you an apology. I came in here like a bull on a leash, and I trampled all over your life with about as much consideration as a bull would show. My life's in upheaval, and that's the only excuse I've got."

"Who does the keyring belong to?" Brad set his empty glass on a dusty wood end table next to the sofa.

"My father. He was murdered when I was little. They convicted my uncle in a kangaroo court, but nobody really knows who did it." I realized as I said the words I believed them, had believed them all my life. My uncle was no murderer. "I'm going to get out of your life, but I need to ask one more question. Who was Mysti's client?"

With Mysti out of the game, her client might have hired another witch, one who knew how to control ghosts.

"Mysti never said this client's name in front of me. She said I didn't need to know. He must have scared her." Brad danced around like a little kid, giving Hannah worshipful glances every few seconds.

"Can your sister see visitors at all?"

"She can, but she won't know you're there." Brad made a pained face. "They have her so heavily medicated."

I remembered my brief stay at a mental hospital. They'd liked dispensing meds there too. I took out a business card and handed it to Brad.

"You remember anything or even if you want to talk about..." I pulled the black opal out of my shirt and showed it to him again and shrugged. "Call me."

Brad pushed my card into a pocket on his shorts and nodded. I figured the card would probably get trashed or washed, but it wasn't my problem. He walked to the front door and opened it. Hannah took one look outside and hauled ass through the yard, yelling at the kids who were using her BMW as a jungle gym. I took one step onto the concrete porch, and Brad stopped me.

"Sometimes my sister has lucid days." He let out a trembling breath. "Next time one comes up, I'll see if there's any more information I can pass on."

"I appreciate it." I gave his arm a pat and walked to Hannah's car. We stopped for ice cream, which neither of us needed, and made the hour's drive back to Gaslight City. I drove straight home from the museum. I was so tired my body ached.

———

THE KNOCK on the door surprised both Memaw and me.

"Who's that?" She wrinkled her nose at the interruption. Odd for her. Usually she welcomed company with open arms, but the dark shadows and her haunted eyes suggested she'd had an exhausting day. *She's getting worse.* The tension came mincing back, locking my shoulders into a painful, yet familiar, rictus. *I need to get it in my head she'll never get better. This is it.*

"Maybe Dean. He's giving a campaign talk to the Main Street Organization. I agreed to come since both Dottie and Julie are members. Maybe he decided to pick me up." I set the knot I'd been making with the crochet hook and the yarn aside and pushed myself off the rocking chair I'd pulled next to the couch so Memaw could coach me. My joints ached as I walked to the door. The day had put its own kind of hurt on me, and the emotional exhaustion had seeped into my body, poison on an open wound. I wanted sleep, but many miles of hard road lay between me and that little luxury. I opened the door.

At first, I just stared at Brad Whitebyrd and the woman leaning on his shoulder. Her arm hung around Brad's neck, his fingers white at the knuckles from gripping her wrist. The woman raised her head. I recognized a rumpled Mysti Whitebyrd from the photo on her website. Saliva slicked her lips, which tilted drunkenly between a grin and a grimace. Her glazed eyes glowed bright with chemicals and madness.

"Help me." It sounded like she was trying to talk around a mouthful of mashed potatoes. I glanced at Brad for clarification, maybe sanity, but a wild light hardened his gaze into something almost as crazy as what I saw behind Mysti's eyes.

"I was reading through some of Mysti's grimoires, and there's a spell to banish evil spirits, but it calls for a protective crystal." He glanced at the black opal around my neck.

"This isn't a crystal. It's a gemstone." I wanted my denial to make him go away so very bad. I'd run out emotional fuel several hours earlier. The prospect of a normal night with Memaw sounded nice, the perfect escape from the truth I had no way out of the craziness in my life.

"But it's magic." Brad's eyes widened for emphasis. "It's powerful. I can tell."

I stared at him. Mysti began to scratch a sore on her arm, digging into the scab. Blood oozed from the wound. I averted my gaze, unable to watch any longer.

"How on earth did you get her out of the hospital?" I didn't ask the real question. Would an ambulance bearing orderlies in white suits come blasting into the yard any second? The middle of Brad and Mysti's drama seemed like a place I didn't want to visit.

"It's not a locked prison ward." Brad frowned and rolled his eyes at the same time. "The facility is voluntary commitment."

"So you checked her out?" My gut said the truth was not yet with us.

Brad pressed his lips together. "All right. I went to visit and snuck her out. But she signed the commitment papers herself, so I don't see—"

I tried to close the door. Brad wedged in one foot. I put my weight on it, watching the pain twist his face.

"Who is it, baby?" Memaw called. "Let 'em on in. I'm all right. Some company might perk me right up."

Not this kind of company.

Brad shoved open the door and stepped over the threshold, shoving me aside with one arm and dragging Mysti with the other.

"Hey," I yelled. "Don't you push your way in my house."

Brad ignored me and made a beeline for Memaw. She stood an inch at a time, her face going blank at the sight of Brad and Mysti. I decided then and there I'd kill both of them if this made her get sicker than she already was. I'd douse them with kerosene and burn them out back at the ruins where Luther Palmore's house once stood. I stomped across the room, came up behind Brad and poked him hard in the back.

"I'm not a witch," I said to his back. "I'm just a clairvoyant, medium, whatever you want to call it. I see ghosts. That's it."

"What's going on here?" Memaw directed the question at me.

"This is a witch someone hired to contact my daddy's ghost." I wished right away I could take back the words. This was too much for Memaw. "Something got into her. She's…" I gestured at Mysti. She didn't need a description. Seeing her was enough.

"Then you have to help," Memaw said. "My mama would have helped them."

Brad turned to me, his face alight with victory. He was lucky Memaw was here. I'd have jammed his nuts up into his sinus cavity had we been alone.

I staggered backward a few steps, thinking maybe I hadn't heard right but knowing I had. How could Memaw, who'd taught me all my life to stay away from magic, to deny what I was, tell me to use magic to help Mysti? It was like being rag doll caught in a tug of war between two huge, angry kids. They pulled me one way. They pulled me the other way. They snarled and bared their teeth at each other. Meanwhile, one of my seams broke, stuffing began to leak out, and I began to break.

I wanted definite answers about what to do and when to do it, and I didn't know how to find them. Every time I thought I had things figured out—no magic in front of Memaw, no mention of paranormal in front of Dean, anything goes with Hannah—the rules changed. Fatigue fuzzed my vision and loosened my resolve. I flopped down on the couch, tempted to take up my ball of yarn knots and pretend to crochet, ignoring them all. I'd seen Memaw do it enough times I thought I could pull off the act convincingly.

"I'm not a witch," I said to nobody in particular.

"It doesn't matter," Memaw and Brad said together. Memaw gave Brad her *you're not the boss here* look and sat back down on the couch next to me.

"Why don't you take your..." Memaw stared at Mysti.

"Sister," Brad supplied.

"Your sister." Memaw gave him a big smile. "Into the kitchen and sit at the table. If you're thirsty or hungry, look around and take what you want. I need to speak to my granddaughter."

Brad shot me another triumphant look. I stuck up my foul finger. Memaw slapped me on the arm and held up one finger in my face as a warning, the way she had when I was a kid. In the pleasantest of voices, the one she'd have used to ask someone if they wanted a sugar cookie, she spoke to Brad. "Now get on in there, or I'll make you leave without any help."

Brad hitched up Mysti on his shoulder and took off, mostly dragging her behind him. Memaw and I watched them leave.

"You can do spells and hexes and whatever else," she said to me in a low voice. "Mama did them all the time, said her mama taught her. She said it's more of a practice, not a talent like you being a medium." I started at her words, having never heard her call my ghost-seeing by its proper name. "Of course, like anything else, some practitioners have more talent than others, and it's a skill to be learned."

But I didn't *want* to. I wanted to find Hooty and Rainey's belongings, stop whoever killed Eddie from killing anybody else, marry Dean, and spend the rest of my life being as normal as oatmeal. *You won't,* a soft voice whispered in my mind. *You can run, and you can hide, but I'll always be here to fuck up your life, to make it hard, to make it scary, to put you at risk.* I tensed at the thought.

"You have to do this, sugar," Memaw said. "I've taught you, even when it costs you something, we help others. What does Lulu at the coffee shop call it? Karma."

"But you're a Christian." I hoped the reminder would put a stop to this craziness.

"Honey, there's a hundred ways to cook biscuits, and not a single one of them is completely wrong." She gripped my arm. "My mama was a Christian, but she also did stuff like this. All ways exist together if we let them. The nature of God encompasses more than we could ever imagine."

The bottom line was I didn't want to do it. It represented the bud of another leaf on a branch I wanted to prune out of my life. If I did this, it was an admission I'd surrendered myself—what I wanted for my future—to *this.* On the other hand, Memaw had her mind made up. She wanted me to help these people, saw it as my duty to them as a fellow human being. She might back down with some arguing, but what would the effort to be angry cost her?

Here's the real question. Will it be easier to live with doing something I don't want to do, to help Mysti, or to have another bad memory of my last months with Memaw? The decision made itself. It wasn't like I ever had to do anything remotely resembling this again.

"I'll help them on one condition. You go to your room and don't come out until it's done. I can't worry about saving someone and worry about it hurting you at the same time."

"Honey, there's not much left that *can* hurt me. Each day is just me prolonging the inevitable."

I chose to ignore the last part. It was better than facing the inevitable. I depended on Memaw to act as my compass too much. There were still things I needed to ask her, jokes we needed to share. The unchangeable future of her lying pale and still in a coffin scared me stupid.

"Will you stay out? Or should I send them away?"

Memaw answered with a harrumph and stood, using my shoulder for balance and holding onto the back of the couch, and left the room. Brad came to the kitchen archway separating the kitchen from the living room.

"Please. Let's do something soon. She's hurting herself."

I squeezed my eyes shut, wishing I could disappear, go somewhere else where life was easier. Then I opened them and got up to do what life demanded.

9

———

I FOLLOWED Brad into the kitchen and had to struggle to keep from reacting. Mysti had raked bloody rows down her face with her fingernails.

"You'll have to tell me every single thing to do." I averted my gaze and stared at the worn linoleum. Mysti creeped me out too much to look at her for long.

"Of course, of course. I couldn't help overhearing. It really is like your grandmother said. Anybody can do this, *anybody*, but you have a little something extra already inside you to make it work even better." He gently pulled Mysti's fingers away from the raw mess of her skin and held her hand in his, ignoring her struggles to get it away from him.

Memaw was right. I couldn't send Brad and Mysti away, no matter how much I worried their weirdness might be contagious. The blight on my conscience would haunt me more than any ghost could.

"What do we do first?"

"Normally, Mysti and I would banish a spirit from the place where it manifested. But this evil spirit—might even be a demon—follows Mysti around. While we sat in here, she saw its form reflected in your toaster oven. It seems to get stronger and stronger."

I glanced at the toaster, curious but not really wanting to see. "Maybe it feeds on her energy or her fear."

Brad nodded. "Before Mysti got really sick, she told me contacting Priscilla Herrera—the witch—went fine, but it was when she contacted your father's spirit that she had trouble. Have you ever had issues contacting him?"

"I've never really tried."

Brad made a puzzled face.

"I've spent my whole life trying to avoid this stuff. I've seen a lot of ghosts I never wanted to see. My father wasn't one of them."

Brad shrugged off my answer. "I'm thinking if we can be near something, especially a mirror of your father's, maybe we could have an easier time drawing him out so we can do the spell."

"I'm not sure if we—"

"The dresser your daddy and uncle shared is still in the barn." Memaw's voice came from the back of the house.

"You're not supposed to be in this," I hollered.

"Don't smart off to me," she returned.

"Come on," I said. "We'll do what we need to in the barn."

The barn sat a good hundred yards behind Memaw's house. I led Brad and Mysti into the stale night air and deep darkness, hands shoved deep in my pockets.

Humidity cloaked us, dampening my skin almost immediately. The barn loomed ahead, a squatting monster in the shadows.

My hand shook as I unlocked the padlock on the rolling door. I avoided this place, especially after dark. A ghost once tried to kill me here. I gathered my courage, gripping the rough wood, and rolled the door open on its track. A wave of pent-up heat rushed into my face, the intensity of it almost knocking me backward. I reached inside and turned on the overhead lights, waiting for them to hum to life, before I crossed the threshold.

"How are you going to find the dresser in all this crap?" Brad eased Mysti onto an upended crate.

I peered into the gloom. Covered furniture lurked in the shadows, ghosts of lives past and lost, sentenced to this raw purgatory. My gaze settled on a familiar shape.

"Right over here." I strode over to it and pulled off the sheet.

Brad put his hands on his hips and surveyed the room, his nostrils twitching at the smell of old horse manure. "We'll set up the spelling area here in this open spot. I'll help you drag the dresser to the edge of where we'll spell."

"It's your show."

We spent the next hour putting together a makeshift spelling area, using a black drop cloth with a white pentagram painted on it. Brad helped Mysti to her feet and walked her onto the drop cloth.

"Would you bring the crate in here? It's unorthodox, but I don't think she can stand."

I obeyed, and he settled Mysti on the crate again.

"Okay, I think we've got everything we need, so I'm going to cast the circle." Brad grabbed a funky little dagger with a shiny handle, pointed its tip toward the ground, and walked around the drop cloth, scattering salt in a circle.

"I'm going to let you set the candles. One at each point of the compass." He held out the candles to me. I walked around the circle, setting them down in the appropriate spots.

"No," he said. "You have the north and south reversed. North is brown. Pick them all up and start again. Go clockwise around the circle."

"What does it matter?" I grumped as I picked them up.

"If you don't take your setup seriously, how can you expect your request to be taken seriously? Come on."

He walked with me around the circle, directing me where to set each candle.

"You drag your father's mirror over here while I cleanse myself. Then we'll cleanse you."

"I don't need it," I said.

Brad snorted. "Yes, you do. You're brimming with negative energy. Come here."

I grumped my way through moving the mirror and finding it something to lean on. Soon as I finished, Brad held his fingers over the incense, then over a white candle he already had lit. He crumbled salt through his fingers and dunked them in a plastic bowl I'd filched from the kitchen and filled with water Brad claimed was blessed. He finished by raising his arms toward the barn's wood plank ceiling and then performed the same ritual on his sister, who'd never quit picking at herself. He turned to me, obviously ready for me, and I shook my head.

"Do I really have to?"

"Look, the fate of my sister is at stake here. I'm begging for your help. I'll owe you, okay? We both will."

I hunched my shoulders in a shrug, wanting to say no and knowing I couldn't. This pushed my comfort level right into the red. It made me feel stupid and inadequate, to boot, made me ask myself what I'd spent the last thirty-one years learning. For all the stuff I knew how to do, I didn't know a damn thing about this part of me who did things science couldn't explain. I'd thought it a small thing, something like a birthmark, but I was slowly realizing it was more like skin tone or blood type—just what I was. I didn't want to use it too much because I feared it would grow like a muscle, getting bigger with use, and one day I wouldn't be able to turn it off and leave it behind so I could live the perfect life I always wanted.

"You going to let me cleanse you?" Brad asked. "Or no?"

Mysti, who seemed to be overcoming the narcotic cocktail the mental hospital had her on, twisted on the wooden crate to see my answer. The naked fear in her eyes shone almost as bright as the kerosene lanterns Brad asked me to light because the place was creepy. I trudged over to Brad.

He walked me through the ritual even though I remembered most of it from watching him. I raised my hands to release negative energy, and something I didn't expect happened. I felt lighter. The feeling almost buzzed in its intensity, filling my head with a high vibration. The black opal around my neck came to life. For the first time, it hummed in unison with my spirit, the two of them twining together like lovers basking in each other.

"Wow," Brad whispered. "I'll cleanse the spelling area, and we'll start." He worked quickly, lighting the candles and sprinkling his blessed water, going in a clockwise motion around the pentagram. The energy I felt inside hummed to life in the room, and the kerosene lanterns seemed brighter and the shadows dimmer. I bathed in the perfect energy, feeling content in a way no chemicals, sex, or love had ever given me.

"Are y'all Wiccan?" I asked at one point, almost embarrassed to enjoy something I believed would ultimately rob me of everything I wanted.

"Hodgepodge," Brad answered. "We're always learning, always evolving. The woman who taught us said these traditions were ancient and had no name. We're ready. Come over here and hold hands with me and Mysti. We—uh—may have to hold her up."

Mysti rose on her own, swaying weakly, and allowed us to prop her up between us.

Brad took a deep, shuddering breath and said, "If any spirits threaten Melissa Denise White, may the spirits of water and fire, earth and air, banish them and remove their powers to the last trace, making them flee and never return to torment her again."

Melissa Denise White. Is that Mysti's real name? How very vanilla. No wonder she changed it, even to something cheesy.

The candles hissed, and each flame burned first blue

then red, and they leapt higher. A metallic odor filled the room, bringing with it a chill breeze. Brad repeated his speech, nodding at me to join in. At first I only said a few words, but after the fifth time, I had them all. Our voices sounded odd, their rises and falls sharp in the tense atmosphere. I caught movement in the mirror out of the corner of my eye and glanced in its direction. A tiny figure moved, seemingly walking toward us, getting larger as it drew closer.

"Keep saying it," Brad ordered, never missing a beat. I began chanting again. The black opal heated, feeling as though it might burn a hole through my skin. The vibration I'd thought pleasant at first increased until I felt like a lightning rod in a storm, every muscle drawn taut, waiting to get hit by a force bigger and stronger than me.

Tendrils of black escaped from the mirror and inched toward us, testing the edges of the circle but not crossing into it. The shadowy form reached the surface of the mirror and stared out at us for several seconds, as though listening to us. Then it stepped out of the mirror, crossed to the circle, and tried to enter it. A flash of light flared and a sound boomed inside the barn. The figure backed away.

The candles guttered, trying to stay lit. The black opal heated to a painful point, and I cried out, trying to wrench my hand from Mysti's. She tightened her grip, taking up the chanting. I tried to ignore the discomfort. The shadowy figure slid into focus, revealing a familiar face. *Paul Mace. My daddy.* I gasped and swayed on my feet. My knees locked, and I struggled to regain my balance to keep from spilling onto the floor. What was my daddy doing tormenting Mysti like this?

"Help me," a voice in my head yelled. "Please, Peri Jean, help me stop this."

I didn't know how to help him stop. Was this the reason his ghost never came to see me? Because he went around looking for people to torment?

I picked up the chant again, concentrating on the power radiating from the black opal. There was no time to try to figure out what went wrong with my father. The candles burned strong again, bigger than I'd have thought them capable, and things outside our circle began whirling around, tossed by some unseen force. The force sucked my father backward. I could have sworn I saw relief on his face as he flew backward, back into the mirror, which went black the same way the one in Eddie's trailer had. Smoke began to seep from the mirror, and it vibrated in place. I could see waves of heat baking off it, the intensity growing until it burst into flames. Brad, Mysti, and I huddled together in the circle watching the thing burn white hot, the glass melting. I broke our human chain and went to cover the fire with an old blanket, ignoring Brad's protests.

"It was my father," I said. "The spirit tormenting Mysti was my own damn father."

Mysti raised her head. She had the clearest, softest brown eyes I'd ever seen, and they were completely sane. "He doesn't want to. Someone is imprisoning his spirit and using it to do bad things."

It all clicked into place then. The ghost who stole the Bruce family journals and Priscilla Herrera's spell book, the ghost who scared Eddie to death and stole his treasure research had been my father. He never came to see me because some bad person captured his spirit and made him commit awful acts. Had this same person murdered him? I intended to find out.

———

THE BURNED SMELL hung in the barn like a noxious fart. Brad bustled around tearing down all our hard work. I left him alone after I folded the black drop cloth wrong and he yelled at me. Afraid to touch anything else, I stood there with my hands on my hips, feeling useless. Mysti sat slumped on her crate, arms around herself, head down, her ribcage rising and falling with hard breaths.

I walked past her and rolled open the barn's huge door to diffuse some of the burned smell. Humidity and heat rolled over me, stale and stifling. Damn August heat. It was never-ending. I grabbed an old folding camp chair from the mess inside the barn, opened it, and went back to Mysti.

"Got a chair for you outside. Might smell a little better." I had to speak to her hunched back. She held out her arm and allowed me to help her to it.

"Talk about a crash course in magic, huh?" The strength had faded from Mysti's voice, leaving it soft and weak.

No shit. Unwanted too. I said nothing. My emotions twisted until they were a tangled mess, bad enough to compete with the worst of my crochet disasters. Weird stuff—magic—had seeped into every part of my existence like a water leak. Had it been water, I'd have gotten down on my hands and knees and wiped it up. I couldn't wipe up this mess, and I couldn't walk away either. I had responsibilities to fulfill, to my friends, to this town, to my long-dead daddy. How did everything end up falling on my shoulders?

Memaw was sick and dying. Barbie had shown up in town. The theft of the Bruce's family heirlooms escalated to Eddie's death. Priscilla Herrera put the fate of Gaslight City in my hands. Learning some pathetic loser had turned my daddy into some sort of spiritual mercenary put a nice, creamy feces icing on the cake. No wonder Eddie mouthed "Paul" at me when I found his spirit in the mirror in his trailer.

"Peri Jean? You all right?" Mysti touched my arm.

"Fine," I said. "Just worrying."

Tree frogs squealed their nightly opera. Usually, I found the sound soothing, something I could hide behind and think. After the events of the night, though, their singing scratched on my nerves, finding sore edges and worrying them. A fingernail sliver of moon hung in the inky sky, hovering over Memaw's house. Was it an omen? If so, it seemed one of hopelessness.

"Worry about tomorrow robs you of your energy to deal with today." Mysti raised her head to stare me in the face. For the first time I took note of the dark half-moons under her eyes and the way she clutched herself. This woman had run a marathon through hell. She needed rest more than she needed to play nursemaid to me.

"I'll clean this up. Let your brother take you home." I turned back to tell Brad to leave it, but Mysti caught my arm, her icy fingers digging in to the soft flesh around my wrist. I barely resisted the urge to pull away.

"No. I want us girls to talk for a minute here. Get yourself a chair and sit down."

I didn't want to have a heart-to-heart with her but couldn't refuse someone so pathetic and broken. Taking the smallest steps I could, putting off the inevitable, I did as she asked.

"Brad says you're a medium in denial." She had a sweet smile, the kind used to getting people to open up, to spill their secrets. I was too tired to fight the invitation I saw there.

"My early experiences with what I am weren't so great. I was put in a mental hospital and diagnosed with schizophrenia."

"I grew up a ward of the state, so I know where you're coming from." Mysti's confession shocked me, and I turned to stare at her. She carried herself like someone who'd always been loved, always felt confident in who she was. How did she get there? "There's nothing I can say to take away the trauma of your early years, but I want you to think about something. Letting those old experiences keep you from finding your true self will never make you happy."

I crossed my arms over my chest. She was sick, and I didn't want to argue with her. I changed the subject.

"Were you hired to find the Mace Treasure?"

"No." She sat back in her chair, frowning. "I want to

help you, but I feel uncomfortable giving you too much information. One of the services I provide is confidentiality."

I sat in silence, stumped on how to proceed.

"But you saved my life and, in doing so, put yourself in danger. Whoever's behind all this will be coming for you." She folded her battered hands in her lap. "Convince me to break my rules."

"There's more to it than the bad guy coming to take me out." I slumped in my chair, the weight of it crushing me. "If the bad guy gets the curse off the treasure, the whole world goes boom."

"Wait a minute. Back up." Mysti's voice smoothed out some of my raw edges. She was good at this.

I started by telling Mysti about my father's ghost stealing the Bruce family journals and the spell book and went from there. Mysti listened without interrupting, squinting her eyes at times, nodding at others. I first noticed the lack of judgment on her face when I explained about the way Priscilla cursed the treasure and how the spirit she tied the curse to would level Gaslight City if released. Mysti's open expression kept me talking until I reached the part where I went to see Julie and got Mysti's name from her. I finished my recitation, and the frogs' screaming filled the silence.

Mysti took a deep breath and let it out. I figured she was gearing up to tell me I'd failed to convince her to do anything but leave and prepared to take the rebuke politely. Much as I wanted to kick little brother Brad's ass the first time I met him, Mysti hit me a different way altogether. I almost wanted her to like me. Almost.

"My employer hired me to contact the ghosts of both Paul Mace and Priscilla Herrera. The purpose was to find the spelling stones and the box you saw in your vision."

Brad already told me that much, but it was a start. "Why?"

"Asking those kinds of questions would put me out of business fast. If I want to make money, I have to keep my lips zipped and do the job." She licked her lips and stopped to think, probably choosing her words carefully. "I contacted Priscilla Herrera at the gallows where she was murdered. I saw her speak the curse you mentioned. I saw her hang." Mysti shook her head.

"The box and the stones?"

"She swallowed the stones while the man was tying her ankles together before they hanged her." She turned to stare at me in the dark, her gaze burning at me. "Her spirit told me the man who buried her stole the box."

"And you thought it might be on the antique circuit so you went to Julie at Silver Dreams." Things were starting to come together, but not in a helpful way. This was all one big, revolving circle.

"That falls under confidentiality to my client." She put her hands up.

Another dead end. I bit my lip in frustration.

"Before we move on, I want to say something that's simply one weird chick talking to another." Mysti's soft voice lulled me into listening. "I can see you feel overwhelmed, even frustrated, by all this, but Priscilla Herrera has some reason she chose you, some reason she thinks only you can do it. She was a powerful witch, and she's still got power as a spirit. When I contacted her, I could feel her controlling what I saw of her last moments alive."

My stomach did a clumsy cartwheel. I remembered trying to contact the ghost who stole the journals—my daddy's ghost. Priscilla kept me from it. Mysti herself got into a nasty mess contacting my father's ghost. Had Priscilla Herrera been trying to protect me? Why?

Help me stop this evil and find peace. The voice came from inside my head, but Mysti jumped and glanced around. Did she hear it too? She put her fingers to her temples and closed her eyes, her whole body rising and falling with her breaths. My body went into overdrive, preparing for unpleasantness. I crouched on the edge of my flimsy chair.

"She's gone." Mysti dropped her hands and raised her head.

Relief surged through me. "That was her?"

"You know it was." Mysti smiled and touched a finger to her split lip. "And you heard what she said just as well as I did."

Help me stop this evil and find peace.

"The law of doing magic is 'whatever you put out comes back times three.' But a lot of belief systems use the same concept. Christianity, for one. 'Do unto others as you would have them do to you.'" Mysti waited a beat for me absorb it. "Priscilla Herrera created some rotten karma when she put the curse on the treasure."

"It was justified." My voice raised, and I cut it off immediately. When I spoke again, it was in a near whisper. "Those sorry bastards murdered her."

"I'll go for the cliché bonus round." Mysti gave me her gentle smile. "Two wrongs don't make a right. Priscilla went to her death with a wrong riding on her, and it compounded as time passed. She is at odds with the universe until it's fixed."

"But why me? You're better at this stuff."

Mysti stared out into the darkness as she thought about it. "The blood," she murmured. "You're a Mace. The treasure was intended for one of your ancestors. Maybe when she said, 'None of you, save one who has the blood, will have the treasure,' she meant only someone from the Mace family could get at it."

Something about Mysti's concept didn't ring quite true to me, but my exhaustion wouldn't let me get at it.

"This connection Priscilla's ghost feels with you might work to your advantage in figuring out who is behind all this." She gave me her soft smile again. "But you don't like contacting ghosts."

No, I didn't.

"Moving on," Mysti said to my silence.

"Will you tell me why your employer had you contact my daddy's ghost?"

She hesitated. "My employer thought your father might have a line on where the stones and the box ended up." I started to speak, but she shook her head. "Now, don't ask me why. We've reached the end of what I can tell you about the job I was hired to do." She glanced at her brother, who'd finished packing up and sat on a sawhorse watching us. "Do you have my cellphone?"

Without answering, he took it from his pocket and brought it to her. Mysti took the phone and tapped out a message. The tension seemed to go out of her body.

"Okay. When I was hired for this job, my client told me specifically *not* to reach out to you for one of your father's personal items to use in contacting his ghost."

My jaw dropped. I wanted to know how Mysti's employer got my father's keychain before this conversation. I was determined to have a sit-down with whoever hired Mysti. Find out who they thought they were skulking around behind the scenes like this.

Her cellphone dinged, and she tapped out a quick response and turned to Brad. "Pack up the car quickly. We have a stop to make before we leave town."

"Car's ready." Brad came back into the barn and stood next to Mysti's chair. She stood, using her brother's hand to help her gain her feet.

"Do you have it?" she spoke to Brad. He handed her what looked like a business card and a pen. She turned it over, scribbled on the back, and handed it to me. "This is my personal number. I want to repay you for your help today by teaching you how to be what you're meant to be."

I took the card and tried to give her a polite smile. She actually laughed at me.

"I understand your reluctance. Really, I do. Had I not met Tunia, it would have taken me a lot longer to accept what I was, let alone learn how to make it work for me."

"Tunia?" I didn't want to address anything else she'd

said because it might mean committing to something permanent.

"It was short for Petunia. She said her mother liked cartoons." Mysti's words broke the tension, and we both laughed.

"How about you tell me who hired you?"

"He said you wouldn't quit until you found out, and he was right. Tubby Tubman. I'm on my way to see him, and he wants you to come too. He said you'd know where to find him."

I wanted to scream and puke at the same time. Tubby Tubman was the last name I expected to come out of her mouth. I wanted to go see him the same way I wanted food poisoning, but I knew better than to refuse. Tubby Tubman gave the Six Gun Revolutionaries a run for their money in terms of ruthlessness and willingness to break the law. Great end to a rotten day.

"I'll take my own car," I said. "You can follow me."

10

I DROVE with the window down and the air conditioner turned off. After ten in the evening, the day's heat had broken, replaced with a velvety coolness I wanted to enjoy while it lasted. Driving below the speed limit and checking often for Brad and Mysti's headlights in my rearview mirror, the trip to downtown Gaslight City took longer than my usual ten minutes. It took even longer to find a parking place where I could convince myself nobody would notice my car.

"We're going to Bullfrog's Billiards," I told Brad and Mysti as they got out of their Toyota sedan. "It's right through these alleys. Dark in there, so stay close."

"How you do know where to find him?" Mysti hovered near me while Brad trailed a few feet behind.

"Let's say I know some things about Tubby the average citizen of Gaslight City might not know." I hurried down the alley, taking small steps to avoid tripping on debris. We ended up in a courtyard piled with beer boxes and wooden pallets. I walked straight to the iron-bar-covered back door.

"This doesn't look like a business," Brad said. "What is it? Some kind of secret club?"

"There's a street entrance," I said. "I'm hoping not to be seen by any of Bullfrog's patrons." Whether my plan worked depended on how much of an ass Tubby felt like acting.

Bunched muscles aching, I raised one trembling hand, knotted it into a fist, and tapped out the code Tubby taught me all those years ago. The door swung open, spilling out a circle of yellowed light. Bullfrog himself leaned out.

"You here to see the man, Peri Jean?" Bullfrog's doughy, pockmarked skin, his massive beer gut, and the distant blur in his eyes made him seem safer than he was, but I'd seen him knife a guy several years ago. Bullfrog jabbed the knife into the guy over and over again, his arm moving like the needle on a sewing machine. The guy crumpled on the floor and a puddle of blood spread around him. Bullfrog wiped the knife on his shirt and went back to his beer. Maybe feeling my eyes on him, he turned, smiled, and blew me a kiss. A couple of his flunkies dragged the stabbed guy away. I never knew if he lived or died.

"He's expecting me."

"You a little long in the tooth for him these days." His lips quirked into an almost-smile. Bullfrog was right. Tubby got older while his companions got younger. I never saw the same one with him twice. The smart ones probably figured out they were sleeping with Beelzebub himself and cut ties. Who knew what happened to the stupid ones? Nothing good, probably.

"That may be so, but he's expecting us."

Bullfrog stared at me. "What's the magic word?"

Oh, come the hell on.

"Lick my armpits?" I forced what I hoped was a nasty smirk onto my face to let Bullfrog know I wasn't scared of him.

He grunted and shut the door in my face. I heard his footsteps receding. The door swung open again, and Tubby Tubman himself looked out at me. I'd come to see him, but having him right in front of me sent my heart into overdrive.

Burns County was too small for us not to have seen each other a few times over the years since that awful night. I'd made a point not to get close enough to take a real look at him. This situation left me no choice.

He stood bare chested, jeans hanging low on his skinny hips. His perpetually bare feet were still bony. One of them sported a tattoo of a cartoon character. A fine layer of muscle covered his bony chest. His crafty eyes had deeper lines etched around them, and a few gray hairs had invaded his dishwater-blond hair. Tub took me in as I studied him, drifting over my body and finally landing on my face. He raised one ropy arm to lean against the doorframe and rubbed a hand over his bicep.

"Well, well, well. We meet again." His nasal baritone sent the wrong kind of chills running down my back. "Peri Jean Mace *and* Mysti Whitebyrd..." He squinted at Brad. "And her lackey."

I heard Brad's gulp and wanted to tell him not to react, but it was too late.

"Come on in." He stepped aside. We stepped onto wood plank floors, stained black from a hundred years of dirty shoes. "My visit with Ms. Peri Jean is gonna take longer, so why don't Mysti and her errand boy come on up, get paid, and we can be done with each other? You can go in the bar, Ms. Peri Jean."

"I don't want to go in the bar," I said.

"Is it because of your association with Burns County Sheriff's Office?" Tubby widened his eyes in mock surprise. I shook my head at him.

"I'm not playing this game with you, Tub."

He laughed and motioned Brad and Mysti to go up the steps to the loft where he conducted business, turning back to me at the last moment. "Sit on the steps and wait then. I don't care." He went up the stairs, giving me a peek at the filthy bottoms of his bare feet. *Nasty.*

I brushed off the bottom step a few times, decided it was no use, and parked my butt on it. Shouts came from the loft. I shot to my feet again and waited for the shit shower to start.

"I don't have to do what you say. I don't want to go down there." The voice was female but not Mysti's. The door at the top of the stairs swung open hard enough to bounce off the wall, and a slim, dark-haired girl was pushed out. She might have been eighteen, but she sure didn't look it. She sneered at me as she thumped down the stairs. I stepped aside and watched her go through the door connecting to the bar. I sat back down.

True to his word, Tubby's business with Mysti didn't take long at all. She came out of his office, eyes wide with shock but tucking a thick envelope into her purse. I waited until she got to the bottom of the stairs to speak to her.

"You okay?"

"We're square." She pulled me into her arms for a quick, soft hug. "Thanks again for saving me, and please call me. I'd love to teach you."

I nodded even though I still wasn't sure. Tubby beckoned to me from the top of the stairs. As soon as I stepped into his loft, the smell of dope and sex assailed me.

"Can we open a window?"

Without speaking, Tubby opened one of the windows and turned on a fan. "Better?"

I nodded.

"Why don't you sit down?"

"Which of these chairs has the least bodily fluids on it?"

He laughed at that and went into the kitchenette and brought out a wooden chair. Then he returned to the tiny bar and fetched one of those sanitary wipes and cleaned the chair. The thing came away black with dirt. He motioned to the chair with a grand wave. "Your throne, darlin'."

I sat. Tubby watched me get settled, one side of his mouth tilted in what might have been a smile. Having it directed at me produced the creepiest feeling in the world. I pretended not to notice him, and he shrugged and went into the kitchen and got another, identical chair and sat on it without cleaning it.

"I'd like us to reach an agreement," Tubby said.

"I wouldn't, but I would like to know how you came to have my daddy's keychain."

"We could bargain for the information."

"I don't dance with Satan's stepson any more, Tub."

"My step-dad's name is Roger." The expression on his face never changed. It was like being watched by a crocodile.

Impatience built in me, but I fought against it. Had to. No matter how long I stayed away, some things never changed. If he gave me anything, I'd have to give him something back, and he'd want something big. This could get bad fast.

Worst part was I had no idea what Tubby wanted from me. At the same time, I knew he knew exactly what he planned to ask of me. I flashed on things Tubby could want and came up with one thing. The Mace Treasure. He obviously had an interest in it. If he thought I could help him find it, he needed to go find another monkey and another circus.

"There's nothing I can do for you, Tub. Can't you help me for old time's sake? I never tried to stick you when Chase was in a mess. I always paid up."

"If Chase is your old time's sake, you can lick my sugared ass." He snorted. "You forgetting what came before Chase's problems?"

I'd hoped it wasn't memorable enough for him to bring up. The thought of those dark months chilled me, and I twisted my legs around each other, crossing my arms over my chest in the same motion. Tubby raised his eyebrows, this time smiling a real smile, the kind sane people ran from.

"You think I'm gonna give you a free pass and act like nothing happened? You ignored me for seven years. I don't owe you shit."

"We don't need to rehash our friendship, Tub."

"Friendship? Give me a fucking break. I kept you from falling off into the abyss after your husband dumped you—"

"Don't say it," I said. "If this had nothing to do with my father—my murdered father—I'd get up and walk out of here. You can talk shit to me all you want, but don't you dare bring up Tim and what he did to me—"

"Fine. The end result was that you came back to town all broken and fucked up, and *I* helped *you.* Then, when you were done, you just walked off."

"Y'all stabbed somebody down there in the bar." Voice raising, I swung my arm at the door leading downstairs. "Plus, you were bored with me. You'd had enough and were moving on. I wasn't so stupid and naive I couldn't see it. It was time to end things before we hated each other."

"*I'm* the one who ends things, and I never told you I was finished."

I rolled my eyes, ignoring the way his eyes flashed anger and his fist curled. This had to be the stupidest argument of my life. All these years he'd been angry because I walked away and didn't give him the chance to dump me? I wanted to tell him to pound sand and walk out, maybe breaking something on the way. Had it not been for my daddy's keychain, I would have.

"Tub, if you let me up here so we can rehash a fling we had when I was at the lowest point of my life, I'll leave. We're wasting each other's time."

"Naw. It ain't why I let you up here, but I wanted you to know I ain't forgot."

For the first time in a long time, I let myself really think back to the spring and summer I spent with Tubby. This was the stuff I'd never tell Hannah if I could help it. I never spoke of those months to anybody—not even Memaw—and tried not to think of them. I saw a lot of things I shouldn't have seen and did a lot I shouldn't have done. Tubby did one thing right, though. He really saved me from falling off a bottomless cliff, just like he said. He paid for my divorce too.

"I'm sorry I did you like I did, Tub." I watched his face to see if the apology made any difference. He still looked the same to me. "We had fun, and you helped me."

Some of the darkness left his face. He'd been making one of his awful hand-rolled cigarettes while we talked. He licked it and fired it up. He scooted his chair closer to me and took my hand.

"What I want from you, darlin', in exchange for the conversation we about to have, is for you to keep me abreast of Deputy Dean's investigations, let me know if he's ever getting close to putting old Tub in jail. Ought to be no problem since you his girlfriend."

I clenched my jaw, not out of fear, but to keep from honking laughter at him referring to himself in the third person. Had I not had the feeling I'd screwed up irrevocably, this whole thing would have been hysterical. My muscles twitched, begging me to get my hand away from him before he ate it, but I knew better. If he was angry about me killing our ending romance softly all those years ago, he'd pitch a wall-eyed fit if I didn't let him manhandle me.

"Knowing where you got my daddy's keychain isn't worth it." No point in saying I wouldn't betray Dean. Tubby didn't care about loyalty or doing the right thing. I tried to stand, and he tugged me back down.

"I got more'n info about the keychain. I know you're looking for what got stolen from the museum and Eddie's missing treasure notes. I got something might can help you." He held onto my hand and smoked his cigarette, watching my face.

I wanted to tell him to forget it, really I did, but it was no longer just about finding the stolen Bruce heirlooms. It was about Eddie's murder. It was about my father and saving him from an afterlife I couldn't imagine. It was about revenge for whoever robbed me of my daddy and a normal childhood. Lastly, it was about what Priscilla Herrera could bully me into doing. Besides, I was still naive enough to think I could wiggle out of a bargain with Tubby Tubman. I nodded.

———

TUBBY BROUGHT my hand to his lips and kissed it. I shuddered, stomach roiling, and pulled my hand away from him. He laughed and got up to get a backpack leaning against the wall. He sat back down, took out a generic laptop, and clicked a few keys.

A familiar face filled the screen. It took me a few seconds to place it, but when I did, my body went loose as jello, and I nearly flopped out of the chair. The face on the screen was my father. Next to him was an ancient African-American man who I'd bet every nickel I had was related to Hooty Bruce. The two sat side-by-side on a rickety, slightly familiar porch. Tubby started the video and everything changed again for me.

"It's ready," said a voice off camera. "Y'all start talking."

The video was the blurry quality I associated with people's old homemade VHS tapes, but there was my father, the man who'd been a mystery all my life.

"All right." My daddy had a soft but deep voice, his thick accent drawing out the words way longer than they were ever intended to be. "If you got it going, Jesse, you come on around and sit with us in case you think of something to ask Mr. Bruce."

Jesse ran around the camera and sat on the other side of what had to be Hooty's grandfather. Even on such a low-quality recording, I could tell a difference between my uncle and my father despite their identical appearance. Jesse fidgeted constantly, tapping his legs, shifting around while my daddy sat stock still, his expression so serious I thought he was going to morph into Memaw any second and start shaking his finger.

"Okay, Mr. Bruce. You ready?" Paul asked.

"I am beyond ready, Mr. Mace." Mr. Bruce had the kind of hoarse voice I associated with people who yelled and smoked a lot. "I always wanted to be in moving pictures when I was younger. Thought I was right good looking, but they didn't have many parts for a black man back then. Figured I'd be better off raising a family here." He laughed and sort of clapped his hands. "This goes to show you never know what you'll get to do if you live long enough."

Paul grinned, and my breath caught in my throat. The smile brought back fragments of memories, the way my daddy'd played with me and talked to me. I forced myself to concentrate on his words. "Mr. Bruce, why don't you tell us your name and age so we can have a record of it."

"Awright. I'm Isaiah Bruce, and I'm 94 years old. Lived in Gaslight City all my life except for the time I spent in The Great War." Isaiah Bruce might have been old, but a bright, sharp light shone in his eyes. He knew exactly what was going on and was excited to be part of it.

"Today is June 3, 1989," Jesse leaned forward to talk to the camera, a smart-assed grin forming on his face. It made me think of his daughter, Rae, who died because of me. "Just for the record."

"What have you got there in your hand, Mr. Bruce?" Paul asked.

I squinted at the video and got a glimpse of the journal my father's ghost had stolen from Burns County Museum what seemed like a lifetime ago.

"This was my daddy's journal. Hezekiah Bruce was the first black business owner here in Burns County. I remember him writing in this book and books like it all my life." Isaiah opened the book to a marked page. "Y'all want me to read about old Bert Holze lynching the witch used to live down the road there right now?" He stuck out one dark arm and pointed somewhere off-screen.

"Yessir," both Paul and Jesse said at once.

Isaiah Bruce began reading the same passage I'd heard Hooty read on the board meeting video. He didn't have Hooty's training as a public speaker, but his dusty voice added a new dimension of horror to the story because, if my calculations were correct, he was old enough to remember the day it all happened and probably witnessed some of it. I glanced at Tubby, nodding to indicate I knew about this. He pressed pause.

"Hell. And here I thought this would be a surprise to you. Dayum."

"Do I get my money back on our bargain?"

He grinned like a dead fish. "Let's finish watching this here video. I think you'll learn at least one thing you didn't know." He started the video playing again.

Isaiah read the last words of his father's account of the lynching and closed the book. "One thing this book don't talk about is the feller who buried poor Miss Priscilla. I don't know why Poppa didn't include it. I was right there when old Archie Mahoney told it."

I jerked in my seat. This had to be the Mahoney on Eddie's note. He'd known Julie was a descendant of this Archie Mahoney. Eddie must have wanted to ask Julie if she had any idea where the box ended up. She obviously didn't, but I'd make a point to mention the name to her.

"What did old Archie Mahoney tell you?" Paul asked Isaiah on the video.

"Well, sir, old Archie was the county sexton." He

grinned a toothless smile at the expressions on Paul's and Jesse's faces. "He did all the county's burying, don't you know. That's a sexton's job. Mahoney told my daddy he pulled all the gold teeth out of poor Miss Priscilla's mouth and took the box out of her pocket." Isaiah shook his head, a grimace puckering his wrinkles even further.

"What happened to the box?" Jesse asked.

"Greedy old so-and-so kept it. Tell you something spooky, though. Mahoney's luck changed, starting the day he robbed that box off poor Miss 'Cilla's body. He fell into one of his own graves and broke his leg. Leg didn't heal right, and he lost his job." Isaiah knocked on his own leg. "Became the town drunk, Archie did. I could have forgot Miss 'Cilla's box on my own, but Old Archie wouldn't let us forget. Every time he got on a toot, he'd go to talking about the box, how he was sure it'd lead him straight to Reginald Mace's treasure. Old Arch tried everything to get the box open over the years, but it was stuck tighter than a Sunday school teacher's knees." Isaiah paused here, staring off into the distance.

"He never got it open?" Paul's question seemed more to get Isaiah back on track than out of curiosity.

"Not that I know of. He finally died, and I guess his daughter got it. Beverly, her name was. She cared for Archie in his final years. Poor thing got killed in a gunfight with another woman over some worthless man. No telling where the box fetched up." Isaiah's eyes went unfocused again. Used to seeing the same look on Memaw, I guessed the old man was getting tired. His body and mind were worn out beyond what I wanted to imagine. Soon, he'd want to rest.

"But I almost forgot to tell you boys the best part," Isaiah said. "Old Archie never made no mention of Miss Priscilla's spelling stones."

Paul cocked his head, looking for all the world like me when I'm surprised. "What's that, Mr. Bruce? Stones?"

"Yessir. Miss Priscilla had her these stones she used to do her spelling. I wouldn't know 'cept my baby sister was born sick. Momma and Poppa was sure she'd die, didn't have no money, so they called on Miss Priscilla. She come and laid out those stones, gave my sister something to drink, her whispering in some language the whole time. I was no more than a little boy, but it scared me right and good. We were churchgoing folks, don't you know. I'd done heard what a witch was, and I knowed for sure I was seeing one that day." He chuckled. "It's funny how you get older and realize how ignorant folks can be. Whatever Miss Priscilla did worked. My sister got better. Grew up and married a nice young man from Florida. Still living there. Guess I won't get to see her again."

Paul and Jesse exchanged an eyebrows raised glance.

"What do you think happened to the stones?" Jesse asked Isaiah.

"She had to have hid them on her property, which I now own," Isaiah said. "Now, I've done told you boys you can go over there and poke around, and now I'm telling you what I think you might find. Keep what you find, long as you tell folks I helped you find it. My daughter gives you any trouble, you tell her to come up here and talk to me."

Tubby turned off the video again. "There's not much more. They thank each other."

"You think you'd be willing to give me a copy of it? I don't have much to remember my father by."

Tubby nodded and set about making a copy of the video, looking so much like the young man I'd spent a long-ago summer with, the one who helped me forget a horror I still didn't like letting into my mind, it made my heart ache for what we'd both lost as we learned the ways of the world. He caught me watching him.

"Was I right? Did you learn something you wanted to know?"

"I did. Now tell me how you came by the keychain and the video."

"You know my momma moved out of Texas last year?"

"Yep. I helped her haul a bunch of old furniture to the dump." Mrs. Tubman told me her wonderful, sweet son bought her a condo in a Colorado resort town. She couldn't wait to escape the Texas summers.

"She didn't clean out half what she had. I found this box of stuff in her house after she left. Had the video, your daddy's keychain, and a couple other items."

"What was the other stuff?"

"I'd be willing to show you for a price."

"Forget it. How'd your mother get the box?"

"I wondered the very same thing and called her. You remember we both lived on the road that goes to the cemetery when we were real young?"

I nodded even though I'd forgotten until he mentioned it.

"Momma said she saw Barbie set the box out with the garbage the day after Paul died. Momma can't resist digging through junk, trying to find something valuable, so she picked it up. Once she figured out what was in it, she kept it, planning to give it to you when you were old enough. Guess she forgot."

And Tubby Tubman sure as shit wasn't going to honor her wishes after the fact. More than ever, I wanted to get away from him so I could think this through. Plus, I worried if I hung around too long he'd blackmail me into burning down the town for him.

"I won't say it was a pleasure, but it sure was an education." I stood and held out my hand for him to shake. He took it and gave it a squeeze.

"Come again sometime. We'll catch up."

I dropped his hand and walked out of the room without answering. Tubby's teenage girlfriend was standing on the stairs, right outside the room. It wasn't hard for me to guess she'd had her ear pressed to the door, trying to hear what she could.

"Whore," she hissed at me.

"What did you say to me?" I widened my eyes and got in her face. My pity over her bad taste in men didn't extend to me taking crap from her. She tried to dart around me, but I blocked her way. "Say it again."

She refused to look at me, hunching her shoulders.

"Look at me." I waited until she did. "It's not a good idea to talk shit to people when you don't know what they're capable of. You're with dangerous people."

"Yes, ma'am," she squeaked out. I moved my arm and let her by, wondering why I bothered.

Seeing it was after eleven and too late to call Julie, I left a message for her at Silver Dreams antiques saying the box I was looking for was once in the possession of an Archie Mahoney and to call me with any information she had. I walked out to my car, still enjoying the somewhat cool night air.

11

———

I TRUDGED through the dark alleys and across an unlit side street to get to my car, crossing into the pitch black parking lot behind the Catholic church.

"You embarrassed me tonight." Dean's voice coming out of the dark scared me into dropping my phone. I caught it before it smacked down on the concrete parking lot. "I stood around waiting and waiting at the Main Street Association meeting, and you never showed. I tried to call you and no answer."

I glanced at my phone and saw I had five missed calls and five voice messages from Dean. I cringed. I'd been so wrapped up with Mysti and Brad, I'd never even heard it.

"I'm sorry. Something came up. The whole thing slipped my mind."

"I was worried about you, so I called your grand-mother. She told me you'd gone out with some people I never heard of before." He slid off the hood of my car and walked toward me. I stood my ground, my heart speeding away in my chest. "I went looking for you. Saw you drive to this parking lot with those weirdos right behind you, stand around talking a while, and then go in Bullfrog's."

My cheeks and lips went numb as adrenaline rushed through my veins. I swallowed hard. After all the trouble I went to, the one person in the world I didn't want finding out what I was up to had seen me.

"What? The three of you go drinking in Bullfrog's?" He jammed his hands on his hips the way he did when he was super pissed. "You said something came up. What was it? Your friends looked like a couple of burnouts."

Anger caught fire and burned quickly, warming my insides, eating away some of the tiredness. Dean didn't know Mysti or Brad. He'd simply made a judgment about them because he was Mr. Cop, and he knew all about everybody with a glance.

"The woman's been under treatment at a mental health facility. She just left today." It wouldn't do to tell him she'd been driven batshit by an evil spirit—who happened to be my father, by the way—and her brother broke her out so I could use my black opal to banish said spirit.

"She was probably in there for abusing drugs. The guy's probably her dealer." Certainty hardened the lines around Dean's eyes and thinned his lips. This was his cop face, and it made me want to punch him in the throat. Working with people gave him a lot of practice, but sometimes he missed the mark, and when he did, he couldn't be budged even if someone proved him wrong. My general policy was to let it go. Arguing with him wasted minutes of my life I'd never get back. I was in enough of a mood to try to teach a goat to floss if it came up.

"Mysti is not a dope head," I said. "She had a mental breakdown."

"Whatever." He turned away from me.

"Why don't we change your name to Dean Whatever? Tell you what, I'll go get my magic marker and run around town crossing off Turgeau on your campaign signs and writing Whatever after Dean. What do you think?"

"Sometimes I forget how young you are."

"Sometimes I forget what a petty jerk you are."

Dean's face fell, and I immediately regretted my words.

"Let's not do this again," I said.

"Your choice." He still had his hands on his hips.

"Please accept my apology for missing your campaign talk. Eddie's death really threw me for a loop." I'd dealt with way more, but this was the only thing Dean would allow himself to process and relate to. "When my friends showed up asking for help, I got distracted."

"How could you possibly help those two losers?"

"It's to do with my being a medium." I almost enjoyed how official and un-crazy the word sounded. Dean flinched and paled beneath his tan.

"I can't have you—"

"Running around playing paranormal Nancy Drew," I finished, keeping my voice as steady and confident as I could. "I know how you feel about it, but I call the shots about what I do in my life."

"Even if it drags you down?"

I stared stupidly at him, not getting it. Helping Brad

and Mysti felt right. My muscles and mind ached with fatigue, and the whole thing had scared the pudding out of me, but I survived and learned. I had no plans to seek out another situation like that one, but I sure didn't want Dean telling me I couldn't or shouldn't. He had no idea how it felt to be a freak, an oddity, and to finally find a good use for the freakishness.

Dean wanted me to change to be more like him. Normal, straight-laced, and firmly planted in the here and now. For our entire relationship—my entire life—I'd wanted the same thing. Still did, but I also wanted to feel like this night made me feel over and over again. I wanted to help people who needed it and enjoy the accomplishment of facing and beating my own personal demons. I stared into Dean's stormy blue eyes, looking for a shred of reason or flexibility and finding only unyielding ice.

"Exactly how you did you help those two losers by taking them into Bullfrog's Billiards? What does going in there have to do with you being a *medium*?"

Gulp. My thoughts ran a wild, lightning fast lap around my head, looking for the way to explain the night's events while not getting myself any deeper into Dean-doo.

"See, baby? The panicked look on your face is all the answer I need. You go around doing all kinds of stuff, never thinking about how it affects me. You associate with all kinds of people, never thinking about how it looks. If people see you hanging out in Bullfrog's—"

"They're going to wonder what kind of sheriff you'll make." I waited for the guilt to come, but it didn't. Maybe I was too tired. I still wanted Dean to win the office of sheriff more than anything. He was an honest man who'd do his best to serve the people of this county. Losing this election would destroy him both emotionally and financially. Dean had a lot on the line right now, but I did too, dammit.

"This is a small town, and small towns thrive on gossip. They love a good scapegoat and all the drama that comes with it." He reached out to me, glanced at my face, and dropped his hand. "Some people here would fight to the death for you, but others still..."

I slumped as the truth of his words sunk in, poisonous hooks stinging. "I'll always be Gaslight City's favorite little Satanist, even though they don't know what a Satanist is."

He snorted, but the stern expression stayed on his face. "All I'm saying is people will look for any reason not to vote for me. They decide you really are sort of weird and not in a good way, and then they think maybe I'm too weird to be their sheriff because weirdness is a scary thing."

I wanted to tell him he was wrong and couldn't. Sheriff Joey Holze was the third generation of his family to hold the office of sheriff in Burns County. No matter how bad a job he did, no matter who he pissed off, the name Holze was synonymous with law enforcement in this county.

My responsibility to help Dean warred with my responsibility to stand up for my own interests, and there was no clear winner. I had to find out who was behind everything from the theft of the Bruce family journals and Eddie's death to somehow imprisoning my father's spirit and making him do awful things. Not to mention what Priscilla Herrera's ghost claimed would happen. Walking away would be a betrayal—to my friends, to my family, and to myself. I didn't see why I couldn't do both things and do them well.

"Seeing you here tonight disappoints me. There are a thousand ways you could use your time more productively. If you want to help people, if you want to improve yourself, you could volunteer." He waved his hands while he talked like some TV preacher working himself into hollering until he frothed at the mouth. "Hell, you're one of the smartest people I've ever met. You could go back to college, get your degree, and get into a helping profession. I'd pay for it." He smiled, and I recognized the smile as one he used when he talked to kids he considered at risk. "You're not going to like what I'm about to say, but step one to having a better life is throwing away old memories of slumming with Chase Fischer. Step two is getting people like those losers I saw you with tonight out of your life. Step three is to quit hanging out with Wade Hill and the Six Gun Revolutionaries. Get the garbage out of your life. They'll turn you into what they are."

His words shocked me as much as if he'd thrown ice water in my face. All the guilt and understanding building in me did a nosedive into the black void of my growing fury. I crossed my arms over my chest, trying to hold in the hateful things I wanted to say, hoping much of what Dean said tonight came out of anger and hurt over my forgetting his campaign event. I opened my mouth to speak, but anger flashed, so strong it almost blinded me, and I closed it again and swallowed hard. Dean took the opportunity to keep driving home his point.

"Chase is gone. Eddie is gone. There's nothing to keep you from turning over a new leaf."

Eddie? Dean thinks Eddie wasn't worthy too? Fury cauterized the festering sore of my indecision, closing it off from further infection. There was no way I'd let Saint Dean Turgeau tell me what to do. He could go sip some monkey butt juice.

"Dean, go home."

"Wha—"

"Please close your mouth and go home. We'll talk about this some other time."

The confidence slid off his face, and anger pinched his handsome features. "Fine. I'm wrong and you're right. I'll go home, sleep alone like I do most of the time anyway, and then we'll do things your way tomorrow."

It was damn good bait. I actually wanted to assure him this wasn't about getting my way but was about this not going further than it had, but I knew him too well to fall into his trap. One word of explanation, one word of self-defense, and he'd be off to the races, telling me everything I'd ever done wrong in my life. So I said nothing. A loud engine cut the silence, slowing as it approached. A lone headlight appeared at the edge of the parking lot.

I stared at the headlight, the muscles between my shoulder blades knotting painfully. The stiffness moved down my back and settled in the spot where Veronica Spinelli kicked me last year. I groaned and put my hand to my back as the pain took up residence. The motorcycle made slow progress into the parking lot and to the spot where Dean and I stood scowling at each other. I closed my eyes and wished I could be somewhere else. There were only a few people I knew who rode motorcycles, and all of them were the kind of people Dean just finished chewing me out for knowing. Next to me, Dean let out a nasty snort.

"Hey, looks like the whole gang is here." He raised his eyebrows and smiled in a mockery of happiness. "Guess I do need to go so I won't put a damper on the party." He waited for me to answer, but I knew better. His fake smile dropped to a glare. He stomped away from me, got into his Trans Am, and slammed the door way harder than necessary. Wade Hill drove his motorcycle up to me and shut off the engine.

"What's his problem? He lose the Short Man Syndrome poster child contest?"

"Cut me some slack, please." I leaned against my car and took out my cigarettes.

"You okay?"

"How is it you always show up when I'm in trouble?"

"Trade secret." He lit his own cigarette, and we stood polluting the air together. He finished his cigarette, dropped it, and stepped on it. "Sorry I made it worse between you and Dean."

"I'm not sure you did. You might have saved me from saying something I'd regret later."

He got on his bike. "You want me to follow you home? Make sure you get there okay?"

"Nah." I opened my car door. "I need to cool off. I may go drive for a while."

Wade nodded and left in a roar of tailpipes. I got in my

car and started it, not sure at all where I wanted to go or what I wanted to do, so I cruised.

I drove down streets I hadn't been down in years, took little used cut-throughs, and went past Dean's house. All the lights were on. He was probably inside sulking, watching TV with the sound off. The thought I could go knock on the door and apologize made me slow down and stop a few houses down. Past experience and arguments exactly like our most recent had taught me Dean would accept my apology without offering one of his own. I put the car back in gear and drove on, turning left on Blackburn Street.

I didn't need Dean in my head. More than anything, I needed to figure out the next step toward setting this whole mess straight. Learning Archie Mahoney stole the mini treasure chest didn't help me unless Julie could figure out if one of her distant relatives still had it. I crept down Blackburn, unable to shake how Tubby said he got my daddy's keychain. Barbie throwing my father's stuff away didn't surprise me exactly. She threw me away and acted like it was the normal thing to do.

Mosby Circle came up to the right, and I turned at the last second. The Gaslight City gossip grapevine said my mother had rented the old Sugar Shack on Mosby. I wondered if the woman who didn't want me was home and if I should stop and pay her a visit. She said, after all, she wanted us to start over. Maybe this was a good time.

———

I DROVE past 9811 Mosby two times, circling out to Blackburn and coming back to the street's other entrance, before I decided to pull in to the empty driveway where I sat in my car contemplating my next move. The lights gleamed from inside the 1910s era Sears and Roebuck six-room house, the TV flickering in the living room. Barbie might have left her car with a mechanic. Maybe she was sitting inside the little bungalow watching TV or looking at herself in the mirror.

Who was I lying to? Her car wasn't in the driveway, so she likely wasn't home. I got out of my car and went up to the front door and knocked and waited. No footsteps inside the house. I went around back, letting myself into the fenced backyard, walked up the concrete steps to the stoop, and looked underneath the ceramic frog. Sure enough, the key was still there.

The Sugar Shack's owner rented the little cottage out to tourists or short-term residents. She hired me to clean up after guests when her regular cleaning lady was booked and always said, "Use the key under the ceramic frog but be sure to put it back."

The six-room house rented for $1000 a night—not much less than the cost of the original materials to build the house. Nobody could afford to stay too long. I stuck the key in the backdoor's lock, turned it, and twisted the knob. The door's hinges whined as I swung it open.

"Hello? Barbie? Mom?"

The sound of the TV was the only answer I got, so I went on inside, not sure what I expected to find in my mother's rental. Why was I breaking and entering for the second time in one week? Because I had a hard time believing a woman who'd dump her kid and throw out her recently deceased husband's belongings for the trash to pick up would show up twenty-some years later searching for redemption. People like Barbie didn't change. They got slicker at playing their games.

Her showing up in town right when this whole mess started hadn't escaped my notice. She sure as hell didn't have the magical umph to make a ghost steal for her. Hell, she acted like I scared the stuffing out of her every time she got around me. I couldn't picture her hiring a witch the way Tubby had, but something Hannah said about her uncle Joey kept coming back to me. Hannah said, in not so many words, her uncle and his family would do anything to achieve their means, even if it meant being a hypocrite. The thing Barbie cared about was money. She'd do anything to have a steady supply of it, and the Mace Treasure promised untold riches.

I crept through the recently redone kitchen. A full cup of coffee sat next to the coffee maker. Both were still warm. She hadn't even drank any of her coffee before she left. Had she left in a hurry? No way to know. A flyer advertising a Dottie's Burgers and Rings sat on the tiny wrought-iron breakfast set. Barbie had scribbled some notes on the back of it.

Istanbul $1350
Rarotonga $1341
Buenos Aires $1270
Luxembourg $1457
She'd listed several more cities and put prices right

after them. If I had to guess, I'd have said they were flight prices. *She doesn't plan to stay after all. She's here for something. Like the Mace Treasure.* I put the piece of paper back where I found it and went deeper into the house.

Barbie's suitcases lay all over the floor of the bedroom closest to the house's one bathroom. She hadn't even bothered to put her clothes into the antique dresser with its cut glass pulls. I touched the silky fabric of a blouse lying across the bed. Nicer than anything I could afford. I knelt on the floor and ran my fingers along the edges of her suitcase and underneath her clothes. Other than a dainty pink vibrator, I didn't find anything of interest.

I went out to the living room, staying close to the walls and avoiding the sheer curtained windows. A laptop sat on the coffee table in front of the TV. I grabbed it and took it back into the kitchen so I could get away from those windows. I set the laptop down on the breakfast table and didn't do anything for several minutes. I wasn't a computer whiz and knew how easy it would be for me to push the wrong button and leave proof someone had been in here snooping. Finally, I pressed the space key.

The laptop woke up. I expected to see an internet browser page for flight booking or maybe passport renewal, since Barbie seemed ready to leave the country. Instead, I found her word processing program open and a half-written letter.

Jesse,

I wish you'd reconsider letting me come see you. I'm back in Gaslight City, trying to reconnect with Peri Jean. She is such a hard young woman to talk to, so distant. I keep thinking she might open up more if I could tell her something positive about herself. Not long before Paul died, I heard you and Paul discussing her. Paul said she was the key

The key to what? Barbie hadn't finished the letter. I wondered if there was a way I could get back in here another time and look again. The answer was probably no.

Headlights flashed over the kitchen wall. I jerked away from the laptop as though scalded. I needed to get out of here and do it fast. I returned the laptop to sleep mode and took it back into the living room. Through the window, I saw a car next to mine. The dome light came on as the driver opened the door, illuminating Barbie.

My legs went light and wobbly, and I fought the sudden urge to pee. I hunch walked to the coffee table, put the laptop back where I found it, and hurried through the kitchen and out the back door. I made sure to lock the door and hide the key under the frog. I sat down on the concrete stoop and lit a cigarette.

There was no way Barbie didn't see my car. She parked right next to it. My one way out of this was to pretend I'd come by for a visit and hope I could be convincing enough for her not to suspect.

The back door opened behind me. My mother said, "Peri Jean, honey? What are you doing here at this hour?"

I turned, hoping I didn't look as guilty as I felt, and tried to smile. "I heard you'd rented this place. I drove by, saw the lights on, and stopped. Saw you weren't here and decided to sit out back and look at the stars. Thought you might be back pretty soon."

"And here I am." She came out and sat on the steps

with me. "It is a pretty night. I love the moon when there's just a little fingernail of it."

I nodded and kept smoking. What on earth could I say to this awful woman?

"I'm really surprised to see you here. Frankly, if I were in your shoes, I'd be somewhere alone with that gorgeous man of yours." She nudged me, and I had to work hard not to scoot away from her. "Y'all fighting?"

"I've been flakey since Eddie died, and he's tired of it." *Crap.* Why did I tell her my business? I could have kicked myself for opening up to her, even a little bit.

"I sure was sorry to hear about Eddie. He loved your father. Would've done anything for him."

I wanted to ask Barbie about her letter to Jesse but knew there was no way to even casually work it into our conversation. Maybe I could get there by asking about my daddy.

"I don't remember much about my daddy."

"I guess you don't. You were so young when he died." She sat gazing into the night with her arms splayed over her legs, using one hand to prop up her head. Realizing I was sitting exactly the same way, I shifted positions.

"What do you remember about him?"

"Those black gypsy eyes and hair." The answer came faster than I thought it could have. "How excited he was when we found I was pregnant."

"How old were you then?"

"Eighteen. If I had been any older, known any better, I'd have...well, never mind." She patted my back. Her touch burned my skin, and this time I did flinch away. She didn't seem to notice. "Hold on a minute." She got to her feet and ran into the house. A few minutes later, she came back holding a wallet and her cellphone. She opened the wallet on her lap and set the phone to flashlight mode. "See? There's a picture of you and your father on your birthday."

Sure enough, the picture showed my daddy, impossibly handsome with his olive skin and five o'clock shadow, hugging me to him. Both of us were laughing. Feeling Barbie's gaze on me, I turned to her and found her staring at me with no expression whatsoever on her face. She quickly rearranged her face into a smile and hugged me to her.

"You take this." She took it out of the plastic and handed it to me. "It's a good picture of you with your daddy, and you ought to have it."

"Do you know what happened to my daddy's things? His personal items? They're not at Memaw's." I couldn't help myself. I wanted to see what she'd say.

"We lived in the duplex your daddy and I rented for a couple more months after he died. Cheap as it was, I couldn't afford it. I know I packed his things up and took them with us, but I sure don't know what became of them after I left town."

She was a good liar. I'd have believed her had Tubby Tubman not told me different. I faked a yawn and stretched my arms wide. The yawn became real about halfway through. How long had it been since I'd slept all night? Or even had more than five hours of sleep? I stood.

"Thanks for talking to me, Bar—Mom. I mean Mom."

She beamed and pushed herself to a standing position. She held her arms open, and I went to her, letting her hug me.

"Come back sometime soon. I'll tell you all kinds of stuff about your father. Like the time he turned over his boat in Piney Lake and almost drowned. Or how mad Leticia was when I got pregnant and what he said to her."

I sort of wanted to hear those stories but knew I couldn't trust Barbie. I promised I'd come back and got out of there as fast as I could. This time, I headed straight for Memaw's house. All the lights were off, and I cut my headlights before they shined into the house. I sat in my car after I turned it off, thinking over the night's events.

Barbie was a consummate liar. I couldn't take anything she said seriously. All I could trust for sure were the things I saw with my own eyes. There was no denying her letter to my uncle Jesse. It was right there on her laptop, plain as day.

For the first time in my life, I wanted to go see my uncle Jesse in prison. Hooty Bruce told me numerous times he'd arrange a visit any time I wanted to see my uncle. I texted Hooty. He always told me his mind wouldn't quit thinking new thoughts even when it was bedtime. It was time to see if he was telling the truth.

You awake?

The reply came back almost immediately. *You know I am. What's up?*

What if I wanted to go see my uncle Jesse?

A pause. *Warden's an old college buddy. I'd pull some*

strings with him and get you a visit as fast as possible. You're on Jesse's visitor list anyway. Is this about the stolen books?

In a roundabout way. I wasn't sure it was at all, but I had to try to figure out what mischief Barbie had planned.

I'll call you when I get it set up.

Thanks.

12

———

Worried Hooty would want me to leave at a moment's notice, I got dressed and ready to leave before daybreak. Turned out to be a good thing.

As the first light of dawn pinkened the sky, when a shadow of fog still clung to the dew sparkling grass, Mysti's car turned into the driveway. I stubbed out my cigarette in the plastic dollar store ashtray I kept on the porch and stood.

The car came to a stop near the chain-link fence surrounding the house, turning on the dome light. Mysti held up one hand to Brad and shook her head. He said something back, wagging his head side to side. She pushed open the car door, fingers hung over the top to pull herself up off the car seat. I hurried out to help her. Brad got out of the driver's side and rushed to his sister's aid.

"I'm so glad I caught you awake," Mysti said. "Brad told me to call first, but I thought maybe you'd want to sleep late."

"You sure didn't sleep late." I took one arm, and Brad grabbed the other. We helped Mysti down the brick path leading to the porch, and Brad lifted her over the steps. She sat heavily in one of the metal chairs.

"Brad can't wait to get back to the city. He wanted an early start." Mysti gave her brother the eye. "Of course, we had time to drive past the museum to see if Hannah Kessler had it open yet."

"Brad, you're such a fangirl," I said.

He curled his lip at me and walked to the edge of the porch to look out at the fog swirling in Memaw's pasture.

"Don't see how y'all stand it here," he muttered.

"Yep, I'm really missing the smell of car exhaust and hot pavement." Mysti waved off her brother and leaned close to me. "I woke up at three o'clock this morning and realized something."

"Hit me with it," I said.

"I forgot to tell you something."

Her words sent a shock through my foggy brain, and I sat up straighter.

"Oh, really? I thought you couldn't tell me any more than you did because you were working for Tubby."

"I don't see how it's unfair to Tubby for me to tell you this stuff." Mysti stopped speaking and studied my face. "You do want to know, don't you? You've got the air of someone about to face the unknown, someone taking a journey. You might be able to use this stuff."

Or it might drive me crazy, or make me feel rotten, or something else bad. I weighed the possible good against the possible bad. It all sounded awful and scary. I needed a different measuring stick. What if whatever Mysti had to tell me got me what I wanted?

"I want to hear it," I said.

"When I contacted your father's spirit—and it took a lot to do it—I ended up in this colorless, windowless, and doorless room. Sort of a prison." Mysti's face paled as she remembered, and a fine gloss of sweat appeared at her neck. "I surprised whoever has Paul trapped. I felt it. They thought nobody could get in, I think." She shuddered and rubbed her arms. "Your father showed me a butterfly he had in his hand. One of the black ones with blue markings on the bottoms of its wings. But then all he did was try to get me to leave. Does the butterfly mean anything to you?"

A sharp, stabbing feeling, worse than any ice cream headache ever, worked its way through my brain. I clapped my hand to my forehead and writhed in the seat.

"Oh no. Your nose is bleeding." Mysti leaned toward me, getting into my face. She took a tissue out of her pocket and shoved it at me.

"Not the bleeds again." I leaned my head back, pushing the tissues into my nostrils.

"This has happened before?"

"Happened last time I messed with the Mace Treasure." My voice came out in a weird honk.

Brad's footsteps clunked across the porch. "She all right?"

"I'm okay." I opened my eyes to glare at him. "Maybe Priscilla Herrera changed her mind and wants me to stay away from it."

Priscilla Herrera's name no sooner left my lips than

several ravens landed in the front yard, making their weird, creaky caw and pecking at the dead grass. From behind us came the sound of someone beating on the window. We all turned to see Memaw shaking her fist at the birds. She realized we were watching, gave us a phony grin, and disappeared from the window. Mysti glanced between me and the birds, a line appearing between her eyes.

"Maybe, but I have a different theory," she said.

I waited for her to tell me what it was, but she didn't speak. Did she want permission to speak? Reassurance I wanted to know? She had me hooked. I couldn't not know. "Well, what is it?"

Mysti bowed her head for a second and then raised her gaze to mine. "Have you ever read much about your uncle's trial? About why he couldn't defend himself against the charges? Why he accepted a plea bargain?"

"Why are we talking about this?" My initial shock faded, and the usual anger I felt when people got too deeply personal took its place.

"Did you see your father the day he died?" Mysti leaned forward in her seat and grabbed my wrist.

Had I? We lived in the same house. Surely I saw him over breakfast before he left for the day. What day of the week had he died? A weekday? A weekend? Nothing came. It was blank.

"I don't remember," I told Mysti. "The last clear memory I have of him is from my birthday, a few days earlier. He took me to ride a pony. What does all this have to do with my uncle's conviction?"

"Your uncle said he had no memory of the day his

brother was murdered. None whatsoever." She started to say more but shook her head. "Do you feel an aversion to reading about your father's—what happened to your father?"

I thought about it. Why had I never searched online for articles about the murder? Or dug up old issues of newspapers? I always thought I just didn't want to know, but maybe Mysti had a point.

"I've got a theory," Mysti said. "I think whoever murdered your father somehow stole both your uncle's and your memory of the day because the two of you know who did it."

"Same as they stole my father's ghost."

"Maybe. Here's something to think about." She clasped her hands together, and the first rays of true sun hit her, highlighting her hair and making her appear to glow. "Your father's ghost is kept somewhere. What if your memories are, too? I've heard vague stories—the witchcraft equivalent of old wives' tales really—about spells to suck memories into a hidden place in the mind. You just have to find a way to unlock the door."

I remembered the little room in my mind Priscilla Herrera took me to when I tried to contact my father's ghost. Had the memories been there? Even if they were, I didn't know how to get back there.

"Furthermore," Mysti said, giving my shoulder a little shake to make sure I hadn't drifted off in my thoughts, "I think the butterfly might have something to do with it."

"How come?" The mere thought of the butterfly sent another stab of pain into my head, but my nose didn't gush this time. One of the ravens flew up to sit on the porch railing. The bird cocked its head at me.

"Want me to run it off?" Brad asked. "I don't think Memaw liked it."

"She's not your memaw, fartwinkle, and leave the bird alone," I told him.

"You are absolutely disgusting." Brad wrinkled his nose.

"Shut up," Mysti and I told him at the same time.

I turned back to Mysti. "Tell me about the butterfly."

"Nothing to tell." She shrugged. "Just got a gut feeling. Sometimes they're wrong, but when they wake me up at three in the morning, I gotta share 'em." She pushed herself off the metal chair, and Brad rushed over to help her stand. He kept hold of her arm, steadying her, and I again glimpsed the love he felt for his sibling. It made something inside me ache.

"We need to get going before Bradley has a hissy fit." Mysti stood on tiptoe and stretched until she could peck her brother's stubbly cheek. "But I've got one last thing to ask you."

"What is it?" I took her other arm as she descended the steps.

"You still got my business card? Or did you trash it?" She winked at me.

"Nope." I let go of Mysti's arm and took the little metal business card case I always carried from my pocket and showed her the card she'd given me.

"You call me, girl. I'm serious. Even if all you want to do is jaw." Her gaze probed me until I nodded my assent.

I hurried ahead and opened the car door for her and held it open until Brad got her settled inside. The two of us exchanged a glance.

"I can call Hannah, see if she's up. She might agree to an early tour of the museum." I wanted to erase the tension between us. We didn't have to be friends, but I didn't want to part on less than favorable terms.

"Thanks for the offer." Brad actually smiled at me. "But I look slept in. In fact, these are the clothes I wore yesterday."

"Fair enough," I said.

Brad got into the car, started it, and drove back down the driveway. I waved as they left, half feeling like I ought to run after them and beg them to stay. I was in over my head, and Mysti was the first breath of anything like sanity I'd had since this whole thing started. The car pulled onto the highway and disappeared from my sight.

My cellphone rang. I snapped to attention and grabbed it. *Oh, please let this be Mysti telling me she'll stay and help me through this.* No such luck. It was Hooty. He started talking as soon as I picked up, not even giving me a chance to say hello.

"I called the warden at home this morning. He agreed to set up the visit if we get there by ten. The drive's a couple of hours, and we're going to have to hurry. When can you be ready?"

"Fifteen minutes." We said our goodbyes and hung up.

I went inside to tell Memaw where I was going and to have our usual argument over getting one of her friends in to spend the day with her.

I PACED BACK and forth on the porch while I waited for Hooty to pick me up, feeling more unprepared than I ever had in my life. This man who I didn't remember at all might not even want to answer my questions. He might hate me for getting his daughter killed. All I could do was hope for the best.

Several minutes later, I lounged on the soft leather seat of Hooty's silver Cadillac, listening to flute music on the stereo system. Hooty reached over and flicked off the sound.

"What, exactly, do you think Jesse might know to help you figure out who took the journals?" He flashed me a grin. "If you don't mind telling me."

I stared at Hooty's round face, searching for an assurance he wouldn't call me crazy. I saw the gray hair at his temples, and the deep lines taking up permanent residence underneath his brown eyes. Nothing more. I had to trust him, and that was a tall order. But this man had always taken time for me. He deserved a few answers.

"I think whoever's behind the theft of the journals killed my father."

Hooty sucked in a deep breath, and his hands tightened on the steering wheel. "How?"

I told him, and the telling took a good part of the trip to the prison. Hooty asked a few questions here and there. Mostly he listened. When I got to the part about my daddy's ghost driving Mysti crazy, Hooty began to sweat. His reaction worried me. Hooty had never been thin, and middle age had spread him even thicker. I concluded the tale before he worked up a stroke.

"Well, I'm going to give you my advice, even though you didn't ask for it." Hooty took one hand off the wheel to wipe the sweat off his forehead. "Your uncle probably won't have much to say about the day of the murder. Have some back-up questions."

Oh, I had a back-up question, all right. I wanted to know what my father thought I was the key to and why.

The guard at the prison searched Hooty's car. The act initiated a quick bolt of panic and paranoia. It was like a flashing sign reminding me I was crossing the threshold between the free world and the world of the incarcerated. My experience in the mental hospital taught me to fear any kind of lockup. Once there, I was at the mercy of those in charge. I twisted in my seat to stare longingly at the road on which we drove into the prison complex. Hooty parked the car and led me into a building I'd have never found on my own.

There began a test to my moral and legal character. I removed my shoes, turned out my pockets, and allowed a prison official to wand my clothed body and pat me down. I showed my ID to prove who I was, filled out a paper, and waited quietly.

Finally, a female correctional officer led me into a sad room where a row of industrial-style chairs facing a clear window awaited me. Each station had an old school phone through which I assumed I'd talk to my uncle because there was no way we'd be able to hear each other through the thick window. The room was empty except for me.

Hooty's connection to the warden managed to get me in for a visit even though regular visiting days were on the weekend. For a few seconds, I stood still, completely shell-shocked. I'd expected an open room with tables, had even planned what I'd do if Uncle Jesse wanted to hug me. People fostered relationships in this room?

The correctional officer directed me to one of the stations. I sat in the chair and stared at the empty space across from me, exposed and spooked by all the official procedures. Visiting an offender in prison was nothing like bailing Chase Fischer out of jail for public intoxication. A hopeless heaviness hung over this place, cold with fear of the unknown and desperation.

A door on the other side of the glass opened, and I straightened, heart thudding and anticipation crawling over me. A small man with his hands cuffed behind his back walked in. The door shut, and the man backed up to the door. The guard uncuffed him. A second or two later, he stepped forward, arms by his sides. His heavily tattooed forearms stood out against his white uniform. The amount of salty white in his black hair struck me as did the lines that started at the corners of his eyes and creased down his cheeks. My uncle looked much older than Hooty even though they graduated high school the same year. He eased himself into the uncomfortable chair on the other side of me.

I froze as I stared into his black eyes, a soft memory of laughter—the side-splitting kind—playing just out of reach in my head. I'd loved this man when I was a little girl. He smiled, and the webbing of lines etched themselves deeper into his cheeks. We reached for the phones at the same time.

"You look like my brother." His voice seemed both familiar and unfamiliar. "But not in a bad way."

"You used to make me laugh." The words came out sounding more hollow and lost than I intended. After all the trouble to get here, I wasn't sure I could talk to this stranger.

"How's Momma? When I found out you arranged a special visit, I worried she might have taken a turn."

"Not good, but there's been no dramatic change," I said. "I'd intended to come, but..."

"Momma said she was working on you." He shifted in his seat. "It's hard to come here, and I thank you for coming. Once Mom's gone, you'll be my last blood connection to where I grew up."

Which is my fault. His daughter, Rae, wouldn't be dead if it weren't for me. I swallowed hard. Should I tell him I was sorry for what happened to his only child? The sterility and finality of visiting a family member in this setting had me off balance. I wanted to say the right things, do the right things, but I didn't know how. My gaze drifted off Jesse's face and onto the little counter in front of me. I noticed it was worn where countless elbows rested on it as they tried to fit a lifetime into a few minutes. Had they felt as empty as I did? I forced my mind back on track. The clock was running on this visit. Time to get down to business.

"I came today because I have some questions to ask you."

"Before you say the first word, let's get one thing straight. I'm not going to talk about the day someone other than me murdered your father." He leveled his gaze at me to make his point. "Last thing I remember was the night before it happened. If you don't remember what happened, you can't expect me to."

The finality in his voice left no room for wheedling. I shrank into my chair, resisting the urge to fiddle with my hair. *Switch gears. Do it fast.* I forced myself to start talking.

"Barbie, my mother, is back in town. I happened to see a letter she was writing—"

"You went through her stuff?" His grin made him look a decade younger.

"Yeah. She said she wanted to come visit you, but..."

"Well, you can tell that bitch there's no way I'll ever agree to see her again." His cheeks reddened. "I ain't got nothing to say to her."

I shook my head. "No, no. I'm not here to convince you to see her. It's about something she said in the letter. She mentioned my daddy saying I was the key to something."

He stared at me through the glass, his expression unreadable.

"The letter indicated she thought I'd open up to her, be more receptive to her coming back into my life, if she could tell me something special about myself."

"And she didn't send you here to try to trick something out of me?"

What? I sat up straighter. He had my interest. "I promise she didn't. We barely speak. She spent my whole life ignoring me."

"Maybe it is time I should tell you." He rubbed one hand over his short hair and tapped his fingers on top of his head. A memory came to me of Memaw telling him he looked like a monkey when he did that. "Paul never intended it to be kept from you, I don't think. He just died before you got old enough to know."

"If it has to do with the Mace Treasure, now might be a good time."

His eyes widened, fear lighting them. "Why's that?"

My father's face loomed in my memory, the same fear brightening his eyes. Then, the moment snapped shut like a door closing. I shook it off and told Jesse about the theft of the Bruce journals, about the book of folk medicine and what it really was. Then I told him the hardest part to tell, the part where I had a vision and saw Priscilla Herrera the day she died and heard her say what would happen if the wrong person tried to take the curse off the treasure. I expected him to scoff at me. Instead he stared at me with an unnerving intensity until I squirmed in my chair.

"You know your gift comes from Momma's family, don't you?"

I nodded, surprised he knew after the way Memaw acted about it. A stray thought burrowed its way into my conscious. *Maybe she acted the way she acted because Jesse and my daddy knowing got them into trouble.*

"Paul thought—in the last month or so of his life—Momma's grandmother was Priscilla Herrera's daughter."

I dropped the clunky plastic telephone receiver. It hit the Formica cabinet in front of me with a bang. Jesse winced and took his receiver away from his ear. I sat there rocking, trying to stave off the dizziness buzzing around my head. Little by little, I collected myself and picked up the receiver again.

"Why'd he think so?" My voice shook.

Jesse reached across his body and pushed up the sleeve on his uniform shirt, showing me his raven tattoo, nearly buried amidst a sea of other art, but almost identical to mine.

Surprise at seeing the tattoo again shook me in my seat. I set the phone down on the counter and gaped. I rolled up my own sleeve to show him my raven tattoo and nodded. I hadn't imagined Priscilla's tattoo. She didn't add it to my vision to make me relate to her. She had the same tattoo as me. My uncle had it. It meant something big in my life. I put my face in my hands and took deep breaths to keep from screaming. The more I tried to cordon off this part of me, the more it crossed barriers and invaded something else.

Jesse, a man I didn't know and never really would, put his hand on the glass between us, and I put mine to it, very aware we looked like some idiotic cliché but not giving a shit. We dropped our hands after a long moment and picked up our phones again. I spoke first.

"Why did my daddy think the tattoo meant we were related to her?"

"He found out Priscilla Herrera had the same tattoo about a month before he died. It was in those books Isaiah Bruce had. As for why, ever'body in Momma's clan's got the same tattoo. Can't be no coincidence."

"Your mother—my Memaw—doesn't have a tattoo like

this one. Since she's been sick, I've seen enough of her to know."

"Not her." One side of his mouth and one eyebrow rose, and despite the surroundings, I saw the mischief I half remembered him capable of. "She left 'fore they could talk her into getting it. Ain't you met none of 'em? Didn't one of 'em give you the tattoo?"

I thought back to the night I got the tattoo, the way everybody seemed so interested in me, and the spooky punchline to the whole experience. Slowly, I nodded at Jesse.

"Bet my momma had a fit over it." A hell-raising smile spread over his face.

I remembered Memaw's anger and horror. A smile crept over my face even though it wasn't funny. My uncle closed his eyes, his body bumping with silent chuckles. After a second, it hit me, too. I took his cue and kept my giggles silent. Maybe it was an unspoken rule of this barren place.

"Memaw only told me about her family last year. How do you know so much about them?"

"She never told *you* because she thinks if me and Paul never met them, he'd never have gotten the crazy idea he could take the curse off the treasure."

My head reeled, drunk on too much information. Jesse took in the expression on my face and held up his free hand.

"Awright. Let's take it one thing at a time. You asked how me 'n Paul knew about Memaw's clan, right?"

I nodded.

"We were awful kids, wild, always sneaking off to Shreveport and Tyler. Sometimes we'd go as far as Dallas or Houston." He stopped talking for a moment and stared at me, smiling at something only he could see. "We met 'em at a—"

"Roadside carnival or fair?"

"Yeah." He cocked his eyebrow again. "It was like they were waiting on us. 'Course they all got...talents. Same way you got talents, right?"

The click of another piece of my life falling into place paralyzed me.

"One of 'em probably knew we were coming. Both of us got the same raven tattoo. Momma like to've had a stroke over it. Never seen her so mad, red-faced and shaking all over. She got on the phone and screamed at somebody named Cecil for an hour."

"Her brother."

He nodded. "Yep. Me and Paul went hunting for them after that. Took us almost a year, but we found them off a backroad outside Livingston, Texas. Uncle Cecil told us some stuff about his grandparents working medicine shows, carnivals, and circuses. Then he told us to get out of Burns County before it killed us. Said his grandparents told him never, ever go to Burns County."

Maybe I'd teach my kids and grandkids the same if I saw my mother dragged away and lynched for being something she couldn't help too. I shivered.

"Those were the kids Priscilla sent away and told never to come back to Gaslight City, Texas."

"I don't know that story. Where'd you hear it?"

I told him about the vision, about seeing Priscilla prepare to be taken away and lynched. I told him about the words she used to set the curse on the treasure. By the time I finished, his olive complexion had taken on a sallow cast. "When the Bruce family journals were stolen, the thief also got Priscilla Herrera's spell book. I think they're planning to take off the curse."

"And those demons'll flatten Gaslight City." He shook his head. "Paul thought he'd found the key to the treasure after reading Isaiah Bruce's journals because he interpreted her words to mean only someone of her bloodline could remove the curse and find the treasure."

"And that's us."

He nodded. "Now you know why you're the key and why knowing won't do Barbara Butthead any good." He glanced again at the guard in the corner. "Time's up. Hey would you tell Rainey Bruce thanks for the reading materials she sent?"

"Sure, but wait a minute. At the beginning of our visit, you said something about me not remembering the day my daddy was murdered. Why would I remember?"

His mouth dropped open, and he stared at me for so long I figured he didn't plan to answer. Then he said, "You were there too. Didn't you know?"

I heard a voice yell something but couldn't make out the words. My uncle put the phone into its cradle, stood, and backed up to the door through which he'd entered, sticking his hands through. The guard cuffed my uncle and opened the door, gripping his arm to take him away.

Jesse slipped me a wink, and I blew him a kiss, sorry our visit had been cut short.

A correctional officer beckoned from the door, ready to escort me back to where Hooty waited. I walked in a daze, Jesse's words echoing in my head.

You were there too. Didn't you know?

No, I hadn't. A lifetime of snide comments and sneaky glances suddenly made sense. How could I have been present at my father's murder and have completely erased it from my memory? How could I be a descendant of Priscilla Herrera? It was all too much, and I shut down, falling into Hooty's arms in the waiting room and letting him hold me like he might have his own daughter.

———

HOOTY GOT us out of the prison complex and turned his satellite radio to an '80s hard rock station. The sound of his rich baritone singing along with bands like Guns N' Roses and Winger lifted some of the hopelessness off my shoulders. I even laughed at the way he tried to imitate the more high-pitched howls in the songs. He smiled at me and shut off the radio.

"Would you like to talk about your visit with your uncle?"

My arm twitched once, then twice, then three times, the muscle cramping. I rubbed at it and realized the sensation was coming from the tattoo Jesse and I shared, the same one my daddy had, and the same one Priscilla Herrera had. We passed a raven or some other kind of big, black bird sitting on a fencepost. It turned its head to watch us go by.

It's all too much. I couldn't process it.

"Why don't you start with one small thing and go from there?"

I wasn't ready to deal with Jesse's theory about our blood connection to Priscilla Herrera, and it had nothing to do with Hooty anyway. This weirdness, this otherness, was my lot in life. I'd never be any different, no matter how much I or other people wished I could. A great sense of loss settled over me. Once I accepted it, a realization hit me. I had the answer to the identity of the person causing all the problems.

"Jesse told me I was present at my father's murder."

Hooty drew in a deep breath.

"You knew, right? Everybody but me knew, right?"

Hooty gripped the wheel and wouldn't look at me. "I wish he hadn't told you. Your grandmother will be fit to be tied."

"What's the big secret? Why didn't they use my testimony to clear Jesse?"

"Do you remember any details of what happened?" Hooty pulled over in the parking lot of a closed gas station.

"I know Jesse didn't do it."

"But do you know who did?" He took off his seatbelt and faced me.

I tried to remember the day my father died, tried to picture what happened right before the awful moment when someone killed him. I tried with all my might.

Hooty grunted and dug in his console, handing me a

plastic packet of tissues. "Your nose. There's blood." He watched me clean myself. "This is why we quit asking you questions. My father used his powers as a judge to suppress your presence at the crime scene. Your uncle agreed not to make you testify on his behalf since you remembered nothing."

"The sheriff didn't insist?"

"You don't remember Joey Holze's father, do you? He made his son look like law enforcer of the year. He didn't care, long as the case got closed."

"The witch Tubby Tubman hired speculated both Jesse and I were somehow spelled to forget."

"My religion does not make room for such beliefs." Hooty took his keys from the ignition and weighed them in his hand. "That said, my life has taught me not to close my eyes to something without carefully examining it. Did she say more?"

"She thought the memory was still in my head, locked away from where I could easily access it."

"If this is true, and you could find a way to access it, you'd know the identity of our troublemaker."

I shivered. "He or she is way more than a troublemaker. But yes."

Hooty stuck his key into the ignition and started the car. He pulled back onto the busy highway without speaking. We drove for several miles.

"I have a suggestion, but I almost don't want to say it because it would be a horrible thing for you to put yourself through."

"Say it anyway. If our troublemaker, as you call them,

releases the curse from the treasure, we're screwed anyway."

"Start with the case file at the sheriff's office." He let out a deep sigh and shook his head. "It'll have the crime scene photos. Those alone may unlock your memory."

I took out my cellphone and called Dean. He answered on the first ring.

"I am so glad you called. I owe you an apology for last night. My behavior was completely uncalled for."

"Mine too. We need to talk about it, but I'm with Hooty."

"Oh? What's up?"

"I need a favor. I want to see the case files for my father's murder."

"Wh-uh-why? Knowing what your uncle did won't help you. It'll just upset you."

"I need to know. I'm pretty sure it's part of the Texas Public Information Act. If I need to go through Rainey—"

"No, no. Save your money. I'm getting off shift in a few minutes. Meet me at the SO."

Hooty dropped me off at Memaw's where I picked up the Nova and drove to the sheriff's office. I waited in my car until Dean rolled up in his cruiser. He had a brief conversation with his patrol partner, Brittany Watson, pointing at me. She gave me a little wave and took off inside. I climbed out and met Dean at the front door. He approached me warily but held out his arms for a hug. I went to him, and he kissed me. I almost forgot why I wanted to do anything but meet him at his house for a late day tryst. He broke the kiss first.

"Please accept my apology. I'm letting the stress get to me and taking it out on you." He stroked my cheek with his thumb.

"I shouldn't have taken the bait. Let's forget it." I lit up a cigarette. Dean watched with a pained expression on his face.

"Smoking's tough on your heart, sweetie. Do me a favor and think about cutting back. We've been talking about having a baby. You'll have to quit then anyway. Don't you want to get a head start?"

Dean liked fixing things—people, animals, situations. He sincerely wanted to help. This wasn't the time. I dragged hard on my cigarette, enjoying the burn of smoke at the back of throat.

"I've been thinking about your request to see your father's case file. Are you sure you want to? I hate to think about you looking at it."

"If we're going to have kids, I need to know what I want to tell them about my daddy and Jesse." Truth was, I'd told Dean no more than an edited version of my reproductive health. When he said if I wanted kids, he wasn't getting any younger and wanted to get started soon, I simply nodded. I figured I'd climb the mountain only if I had to.

Dean nodded, his deep blue eyes thoughtful and suddenly sensitive. He took my arm and gently led me inside the building, motioning to Brittany to join us. She gave me a quick hug, which I returned, feeling old, old, old because I used to babysit this young woman.

"Deputy Watson, this citizen wants access to the Paul Mace murder case files, which is her right by law since it is a closed case. I'll walk you through the process." Dean went into teaching mode, and I allowed him to settle me at his desk. I zoned out, letting the activity around me buzz my mind numb. The sound of raised voices pulled me back to earth.

"What's she doing here?" Sheriff Joey Holze limped toward me, leaning heavily on the cane he'd started using the last few months. The gossip grapevine said his diabetes, exacerbated by his obesity, had affected his feet and might cause the loss of his toes if he didn't watch out. "Y'all finally find something to arrest her for?"

He guffawed. Everybody in the room ignored him. Everybody, that is, except his son, a lousy lawman who only kept his job because of workplace nepotism. I kept my face empty of expression, remembering the time Joey Holze told me he'd love to see me in jail right next to my murdering uncle.

Dean came from the back of the office, face set and legs pumping fast to get him between Joey and me. "Sheriff?"

Joey turned to Dean. "Thought I told you not to bring her in here. Meet her somewhere else if you got to associate with her."

"Sheriff, she's here as a citizen of Burns County, requesting to see the Paul Mace murder case files. We can't refuse her." Dean, bless his heart, was still in teaching mode. Joey reddened, and his hand tightened on his cane. For a second, it seemed like he was gearing up to raise it and hit Dean. I sort of hoped he would. It would expose the meanness inside him for everybody to see.

"I know what the damn law is," he hollered. "I been

practicing it since you was smoking dope and chasing girls."

Dean closed his eyes. I knew he was counting to ten, a trick he'd learned from me. When he opened them, he smiled and straightened.

"Of course, sir. Sorry about that. We can't find the Paul Mace file. There's no record of it being checked out either," Dean said.

"So?" The sheriff jutted out his chin, looking for all the world like a bull about to charge.

"Do you happen to know where it might be? Sir?" The cords in Dean's neck stood out. He'd told me his opinion of Sheriff Joey's law enforcing skills enough times for me to figure he wanted to jump up and down and demand answers.

"Well, hell no, I don't." I've seen TV police talk about knowing someone was lying and always wondered what they meant. No more wondering for me. Sheriff Joey knew exactly what happened to my father's case file. "Who really cares? Every Mace I've ever known was about one step above white trash."

Dean opened his mouth and closed it with a pop, his face turning red and a vein in his forehead thumping.

"Get her out of my office." Joey leveled a thick finger at me. "You ain't sheriff, but I am, and I want her trashy bee-hind out of here."

I stood, gathered my purse, and walked out of the sheriff's office. I could have stayed, could have made Dean defend my honor, but the election was soon. If Dean won, Joey would be out of the office for good. If he didn't, well,

Dean would probably be out of a job and none of it would matter anyway. Footsteps pounded behind me, and Dean caught up to me. He put both hands on my shoulders.

"I'm sorry. Usually he's gone home by this time of day."

"He knows where the files are," I said.

"I know. I know. But what can I do? Unless I can prove he has the files or did away with them, I'm stuck." He opened my car door. "In a few days, everything will be different. One way or the other. Even if I lose, I'll be glad. Not a day goes by without him telling me how honest he's being by letting me keep my job."

"He'd look like a tyrant if he fired you. Can't believe he's got sense enough to know it." I got into my car, wincing as a wave of stale heat hit my face. Sweat oozing from my pores, I started the car and used my cigarette lighter to turn the air conditioner on high so the knob wouldn't burn my fingers. Dean leaned into the car and trailed his fingers down the back of my neck. The usual heat ignited in me, but the whereabouts of those files kept me from really getting into it. Some damn good dirt must have been in that case file. Gone now, thanks to Burns County's dirtiest cop.

Dean continued stroking my neck, probably mistaking my pondering for hurt feelings. "I've got a little paperwork to wrap up inside, but why don't you meet me at my place? A couple of hours?"

I forced myself into the moment and put my hand over his.

"I'd like to spend some time with you." The heat in his eyes melted me. "Some alone time."

My brain short-circuited. Memaw's health had dictated the physical side of my relationship with Dean for the last couple of months. The idea of spending a few uninterrupted hours in his rundown house almost made me forget why I'd come to the sheriff's office in the first place.

"Two hours?"

Dean nodded, and I started my car. He waved and went back inside the building, where sharing space with Sheriff Joey Holze must have been more hellish than the August heat. I sat in my idling car, enjoying the blast of the air conditioner and thinking of ways I might be able to find out more about the sheriff's investigation of my father's murder. The official papers were obviously lost to me. I decided to go with an internet investigation and put my car in gear. My cellphone rang. I put the car back in park and dug it out of my bag.

Julie. I'd forgotten about the message I left her. I answered.

"Good news. I found the box. One of my distant cousins has it. He doesn't sound real interested in letting go of it, but he's got back taxes due on his property. You want to go see him?"

"I'll be at Silver Dreams in five minutes." I intended to get this guy's address off Julie and go use whatever means needed to get the box from him. I sent Dean a quick text message.

Sorry, babe. I've got to cancel. Maybe another time?

He didn't reply.

13

———

On the short drive to Silver Dreams antiques, I worked through my strategy.

This cousin of Julie's might be ready to get rid of the box to cover his expenses. But I wouldn't hold my breath. Considering how long this family had held onto the thing despite the horrible fortune they'd experienced, I expected the opposite reaction.

There were two ways I could play it. On the bottom of the box was an image of the same raven I wore tattooed on my arm. I still had the picture of Priscilla Herrera as the tattooed lady on my cellphone. Her matching tattoo was blurry but visible. It was, at best, shaky proof of our shared blood. It might work, but only if Julie's cousin already wanted to get rid of the box.

The second ploy had a better chance of working, but I didn't want to do it in front of Julie. If all else failed, I'd use my freakishness—the same stuff I'd inherited from

Priscilla herself—to scare this guy into selling me the box. If he even half believed his family's bad luck had originated with the box, I figured I had a good chance.

I swung into a paid parking spot in front of Silver Dreams and walked inside without feeding the meter. I hoped to be back in my car and on the road before I got a parking ticket.

I almost ran right into Barbie. She smiled and threw her arms around me, squeezing me so hard my back popped. I pushed away from her, resisting the urge to snap at her not to touch me.

"You excited about the final debate tonight?" She wore a cheap button on her blouse endorsing Joey Holze. Following my gaze, she giggled and clapped her hand over it. "He and I were friends back when I lived here, and he personally asked me to wear one. You know me. I can't say no."

Thinking of the men revolving through her life, I felt my lips stretch into a nasty smile until I realized I did pretty much the same thing before I met Dean. Cheeks heating, I crossed my arms over my chest and slumped.

"So you and Julie are going on a buying trip? You don't strike me as an antique lover." She scrunched up her face, somehow keeping her smile intact while she did it.

"I have some expertise on this one item."

Barbie waited for me to explain, but I turned away from her, looking for Julie and thinking about shouting for her. I might have done it had the shop not been full of middle-aged yuppie tourists.

Julie thundered down the stairs from the loft, her purse in her hand.

"You don't have to waste the time to go with me," I said. "I can get his address and go by myself."

"He made it clear he wouldn't talk to anybody other than me about the box. It's been in the family since—well, you know." Even with estranged, distant relatives, Julie hesitated to call them grave robbers.

I closed my eyes and shook my head. *Can this possibly get more complicated?* Julie never hesitated to hire me for odd jobs. Though I suspected Eddie used their friendship to convince her to try my services, I'd done everything I could to earn her trust. She gave me a steady twenty hours a week work in her shop during tourist season. We got on well. She once told me, however, she was really surprised and impressed how down to earth I was considering the rumors she'd heard about me. If I played this wrong, she might never speak to me again, much less hire me. No telling what she'd do to me socially. I might never get hired for day labor again in Burns County.

"You ready?" She motioned to the back door where she kept her delivery truck. Why on earth would we need that big, old behemoth? Barbie hurried to the counter and grabbed the huge water bottle Julie kept with her all day and gave it to Julie who nodded her thanks.

"I need to move my car, or I'll get a ticket. Meet you out there." I gave Barbie a half-smile and hustled my bacon outside.

I found Julie waiting in the passenger seat of the delivery truck.

"You mind driving, baby? I barely got any sleep last night. I am so sad about Eddie."

There wasn't much I could say. I climbed in the driver's side, reminded myself about the huge blind spot on the truck, and started it up.

"Why take this thing?" I had to yell over the engine's roar. "The box isn't that big."

"I've got to make it look legit." Julie held up both hands. "He runs sort of a curio business. If we show up bulldozing him about the box, he'll probably throw us out."

It was going to be a long morning.

We got on State Highway 59 and boogied south for fifty miles. The delivery truck drove like a tank with no power steering. Within ten minutes, my arms felt like overcooked pasta and my hearing had a permanent hum from the vehicle's constant rattle. Julie somehow dozed off and slept all the way to Panola County, waking to direct me off the highway and through a maze of farm roads until we reached her cousin's house. I stopped short of pulling into the driveway.

"How long's it been since you saw this guy?" I couldn't take my eyes off the tableau before me. I'd never seen anything like it and hoped to never see anything like it again.

"I met him a few times at family reunions." Julie looked as shocked as I felt. "She turned in her seat and peered at the other properties on the narrow, white sand road. "This has to be the right place. Sign says 'Mahoney Antiques and Rarities.'"

I pulled into the driveway, bracing myself as we hit the first pothole, worried my head would hit the delivery truck's roof. Mahoney Rarities and Antiques turned out to be an unpainted frame house, the front yard filled with rusting hulks of antique cars and farm implements amidst doorless refrigerators, tangles of scrap iron, and dangerous, sharp junk camouflaged by the overgrown, dry grass. The most eerie decoration by far was dozens of decapitated doll heads impaled on the chain-link fence circling the house.

We surveyed the tangle of junk in the front yard, and Julie pursed her lips and shook her head.

"It's just salvage. I thought he might have some real antiques, way he talked on the phone."

I turned my head to stare at her. *I* thought we came here to get Priscilla Herrera's curse box. Julie seemed to have woken into a different reality after her nap. She unbuckled her seatbelt, moving slowly and deliberately. We climbed out of the truck.

The doll heads drew my gaze. Mildewed and cracked from exposure to the intense Texas sun, the light wind made them move like bobble heads. Staring at them too long made me feel dizzy and sick. I swiped a cold sweat off my face and tried to tear my gaze away. I couldn't. One doll's eyes opened, displaying human eyes which followed my movements. Cold fingers crawled up my spine.

"You need to make up your mind we probably won't walk away from here with the item Eddie wanted. It's been in our family for years and years, and he didn't sound too interested in letting go of it."

Then why are we here? She couldn't be interested in playing "remember when" with this dude. Otherwise, she wouldn't have waited so long to come see him. Had she really thought this would be a big antique buy for her?

"I know this is something Eddie wanted you to get," she said. "I also know the other woman looking for it creates some urgency in your mind, but you've always been levelheaded, Peri Jean. Don't get caught up in a buying frenzy and waste your money on an old trinket."

"It's not just an old trinket. It has to do with the Mace Treasure."

"Oh, I know. With Eddie, all roads led back to the Mace Treasure. Don't let yourself get caught up in it too."

But it's more than just the treasure, I wanted to say. It's the person who murdered my father. If they get this box, they're going to start the apocalypse right in Gaslight City. Best keep my mouth shut for the moment. The less Julie knew, the better. I didn't want to test her loyalty to Eddie by challenging how she felt about me. The answer might hurt my feelings.

Hinges screamed from the direction of the house, and an ancient wood frame screen door scraped along the porch boards. Too warped to open all the way, it stopped halfway. A stooped man, his white beard hanging halfway down his chest, stepped out onto the porch and stared at us. He wore a pair of faded overalls with a white ribbed T-shirt underneath. Yellowed, overgrown fingernails capped his twisted fingers. Julie gave me one last glance, an odd expression on her face, and slipped out of the truck.

This is going to go over like telling your Sunday school

teacher you have the clap. I hopped down from the delivery truck's cab and tagged after her.

"Carl? Is that you?" Julie managed to paste a toothy smile on her face as she picked her way through the yard.

"Yep. Ain't seen you in—what?—forty years?"

"Can't be that long. I'm only thirty-five." She laughed, but her cousin didn't join in. He simply watched through watery blue eyes. We made it to the porch without breaking any bones or giving ourselves tetanus on the rusty junk. The cousin's gaze flicked to me and then back to Julie, a silent question.

"This is Peri Jean Mace," Julie said. "She's the one interested in the little box you have."

I held out my hand to shake.

"Carl Mahoney." Ignoring my hand, he opened the door and motioned for us to come inside. Next to the door sat the skeleton of a small animal which had been painted gold and turned into a decoration. I shivered.

"Come on in the kitchen." He moved along the tiny path through the junk as though it was a mile wide and turned on a light at the other end.

Julie and I picked through what must have been the living room. I had to put one foot exactly in front of the other so I didn't risk tripping on anything.

"Got beer or sody-pop," he called from the kitchen. I heard a refrigerator open. *Is he kidding?* The smell of cat urine had already permeated my mouth and cemented itself onto my tongue. I didn't want to put my lips to anything in this house. I'd have to bleach them when I got back to Gaslight City. Our trek through the living room spit us into the kitchen. Compared to what I'd already seen, it was moderately neat. It only had one row of boxes stacked along its perimeter. Carl held an unlabeled brown beer bottle in his hand, already opened and with some of the liquid gone. He took another swig.

"Want one?"

"Ah, no sir. Don't want to have to find a restroom on the way back to Gaslight City." I smiled. The expression on Carl's face stayed the same. Maybe he didn't know what a restroom was. Maybe I should have said "john" or "outhouse."

"Same here, Carl." Julie stood in front of the Formica and chrome table sitting in the middle of the kitchen. The chrome legs had a few tiny spots of rust, but it was otherwise in great condition. She pulled out one chair. The sparkly vinyl covers wore a thick coat of dust, but I saw no tears or dry rot. I figured she'd love to have this set for her shop in Gaslight City. A nice set like this could bring a few hundred bucks.

"Go on, sit down." Carl took a chair across the table.

Julie continued staring at the dusty seat, probably wondering if she could wipe it off without offending Carl. I wondered the same thing about my seat, though I wasn't as worried about my jeans as Julie probably was about her pastel colored linen pants. At long last, she took out a tissue, gave the chair a few swipes, and sat down, smiling uncomfortably. I took my seat without cleaning it. I'd have to take ten hot showers to wash this place off anyway.

"I been thinking 'bout the box you asked about ever since you called." He flicked his rheumy eyes in my direction. "I cain't let it go. Been in the fam'ly over a hundred years."

"I understand," Julie said. "I told Peri Jean it was a long shot, but she wanted to try anyway. Now about this dinette set—"

She just threw me under the damn bus. I sat in shocked silence while the two haggled over the dinette, Julie explaining how it would take a while for the right buyer to spot it and how it did need a little work and Carl arguing people were clamoring to get their hands on these things.

It didn't take me long to start thinking about the exact way Carl's family had come into possession of the box. My hands balled into fists on my legs. Hell, I'd have done better coming here on my own. At least I could have threatened him with a busted nose. I could have brought Wade Hill as my bruiser.

Carl and Julie reached a price on the dinette set. Knowing the price she'd put on the set in her shop, I thought she'd gotten a bargain. Carl dragged over one of the boxes and opened it to show Julie a bunch of Vaseline glass wrapped in newspaper. Julie clapped her hands to her mouth and squealed. I'd had enough.

"Mr. Mahoney, why don't you tell me how your family acquired the box I came here to buy."

"It doesn't matter how they got it," Julie said. "All that matters is Carl has it and isn't willing to sell. We discussed this on the way over." She narrowed her eyes at me, a sure signal to shut up.

I had enough sense to know how much pissing Julie off could cost me. I'd lose more than the work I did for her.

She had the pull to erase a lot of my money-making opportunities. All the filling in I did at bed and breakfasts would end. The day work waiting tables in diners when somebody didn't show up would dry up. My best bet might be to let it go, wait and see if there was another way to skin this particular turd.

A drumming on the kitchen window yanked me out of my own head. I turned to see what it was. A huge black bird perched on the window sill. Soon as it was sure I saw it, it pecked the window and let out a funky caw. Seeing the bird injected a breath of determination into me, helped me remember I had proof of my claim on the box. I turned to Carl, ready to present my argument, but found him staring at the window, his mouth open. His teeth hurt to look at.

"Son of a bitch. I hate these damn things. Always showing up. Eating my garden, shitting on the deck. They're bad luck." He grabbed a wad of newspaper from the box of Vaseline glass and threw it at the window. The ball ran out of steam and dropped to the floor several feet away. "Get the hell out of here."

The bird sputtered and flew away. My muscles gave a little jerk. For completely irrational reasons, I wanted to grab the collar of his shirt and yank him into my face, bare my teeth at him, and tell him how it was going to be. Keeping my mouth shut was out of the question.

"The residents of Gaslight City lynched the woman the box used to belong to, and Archie Mahoney robbed her defenseless corpse. Isn't that how your ancestors ended up with it?"

"The box is staying where it is. In the Mahoney family." Carl pointed one finger at me. "You calm down and shut your mouth."

"Peri Jean Mace! You can't talk to people like this, especially not my cousin." Julie laid one cool hand on my arm.

I sat as still as I could. If I moved one muscle, I would slap her cool hand right off me. Julie let go of me and turned to Carl.

"A man we both know—one who was like a father to her—died a couple of days ago. He was looking for your box when he died." Julie did a combo head shake and eye roll. "I think she wants it out of some sense of duty to him."

Carl grunted and gave me a nod, his watery eyes still hard with anger.

"If you stop right now, I'm willing to forget all this." Julie's voice was sharper than I'd heard it since the day a tourist's child broke an expensive carnival glass vase and the parents got snitty when Julie expected them to pay for it. The moment of truth was staring me right in the face.

Am I ready to die on this hill? Lose my business over this? No.

I had bills to pay, financial responsibilities. I worked too hard building my day labor business to piss it away in one day. There would be no starting over. I'd have to look for minimum wage shift work at something owned by out-of-towners. No Gaslight City natives would hire me and risk Julie's wrath. It took every bit of self-control I possessed, but I clamped my mouth shut and sat back in my chair. My ear canals burned as though little jets of steam could shoot from them any second.

"Are you finished?" Julie stared at me.

My pride wouldn't let me answer, so I stared at my lap, the back of my neck on fire. What I saw in my ex-friend's eyes dug at me more than anything she could have said. Flat-out-don't-give-a-shit shone out of Julie's windows of the soul. She'd decided her cousin should have Priscilla Herrera's curse box, and the deal was done in her mind. Aside from forcefully taking it, nothing I said would do a damn bit of good.

Something moving in the yard caught my eye, and I gladly turned away from Julie and peered out the dirt-caked window, unable to see much detail. A huge shadow moved across the yard, coming toward the house, darkening the ground as it went. It didn't look good.

SOMEONE WAS YELLING AT ME. I turned to see Julie all red-faced. She glared at me and set her jaw. "I'm asking if you're finished, Peri Jean."

"Shut up and look out the window." I pushed back my chair and ran the few steps across the kitchen, getting as close to the filthy window as I could without touching it in hopes of widening my field of vision. A short distance from the house, the sun still shone. The darkness only covered the house and yard. A strong wind whipped through the murky dusk, almost laying the tall grass on its side. The lighter items in Carl Mahoney's junk collection blew around. The dollheads jittered on the fence, their eyes opening and closing. The window began to rattle in its frame. I heard dishes in the cabinets clinking together. I took several steps backward, though I knew it wouldn't help if push came to shove. We needed to get into a windowless room, preferably in the middle of the house. "Storm's coming. Fast."

"Ain't no storm." Carl's beer bottle jittered on the table in front of him and overturned, the beer foam rushing into his lap. He slapped it away and stood. "I checked the weather."

The back door blew open, and Julie bleated. About a hundred yards from the house stood an unused well. A concrete disk covered the opening, indicating the well was no longer in use. The disk rattled on top of the well, jumping until I could see space between the well and the concrete. Bony fingers appeared at one edge of it and pushed the disk aside like it was nothing. It thumped onto the dirt next to the well.

My heart tried to climb up my throat, gave up, and started banging against my ribcage instead. The disk would weigh a hundred dense pounds. Heavy enough I'd have had a hard time moving it alone. The whipping air carried an almost electric current, which turned the fine hairs on my arms into tuning forks, standing them rigid. My muscles bunched. I was ready to run but couldn't make myself move a muscle. The only part of my body moving was my trembling knees.

Skeletal fingers hooked over the edge of the well, and I knew something on the other side was climbing up to join us. A small skull appeared, rising over the well's edge, hooking its arms over and pulling itself out. Carl joined Julie in screaming, though his screams had words.

"Stay down! Stay down! Stay down!" The man's eyes were so wide I wondered if it was possible for his eyeballs to pop out. Even if they didn't, I bet his heart would give out before too long. My muscles tightened to the point I thought I might pee my pants, but still I couldn't move. The skeleton threw one bony leg over the side of the well and hefted itself over the side.

"Stop it, Peri!" Julie came to stand next to me. "You stop this witchcraft or whatever it is."

"You think I'm making this happen?" I touched the black opal through my shirt. It was cool and calm. Unusual in the face of something paranormal. Usually it heated up and burned me. "You're crazy if you think I'd do this."

Julie's mouth popped open like one of those candy dispensers. "How dare *you* call me crazy."

Her words slammed into me, hurting to the deepest, most hidden part of my soul. Crazy. The thing I feared people saying to me, thinking about me. A hundred years ago, they'd have done me the same way they did Priscilla Herrera for the same reasons people kill spiders in their houses—just in case. I tore my gaze from Julie to check the progress of the skeleton.

It crawled across the yard, growing tattered, parchment-colored skin as it came. The skull filled in, revealing solid black eyes with no whites and cracked, broken lips. Its proximity allowed me to see the femurs had been broken and the back of the skull was bashed in. Using fingers covered with broken and cracked skin, the skeleton gripped the door jamb and pulled itself to a standing position and stepped into the house.

The black opal finally came to life, going from cool to ember hot. I yelped and pulled it away from me. Instead of the power I usually felt coming from it, I felt a sucking sensation, making me think of water running out of a sink. The skeleton dragged itself a few more feet forward and grabbed my ankle. I recoiled, choking on the spit flooding my mouth, but the hand held me fast. A voice filled my whole world—the house, my head, even the outdoors.

"Who has my box?" The voice sounded garbled like a thousand voices all talking at once, using each other to form the words.

I tried again to shake off the horror holding onto me. It tightened its grip. I bent at the waist, intending to pluck its hand off me even though I could barely stand the idea of touching the thing. The black opal's heat increased to an unbearable level. As soon as I made contact with the bony hand, light flashed, and the skeleton fell away, the false life in it gone.

I fell backward, dizzy and devoid of energy, gasping as though I'd been exercising. Another gust of wind hit the house, making the old boards cry out. The skeleton twitched, once, twice, three times. It rolled to its knees and got to its feet and lurched at me. We weren't done. I held my arms out to ward it off, unprepared for the next attack but too ignorant to know what to do.

"Peri Jean Mace, I am the future of this town unless you fulfill your destiny." Its teeth clacked together as the words came, even though the words didn't seem to come from the bones.

The skeleton opened its arms as though inviting me to give it a hug. I pushed myself backward and hit the wall. Imaginary ants swarmed over my skin. My lips and cheeks tingled. I wanted to turn my gaze somewhere else, to relieve the terror, but I couldn't. The skeleton came closer, its coal eyes fastened hungrily on me.

Red flashed behind my eyes, and my vision turned inward. I saw Hannah Kessler sleeping in her bed. The skeleton came from under the bed and reached up one bony arm to grip her leg and raise itself onto the bed. Her eyes flew open, and her mouth opened to scream as the skeleton opened its mouth to bite into her. A black hound with red eyes chased Kansas Fischer, the son of my dead best friend. Tears streamed down the boy's face as he tried to outrun the thing. The animal launched itself and slammed into his back, forcing him to the ground. Its mouth ripped into the back of his neck. Rainey Bruce sat locked in her car, her eyes wide with fear, her mouth opened in a scream as flames engulfed her.

"No more, no more." I forced myself out of the vision and back into Carl Mahoney's filthy kitchen.

"Where is my box?" the skeleton screamed.

I glanced at Carl Mahoney. The horror turned on the man, opened its mouth wide, and let out a roar. Carl tried to run but tripped over his own feet and hit the floor. The man whimpered and tried to scuttle away, using his hands to slide himself toward the living room. The skeleton jerked and stumbled after him. Carl backed himself against a pile of crap. His legs kicked wildly as the skeleton stood over him.

"Give up your ill-gotten gains, thief." The skeleton's hiss shook the room.

"Do it, Carl." The steadiness of my voice surprised me.

"No, no, no." He whined. "It can't have my box."

His words were like a cold slap on my face. *Your box?* After all this, Carl still thought it was his box. Unbelievable. I wanted to run over and kick the old man cowering on the floor, but a whine filled my head. It hurt worse than any screech I remembered hearing and gained in intensity each second. I clapped my hands over my ears, which did nothing to block it out.

A shadow fell over me, and the young, tattooed version of Priscilla Herrera leaned over me. She offered her hand. I took it without hesitation and let her pull me up. Then she stepped into me, the chill of her deadness inundating me, filling every nook and cranny. The whine turned to a sweet sound, the call of an old friend. I knew I had to follow it.

I ducked past the skeleton and Carl and stumbled toward the sound, bouncing off piles of crap in the living room. A stack of magazines toppled and slid across the floor. I tried to plow through them but they slid underneath me, throwing me off balance. I grabbed the nearest thing, which was a stack of jigsaw puzzles. Boxes went flying, and I hit the floor with them.

"Son of a syphilitic bitch," I screamed and slapped the floor. I rolled onto my stomach, preparing to get up and saw what sat in front of me. The box was as I'd seen it in my vision, though a lot worse for the wear. It bore dings and punctures where generations of greedy-assed Mahoneys tried to get into it. Though the world raged around me, the box drew my full attention, shutting out the chaos. I picked up the box, and energy flowed into me, restoring the energy the skeleton took to become animated. *The skeleton.* What happened to it? I turned to stare at the animated corpse. Its limbs tangled with Carl Mahoney's, keeping him away from me.

Priscilla Herrera's voice spoke in my head. *Time to send my servant home.* Knowledge of unfamiliar words and phrases, of frustration and fear, exploded in my head. The deluge overrode everything not of it. Nothing belonged to me anymore. I became an observer in my own body. My legs marched me straight to the skeleton. Though I wanted nothing to do with the awful thing, I saw my hand reach down and grab its arm, tearing open the thin skin, making black ichor ooze. My muscles strained as I hefted it off Carl Mahoney.

Words I didn't plan came out of my mouth. "Be gone. Go where you can rest until I need you again."

A whirlwind filled the room. Cabinet doors opened and dishes crashed to the floor. The water faucet came on, blasting water into the sink. Light radiated from somewhere near me. I glanced down and saw it coming from underneath my T-shirt. The light pushed at the wind swirling around the room, sweeping it out the door. I added my own will to it, pushing at the force, willing it to go the same way I had helped Mysti. The house shook around us, so hard I imagined it coming off its underpinnings and flopping over on its side. The burners on the gas oven came to life with a soft whump, their flames burning high.

"Turn it off," Carl screamed at Julie. She tried to make her way to the oven but the wind pushed her down, blowing her against the wall.

The skeleton pulled itself out of my grasp and jerkily made its way back to the well, climbing in and disappearing from sight.

"This box is mine," Priscilla Herrera and I yelled as one. "You will never have it again, and you will not stop me from taking it." The heat from the black opal burned my skin, and I wanted to reach to pull it off, but my arms didn't work.

The storm left the house in degrees, the same way it came in. It passed out of the yard, the cloud cover going with it. The power still thrummed through me, pulling everything so tight it ached.

You must learn to do for yourself. Priscilla's voice was soft, no louder than a whisper. *The day will come when you have no one to help you.* With that, she left. I slumped to the floor, too weak to move. The curse box rolled from my hand and stopped a few feet from me. Carl Mahoney's gaze fastened onto it. I gathered the last of my strength and snatched it up before he could even think about beating me to it.

"Get out of my house," he said. "Both of you crazy bitches."

I thought he had a good idea. I rolled to my knees and slowly gained my feet, my legs shivering with the effort.

"What are you doing? That box belongs to me. Been in this family for generations."

"Put the box down, Peri Jean." Julie got to her feet.

"Want to fight me for it?" I didn't feel strong enough to whip either of them, instead banking on them being afraid of me. They both swiveled their heads away from me, first looking at each other, then at anything but me. I limped out the door, feeling as though I'd been working hard for many hours, and went to lean against Julie's delivery truck. I heard her footsteps coming across the yard and felt her stop next to me but refused to look at her. I'd thought her an ally. *How can I be so damn dumb?*

"I don't want you riding back with me. I—I can't be around you."

I made myself look at her face. I saw the fear I expected, but I also saw another emotion. Was it disgust? If not, it was a close cousin.

"Why'd you bring me here today? You knew he wouldn't want to sell me the box."

"I let it go as far as it did out of loyalty to Eddie."

Her answer made absolutely no sense to me, but I knew better than to ask for clarification. It wasn't my first ride in this particular rodeo. I turned away from her and began walking, looking at my phone and praying I could get a signal out here. Julie walked back to the house, her voice and Carl's mingling as I walked down the driveway. By the time I got out to the dirt road, their voices faded. A few minutes later, Julie passed me in the delivery truck, never even glancing my way. Two miles up the road, I found a spot where I had a good signal. Rainey answered her phone. I explained the situation, gave her the GPS coordinates off my cellphone, and heard her clicking a keyboard.

"There's a convenience store three miles north. Get to it, and I'll send someone to pick you up."

I thanked her and started walking.

14

Just my luck. Julie dumped me in late afternoon, the hottest part of the day. The sun, though low in the sky, still beat down with dangerous intensity, turning my uncovered head into a heavy oven. Within five minutes of walking, a thin coating of sweat slimed my body and made my clothes cling to me. My exposed skin burned, not with sunburn but from the heat. Mosquitos hovered over the water in the ditches, zooming after me and buzzing in my ears. I gave up on slapping at them by the time I'd walked ten minutes.

My mind gave me an encore presentation of the dissolution of my friendship with Julie. My stomach hardened as it played in agonizing detail. I could have kicked myself for trusting Julie with all this. *Did a lifetime of this garbage teach me absolutely nothing?* After I saw Carl had no intention of giving up the box and Julie had no plans to try to convince him, I should have dropped it, ate my shit with a knife and fork like a good girl.

An approaching engine knocked me out of my mental rant. I twisted for a glance behind me and saw a single headlight approaching. A motorcycle. *Please don't let them stop.* Relaying an edited version of how I came to be walking down an isolated highway in the woods to a good Samaritan would suck. Fending off an attack from an asshole who saw a perfect opportunity could end with me dead.

I reached into my bag and grabbed the handle of the screwdriver I carried around, praying they'd drive on by. The engine slowed as it neared me. Heart slamming so hard I could barely breathe, I gauged the distance between me and the trees. I could get to the woods before the motorcycle rider stopped if I ran. *But where will I go once I'm in the woods? I don't know these woods.* If the guy didn't catch me—big if—I'd likely end up lost, maybe with a nice snakebite for a souvenir. The motorcycle pulled alongside me. *Oh well. Too late now.* I turned to face the rider and laughed, body going weak with relief.

"What are you doing out here?" I asked Wade Hill. His being here made no sense. Even if Rainey'd called him to come pick me up, which I doubted, he hadn't had time to get here from Gaslight City.

"Just in the neighborhood." He stared at my face, studying me too hard for someone who'd come upon me by coincidence.

"What are you really doing out here?"

He shrugged. "Want a ride? Long walk back to Gaslight City."

I thought about holding out for the truth, but Wade

could drive off and leave me stranded for another hour. I quickly texted Rainey I'd found a ride home and climbed onto the back of Wade's motorcycle.

The motorcycle's roar and the scenery flying by provided background music for my pity party. Why oh why hadn't I agreed to let the box go? I soon remembered I'd been ready to let Carl Mahoney keep the box when things went to hell. The career destroying scene happened because of my willingness to roll over. Priscilla Herrera wanted the box in my hands, so it was. Then things went the way fate had planned. As soon as Julie saw the skeleton crawl out of the well and saw me after Priscilla Herrera took over my body, I was cooked.

Priscilla Herrera. I squeezed closer to Wade, suddenly cold despite the hundred-degree heat. She was one scary woman. There was no way to escape someone who knew how to access the workings of my mind. Both the abomination that came out of my cellphone and the skeleton from the well came straight from my nightmares, ones I had after watching horror movies. Priscilla knew exactly when I was ready to give up and let Carl keep the box.

The way she stepped into my body and used it as a broadcasting device both creeped me out and physically exhausted me. The experience left behind many of her emotions and made me want to somehow make things right for her. Mysti's talk about Priscilla Herrera trying to make up for her wrongs came back to me. Everybody wanted a second chance. What if I didn't have the skill to give Priscilla her do-over? What would she do to me then? Would my death at the hands of the treasure's demonic guardians be worse than anybody else's? Somehow I thought it might.

My mind stubbornly returned to Julie. The expression on her face outside Carl Mahoney's house flashed behind my eyes over and over. The unfairness plaguing my entire life had sprouted another head and found a new way to drop shit bombs all over me, and Julie's horrified face with its thin lips and wild eyes represented it. I wished I had kneecapped her right then and there. I had no doubt she was blabbing the whole experience to someone in Gaslight City who'd turn right around and tell someone else, and they'd tell a few more people. By the time I got back to town, the already fantastic story would be even weirder and might even have my head spinning around backward.

The Gaslight City limits sign came into view. Wade slapped my leg to get my attention.

"Where's your car?" he screamed over the motorcycle's deafening roar.

"Take me home," I hollered back.

He obediently took a cut through to the road Memaw and I lived on. I'd go pick up my car late tonight, long after Julie took her sorry, sanctimonious ass home. My cellphone vibrated in my pocket, and I removed it, gripping it tightly to keep the rough ride from jarring it out of my hand. It was a text message from Dean. Figuring it was a nasty-gram paying me back for standing him up again, I took a deep breath and opened it.

"Don't forget debate tonight. Civic center. 8 pm."

I slumped and squeezed my eyes shut. I'd have to face

the whole town. The chewing out Dean surely had in store for me would have been preferable.

Wade drove down Memaw's driveway. I noted with relief her car was gone. She'd probably find out what happened at Carl Mahoney's before I had a chance to tell her, but at least I could lick my wounds and prepare to talk to her about it before I had to. The motorcycle's engine cut off. Wade and I both stayed where we were.

"You okay?" he asked after several minutes had passed.

"No." Tears, both of anger and sadness, stung my eyes and before I could stop myself I unleashed a gout of verbal diarrhea on Wade. Getting down off the motorcycle so I could pace and wave my arms, I ranted about the morning's horror in great detail, showing the box to Wade as though he'd demanded proof. He took it from my hand and quickly handed it back as though it burned him. Inwardly cringing, I finally came to Julie's decision to unfriend me.

"It's not like I expect any less. I let myself get complacent this last year and forgot how people in this town see me. I forgot to be careful." I glanced at Wade, expecting him to say I shouldn't have to be careful but saw only understanding. "The worst part of all this is Julie knows a lot of the business owners in this town. The chances she won't blab this story all over are so thin, I can see myself through them."

"Who cares? Go on with your life. Don't let it matter." Wade spoke with conviction, but I saw hurt in his eyes. I bet he'd experienced the same thing. Maybe more than once. Go on with your life meant he'd survived, and I would too. But with what new restrictions?

"No other choice, but it's going to hurt both Dean and me. The debate between Dean and Sheriff Joey is tonight. Way the sheriff's been slinging shit, you know this is bound to come up."

Wade snorted, and it turned into a full blown laugh. I put my hands on my hips and glared at him.

"If this is part of your testosterone war with Dean, I'm not amused."

"No, no. It's about the sheriff. People who live in glass houses need to stay the hell away from rocks. Sheriff Joey Holze is such a crooked cop, I'm surprised he doesn't put his clothes on backward in the mornings."

Huh? All I could do was shake my head and hope Wade knew I meant I didn't understand and wanted to hear more.

"Remember the Bearden murder/suicide last Christmas?"

I nodded. Boy did I ever. Cody Bearden, a well-liked home builder, had hired a private detective to see if his wife was cheating on him. Once the results came back positive, he took the day off and waited for her to come home from work. When she did, he beat her to death with the business end of a claw hammer and then drank a bottle of drain cleaner. Their teenage daughter came home from an overnight with friends to find the mess.

"One of the guys from the Six Guns was the wife's brother. He was the closest relative, so he had to help his niece pick up the pieces. She asked about a bracelet her mother wore all the time. Claimed to have seen it on the body before the sheriff's people got there. Guy asked the sheriff's office about it." Wade got off his motorcycle and crossed his arms over his chest, using one hand to stroke his beard and frowning.

"And?" I'd never heard this story, had no inkling any of this ever went on.

"Holze and son blew him off, threatening to haul him in on some bullshit. He dropped it, helped his niece liquidate her parent's belongings, and got her settled with his parents in Austin. Couple of weeks ago, he saw Felicia Holze wearing the same fucking bracelet right there in HEB, buying her groceries and talking up a storm to everybody she saw."

"Did he confront her?" I hoped the answer was yes even though I didn't see how it would be.

"Hell, no. The stuff the sheriff's office suspects him of doing—"

"Is stuff he actually did?"

Wade nodded.

"Holze and his family have hollered a bunch of rumors during this whole campaign. It would serve them right if I found a way to make them look awful." I imagined myself humiliating the Holze family all over Gaslight City. Then Dean's face flashed into my mind. He wasn't smiling.

"There you go." Wade smiled. "Give 'em some of their own medicine."

"I can't. Dean would be furious at me if I had an outburst like what you're talking about."

"Then he doesn't want to win enough." He stared at me until I turned away. "What's really bothering you?"

"You think what I told you isn't enough?"

"There's more. You might as well tell me. I'm a good listener."

I let out a shuddery sigh. "The other thing Julie's gossip will do is cost me jobs. She's a respected part of the business community." I thought about all the Main Street Association meetings I'd attended as hired help. Julie always ran the show. "If she comes back from a road trip saying I really am as weird as she always heard and then blackballs me...I'm toast."

"Individuals hire you too."

"But I make the real money with businesses."

Wade shook his head, indicating he didn't understand.

"They pay me for a few weeks during their busy times, and it's a big chunk of money for me. It's win-win because they don't have to have the expense of a year-round employee." I sat down on the dirt, dug my elbows into my thighs and rested my chin on my hands. "If Julie blackballs me, so will the bed and breakfasts, the downtown businesses including the cafes, the junk shops...you name it."

"So you figure out another way to make money. I've done it a couple dozen times."

But I worked so hard to turn my odd jobs business into a full-time income. I kept the words to myself because they sounded whiney even while they were still inside my head, which was always a bad sign. The sentiment from the words stayed in my head anyway. I didn't want to face the humiliation of failing at my business and having to go to work doing something I hated.

"Girl we had tending bar at Long Time Gone quit night before last. Corman's doing the work for now, but he won't last. He punched a dude in the mouth last night for saying the beer was warm. Guy lost both front teeth."

I still said nothing, and he gave me a shove.

"I'll talk to King for you."

"I don't want to owe any more favors to your motor-cycle club."

"It'll just be a job. I promise you."

Thing was, I didn't want the job. I wanted my old life back. I wanted none of this to have ever happened because it was destroying me, both professionally and personally.

Memaw's old car sped down the driveway. Either she needed the bathroom really bad, or worse, she'd already heard all about my morning adventure with Julie. Soon as she pulled into the carport and shut off the engine, she rolled down her window.

I got up and slunk over to her.

"What are you doing out driving around by yourself? Why didn't you ask Esther Bruce to go with you?" I wanted to avoid talking about my problems as long as possible.

"Mind your own damn business. I'm the grownup here." She barely raised her voice. We both knew it was all for form. Memaw would die doing what she wanted. She grabbed my wrist, her skin so cold it gave me a shock. "I heard what happened. Damn Julie Woodson. Damn her. You all right, sweetie?"

I nodded, noticed I was clenching my jaw, and forced

myself to stop. She got out of her car and hugged me so tight her muscles shook with the effort. Her body was giving out. She wouldn't last much longer. Along with everything else in my life turning to shit, I was losing the only woman who'd ever mothered me. She let me go and turned to Wade.

"Thank you for being there for her, sweetie." She stood on her tiptoes and reached for his cheek. He had to lean down to let her touch him. "Such a good boy."

"Let's go in," she said. "You can tell me all about it, and I'll fix you hot chocolate. You too, Wade."

"I can't stay," Wade said.

"You can't?" Memaw, who'd already started across the yard, stopped and turned.

"No, ma'am, but thank you anyway. I got some business on down the road." He got on his motorcycle and started it.

Memaw motioned me to follow her. I did, even though I'd never be ready to listen to her try to console me or to listen to her relay every awful thing she knew about Julie, but I had no choice. Just like the rest of my life.

———

THOUGH THE GASLIGHT CITY CIVIC CENTER had modern air conditioning, the hundred-fifty-year old-building didn't have modern insulation. The day's intense heat lingered in the high-ceilinged room, absorbing the air conditioner's cool air faster than the unit could pump more out. Made me glad I talked Memaw into staying home. Hannah positioned her handheld fan so it blew on both of us, but I continued fanning myself with the program Rainey Bruce handed me at the front door.

A few streets over, the Catholic church's bells began chiming the hour. It was eight o'clock, time for the debate to begin. I shifted in my seat, trying to find a place where my bony ass didn't pinch my screaming nerves. As Dean's campaign manager, Rainey'd advised me to keep my mouth shut, no matter what was said, to be quietly supportive of Dean. I intended to take her advice no matter how bad things got. The house lights dimmed, and the lights on the stage brightened.

Dean walked out wearing his Burns County Deputy's uniform, his hat held in both hands in front of him, and went to the podium on the far side of the stage. A smattering of applause rippled over the room. Dean gave a short wave to acknowledge it. Sheriff Joey waddled out, leaning heavily on his cane, sweat beaded on his red face. I didn't like the man at all, but even so I worried he might stroke out at any moment. Somebody needed to bring him a glass of cool water.

Benny Longstreet stepped to center stage, wearing his trademark cowboy suit, his silver belt buckle and jeweled bolo tie blinding in the stage lights. He grinned, showing his big, horsey teeth, and waved to the crowd.

"His getup's uglier than a possum's pecker," I whispered to Hannah.

She elbowed me but giggled. "How would you know what one looks like?"

We both clapped our hands to our faces and snickered as silently as we could. I owed what little sanity I had tonight to Hannah. She came over to Memaw's as soon as she heard the news and helped me through the hours before the debate, not with false promises of how it would be okay but with a frank story about the humiliation she felt when her name was all over the tabloids because her famous athlete husband had fathered a child with his mistress. Hannah found out the day the tabloids hit the stands. She quoted Kris Kristofferson, telling me not to let the bastards get me down.

"All right, folks, we're about to get started." Benny took out a stack of index cards. "Everybody who ain't found a seat, please do so."

"Ain't enough seats, Mr. Benny," some man hollered from the back.

"Oh, hell," Benny said. "This is exciting, ain't it? Would you younger folks let some of these people who can't stand for the duration of the debate sit down?"

The room filled with shuffling as people craned their necks, hoping they didn't have to give up their seats. I glanced at the people lining the wall next to our row and motioned to Mrs. Elaine Watson and the elderly lady with her to take Hannah's and my seats.

"Come on," I told Hannah. "I know where there's an air vent. It'll be cooler."

People stilled again, and Benny introduced the candidates and asked the first question. "Deputy Dean, how do you intend to improve the way the Burns County Sheriff's Office solves crimes?"

Dean cleared his throat. "Over the year and a half I've worked in Burns County, we've had numerous issues with narcotic manufacturing. We've broken up three large operations and at least a couple dozen smaller ones." He paused to let this sink in. "I plan to reallocate funds to hire additional personnel so we won't be stretched so thin. I also plan to buy more computers and get us some up-to-date software to help us do our jobs better. Some of the people we arrested had probation violations we should have been aware of and would have been aware of if we weren't operating on outdated equipment."

"Now wait a minute," Sheriff Joey broke in. "All this modern technology crap is just an excuse for not doing the actual work of law enforcement."

A cheer somewhere near the front of the room erupted and went on until Joey, smirking, held up one chubby hand.

"This job is pounding the pavement. Not sitting behind a computer. It's about knowing the citizens of this county and understanding their needs—"

Elaine Watson shot up from my former seat. "Sheriff Joey, I got a question."

"Go ahead, Miss Elaine." Joey's voice could have dripped sugar.

"If you know me and understand my needs so well, why did you shoot my dog for no reason?"

His face reddened. "Miss Elaine, that was an honest misunderstanding, and it was a long time ago. I thought that dog was responsible for some reports of attacks we'd had—"

"Folks, let's get back to the debate." Benny tapped his microphone to make more noise.

"You don't tell me what to do, Benny Longstreet. I used to hire you to mow my yard." Elaine yelled. "I bet Deputy Dean would have investigated a little to find out what was going on instead of shooting my damn dog so he could leave to go fishing in Galveston."

"I'm voting for Deputy Dean because he stopped and helped me when I was stranded on the highway because I had a flat tire on my van," Lulu Dillahunty yelled. "Sheriff Joey has never stopped to help me, even though I lived across the street from him for forty years."

Joey's face turned even redder, and his lips flapped open and closed. He glanced at Benny, motioning for him to get control of the crowd. Benny gave him a miserable shrug as the crowd shouted at the stage.

"Hey, folks, let's show a little respect for this process," Dean said into his microphone. "I think there's time at the end for the attendees to ask questions. Isn't there, Benny?"

"Yes, there is." Showing his huge teeth again, Benny leaned into the microphone to speak. "Next question—"

The crowd quieted, and Felicia Brent Holze picked that moment to strike.

"All you folks who are mad at Sheriff Joey over some silly little incident need to remember one thing: if you elect Dean, you're getting her too." She pointed one finger in my direction, and every person in the big room turned to see who sat at the end of Felicia's nasty, booger-picking finger. "At least my father-in-law has a family of good, church-going Christians behind him and is not intimately involved with a Satanist who practices witchcraft and uses it to put other people in danger."

Mutters and whispers created a kind of white noise in the room, competing with the roaring between my ears. I pressed my back against the wall, wishing I could be anywhere else, even back in Carl Mahoney's house of horrors fighting over the curse box. People turned completely around in their seats so they could stare at me, their eyes lit with a nasty, hungry kind of curiosity. I imagined the spectators at the Roman Coliseum wore the same expression. Through the mutters and whispers, a few voices came through loud and clear.

"Well, you know what Julie said happened."

"I remember the whole business about her saying she saw Adam Kessler's ghost."

"No telling what the truth is about her. Might be something to think about tomorrow at the polls."

Without thinking about what I was doing, I started walking to the front of the room. I felt Hannah's fingers on my arm for an instant but brushed them off. People shrank away from me, not wanting to get my kind of crazy on them, I guessed. I reached the stage and climbed onto it, ignoring the horror on Dean's face, and walked over to Benny Longstreet and stared at him until he moved away from the microphone.

"You can't come up here, Miss Peri Jean," Sheriff Joey said from behind me. I ignored him, shocked he had the gall to call me "Miss Peri Jean" after all the other things he'd called me over the years.

"I'm sick of people saying untrue shit about me and running around like a bunch of villagers afraid the sky is falling because they don't know what I am." Feedback blasted from the speakers, and I lowered my voice. "Let me start with what I'm not. I'm not a Satanist. I'm not out to harm any of you, steal your souls, or cook your kids and eat 'em. But every rumor has some truth, and I'm not going to sugar-coat the truth any more. The truth is I communicate with dead people."

A collective gasp came from the audience. I wanted to roll my eyes. I'd withstood the rumors all my life, listened to the whispers, tolerated the silly jokes. Why pick this day and this situation to act like they never knew anything was different about me? *Puh-leeze.* People in the back pushed forward, jostling others to get a closer look at my tantrum. I made a point not to look at any of their faces because, if I did, I was afraid I'd shut up and never have the courage to defend myself again.

"What I can do is not bad or evil. It just is. What happened this morning—the thing Julie's running all over town telling everybody who'll listen—is something I didn't expect or plan. It happened because of my connection to the spirit world, and I couldn't help the way it went down." I found Julie's hateful face in the crowd and glared at her, daring her to accuse me of stealing the box. She wouldn't even look at me.

I felt another stare on me and found Wade Hill's huge form. He gave me a thumbs-up. I stood a little straighter.

"I am weird. I'll never deny it." I waited while a few people laughed and agreed. "But I can do good things with this weirdness inside me too. Last year, I solved Rae's murder. A few months ago, I helped solve Dean's sister's murder...didn't I?" I glanced at Dean for confirmation. His face turned red, but he nodded.

"Dean's sister was missing for twenty years, but her spirit contacted me, and I found where her body had been hidden and exposed her murderer." I trailed off because I realized the room was so quiet I heard a clock ticking somewhere. Every gaze in the room pinned me in place. Finally, I let myself see them. Some faces wore expressions of disgust or disbelief. Some wore pity. A tiny number wore open, interested expressions. The negative ones hurt more, but I tried to burn the image of the interested ones into my mind. "I'm not a monster. Y'all know I'm not. You've lived alongside me. You've hired me to work for you. You know I'm honest and good."

The total silence gave the room a surreal feeling, and I wondered if I was dreaming.

"Here's the thing you're all forgetting." I made myself make eye contact with the people in front of me. "Dean will do the job of sheriff if you elect him...not me. You all know Dean is both a good man and a good law enforcer. He's honest, he's kind, and he looks damn good in his uniform."

A few laughed, and some of the women cheered.

"If you don't elect Dean because of me, you're no better than a bunch of junior high kids trying to decide who's king shit of turd mountain. When you go to the polls tomorrow, decide who'll do the best job. Voting for or against *me* because of fear and ignorance is the same as voting against yourselves."

"Or the same as protecting ourselves from a spiritual

threat." Felicia jumped up, both arms raised like an athletic coach lecturing a team.

"See the bracelet on her wrist?" I made sure my voice carried through the room. "It came from the Bearden crime scene. When the Bearden family asked for its return, your sheriff and his son stonewalled them. Think about who you're voting for and why, folks."

Sheriff Joey began sputtering and protesting behind me. Felicia screamed a not very nice name at me. Ignoring them both, I blew a kiss at Dean, hopped off the stage, and left the building.

15

Th e f i r s t c a l l came around seven the next morning.

"Business is slow, hon, and I can't afford to have you help me today," said Alice Meeks, owner of the Delectable Dairy Ice Cream Parlor. "Ain't that I don't need the help. Folks don't spend enough money."

It shouldn't have surprised me, but damn my naivety to hell, it did. Calls poured in after my short conversation with Alice. Each time my cellphone rang, I flinched, the hollowness inside me growing. This wasn't after-school money for me. This was how I lived. I wanted to scream at the people telling me they no longer needed my services, to call them sheeple, to tell them I was the same person who'd worked for them on and off for the last few years. There was no point, though. It was what it was.

"How many's that?" Memaw asked.

"Don't matter. This'll free me up to help Hooty and Rainey with election day stuff today. Once the election is over, you and me can spend more time together." I worked to keep my voice even.

She stared at me, her dark eyes sharp with pity and sorrow. "Fine. I'll get dressed and ride to town with you."

I sank onto the couch as soon as she left the room and put my hands over my face, taking deep breaths and trying not to cry. I'd done this to myself. Crying wouldn't help. Oh, but I wanted to do it so badly. There was no way there'd be a full boycott of my services by everybody in Burns County, but enough would blacklist me to prevent me from earning the living I had for the past several years. *What's next? What do I do next?* My thoughts scrambled into meaningless, hysterical mish-mash. I had no choice other than to go about my business, acting as though everything was superfly, and keeping my eyes and ears open for the next opportunity. Wade had mentioned tending bar at Long Time Gone. I'd have to suck up my Texas-sized pride and do it.

Election day passed in a flurry of exhausting hurry up and wait activity, most of it spent outside roasting in the blazing sunshine. The reports we got from early ballot counters said Dean and Sheriff Joey were running neck and neck. Dean kept smiling and slapping backs, but I saw the worry in his eyes. The question would hang in the air until the final votes came in. The polls closed at seven in the evening, and the intensity of the situation multiplied exponentially. Waiting gnawed at me, made my hands twitch and my muscles ache. We huddled together in an old storefront Dean rented for the campaign all of us drinking too much coffee and trying to pretend it wasn't making us irritable. Around ten, the phone rang, and Dean answered.

"I see," he said. "We'll be over there shortly." He hung up the phone and stood with his back to the room for several long minutes. My heart dropped. He'd lost. I knew it. All this effort for nothing. We'd let the campaign drive a wedge between us. Dean would be out of a job tomorrow. I walked across the room, almost afraid to touch him, but knowing I had to do what I could to smooth the way for him.

I stepped up beside him, facing a wall plastered with campaign posters showing his smiling face, and dared to glance at him out of the corner of my eye. I gasped. The wild smile on his face told me I'd been wrong. I gripped his arm in congratulations and tipped my head at the people waiting behind us, the ones who'd worked so hard to make this happen. We turned together. The room erupted into cheers and howls. Rainey rushed at us and grabbed Dean in a hug. The two of them jumped up and down together. She pushed him away from her and beamed at him.

"We did it." She gave Dean a hard shake. "Oh, we beat that awful man." She turned to me. "I think your little speech last night tipped the scales. I know it cost you, but I am proud of you, so very proud."

"Is the sheriff coming by to congratulate you? Or do we just go on down to the courthouse square?" a young teacher from the high school asked.

"The Holze family has gone home for the evening," Dean said. "Let's get our stuff together and meet back up at the square."

People exchanged glances, surprised at Sheriff Joey's rudeness. I wasn't a bit surprised.

"Where's Miss Leticia?" Hooty asked me.

"Sleeping in your RV out back in the alley. It got late for her." I'd actually forced her to go out there and take a nap, having no idea when we'd be able to get home. "I'll go wake her and push her to the courthouse in her wheelchair."

"Better you than me getting her to ride in the wheelchair."

I rushed to wake Memaw, we argued about her using her wheelchair, but I won out and wheeled her to the town square where a bandstand had been constructed for the winner to make a victory speech.

Dean's campaign team had already assembled on the stage. Deputy Brittany Watson, who had never wavered in her support of Dean, set out metal folding chairs. Hooty circulated, shaking hands and laughing. Dr. Longstreet stood off to the side, arms crossed over his chest, grinning more widely than I'd seen him do in a long time.

"What are y'all waiting for?" Deputy Brittany leaned down.

"There's no ramp." I walked around the stage for a second time.

"Joey expected to win," Memaw said. "Nobody in his party needs a ramp."

She was right. It made me blaze with anger even though we'd won the fight.

"We'll just stay down here." I squatted next to Memaw's chair, sweat squelching behind my knees.

Dean mounted the steps to the bandstand, holding his uniform cowboy hat in both hands. His eyes moved over the audience, looking for me. I waved, and a grin split his face. He moved to the edge of the stage and leaned down.

"Come up here with me," he said. "I wouldn't be here if it wasn't for you."

"No ramp." I pointed at Memaw.

"You go." Her rough voice trembled when she spoke. "I have to let you go sometime."

I turned to her to find tears brimming in her eyes. This was about more than me leaving her side to stand with my man. It was about our time together ending. The grief, embedded deep in my heart, throbbed on cue. I hesitated, glancing between Memaw and Dean.

"We'll stand with her." King and Corman Tolliver appeared at my side.

"Go." Wade walked up behind them. "You belong up there with him." I stood staring at the three men for a long moment. Leaving Memaw there felt so final.

I kissed Memaw's cheek and walked to the stage. People had the steps blocked. Dean leaned over them and held out his hand. I took it and let him lift me enough to get a foothold. One hard yank, and I stood beside him, facing the crowd. He kissed me, and a moment of silence gave me time to worry everyone might boo after my little show last night, but then they cheered. Loud. Above them all, I heard Memaw's booming voice hooting. Dean pulled me to stand with him at the microphone, the flood lights blinding us both. He tapped the microphone.

"Thank you all for coming out tonight, and thank you for your votes." Dean played his good ol' boy accent to the hilt, drawling over his consonants and dropping the endings of some words. "I only hope I can prove myself worthy of your confidence—" The crowd interrupted him with wild cheers.

Dean and I exchanged a glance. My heart swelled at the joy in his face. I gave him an impulsive kiss on the cheek, and his constituents hollered even louder.

A dark murmur roiled though the back of the crowd. I squinted into the blinding lights, unable to see what made them switch gears. Dean and I exchanged a worried glance. One woman screamed, then another.

"Stop right there," Memaw shouted, her words ending in a hacking cough. Gunfire boomed, and the first screams sullied the night.

People ran every which way, their movements like a slow motion film. Deputy Brittany rose from her seat so fast the metal chair fell over, clanging on the wood. She unholstered her pistol and ran to the edge of the stage, squinting her eyes, just as blind as I was. She held her weapon in both hands but didn't raise it. I didn't blame her. Though most folks were running for their lives, she'd have never wanted to fire into a crowd of mostly innocent people.

"Memaw? You all right?" I pushed my way to the edge of the stage to look for Memaw, Dean right next to me. He threw one arm out and tried to shove me behind him. I elbowed him aside. Didn't he understand my grandmother might be hurt? "Memaw?"

Dean, who really was stronger than me, managed to shove me behind him. As he did, a voice came from directly below us.

"Die, witch!" The gun went off again, and footsteps smacked against the concrete as whoever did the shooting retreated into the darkness.

Brittany Watson jumped off the stage and disappeared into the darkness screaming, "Backup! I need backup! Deputy Fitzgerald? Where are you?"

Deputy Fitzgerald came from around the side of the stage and ran after Brittany.

Dean stared at me, his eyes wide and brimming with tears. One shaking hand went to a spot on his chest, and he slowly sank to his knees. I dropped next to him, putting my hand over his.

"Help us," I hollered to nobody in particular, still wondering where Memaw was.

Blood soaked through Dean's uniform shirt fast, too fast. Wade Hill could save him, same as he saved me on the side of the road. This time I wasn't too late.

Everything in me went into overdrive. I needed Wade to save Dean. I leapt to my feet and ran to the edge of the stage. "Wade Hill, I need you. Please help me." My screams ate at the tender lining of my throat with jagged teeth, leaving it raw and burning.

Wade came right away, as though he'd been near all along. He climbed onto the stage as though it was no more than an inconveniently large step.

"Come on. We have to save Dean." I held my arm out to him, willing him to hurry.

The bright stage lights against the inky night made Wade Hill's dark eyes unreadable. His still face betrayed no emotion, and his silence chilled me. He pulled me against him, clapping one heavy arm over me. "Just stay here with me. It'll be all right."

"He's bleeding to death." I twisted in his embrace and yelled into his face, grabbing his arm dragging him with me. He resisted at first, tugging against me, but I turned and yelled, "Memaw says we always help others when they need it, even if we don't want to. You're going to help me help Dean."

He winced and followed willingly, head hanging low. I couldn't believe he'd be willing to let Dean bleed to death because they didn't get along. I glanced back, making sure he was still following, and was struck again by the way he slumped and took slow steps. How could helping someone be such a bad thing? We pushed through the semi-circle of people fanned helplessly around Dr. Longstreet and Dean.

"Move!" I yelled at Dr. Longstreet's back. He turned, eyes widening, and scrambled out of the way.

Wade and I knelt in the puddle of blood spreading around Dean. I put my hands over the bubbling wound on his chest. The black opal against my breastbone began to warm.

"I'm here." I choked on the words. "I'm gonna save

you." I reached for the power of the black opal, finding its burning light with no problem and latching onto it. The stone heated on my chest, much faster than when it reached out to me. I turned to Wade. "Do it."

He blinked once, the movement maddeningly slow. "You sure?"

"Yes!" The warm spot began to sting. I tried to brush away the discomfort, but it stayed. Ignoring it, I focused on Dean's fluttering eyes. He had seconds left. What was Wade's problem? I nudged him with my elbow.

The spot on my chest where the black opal rested throbbed and ached. I thought I smelled something burning. Maybe my own skin. I reached under my shirt with trembling fingers and found the black opal pendant. Its intent leaked into me, as clear as my own thoughts. It wanted to save Dean, the great-grandson of its previous owner. I closed my fist around the burning stone and used the other hand to grip Wade's wrist.

He jumped and cried out when the magic poured into him. A hot summer wind rushed over us, and Wade's skin began to glow from inside. He repeated his words with more force. I concentrated on pumping the black opal's power into Wade, shaking with the effort it took.

Wade put his hands on Dean, his lips already moving. This time I caught a few of the words, especially when he said, "Live."

"Stay back, folks," Dr. Longstreet shouted. I half turned to see a bank of legs standing around us, recognizing both Rainey and Hannah's fancy high-heeled shoes, along with Hooty's shiny dress shoes. They were blocking the view of us from anybody still hanging around.

When I brought my attention back to Dean, I saw the blood running out of his chest had slowed to a trickle. I pushed his shirt open, horrified at the hole there. Wade put his hand over the hole and said his words again, closing his eyes. A vein pulsed in his neck, and he spoke the words again. The bullet came to the surface of Dean's skin and pushed its way out. It rolled off his skin and clattered to the wood floor of the stage. Someone behind me gasped. I stared at the wound. Blood no longer even trickled from it. Either Dean was dead or we'd done it, saved him. Wade pushed to his feet, shoved his way to the edge of the stage, and fell to his hands and knees to vomit noisily over the side. He stayed in his crouch, shivering all over and rocking back and forth. The pulsing magic slowed its circuit through me and finally faded. Without it to bolster me, a heavy tide of exhaustion rolled in. I slumped and had to hold myself up with one shaking arm.

"I'll take over." Dr. Longstreet's voice came from right next to me. "We need to get him to the hospital immediately. Get more blood in him."

I felt hands under my arms, pulling me away so the emergency workers could get to Dean. Brittany deposited me next to Wade, who still rocked back and forth at the edge of the stage. She paused for a second, her face so full of pity I thought for a second Dean had died. Then her cousin, Roland, the medic, gave me a thumbs-up and a wink. Fatigue pressed down on me, a heavier weight than I'd ever felt. The black opal had helped me, but that much magic flowing through me had taken its toll on both Wade and me. I'd have to worry about Brittany later. I turned to Wade.

"Headache." He rubbed at his temples and neck, his face so pale his dark beard created a sharp contrast against his face.

"We did it. We saved him." I squeezed his hand. "Thank you. I can never thank you enough."

Wade said nothing. At first, I thought it was because he was out of breath too. But, even after his breathing slowed back to normal, he still didn't speak.

"Are you okay?"

"I don't know," he said. "Probably not. Look, I need to tell you something."

A few feet away, the EMS workers put Dean into the ambulance and drove away, sirens wailing for the entire block and a half to the hospital. The action died down quickly. I realized I never knew who did the shooting. Rainey Bruce approached us, her face streaked with tears.

"I'm so sorry, Peri Jean." She hugged me.

Sorry for what? Isn't Dean alive?

"Who did it?"

"I don't know." Her voice had all the inflection of a robot.

I couldn't speak. I glanced at Wade, looking for an explanation.

"Peri Jean, there's no easy way to say this." Wade put one hand over his mouth, wiping at his beard. "Your grandmother was shot too."

I jumped to my feet and swayed, nearly falling to the

ground. My nerves stretched to the brink, pulling me in a dozen different directions. Rainey grabbed my elbow and held me up. I took in her tear-streaked face, asking for confirmation. She nodded.

"How? Why?" My mind rejected the information. If I asked enough questions, surely I could make Wade's words untrue. I knew the folly of my thinking, but I couldn't stop myself.

"The shooter had the gun pointed at you," Wade said. "Your grandmother grabbed her arm and got in front of her."

Rainey took a long shuddering breath. "This is so awful," she sobbed.

Then it hit home. Memaw had been shot just like Dean. Maybe she needed help. Wade and I could help her. I'd use the last of my strength to save her.

"Where is she?"

"King took her to the hospital." Wade's voice still had an odd, toneless quality.

"Come on then. We have to get over there."

Wade simply stared at me, shoulders rounded, the expression in his eyes battle weary.

"What aren't you telling me?"

"Shot in the head. Point blank range. Too much damage to—" He choked on his words and put his hands over his face and sobbed.

Anguish kindled and mounted into an inferno in a matter of seconds. Someone wailed in the background. One look at Rainey Bruce's face told me the howler was me. I took off running, leaving Wade and Rainey on the courthouse square.

———

BY THE TIME I reached the hospital, my breath came in harsh gasps from battling the suffocating humidity. Sweat beaded and ran down my body, tickling as it went. I slammed into the emergency room, looking for Memaw. Wade shouldn't be far behind me. He was wrong. There had to be a way to fix Memaw. Together, we could fix her the same way we fixed Dean. King sat in one of the orange chairs, his gray head bowed and his hands clasped between his knees. He raised his head at the sound of my footfalls. Our eyes met, and I saw the answer in their dull depths.

"No." I howled the word, letting it drag out until I ran out of breath. King stared at me, face expressionless, neither shocked nor impressed at my show.

"Dead on arrival." His voice was gritty and dry like he'd been crying. One glance at the tear streaks on his cheeks told the story. "I tried to get in front of her. Didn't realize what was happening in time."

I sank to my knees in front of him, shaking my head. I wailed my disbelief and beat my fists on the floor as my world sank into the abyss. No more Memaw. The cooking and crochet lessons, the talks about life and God, the private jokes—all gone in a flash. I cried harder than I ever remembered crying, chest straining with the effort of it, head pounding from the force of it.

"Ma'am? You can't do that in here," a voice said from behind me. "We have a chapel if you'd like to—"

"You say one more word, you heartless bitch, and I'll cold cock you myself." King's voice remained light and calm, but I didn't doubt him.

"I'm calling the sheriff," she said.

King grabbed me by one arm and dragged me out of the room. My tear-blurred eyes roved over a sea of horrified faces. Many held sympathy, but all I saw were the people who'd made fun of me all my life. Once outside, King lit a cigarette and jammed it between my lips.

"Straighten up. Get a hold of yourself. Quit acting like a fucking baby." He tried to force me to stand up straight. I curled in on myself, trying to get away from him. He held my wrist in an iron grip and gave me a hard shake.

"You think you were the only person who loved that old lady?" he shouted, his voice nearly lost in the roar of blood rushing in my ears. "Hell, there wasn't a dry eye in that emergency room, 'cept maybe that mean bitch who run us off. She's cold as a dildo's been in the freezer for a month."

I glared at him through my tears. He hadn't loved Memaw like I had and couldn't possibly understand. "It's my fault she's dead. Wade said the shooter pointed the gun at me."

"There is no way Miss Leticia could have stood watching you be shot and die in front of her. Any parent would have done the same." He gripped my shoulder, probably getting ready to shake me some more, but I jerked away from him.

"But my grandmother's dead." I sank on the ground and choked back the ache in my throat. "I wasn't...ready." A black hole of pain opened up in my chest, sucking bits and pieces of me into it. The parts of me it left behind bled and screamed in blind pain. My face burned, and I wanted to puke. I wanted to take back all the awful choices I'd made. But I couldn't.

"You're never ready." He knelt next to me. I couldn't let myself focus on the sadness in his voice. I wanted to be mad at King, to pound him with my fists and yell in his face. I had the energy to do none of it. I felt devoid of even the gumption to keep breathing.

A flicker of light, too bright for this nasty old parking lot, drew my gaze. A young couple approached the electric doors and passed through them as though they weren't even there. The girl wore a full skirt which fluffed out like it had a petticoat underneath. The boy wore khaki pants short enough to show his white socks and loafers. The couple might have been going to a costume party featuring the nifty fifties as its theme, but they weren't. They were my grandparents, so young I barely recognized them.

The last I'd seen of my grandfather's ghost, he'd been a middle-aged man, broad-shouldered, face weathered by sun and circumstance. All those scars of living had dropped away. His unlined skin glowed under his Brylcreemed pompadour, his spade sideburns cutting an angle down his jawbones. They stopped a few feet from me, hands clasped. I stilled the same way I would have if I'd crossed paths with a deer and wanted to watch it a few moments before it ran off. I drank in Memaw, staring at her dark eyes and her Liz Taylor haircut. She'd been so beautiful before life wore her down, and she was so again, her face full of light as she smiled up at my grandfather, barely sparing a glance at me.

"Well, I'll be," King whispered beside me. I took in the wonder on his face and guessed he could see them too.

Memaw turned to me, smiling at me more like we were old friends who'd gone to school together than grandmother and granddaughter. She'd changed and was ready to move on down a new road, one with no cancer or pain or loss to make it rocky. She motioned me to get up and approach her. I did, taking slow, small steps, fearful of popping the bubble of this encounter. Her love covered me, hugging me without touching me. She leaned close and opened her hand. Inside was a butterfly. It moved its wings and rose into the black night. Memaw winked and gave my grandfather's hand a tug. He nodded and waved to me. Sobs shook my body, and I clasped my arms around my chest and watched them walk out of the parking lot and down the street. Finally, they disappeared with a little pop of light.

"I don't have anybody left," I whispered.

"Your grandma was sort of one of us." King put his hands on his hips, heaved out a sigh, and spoke as though he was giving me his last penny. "In her honor, if you ever need my help, ask."

Corman came to stand next to me. "I second what Daddy said. You come to us if you need us. No strings attached."

Wade put one arm around me and yanked me against

him. He smelled sour and sick, but I hugged him anyway. Hannah slammed out the door, tears streaking down her face.

"Oh, thank God, you're all right." She ran at me and threw her arms around me, holding me so tight it hurt. She pulled back and stared at my face. "Is it true about Memaw?"

I said nothing but felt my lips tremble.

Hannah threw back her head and cried loud whooping sobs like a child who'd fallen off the swing set. It was then I let myself sift through what I knew about the last moments of Memaw's life. I hadn't seen anything, but I'd heard enough.

The shooter screamed *Die, witch.* It was my fault. Whatever time Memaw had left was cut short by me being me. *Die, witch.* I did nothing but get the people I loved hurt and killed. *Die, witch.* I recognized whose voice had hollered "Die, witch" and knew I'd never wash all the guilt off me. My throat closed, and I put my hands over my face and rocked back and forth. Every single bit of tonight was on me.

Dr. Longstreet came out of the hospital, still wearing the suit he had on when Dean got shot. Bloodstains covered it. Seeing me bent over, he rushed to me, taking my arm and learning over me. "What's happening? What hurts?"

My heart hurts, doctor. Beating me upside the head with a hammer might fix it.

"The shooter was Julie Woodson." Speaking made me realize my lips had gone numb, and the inside of my mouth felt like old cotton.

"I, ah, was listening to the police scanner on my phone." Hannah held up the device. "The sheriff's deputies have her surrounded at the antique store. They're trying to get her to come out and surrender."

"I never realized it would come to this. My memaw's dead because of me." The sobs returned, clawing my throat raw, burning my eyes, and leaving nothing behind but the worst pain I'd ever felt. I cried myself out faster this time, maybe because I knew it wouldn't help ever, and turned to Dr. Longstreet.

"Dean?"

"Tough sumbitch is gonna live," Dr. Longstreet said. "Don't tell me what the two of you did to him. Might ruin my belief in medical science. All he needed was a blood transfusion and a little patching. Got an intern taking care of it. But that bullet should have killed him."

"What did you see? What did the other people see?" Wade loomed over Dr. Longstreet.

"Not a damn thing," Longstreet deadpanned. "We blocked y'all from sight. Nobody saw much."

I understood. They would ignore what they saw because it saved Dean. They had probably already started lying to themselves about it.

"He awake?" My voice sounded like someone had rubbed sandpaper on my vocal chords.

"I sedated him. He was arguing with me about going back to work tonight. It'll take hours to give the blood transfusion he needs."

"Can I see him?"

"You can go sit with him in his room. Come on."

I started to follow the doctor but stopped and turned back to my friends. One by one, I made eye contact with them, thanking them for being there with me when I needed it.

16

I FELT like the walking dead—sort of not there—as Dr. Longstreet led me to Dean's room and got me situated in a chair next to his bed with a blanket. I heard someone else's voice asking the doctor if I should call his family or let him decide when he woke up but didn't even listen to the answer he gave, figuring the other person, the one who sounded so together would take care of it. Instead, I tried to figure out what they'd done with Memaw's body. The thought, though it should have made me scream, just deepened the numbness in my soul.

Over the last year, I'd imagined Memaw's death numerous times. She'd die with me holding her hand. I'd cry, run off, and hide like a wounded animal but eventually come to the conclusion she was no longer hurting. In this scenario, Dean acted as my rock, bringing me back to the land of the living with his strength and pragmatism.

In reality, I sat next to a hospital bed, hovering over

Dean's unconscious form like there was something I could do other than wait for him to wake up. I might as well have been alone, considering how isolated I felt. Losing Memaw so abruptly had scooped out a piece of me as neatly as a shovel digging a hole. I felt sure it would return, along with all the screaming, crying, and hysterics. For this moment, the emptiness held me in thrall. My wonderful Memaw was silenced forever by a bullet intended for me. No wonder her spirit left with my grandfather's so quickly. I think I'd have headed out for greener pastures too.

The idea should have brought tears to my eyes, lodged a lump in my throat, but it did neither. I couldn't form a reaction. I sat there silent and still, watching Dean rest. He had an IV hooked to one arm. A bag of blood and a bag of saline hung from a rolling metal stand next to his bed, the IV tube snaking to one arm. I curled my fingers over the unfettered hand, caressing his fingers with my thumb.

I pulled myself together as best as I could and began a mental list of things I needed to do. Memaw left her final wishes with Hooty, so I'd have to get with him. I'd need to clean out her clothes, pick the ones I wanted to keep, and give away or sell the rest. I'd need to decide if Dean and I wanted to live there in Memaw's house together or if he wanted to keep his house of horrors downtown. Somewhere in there, I must have dozed.

Dean jerked and woke me. I removed my hand from his, worried I was hurting him. His eyes were wide, darting around the room.

"You're okay. They had to give you blood, but it's over and you're going to be fine."

His eyes settled on my face, still wild and too bright. He licked his lips. Realizing he needed something to wet his mouth, I poured water from the mini-pitcher and held it out to him. He shook his head hard, whipping it side-to-side, warding me off with his hands. The empty hole inside me closed, and the cold sting of fear kickstarted my emotions.

"It's okay." I reached out to touch him, to assure him I meant no harm.

He flinched away, cowering from me.

"What is it? Do you want me to call the nurse?"

"Get out." His voice was barely more than a croak, but his words slammed into me as hard as if he'd shouted them. "Don't touch me. You're...you're...unnatural."

I flinched from his words, hurt welling up in my throat. My mind searched for an excuse. Was he having some sort of episode? A stroke maybe? I snatched the call button, but Dean batted it from my hand. I backed away from him, my hand moving to my chest, trying to dam up the emotion flooding me.

He took the water from where I'd set it after he refused it. He took a drink, slopping it on the bed and himself. He seemed not to notice. His attention stayed on me, wary and scared.

His reaction baffled me. He acted as though this was the first he'd ever experienced my abilities, but it wasn't.

"I came so close to dying, my spirit left my body. I watched you and Wade trying to save me. There was this... I don't know...like a nimbus of shadow surrounding the two of you." He paused, breathing hard. A vein in his neck pounded, the skin shiny with sweat. "I was scared of it. And, now, I feel like part of me's still out there. What you did was wrong. You tried to trick nature."

"I saved you." My words came out ragged and and full of broken edges. "I did it because I love you."

"Get away from me." He whipped his head side to side. "I don't want that part of you touching me ever again." He turned his body away from me and stared out the window.

I stumbled backward, my knees loose and shaky, and caught myself on the cheap dresser. I looked back over the past months and saw them in a new light. Nothing had changed about the way Dean reacted to me doing out of the ordinary things. He just ignored them. Sensing his discomfort, I'd kept it away from him. The two of us had been headed for disaster for some time. Maybe some deeper, smarter part of me saw the end coming, because it wasn't the end killing me inside. It was the way Dean had curled his lip when he looked at me, as though I repulsed him. It was the same way Barbie looked at me. Nausea bubbled in my stomach, threatening like distant thunder. I swallowed against it.

"Get out. I can't deal with you today. Maybe not ever."

It hit me then. Dean had compartments for everything in his life. It was why he could be so fastidious in his appearance, so dedicated to being good at his job, but live in a rundown house. What I could do—what I was—was okay as long as he kept it at a distance, didn't let it touch him. But it had saved his life, and he could no longer ignore it. Sadness so deep that it almost blacked out my vision filled me. The door to Dean's room swung open, and Deputy Michael Fitzgerald rushed in, hair standing up in oily spikes and uniform wet with sweat.

"It's over, Sheriff. We heard a gunshot. Investigated, and Miz Woodson had shot herself. Boy feels funny calling you sheriff—" He took in the scene before him, eyes widening at the sight of me and mouth dropping open when he saw Dean curled into the fetal position, his back turned to me. "What's wrong?"

"He's pulling a fit because life ain't fitting into his narrow-assed view of how things ought to go." I used the last of my inner steel to march out of the room. Soon as I got out of sight, I turned to jelly, barely able to see through the tears burning my eyes. I staggered through the hospital like a drunk, brushing against the walls, holding onto them for support. Curious eyes followed my progress, but nobody tried to help. They just let me go. I thought I heard someone calling my name but ignored it, pitching forward, closer to the exit with each clumsy step.

I tripped going out the door and sprawled face first into the parking lot, scraping my hands on the asphalt. I lay there, hands on fire, a spot on my chin stinging. A car whipped into the parking lot and came straight for me. I managed to get to my knees in time for them to see me and slow.

A guy I recognized but didn't really know leaned out his window. "You all right, lady?"

I nodded and forced myself to walk back to the courthouse square, trying to remember where I'd left my car.

Finally, I remembered it was at the museum, in the tiny parking lot in back.

I don't know how I made it to the museum or how I got home. I don't remember stopping at any stop signs or seeing any traffic lights. I rolled under the carport and parked and sat there staring into space. The numbness I worried about earlier had been a blessing. In its place had grown a throb so intense its beat resonated in every inch of my being. I staggered out of the car, left the keys in the ignition and the door hanging open, and walked to the house on unsteady legs.

It was baking hot inside. Memaw wasn't there to run the window units. I'd get them started and make a pitcher of iced tea to drink while I worked, just like Memaw would have done. I put the kettle on the stove to boil and grabbed the matches to light the gas burner, realizing at the last moment I didn't know how to get the stove started. I'd lit it by myself since I was ten or so, but in my haze of grief, I couldn't remember how to work it. Tossing the matches on the kitchen table, I dragged myself to Memaw's bedroom. Fuck the iced tea. I'd make it later.

Opening her closet, I looked through her things, wondering what I'd bury her in. I took out her favorite Sunday dress, the one she'd worn to church on special occasions the last several years in a row. It looked so small. I sat down on the bed, holding it, rocking. The first tear dripped onto the periwinkle fabric, and I tossed the dress over her vanity bench, not wanting to soil it. The angle allowed me to see the light on Memaw's answering machine blinking. She kept it in her room because I never remembered to check it. Wondering how long the message had been there, I pushed the button.

"Peri Jean?" Julie Woodson sounded out of breath.

Deputy Fitzgerald said she'd shot herself. Unless this was her ghost calling, I guessed she must have called during her standoff with Burns County's finest.

"I'm sorry for everything I did and said the last couple of days. When I came to myself holding that gun at the courthouse square, Dean laying there shot, poor Miss Leticia dead at my feet, I couldn't figure out what'd happened. Last thing I remembered was telling your mother not to haggle more than ten percent on merchandise while we were gone to see my cousin Carl. I thought there must be some mistake, so I ran back here, thinking it'd give me time to figure out what to do. More I sit here, though, the more I know I'm sunk. Listen, girl, what I want to tell you is Eddie always believed you and Jesse'd both been spelled to forget what happened the day your daddy was murdered."

Well, no shit. Of course, it had taken me all my life to figure it out.

"It was Eddie's dream to help you remember. The week he died, he called me all excited, saying he thought he had it." The machine beeped off. I half rose from my seat, heart pounding, thinking whatever she said was lost. The machine went to the next message.

"Shit. Didn't realize these things cut off after a certain amount of time. I'll try to be fast. Eddie said for the forgetting spell to have lasted so long, it must have been drawing energy from somewhere. Maybe a person. Maybe an item. Would have to be something—or somebody—you had real strong feelings about. Soon as I remembered that, I went straight to my curio display in the back of the store."

Julie'd set up parts of her store to resemble rooms in a house. Her favorite was an art deco bedroom in the back of the store. The locked curio cabinet housed Julie's own collection of perfume bottles and vanity items from the era. She claimed she had so few visitors at her own house, she kept the items there in the store so more people could see them.

"I didn't quite know what to look for, but I took down my new bottle, the one you said reminded you of a genie bottle, opened it, and there it was. This little rolled up piece of paper was inside, and it had these funny markings on it. I burned the paper, and I—" The message beeped off again but went right to the next one.

"I burned it, Peri Jean. I burned the paper. Then, I remembered every awful thing I'd done over the last couple of days, right up to shooting—" Her voice broke and she wept awful, wracking sobs until the machine cut off the message again. The next message started. By then Julie'd gotten control of herself well enough to speak. "I want to apologize to you for everything I did. I can't believe I treated you the way I did at Carl Mahoney's house. I set the appointment to go over there with full intent of helping you get the little box you'd told me about. And afterwards, calling all those people and badmouthing you. I can't believe it was me saying those awful things. Then, what I did last night...Peri Jean, please believe me, I didn't know what I was doing." The machine cut off.

Did I believe Julie? She'd treated me no better than a hog rooting up her garden. *Wait. Memaw's the one who got the pesky hog treatment.* If Julie was telling the truth, she'd been under someone else's control since the day we went to see Carl Mahoney. I didn't understand how someone could use magic to control another person but then thought about the curse keeping people from finding the Mace Treasure and had to admit magic in the right hands could accomplish some pants-pissing outcomes. One thing was for sure. If someone had controlled Julie's actions over the last few days, the same person had sent her to kill me last night. *Die, witch.* The next message started up, and I forced myself to focus on it.

"I'm going to make my point, honey, because I'm getting real tired of this damn machine. Whoever did this to me must be the same person who made you lose your memory when you's a little girl. You got to find where they hid your spell. It'll be in a place important to you, a place you—how did Eddie say it?—a place you invest with your own emotions." She took a shuddering breath, and I heard Brittany Watson hollering outside, her voice amplified by some sort of speaker system, saying something about busting down the door in thirty seconds. "Well, I can't live with what I've done, so I guess this is the end of the road for me. I want to say I'm sorry one more time. I hope you'll find it in your heart to forgive me." The phone clunked down on a hard surface.

"No, no, no," I muttered, even though I knew it

wouldn't do any good. The gunshot blasted through the answering machine's speaker, and I jumped. The machine beeped, signaling the end of Julie's message, as well as the end of her life. I sat on Memaw's bed, arms clutched around myself, shivering and rocking, too shocked to cry any more.

Instead, I fantasized ways I could have helped Julie, helped her realize what was happening before it was too late. The person who did this to Julie had way more experience and probably more supernatural power than I ever would. Julie was gone, and I'd spent the last hours of her life hating her with all my heart. I couldn't believe I'd been so quick to believe the worst of someone who'd been nothing but good to me.

Then my tears came, and I cried for everybody the Mace Treasure had taken from me. My grandfather. My father. My cousin Rae. My childhood sweetheart, Chase Fischer. Eddie and Julie. Dean almost died because of people trying to get to me.

And Memaw.

I'd made so many mistakes. Fighting for Priscilla Herrera's cursed mini treasure chest had made it worse. It left the person behind all this no choice but to try to kill me. This asshole who'd taken away my life had left me no choice but to try to kill him.

First thing I needed to do was find out what was hidden in my lost memories.

Despite the early hour, the temperature was already in the nineties, the humidity skyrocketing the heat index into triple digits. The chore of getting my keys out of the Nova and closing its door plus the hundred-yard walk out to the barn left me tacky with sweat. It tickled its way down my scalp, dripped into my eyes, and stung. Mosquitos lit on my bare arms for a taste of my blood. Trying to ignore the discomfort, I unlocked the sliding door and rolled it open. A cloud of musty, baked air rolled out, and I stepped aside to let it pass.

Inside the barn, I flipped on the overhead lights. They hummed to life but did little to light the nooks and crannies. I placed the two battery powered lanterns I'd wagged out there on top of an old refrigerator and an old dresser and stood with my hand on my hips. If the spell was hidden in something I had when I my father died, it was either out here or gone forever, possibly thrown away by Barbie. I'd moved my childhood stuff to the barn at the onset of teenage coolness and still remembered where most of it was. All I needed to do was remember what I'd loved. Easy as quantum physics.

I tore open a box labeled "Decorations from Peri Jean's Room" and regarded a collection of dusty stuffed animals. I didn't remember any specific connection to any of them and set them aside. Another box revealed clothes I'd never wear again unless someone used a shrinking spell on me. The way my life was going, a shrinking spell might really come into play later. *Better keep them.* I grabbed another box with my name on it and looked for a place to sit.

Being awake for the better part of twenty-four hours

had whipped my ass. I could barely concentrate on the junk in front of me, much less remember something I valued more than a quarter century ago. My body begged for permission to go back in the house and rest. My eyes drooped, and I swayed on my feet.

"Wake up." I pinched my own arm as hard as I could. The jerk who spelled Julie almost got me last night. One more try might be enough to kill me. I halfheartedly looked through two more boxes, these containing children's books and a scattering of well-used toys. I tried to remember myself playing with them, and fatigue rolled through me again. I dropped the box. It bounced off my legs and hit a sheet-covered object lying on the floor. I couldn't remember what it was and stooped to pull off the sheet.

"My dollhouse. I forgot all about this old thing." I'd seen a show or read a book about a little girl who had one, and Memaw had scoured the garage sales until she found this one. Because each piece was sold separately, I never had much store-bought stuff for it. I'd sort of cobbled stuff together. Like the tiny chair Memaw helped me make out of cardboard and a scrap of felt. Or the hot tub I made out of plastic tubing and a butter container. My dolls consisted of several *Star Wars* action figures and a few ratty Glamour Gals, both found at yet another garage sale.

I sat down on the dirt floor and pulled the dollhouse closer, examining it more carefully. If there had been anything I loved as a little girl, it was this dollhouse, but there was no way the forgetting spell was hidden in here. I got the dollhouse after I moved in with Memaw, when I was eight-years-old. My father was murdered when I was four. Then something glinted inside the dollhouse, and I leaned closer, pulling out my keychain and turning on the flashlight attached to it.

I reached inside the dollhouse, not even thinking about black widow spiders and asps, and pulled out something I'd loved ever since I could remember loving anything. The cheap gold plating on the compact had worn off in spots, but the cloisonné black and blue butterfly on the front still looked as beautiful as I remembered. I turned it over and looked at the engraving as I had so many times as a kid.

To Barbie on her 16th. Love Mom and Dad.

I'd always pretended my mother passed down her compact to me. The truth was, I kept playing with the thing, even after she told me not to, and dented it. She'd come to me screaming and raving and threw the thing in my face, the metal cutting my chin. I remembered how ragged and full of grief her voice sounded when she hollered I could just have the fucking thing since I'd fucked it up. I rubbed the scar left by Barbie's tantrum until I realized what I was doing and touched the cool metal to my hot cheek, the way I always had as a child, trying to let it comfort me. Yes, I'd loved this thing no matter how much pain it represented.

The compact started out with a mirror, but it went missing somewhere along the way. By the time I put it in my dollhouse for my dolls to use as a floor-length mirror, I'd glued a cheap mirror pried off a plastic throwaway compact into the place where the original mirror once was. As an adult, I saw my makeshift repair left much to be desired. For one thing, the mirror was crooked. I'd used the compact's powder puff for a throw pillow on the dollhouse's bed, leaving the spot for the powder cake open.

For the first time, I noticed a tiny indention on one side of it. Holding my keychain flashlight in my mouth, I examined the thing more closely. The gold frame could be raised and removed for the powder cake to be placed in the well. The frame would then be popped back down to hold the cake in place. The manufacturer's instructions, smudged beyond reading, sat at the bottom of the well, protected by filthy netting.

The fog lifted from my brain fast as a fart stinks up a car. *Could this be it? Could the forgetting spell be hidden underneath those instructions?* By the time I was four, this compact already belonged to me. My pulse raced, and I used a game piece from an old set of pickup sticks to pry up the frame. *This won't be it. It's too simple.* I lifted out the manufacturer's instructions and sucked in a surprised breath. My luck was in, for once. Sitting there was a folded slip of paper with dirt on the creases.

The black opal tingled on my chest, signaling the paper had magic in it. I reached for it, hesitating as I wondered if touching someone else's spell against me could somehow hurt me. I could go inside the house for a pair of tweezers. *Nah.* My curiosity held the driver's wheel right then. I pinched the paper between my thumb and forefinger, pulled it out of the compact, and unfolded it. On it was the weirdest scrawl I'd ever seen. The words, if they were words, were written in a type of lettering unfamiliar to me.

Julie had said she destroyed the paper she found in her perfume bottle and her memory came right back. I took out my cigarette lighter and lit the corner of the paper. It caught fire faster than I expected, stinking worse than any other burning paper I'd ever smelled. The black opal heated fast on my chest, as though it somehow absorbed the fire, or perhaps responded to something I couldn't see. Smoke drifted up from the burning paper, and the odor of rot filled my senses. I grunted and tossed the paper on the dirt floor, standing close so I could stomp it if the tiny fire got out of hand. The paper curled in on itself, the flames turning green and sparkling, and finally blackened until it was nothing but flakes.

I waited for my memory to come back, holding on to a support beam in case the force of it threw me off balance. Nothing happened. After several minutes, I got bored and gathered the ashes from the paper into my cupped hand and took them outside and buried them. Then I brought the rake back inside the barn and turned the packed earth on the place where I'd allowed the paper to burn. By my estimation, thirty minutes had passed, and still no recovered memory.

A strong gust of wind hit the barn, rattling the rolling door on its track. I went to the opening, scanning the sky for a coming storm. The sky, white with heat and humidity, looked hot but not stormy. Another gust of wind came, rippling my clothes and caressing my skin like the fabric had come to life. The black opal sent painful jolts into my skin, maybe warning me. I was too ignorant of its power to know for sure.

I scanned the world around me and still saw nothing out of the ordinary. The black opal flooded me with a painful tide of energy, rocking me on my feet. Refusing to learn the black opal's signals hadn't helped me stay normal any at all. I'd still lost everything—Dean, my business, Memaw. I thought of Mysti, Brad, and Wade, so comfortable with what they could do and so confident in doing what needed to be done.

What if I learned how to really use the black opal, faced what I am without apology? I'd lose any hope of normalcy. Drama and negative consequences from supernatural shit would taint everything. Keeping the weird stuff on the outskirts of my life left me a little hope of a happy, normal life doing mundane things.

Another gust of wind blew into the barn, making the junk behind me clatter. A sheet or piece of fabric beat against whatever it covered with the intensity of the wind. I stepped outside the barn, expecting to feel a few stray drops of rain against my upturned face. The air hung still and humid, but there was no rain. I turned back to the barn and peered inside. Had the wind been only inside the barn? I debated the merits of going back inside to investigate and had pretty much talked myself out of it when I heard my car start.

What on earth? I ran across the huge yard to the carport and found my car sitting empty, running on its own. I grabbed an old hoe off the pegs sticking out of the wall, found a bare space and pressed my back against it so nobody could sneak up behind me.

"Who's here? I'll whup your ass you don't quit messing with me. See this hoe? I'll use it."

Nobody answered, but another hot wind raged across me, chilling the sweat covering my body. I listened as hard as I could but heard nothing. No birds singing, no frogs hollering, no crickets fiddling. Muscles tensed and ready to fight, I began to shake, trying to hold the fear back and stay alert enough to defend myself. The black opal quivered against my skin. *I wish I knew how to use it, wish I knew the limits of my powers. Fuck being normal.* When shit like this kept happening, normal was beyond my reach anyway.

The driver door to my car swung open. The dirt next to it indented with the weight of an invisible foot. I pressed my back harder against the corrugated tin wall, gaze darting madly for an escape route. Footsteps crunched closer and closer to me. I could climb over the hood of my car and then scoot through the narrow gap between my car and the opposite wall, but I'd have to act fast if I planned to run.

The scrape of a foot against the floor spurred me into action. I clambered over the car, slamming into a stack of plastic buckets and sending them flying. There was barely any room between the car and the wall, but I knew I could squeeze through. I raced forward, heart slamming hard enough to jar my vision. I saw the passenger door of my car opening and knew it was too late to stop but tried anyway and slammed into the door with my side and hip, the hoe digging into my shin.

The collision knocked my own breath out, and I hunched forward, jabbing the wooden hoe handle into my eye, and falling backward. I hit the ground hard but gave myself no time to recover, scrambling to my knees and slapping my hands against the car, groping for anything I could use to pull myself back to a standing position. Icy arms closed around my middle and dragged me to my feet, staying at my back.

"You shoulda stayed outta this. I can't help you." The almost familiar voice came from within my head, part of me but not part of me, and the black opal vibrated with its timbre. The last time I'd heard this voice was at the prison when I visited Jesse, but this wasn't Jesse. It was my father.

My skin tightened against his touch, and a shudder ran through me. I jerked away from him and spun to face him, breathing hard. I saw he held Priscilla Herrera's curse box in one translucent hand. I reached for it, but when my fingers made contact, it shocked me, and I ended up back on the ground, looking up at my father's ghost.

"You can't ignore this. Time to fight or die...like me."

"Who's doing this to you? Tell me, and I'll..." I didn't know what I'd do. Kill someone? Maybe. This person had indirectly killed my grandmother, tried to kill me.

My father's mouth opened to speak, and garbled noise came out. He squeezed his eyes shut, straining against the force controlling him. His words, when they came, shook the air so hard the hair on my arms moved.

"Memory...of the day...I died." Another strong wind whipped through the carport, making the old tools hanging from the walls sway with its force. My father blew away with it like a stray piece of paper, tilting and whirling in its grips until he disappeared from my sight.

I stumbled to the front porch and sat down on the steps. All my effort the last few days, everything I lost, had been for nothing. The curse box was gone, and the asshole had it. If I did nothing, they'd use it to remove the curse from the Mace Treasure and destroy us all while trying to steal the treasure.

Steal it? Those words sounded an awful lot like I thought there was something to steal. If there was, I didn't want the asshole to have it any more than I wanted Priscilla Herrera's spiritual minions to level Gaslight City. Yeah, I hated a lot of people here, but letting them die when I could stop it was not the way Memaw taught me.

Besides, me and the asshole had a score to settle, didn't we? The asshole had killed my father, Eddie, Julie, and my memaw. The asshole tried to kill me. I'd take a pig shit bath before I let the asshole get away with anything else.

My father's ghost said I had to remember. My memory would tell me the identity of the asshole. The information had been hidden in there more than quarter century. All I had to do was find a way to access it.

I'd done what Julie said—burning the paper part of the curse—but there had to be something else. Exactly how could I get at the memories? I wished I could ask my daddy's ghost, but the idea of contacting him scared me after what happened to Mysti. I didn't have time to let the asshole controlling him drive me crazy.

What if I went to the place where my father died? I couldn't be in any more danger there than I was here alone at Memaw's house. The asshole had proven how easy it would be to get to me. I took out my cellphone and wondered who I should call. *I can't call anybody.* It would do nothing but put them in danger, too.

I picked myself up, went out to my car, and started driving.

17

———

THE PLACE where my father died was on a white sand road less than a mile from downtown Gaslight City. While other outlying areas filled up with housing developments or shopping centers, this little hollow stayed wooded and untouched. I passed the remains of Hezekiah Bruce's general store. Long closed, the building listed to one side. The little shack behind it where the family had lived had gone back to the earth with only a stone chimney to prove its existence.

I slowed my Nova to a crawl. I'd always heard the murder site was right past the store, but all I saw was a bunch of trees. The road went on a few hundred more yards before it dead-ended at Lonnie and Amanda King's driveway. Their huge brick mansion surveyed the quiet landscape from a slight rise a quarter mile away. Priscilla Herrera's homesite had to be in the trees somewhere. I stopped the car and looked around.

Local legend trippers considered the place where my

father died a prime destination. The number of tire tracks on the one lane road attested to the place's popularity.

"What a bunch of ghouls." I got out of the car. "Bet they'd shit their underoos if they saw anything real out here." I'd hoped seeing this much would jog my sluggish memory back into gear. No luck. I didn't remember ever being out here.

The rough croak of a bird came through the woods, sounding as though it was right on the other side, in the clearing I'd come to see. I forced myself to take a few steps in its direction but stopped. This was stupid. Somebody needed to know where I was in case the asshole came to get me. I took out my cellphone and tried sending a text message to Hannah, but it came back undeliverable. I took a closer look at my phone's screen and saw the dreaded No Service in the corner. *Maybe I should leave, come back when someone knows where I am. But what if I get them killed too?*

There it was again. The possibility of more blood on my hands. Nope. Not happening. I pushed my way through the thin screen of skinny pines, sweat already rolling down my back, acid burning the back of my throat. Then I was there, in the place I saw in my vision. The little lot bore marks of the legend trippers' passage—empty beer bottles, cigarette butts, and other basic garbage. The cabin I remembered from my vision of the day Priscilla Herrera died still stood and bore surprisingly little damage. All the window frames stood empty, reminding me of sightless eyes, but the cabin's door was closed tight and looked structurally sound. I tried to swallow and almost gagged.

Settle down, girl, I coached myself. *You won't accomplish anything if you don't calm down. Nobody's here but you and maybe some ghosts. And you can't go anywhere without seeing a bunch of damn ghosts.*

I stood still, closed my eyes, and took deep breaths, trying to control my racing heart. When I thought I had myself under control, I opened my eyes and took stock of the clearing. The pine trees surrounding the cabin were old with thick trunks stretching so high I couldn't make out their tops. Pine trees this tall usually clattered and whispered with some kind of breeze, but these trees were still. I didn't hear any of the songbirds I expected to hear this time of day, either. The only life I heard was a sick-sounding croak near the cabin.

I took baby steps in that direction, wanting to see what I'd come to see but not wanting to all at the same time.

I reached the cabin and peeped into one of the windows. The floor was bare, the boards buckled with time and pitted from years of rain coming through a leaky roof. My memory flashed onto the vision of this room neatly swept with a fire burning in the stone hearth and Priscilla Herrera bustling around, getting ready to die at her persecutor's hands.

A glint from something high in the structure's rafters blinded me for a second, and I jumped away from the window, sure the boogeyman had me in his clutches. Then I realized it was just a piece of glass some creepy wannabe had set up there. A car went by on the road outside, noticeably slowing, probably wondering what my car was doing here. I had to hurry if I wanted to do this. Someone would come soon, pretending to be concerned about me, but really wanting to be nosy, wanting to be the first person to have some new gossip about crazy-assed Peri Jean Mace.

I walked around the clearing, looking for anything to jog my memory, but the site had been trampled and examined by a lot of pilgrims before me. Maybe nothing was left here of my father or of the child I'd been the day he died. Then the awful croak came again, this time very near me, almost even with my eyes. I gasped at what I saw.

Someone—either my father or my uncle—hard carved a heart into the trunk of a pin oak tree. Inside were three initials: P, P, J, and the year, 1989. It was the year all three of us died, really. I traced the heart and then the initials with my fingertips, eyes stinging with unshed tears. The awful thing in the trees croaked again, and this time I thought maybe it was a sick crow, probably dying on the poison in this sad place. Then I heard the voice.

"Daddy, is this place haunted?" Footsteps crunched in the leaves and branches on the ground, and two figures came into view. I almost didn't recognize myself. I was so small, my messy black hair pulled back with a silver barrette, and wearing a matching red shirt and pair of shorts with a cartoon character on them. My tiny shoes bore images of the same cartoon character, who I vaguely remembered being my favorite. I had a Band-Aid on my chin.

"Ain't nothing haunted," my daddy put one hand on my back and gave me a gentle push. "Not for you at least. A place that's haunted is a place that's scary. You see them—

the other ones—and understand them. Nothing scary about it."

Judging from the expression on my little face, I wasn't so sure I believed my daddy. Uncle Jesse entered the clearing, carrying a bunch of shovels and picks.

"Where you think she buried these stones?"

"Dunno," Paul said. "Maybe under the floorboards of the house? She coulda dropped 'em down the outhouse." He gestured at a narrow ramshackle building behind the cabin. "You can look in there, Uncle Jesse. Can't he, baby?"

"Yes!" Seeing the expression on my uncle's face, I jumped up and down, screaming with glee. My daddy liked my enthusiasm and laughed too.

"You see anything here?" He leaned down to my eye level to speak to me.

I stared around the small homesite, my dark eyes serious for someone so young. I seemed to know exactly what I was doing, what I wanted to see. *How did I go from the brave little girl to the scared adult I am now?* I marched around my daddy, my little hand forming into a fist with my pointer finger extended.

"Here." I pointed to a spot on the ground where a tree had fallen. "Something's buried under here."

"What?" Jesse asked.

"What the lady wants you to see." I pointed to the cabin, jumping up and down. "She's in there." Sure enough, there was a figure standing inside the cabin. Neither my daddy nor Uncle Jesse seemed to see her.

"Wanna do it?" Paul asked Jesse. "If we can find this treasure, it'll be fifty-fifty. Me and Peri Jean is getting out of here. I ain't keeping my daughter here. Not after her own mother…" Paul glanced down to see little me watching him, eyes big. He put on a big smile. "Let's get to work."

My daddy tried to roll the huge tree off the spot I'd indicated. Jesse pushed too, both brothers grunting. They stopped, both of them breathing hard.

"Got to get a chain, pull this damn thing out of the way," Paul said.

"Chain's back at the house," Jesse said. "I'll go get it. Bring us back some sandwiches too." He walked out of the clearing, and we heard his truck start up.

"You want to go on an adventure with Daddy?" He squatted down in front of me. I'd been busy scratching at the Band-Aid covering my chin and looking into my brand new gold compact. My daddy gently took it from me and repeated his question.

"Will we go to AstroWorld?"

"Sure. Then we'll find some people like you, who'll help you learn to be strong so you can be happy all your life."

"See there? He's lying to you just like he's lying to me. He's not taking either of us anywhere." The nasty, strident voice came from the woods, but neither big me nor little me needed to see the speaker to know who it was. The little version of me grabbed my daddy's hand.

My daddy stood from his crouch just as Barbie came into the clearing from the thick woods on the other side of the cabin. Another young woman with long, blond hair followed her. The way she moved seemed familiar, but I couldn't quite place her until she scraped a stray lock of her hair behind one ear. *Amanda King. So much for Amanda and Barbie barely knowing each other beyond their hair stylist/client relationship.* Daddy and I backed away from them.

"See what I told you?" Barbie yelled at Amanda. "This cheating bastard told me we'd find the treasure and move to a city, and then he told you whatever he told you. But you heard him: his real plan is to find the treasure and use it for her." Barbie, red-faced and screaming by the end of her declaration, pointed at the little version of me.

Daddy glanced down at me and said, "Go back out where we parked. See if Uncle Jesse left the cooler. If he did, get us both something to drink."

"But, Daddy, she's mad," I whined, shifting foot to foot. "She's gonna hit."

Daddy put himself between my awful mother and me and said, "It'll be fine. Go on." The little version of me left the clearing, glancing back fearfully over her shoulder a few times. From my vantage point, I saw the little version of me never really left. She simply walked a little way into the trees and stood very still so she could listen to the fireworks. I could tell by the expression on her face she was scared for her daddy. From what I knew about the events of this awful day, she had every right to be.

"Barbara, I am sorry for you to find out this way." My poor doomed daddy faced his wife, his expression stony. "It is over between us. You're abusive and neglectful to our child and a horrible person in general. I don't want to be with you anymore."

"You obviously don't want to be with either of us." Barbie gestured to Amanda. "We just heard you saying you were going to take Peri Jean away from this place, so it could be you and her against the world."

"Is this true, Paul?" Amanda's mouth turned down and trembled, and she raised a shaking hand to wipe at her nose. Paul turned to face her and his shoulders slumped.

"Amanda, baby, I do care for you, but I need to get by myself for a while and concentrate on my daughter. You're married to somebody else anyway." Paul backed away from Amanda, probably realizing the shit was hitting the fan, and bumped into Barbie who shoved him away but moved so she could stay at his back. I wanted to scream at my daddy to run away from them both but knew it would do no good. I could only watch, whimpering, as the scene unfolded.

"You've been lying to me." Amanda started blubbering, making it hard to understand her. "Saying the three of us were going to leave town and be a family. You never intended to really do it."

Paul held up his hands in surrender. I didn't know my daddy well and never would, but I knew how a man looked when he got caught red-handed.

"You lied to get me to use magic to help you look for treasure clues?" Amanda's tear-filled voice raised to a choked yell. "You lying, cheating son of a bitch." She ran at him, slapping him and clawing his face. Paul raised his hands, trying to ward off Amanda without hitting her. While he was occupied with Amanda, Barbie took a couple of steps forward, removing a folding razor from her pocket. This time I did scream, but none of them acted like they'd heard me. Barbie raised one arm and slit my daddy's throat. He clapped his hand over the spurting geyser of blood and turned to face Barbie, his eyes huge and fear-filled.

"No," Amanda yelled. She ran around Paul and tried to take his arm.

"Get away from him." Barbie pulled Amanda a few feet from Paul. "You'll get blood on your clothes."

"What did you do?" Amanda screamed, bucking in Barbie's grasp, trying to get away from her. "We're going to jail."

"No, we're not," Barbie said. "Joey agreed to help us cover this up. All we have to do is sort of make it look like Jesse did it."

"No, no, no." Amanda put her hands over her face, letting out loud, honking sobs.

"You agreed to this." Barbie shook her finger at Amanda, going into full-on bitch mode.

"No, no, no. I didn't agree to kill him." Amanda shook with her sobs.

"But you did agree to help me get the treasure, and we're about to get it. He was digging right there." Barbie pointed. "I heard him tell Jesse all they needed was chains to pull this tree out of the way. We'll wait until Jesse gets back, incapacitate him—didn't you say you had a spell to do that?—and find the treasure. It'll be over."

The little version of me—oh, how I wanted to not be her—climbed out of the bushes and ran to her father who was still choking on his own blood, dying. She knelt next to him and began weeping. It was the saddest sound I think I've ever heard. The real me, the big me, clapped my hands over my mouth to keep from screaming, even though I knew none of them would ever hear me.

"Shit. I'd forgotten about her. I wish I could forget her forever." Barbie scooped the knife from the ground and walked toward her child.

Amanda grabbed her around the waist from behind, holding her arms away from little me. "I won't let you kill her. No matter how I feel about what Paul did, she's only a little girl."

"She's creepy and weird, and she's ruined my life," Barbie screamed.

"L-l-let's make her forget. I can make a spell where she'll forget even seeing Paul's murder. All I need is something she loves."

"All she loves is Paul and his damn mother," Barbie said.

"What about her little compact?" Amanda said. "There it is lying on the ground. She's always playing with it when you come to get your hair done."

"All right." Barbie went to get the compact. "What do we do?"

Little Peri Jean, realizing something bad was about to happen to her, tried to run from Barbie. The bigger woman caught her after a few steps, grabbing her daughter by the foot and pulling her down. She dragged the screaming child back to Amanda, who watched the whole scene with a pained expression on her face.

Amanda took a slip of paper out of pocket and began writing on it, saying stuff about forgetting. Barbie stopped her.

"How do I know you won't remove the spell to get her to remember so you can send me to jail?"

"You'll hold the focus of the spell, the power that holds it intact." Amanda shoved Barbie's hand off her. "You'll have to make a point to make physical contact with Peri Jean, frequently at first, but later—once this memory would have naturally faded anyway—every ten years or so should do it."

"What about for Jesse? You said you'd make him forget us stealing the treasure from them. The forgetting has to be really good or we can't frame him for killing Paul."

Amanda sagged. "You planned this all along, didn't you? No, don't answer. I see it on your face."

"I can kill you too, keep the treasure all for myself."

Amanda shook her head and kept preparing the spell. Barbie walked over to her and kicked her to get her attention. Amanda spun to face her, red-faced and pissed, but stopped short of giving my mother exactly what she deserved.

"What about Jesse?"

"You'll hold the focus of his spell too. If you can't make physical contact with him, send him letters every once in a while." Amanda took the compact apart and hid the slip of paper inside as she talked. "All we need is some physical item he loves and hopefully won't get rid of, but we can hide the ticket—the spell itself—well enough so it hopefully won't get destroyed even if Jesse gets rid of the item." Amanda touched her hand to little Peri Jean's head, said some words, and the vision ended.

"Find what you were looking for out here, kiddo?"

Barbie's voice came from behind me. I turned, still shaky from the intensity of what I'd seen. She stood in front of me holding an axe handle and grinning. She brought the axe handle up. Fury welled in me, sharp and hot, and I swung one foot out to kick her at the same moment she swung the handle. I don't know where she intended to hit me, but it caught the top of my head. The whole world went white and filled with the sound of the stupid bird croaking, croaking, croaking.

———

HEAD THROBBING, I listened to Barbie and Amanda grunt as they dragged me to the base of a slim tree. They leaned me against it and looped a length of nylon cord around my chest. The rope tightened until it dug into my skin through my shirt.

"Hold her hand out," Amanda said in the same businesslike tone I'd heard her use in her hair salon.

Barbie grabbed my wrists. I struggled against her, but the blow to my head had made me weak, and I ended up slapping at her like a kid in her first playground tussle. She deflected my attempts with no more effort than a fly dodging a flyswatter. I shook my head, trying to get some sense back into myself. It just made me dizzier.

Amanda drew a wickedly long dagger out of a metal sheath attached to her belt. The jewels on its handle winked in the sun, blinding me and making my head hurt even worse. Barbie's grip tightened on my wrists. Realizing what Amanda intended, I knotted my hands into fists.

"Please don't." In my panic, my voice paled to a whisper. "I won't do...I don't know. Please don't."

"Get her hand open, Barbara."

The woman who gave birth to me dropped one of my hands and focused her grip on the other. Fast as a snake striking, she jammed her thumb in the webbing between my clenched middle and ring fingers. It felt like someone was driving a nail into the bones. I gritted my teeth, straining against the pain, until I shook all over. My hand suddenly let go without my permission. Amanda grabbed my fingers and used her dagger to lay open the skin nearly to the bone. Blood slowly welled in the cut, and the first throbs made me mewl. Amanda grabbed an ornate silver goblet and motioned Barbie to hold my hand over it. They milked blood out of my hand. Ashamed of myself, I screamed each time they put pressure on my wound.

"Okay. I think we've got enough," Amanda said. "Tie her wrists so she can't get away and come help me with the rest."

"You said we were going to end her so she couldn't interfere." Barbie, eyes wild, stood over me holding another length of nylon rope. "Why not kill her this second? You've got the blood to unlock the curse."

Kill her this second. I went cold at Barbie's words even though they shouldn't have surprised me. She'd wanted to kill me when I was a little girl. I tried to swallow and almost choked.

"Because I want to collect her spirit. Use it like I have her daddy's. She's much more powerful than he was." Amanda handed the goblet to Barbie, leaned forward, and pulled the black opal necklace over my head. She kissed it and put it on herself. Then she winked at me. I wanted to kick her teeth in.

"Perfect," Barbie muttered and looped the nylon rope around my wrists, pulling it way too tight. My fingers began to tingle almost immediately. The pain from my hand wound and the discomfort from my bonds swept some of the fog out of my head. I waited until she had some tension and yanked my arms, throwing her off balance. She kicked me in the stomach twice. I brought my knees up too late to deflect the kicks and shuddered as the pain spread through me, aching in my bowels. It felt like she'd implanted a fiery ball in my belly, and it weighed six hundred pounds. Barbie wrapped my wrists with the precision of a rodeo barrel racer and sneered in my face. "You ain't the only one who can win a fight, Peri Jean."

I sneered right back and said, "We ain't done...*Mom*."

She raised her eyebrows in challenge.

"Leave her alone." Amanda walked across the home-site to the path where I'd entered. "I have to draw these dimming symbols in the road and on the path so people'll drive on by."

"I'm not helping you do magic. That's not the deal we made."

"I'm not asking you. I'm telling you this is what we have to do—and fast—if we want to take care of our business here. If we don't remove the curse, we'll never find the trea-sure, and we'll both die penniless. Sound fun to you?"

Barbie followed Amanda grumbling, and the two of them used sticks to draw something in the white sand,

Amanda speaking in a low voice and sprinkling water on the drawings. They came back to where they'd tied me, and Amanda began setting up a spelling area. I recognized some of the things she did from the night I helped Mysti.

"You two murderers are still looking for the treasure after all these years?" I struggled against my ties, letting them grind into my skin as I tested their strength and wilting when there wasn't any give at all. There had to be a way out of this. Had to.

"Your mother only found out half the story before she killed your daddy. She never has the patience to plan things out. Everything's done on impulse." Amanda rolled her eyes at the heavens.

She returned her attention to her altar and set a worn, leather-bound book next to the mini treasure box she'd stolen from me. Priscilla Herrera's spell book. I recognized it from my vision. Amanda must have managed to remove the glamour making it appear to simply be a book of folk remedies. She opened it and ran her finger down the page. She placed the cup of my blood and the dirty dagger on the opposite side of the makeshift table. Then she turned to me, crossing her arms over her chest. "Your father was looking for Priscilla Herrera's spelling stones the day Barbie killed him, not the actual treasure." Amanda paused to glare at Barbie, disgust pulling her mouth down. "Paul told me he thought Priscilla buried them here on the home place before she was taken to town and hanged."

I didn't have to ask if my father's theory had been wrong. I knew the answer. The stones were wherever

Priscilla Herrera's body rested unless someone had cut them out of her stomach.

"What was under the tree then?" I remembered my insistence the lady in the cabin wanted us to see what was buried under the tree.

"A big-assed dead bird," Barbie said. "Soon as we dug it up, a bunch of crows—"

"They were ravens," Amanda said.

"Who gives a shit?" Barbie yelled. "A bunch of big, ugly black birds came down on us like the wrath of God." She pulled up her three-quarter sleeve and walked over to me. "Bit me here. Still got the scar. See?"

I turned my head to look, and she popped me across the cheek with her open hand and hissed her sour breath into my face. "I know you made it happen somehow."

I kicked out at her, wanting so badly to do her harm. She danced away and used her foot to sling dirt in my direction. It peppered my face, and I spat, which did nothing to clear the grit from my mouth.

"You're not going to remove the curse without the spelling stones. I saw Priscilla Herrera do the curse in my vision." I knew I might have been telling too much, but I'd do anything to stall the proceedings. I didn't want to see what would really happen if Amanda managed to separate the dark spirits from the mini-treasure chest.

"*You* accessed a vision of what happened the day she died?" Her gaze sharpened and fastened onto me. She shook her head. "If you weren't so stubborn, we could work together instead of this." She clicked her tongue and shrugged. "I don't think I need the stones. The spell book says she used blood to seal—or protect—the spell. I'm going to use your blood to unseal it."

"What do you think is going to happen once the curse is unsealed?" I heard the tremor in my voice as I imagined every kind of hell breaking loose.

"The entities Priscilla Herrera attached to the treasure to carry out the parameters of the curse will be detached from it." She paused to light her candles.

"You're forgetting I saw her attach them. She gave them instructions to destroy Gaslight City and everybody in it if anybody but her detached them. You're going to kill us all."

"No." She turned to me, and the expression on her face chilled the August heat away in an instant. "Just you. I can use your blood to detach them from the treasure *and* to attach them to you all at once."

Vertigo spun me. If the ropes hadn't been holding me up, I'd have fallen. I hung there, ropes holding me up, and a wild hope hit me. Maybe I could lie my way out of this.

"It's not going to work." I said the words like I believed them. "The curse Hezekiah Bruce wrote about left out one big detail that I saw in my vision. The person who removes the curse has to have Priscilla Herrera's blood. Mace blood might be needed to find the treasure, but Herrera blood is needed to remove the curse." I widened my eyes for emphasis. "My blood isn't going to help you."

Amanda smiled at me, eyes crinkling at the corners. "It really is too bad I'm going to kill you. You think fast under pressure."

"I figured out you were the Herrera heir when I eavesdropped on your conversation with Julie at the antique store, you nitwit." Barbie pursed her lips and shook her head at me. "That's why I asked about your ugly fucking tattoo."

Her words washed away the last of my hope. I bit my lip because I didn't want to cry in front of her.

"Look at this way, Peri Jean. You're not dying in vain. Amanda and I'll have access to all the clues Reginald Mace hid around town—I'm talking about the real clues, not the false paths." Barbie clapped her hands and hurried into the cabin. Amanda watched her go, the expression on her face wary. Barbie came back out holding a small piece of glass in her hand. As she got closer, I saw it was a mirror, and not just any mirror. It was the missing mirror out of my compact. She held it out to me. I winced away, not understanding what it was or what she meant to do with it.

"So your daddy can watch what happens to his precious baby."

Her meaning sank in. My lost hope came back as red fury. My jaw clenched. I wanted to put my hands around her throat and squeeze the life out of her. Both of them.

Just as Amanda had used one part of the butterfly compact to imprison my memory, she'd used another part —the mirror—to trap my daddy's spirit. Barbie, the poisonous bitch, perched the mirror at the fork of two branches and angled it to reflect my face. She studied her work, almost smiling, and nodded. The ice in my veins melted and boiled. I would not die without a fight.

"You might kill me, but Rainey and Hooty and Hannah are going to want to know who did it. Eventually, they'll figure out it was you two losers."

"We're going to make your death look like the work of a certain group of motorcycle riders," Amanda said. "I've gotten better at framing people over the years and no longer need the cops to look the other way." She smirked at Barbie, who glared right back.

While they fought their silent fight, I focused on the black opal hanging around Amanda's neck. It was my only hope. Most of the time, it followed wherever I went. I used my will to pull at it. Nothing happened.

"Your friends will be furious over your death." Amanda slipped me a wink, as though she knew exactly what I had in mind. "They'll forget all about the Mace Treasure long enough for us to find it and be gone."

"I know why Barbie wants the money. Her husband finally figured out he married the human equivalent of a black widow spider and got away while he still could." I knew my time was running out. I had to stall things. I screwed up my face at Amanda. "Why do you want to mess with the treasure? You're rich."

"We were," she said. "Lonnie's death did me in. I had no idea how to run King Ranch Chicken, so I hired somebody. The prick embezzled from the company. I'm on the verge of declaring bankruptcy and closing the doors. I doubt King Ranch Chicken will last another six months."

"I've wanted you dead since I found out I was pregnant with you." Barbie's eyes glittered with hate. "I can't wait for this."

"Fuck you." I wanted to beat Barbie until she couldn't even grunt when I hit her. All these years, and I never realized the bitch had been the one to rob me of my father.

Barbie slapped me hard enough for my teeth to cut the inside of my mouth. I spat blood in her face. She backed up and kicked me in the thigh, making the muscle seize. I writhed in pain and glared at her, wishing I could turn my hate into a death ray.

"Stop it," Amanda yelled. "Let's start the spell. Come over here and help me."

"Wait, please." My breath came in gasps, and a light-headedness had me so dizzy my thoughts were like helium balloons, floating off into the distance.

"Wait for what?" Amanda turned her back to me and dripped some of my blood on the mini treasure chest. The air in the little clearing came to life with power, as though Amanda had flipped a switch. A thunder of bird wings flapping filled my ears, and dozens of black shapes lighted in the trees. Amanda craned her neck to look at them, her face turning white. Barbie shifted foot to foot, no longer focused on my fear and discomfort. The skin on my face had the pins and needles feeling I associated with a numb appendage. My raven tattoo flamed to life, itching as though it was brand new, even though I'd had it the better part of a decade. Amanda took her attention off the birds and went back to her altar, her movements hurried and clumsy.

"As my power meets Priscilla Herrera's curse and Reginald Mace's treasure, I release the guardians of darkness to go into this blood and its source, consuming it as your reward." She closed her eyes and leaned back her head, repeating the words until they assumed an odd rhythm and made no sense.

The mini treasure box popped open, issuing the black smoke I remembered seeing when I solved my cousin Rae's murder. The smoke curled and snaked around Amanda, making her hair move around her shoulders.

A distant shouting drew my attention away from the scene in front of me. Hoping someone somehow knew where I was, I peered into the thick woods. I heard the shout again and realized it was coming from somewhere closer. Remembering the mirror in which Amanda had trapped my father's spirit, I turned my gaze onto it. Paul's tiny figure beat at the glass from the inside, shouting something the distance between our dimensions kept me from hearing. If I'd had the black opal, maybe I could have heard him, but Amanda had it.

I tried again to will the black opal to me, straining with the effort until I shook. All I did was make the ravens holler louder. Amanda had to be using some kind of magic to keep the thing around her neck. Any other time, I'd have it as soon as I thought of it.

My daddy's faint voice reached my ears again. I turned back to the mirror to see what he wanted. He did a crazy dance, running around and flapping his arms. Maybe the prospect of watching me die had driven him mad. I was mad too, but mine was the kind where I wanted to give out knuckle sandwiches.

Amanda stood very still, eyes still closed, the black smoke wreathing her and moving around her like a pet snake. She'd taken everything from me. My relationship. My grandmother. Even my black opal. She'd attacked me and stole the cursed box. All so she could have the Mace

Treasure. The treasure my family hid. The treasure my ancestor, Priscilla Herrera, cursed and died for. I'd die for it if Amanda had her way.

There she stood, preparing to take it all, as though it was hers by rights, and there was nothing I could do to stop her. I strained against my bonds again to see if they'd loosened. No such luck.

"Listen to me, guardians of the darkness. I release you from this task," Amanda, the queen of stinky butt crack, intoned.

She'd take the treasure like it was hers all along, and there was nothing I could do. Was there? I glanced back at the mirror. My daddy stood where I could see him, still flapping his arms. The raven's calls echoed from above me, as though reminding me just who the hell I was. Peri Jean Mace, by God, freak extraordinaire.

The black opal swung at Amanda's neck, sparkling with magic. I mentally reached out to it again. Maybe I could use its power even if it hung around someone else's neck. The sharp static of its magic connected with me in answer. *Amanda better get ready. I'm about to throw some fuckery her way.*

I might not have had training in casting magical spells, but Mysti said it was more about intent than anything else. I shut my eyes and concentrated on the thrum of power filling the clearing, the burn of magic from the black opal, and said the first thing I could think of.

"I, Peri Jean Mace, claim the magic set forth by Priscilla Herrera, my ancestor, because the Mace Treasure is mine by rights and by blood. I order the guardians of darkness to attack this trespasser and to punish her for trying to steal from me."

Amanda began to yell her incantation over mine, her voice strident and panicked. I responded by yelling back, repeating myself until my throat was raw. Soon, I noticed the flaw in my plan. Every time Amanda spoke, the black opal's power waned. She used it to fuel her magic too. I had to get it back. I concentrated on the power, pulling it as hard as I could.

"I want my damn black opal back," I screamed.

Barbie yelled at me to shut up. I opened one eye to see her rearing back to kick me again. Behind her my daddy jumped up and down in the mirror, punching at it, trying to break it. I braced myself and took Barbie's kick in my shin. Bitch kicked hard. The blow took my breath away and made me shudder.

"I want my black opal back," I screamed again and imagined it around my neck.

A black shape flew out of the trees and descended on Amanda, wingspan hiding what it was doing. Amanda howled in pain and fury, her arms pin-wheeling. The bird let out a squawk and flew away from her. It swooped down, diving toward me. Something hit my hand. I took my eyes off the bird and saw the black opal sitting there. Closing my eyes, I imagined the mirror smashing into a million little pieces and concentrated on the image until I heard a loud crack right near my head.

The shards of the mirror caught sunlight and sparkled as they dropped to the ground. Barbie's eyes widened and rounded, her mouth dropping open. It would have been funny had I not seen the figure of a man rising from the broken glass. Paul doubled up his fists and charged in Barbie's direction. She ran from him, and he followed. A figure stood at the door of the cabin, watching it all. She turned her head to stare at me, and her voice cut through the black opal's static in my head.

"Keep saying it. Don't let the other witch recover."

I did. I repeated my made-up incantation again and again, while Barbie ran around screaming her empty head off.

"I, Peri Jean Mace, claim the magic set forth by Priscilla Herrera, my ancestor, because the Mace Treasure is mine by rights and by blood. I order the guardians of darkness to attack this trespasser and to punish her for trying to steal from me."

The black smoke, which at first seemed to caress Amanda like a pet, changed before my eyes. It churned around her, tightening and squeezing as her eyes filled with horror and pain. She opened her mouth to scream, but her cheeks caved in, and her skin began to dry and flake.

Barbie sprinted around the cabin several times and was running out of steam. She stopped and gasped for breath, and Paul's ghost jumped on her back. His see-through arms merged with hers. She shook him the way a dog shakes water off his back, but he hung on. My mother saw me watching.

"Peri Jean, sweetie, come help momma. I know you can do it." The tears streamed down her face, but she tried to smile. "Please?"

"You tied me up." I pushed against the bonds to show her. But the truth was, I wouldn't have helped her even if I could have. She hated me. No matter what she promised, the time would come when I wound up dead by her hand.

Paul gained the upper hand and began to pull her into the earth an inch at a time. She whipped her arms and legs, her struggles only digging her deeper. The earth covered first her feet, then her calves, and rode up to her thighs like the swell of a gritty sea.

"You useless little brat. Use your magic to get loose and help me. Peri Jean Mace! I am talking to you." Her eyes rolled from me to the dirt covering her and back again. Then the earth was over her torso and touching her collarbone. Her glare locked on me. "I wish I'd had an abortion. You weren't worth any of it."

She threw up her head and keened at the sky until a mouthful of dirt cut it off. The most horrifying part was the last few seconds view of the top of her head, the gray at the roots reminding me this was a human being. I wondered what she thought about as she choked to death on dirt. At the last second, a ghostly hand reached up from the dirt and pushed her the rest of the way under.

Heart pounding, fighting the blackness at the corners of my vision, I turned back to Amanda. One pain-filled eye rolled to stare at me. The black smoke had sucked her dry until she looked like she was the one dying of cancer. Something pulled my gaze back to the figure in the doorway of the cabin.

"Finish it," said the disembodied voice in my head. I took a deep breath and yelled the words again.

"I, Peri Jean Mace, claim the magic set forth by Priscilla Herrera, my ancestor, because the Mace Treasure is mine by rights and by blood. I order the guardians of darkness to attack this trespasser and to punish her for trying to steal from me."

The ravens flew from the trees, seeming to number in the hundreds. They swarmed around Amanda, pecking at her flaking skin, eating bits of her. I had to turn away when one of them ripped out her eyeball.

A heavy hand fell on my shoulder. My body jolted, using the last bit of adrenaline I had left. I screamed. It was girly, and it was weak, but I was too tired to keep myself from it.

"It's all right." Wade Hill pulled a butterfly knife out of his pocket, flipped it open, and sawed at my bonds. "I'm here. I got you."

He cut through the ropes and unwound me, dragging me a short distance from the melee. We crouched together watching in horror as the ravens consumed the rest of their meal, croaking at each other. I checked the cabin to see if Priscilla Herrera's ghost still watched, but it was empty. I hoped she was gone for good but would bet my last twenty dollar bill she'd be back.

The ravens consumed all there was to eat of Amanda King, fighting over the leftover bits. They flew away a couple at a time until only one remained. He watched me out of one eye, the way birds do, tilting his head at me.

"Thank him," Wade whispered.

I gave the bird a nod of appreciation, and it flew away. The old homesite felt different than when I first stepped foot into it an eternity ago. It felt almost peaceful, no longer a haunted, spooky place, but just an old place with an abandoned house on it.

"We've got to clean up this mess," Wade said.

There was really not much left to show Amanda or Barbie had ever been to the site. Amanda's candles and her goblet and dagger went into the Nova's trunk. I'd figure out what to do with them later. I knew I didn't want to keep them. No telling what kind of evil she'd managed with them. Wade and I packed my belongings—the cursed mini treasure chest and the spell book—into the passenger seat of my car.

"Do you think we can break into Amanda's house? She must have Eddie's treasure notes. If I don't get them now, it'll end up being an ordeal."

"What makes you think I know how to break into anybody's house?" He frowned at me.

"Please." I rolled my eyes at him. "She lives at the end of this road. Nobody'll see us."

Turned out, we didn't need to break in. We let ourselves in the unlocked front door. The state of things indicated Amanda'd left in a hurry. She must have felt it when I broke the memory spell and come running.

We found Eddie's research trunk and the Bruce family's journals in Amanda's study and carried them out to my car. I didn't want any stuff belonging to me or my friends to ride in the trunk with Amanda's candles and dagger and goblet, so I returned those to her study. By the time I came back out, Wade had Eddie's trunk in my car. Neither of us spoke on the ride back to his motorcycle. He started to get out of the car, but I grabbed his arm to stop him.

"How'd you find me?" I turned to Wade.

"Last year when I lost you, it scared the shit out of me." He pulled a muslin bag out of his pocket and waved it at me. "I made this little bag as sort of a homemade tracking device."

"What's it got in it?"

"You," he said. "Beyond that, you don't want to know."

"That why the Six Guns call you Mojo?" I gave him my patented Don't Fart In My Car glare. "And don't say it's a trade secret."

He leaned his head back on the seat rest and stared at me, his eyes hooded. A long silence passed. He swallowed hard. "Yeah. Some of it."

I took my hand off his arm, and we went our separate ways.

18

———

On the way home, I made a stop by Eddie's trailer and used my key to let myself in. Breaking the mirror where Amanda had trapped my father set him free. If Eddie was trapped in the mirror where I saw him, I wanted to do the same for him. I walked through the stifling tin can, the smell of mildew nearly overpowering me, and stopped short at the end of the hall. The remains of the antique mirror lay on the carpet in sparkling shards as though something had burst out of it.

"Eddie? Did you hang around?"

No answer. The hurt welled up inside me and overflowed. I slumped back to the front door, tears spilling down my cheeks. Everything I loved and cherished was lost to me. I closed my hand on the doorknob's warm metal, and a freezing hand fell on my shoulder.

"Loved you like you's my own," said Eddie's voice. The hand squeezed.

I spun to face him, to say all I needed to say, but he was already gone.

I drove home crying and sat in my car a long time after I got there. The house looked so empty and deserted. Finally, I made myself go inside.

The numbness I felt right after Memaw's death returned in full force. I couldn't manage to do any more than to go sit in Memaw's room, looking at her things, and wishing she were with me again. My phone beeped, and I realized I'd been hearing and ignoring its intermittent beep for hours. I had a dozen missed calls and four messages, most of them from Hannah. I needed to call her but wasn't ready yet.

My body felt like it had gone ten rounds with an iron gorilla. Scratches and bruises covered every visible inch of skin. The hand Amanda gashed to do her spell throbbed. I needed to find my own way to close the cut or go to the hospital and get stitches. However bad my body felt, my mind hurt worse. It snarled like a hundred snakes with their tails tangled. Past events flashed before my eyes, making more sense than ever, my reaction to some of them causing me great shame. I hunched over and hugged myself but found no comfort.

The boom of a vehicle's door slamming pulled me from my pity party, and I caught a glimpse of myself in the mirror over Memaw's dresser. Tear streaks shone on my cheeks. Someone knocked on the door. I rushed to answer, rubbing the tears off my cheeks and wishing I could ignore the knock.

I opened the door to find Wade Hill on my porch.

"Did you forget something?"

"No." He picked up two suitcases. "I'm here to stay. I'm your new roommate." He came toward me, and all I could do was step out of his way or get run over.

"No, you're not. I don't want a roommate." I followed him down the hallway where he stood in the open doorway of my bedroom.

"I'll take this one. I'm afraid I'll ruin your grandmother's furniture."

"But I don't want a roommate," I repeated.

"Read this." He pushed an envelope at me and headed back out the door, probably to bring more of his crap into my house. I tore open the envelope, recognizing the handwriting immediately. Tears stung my eyes as I read.

Peri Jean,

If you're reading this, I am dead. I hope my dying went quick and didn't cause you too much trouble. I know my time is about up because even I, who can't see ghosts like you can, have caught glimpses of your grandfather wandering around, waiting to help me make the passage. George was such a nice man. I've missed him greatly and am looking forward to seeing him once more.

Now let's get down to business.

First thing's first, let Wade move in. Please. His special gift gave me a few extra months with you. This was the only way I knew to repay him. Took me forever to get him to agree, but I know he needs this. Now, I can no longer force you to do anything you don't want to do, but I wish you'd at least give it a try. I think the two of you could be good for each other. If you don't kill each other being stubborn.

This second thing's a little harder.

You know what's funny about life, my beautiful grand-daughter? You've got things you know you ought to do. You've got plenty of time to do those things. But you end up letting the clock run down and never do them. If I could offer you any one piece of life advice, it would be to do it all before it's too late. Experience everything you can, even if it ends up making you want to curl up in a ball and die.

I am telling you this because it goes against everything I taught you ever since I took custody of you. After seeing what I saw growing up, hearing my parents' stories, and then seeing it happen to you when you told your schoolmates about seeing Adam Kessler's ghost, I thought the way to protect you was to teach you to hide what you are.

You were such a good student. You built a wall around your-self and did everything you could to keep people out. I thought this was the truth of your existence. It made me sad because I knew most people would never understand how special and kind you are, but I thought your survival depended on keeping yourself separate.

Then your cousin got murdered, and you took it on yourself to solve the murder. Somehow, your wall started crumbling then, and people started coming in. I could see how special you were to them and how special they were to you.

Then I saw the way you tried to make yourself normal for these friends of yours. Especially for Dean.

(Another thing I know if you have this letter in your hands is you and Dean are finished. I don't know how it happened, but I can guess why.)

I wanted so much to tell you to just be yourself and let Dean work out his own issues. I couldn't because you were right in the middle of being in love with him, and the timing was wrong. He needed you to be a certain way so he could love you. If you were willing to try, who was I to preach at you? I spent my entire adult life trying not to be the person I was born as.

Since you and Dean are finished, let me tell you what I wanted to tell you the whole time you were with him.

Be who you are without apology. Never, ever let someone else try to change the core of what you are. Just like a tiger can't change his stripes, you will never change being able to communicate with the spirit world. You have more otherworldly power than anybody I've ever seen, including my mama. Don't ruin your life trying to be what someone else thinks you ought to be. Learn who you are and live your life for you.

I've done my best to keep you away from my family for your own good. But if you want to learn who you are, they might be a good place for you to start. Look for them, and you'll find each other. If you're going to do this, be careful. Listen to your inner voice. Look for danger and run if you see it coming.

Third thing. Your uncle Jesse said he told you about the tattoos. It is a mark many members of my family carry. My mama told me our family had a long relationship with the raven, going back before her family ever came to this country. She believed the birds brought her messages from the spirit world. She said sometimes they offered protection. When I was growing up, they were always around, even when we lived places ravens weren't supposed to be.

When I grew up and moved away from my family, I left behind the ravens too. I never saw them again until you were born. Then they came, looking in the window at you, watching you play. I shooed them away, even shooting at them. Finally, they stayed away. My life is drawing to a close, though, and I see them more and more. Make your own choice about your kinship with them. It's in your blood.

Love now and forever, my darling girl,

Memaw

Wade tromped into the house with a box of junk, stopping to stare at me, asking me silently if he could stay. I simply stared at him, too shocked and tired to commit to anything. He went to my bedroom. I followed and watched him put down the box, which held books. Lots of them.

"I don't want a roommate," I said again.

"You've said that twice now." He opened one of my dresser drawers and made a face at the clothes inside. "I can help you move your stuff into Miss Leticia's room if you want."

"I don't want—"

"A roommate," he finished. "Even if Miss Leticia—your memaw—hadn't insisted on this arrangement, it would be a cold day in hell before I left you out here in the woods to walk around like a zombie. Let me stay a month, get you through the worst of this. If either of us hates it, I'll go."

Anger flashed over me. Finally, an emotion I knew how to express. I marched into the room, yanking a drawer out of the dresser and carrying it into Memaw's room and dumping it on the bed.

"Don't get mad at me." Wade followed me through the house and into Memaw's room. "I know this is a big change. Like I said, if either of us hates it, I'm gone." He turned me in his arms and held me tight. I pushed against him at first, but he wouldn't let go, so I gave up and let him hold me. I laid my head on his chest and breathed in his scent. Sunshine, open road, and gasoline. I closed my eyes and hugged him back. We separated, and I sat on the bed. Wade sat on Memaw's vanity bench. He looked like a gorilla on a tricycle.

"Why do you need a place to stay?"

He shrugged.

"You're not going to tell me."

"Miss Leticia said you'd have a hard time keeping up this place alone, and she hated to think about you out here alone after she was gone."

There was more to it than he was telling. Memaw's letter implied she believed she was doing Wade a favor. I let it go for the moment because I didn't have the energy to fight with him. Whatever the reasons Wade needed a place to live, Memaw'd been right. The cost of maintenance on an old house would be too much for me alone. I still wasn't sure I wanted to live with Wade. His Six Gun Revolutionaries stuff aside, I wasn't sure what he expected from a female roommate.

"Don't expect me to clean up after you, do your laundry, or cook for you. I'm not your maid—" I broke off as another thought crept into my mind, this one more primal. I stared at the tuft of black hair peeking out of the collar of Wade's shirt and inhaled his musky scent.

"I don't expect any of it." He gave me a raunchy grin accompanied by a stinky wink. "Or the other you're thinking about but are too chicken to say."

"You don't know what I'm thinking." My cheeks burned at being caught, but I'd never admit to it.

"It is all over your face." He laughed. "You could never play poker. Listen to me. I want friendship more."

I gave up and went into the bathroom. I washed the grime off the cut on my hand. The wound hung open. It needed stitches. To hell with that. I wasn't going back to the hospital. I glanced at the door. Wade could heal it.

Then I thought about him puking off the stage the night before. The magic had been hard on him, maybe even hurt him. No. I could handle this myself.

I dug under the sink until I found a bottle of alcohol. Jaw clenched, I poured it onto the cut, taking shallow breaths until I knew I wouldn't scream. Once I could move, I took a much needed shower. I looked like I'd crawled out of a grave and smelled worse. It was time for the bad part.

I removed the brand new tube of super glue I kept for this purpose from the medicine cabinet and cut off the top. Gritting my teeth, I pushed the edges of the cut together, and spread the glue over it. This burned a thousand times worse than the alcohol. I used every ounce of my self-control to not let even a single moan escape. When the glue was dry, I bandaged the hand.

Wade coaxed me into cleaning out the rest of Memaw's clothes and personal belongings. While her bedclothes washed and dried, we polished all her furniture and cleaned the floor. By the time we remade the bed, the room was like a new place. I moved what little I owned in there and took a long, slow look around.

I'd always loved this bedroom furniture. It had much

more character than the cheap, mass-produced particle-board set in my old room. Wade got one of his books and sat down at the kitchen table, smoking and reading.

Someone knocked on the door. Wade stood faster than I thought a man his size capable and put one hand under his jacket. Who was he expecting?

I turned on the porch light and opened the door. Hooty and Rainey and Hannah stood on the porch, their faces drawn and long. I shifted on my feet, suddenly too hot. I should have called one of them.

"I'm sorry to barge in on you like this." Hannah drew me into a hug. "I know what happened with Dean."

"It's all over town, of course." Rainey made a face and shook her head.

"We wanted to give you your space," Hooty said. "Then none of us ever heard anything. We were worried." He tapped a file on his leg. "Plus, I need to look over Miss Leticia's funeral arrangements with you."

"Come in." I held the door open.

They filed in. Hannah's eyes widened at the sight of Wade sitting in the kitchen smoking and reading. She raised her eyebrows and cocked her head to one side. If I hadn't felt so shitty, I'd have laughed. Neither Hooty nor Rainey showed any reaction to Wade. Either they'd seen so much weirdness from other people in their lives they didn't care, or Memaw had spoken to them about her plans. Wade nodded at our visitors but went right back to his book.

"I've got something for the two of you," I said to Hooty and Rainey and left the room. I came back carrying

Hezekiah Bruce's journals. Father and daughter leapt to their feet, faces split in smiles. Their voices tumbled over each other as they asked too many questions at once.

I tried explaining what happened. At the end of my story, all three of my friends sat in stunned silence.

"Should we call the sheriff's office?" Hannah asked. "Tell them what happened to Amanda and Barbie?"

Rainey pressed her lips together and glared at Hannah. "What do you think the answer really is? We can't tell anybody what happened to them."

"Eventually, they'll be reported missing," Hooty said. "We're all likely to be questioned."

"We'll work it out when we get to it," Rainey said. "No need to worry about something we can't change."

"If it's settled, I have something I need to tell the three of you."

Three sets of eyes focused on me, all wary about what I might say next.

"When I was fighting for my life in that clearing, I realized something." I took a deep breath, still unsure about what I was about to say. "I want to find the Mace Treasure. People are never going to quit hunting it. Some of them are bad people, willing to kill over it. I can't live with anybody else I love getting killed over some money that might or might not exist." Thing is, for the first time in my life, I thought it did exist. Maybe it had never been found because the best camouflage in the world—magic—was used to hide it. My takeaway from this whole ordeal was that I had the talent to find it.

Hannah smiled. "I'm going to help you."

"I am too," Hooty said. "We'll either put the myth to rest or get rich."

"I'm in," Rainey said.

Wade ignored us all, still pretending to read his book. I didn't blame him.

Hooty showed me Memaw's funeral plan, and I signed off on it, tears streaking down my cheeks. My friends said their goodnights and left soon afterward. I followed Rainey to her car, ignoring Hannah's curious stare.

"Barbie and Amanda killed my daddy. Uncle Jesse can't stay in jail for it." I put my hand on the door of her Mercedes so she couldn't jump in and drive away. She closed her eyes and exhaled through her nose.

"I've been working on his case since I passed the bar," she said. "I don't want him there any more than you do, but to get him out, we have to prove he didn't kill your father."

"But I'm standing here telling you who did it." I wanted to shake her.

"There's nobody left to back up your story. You killed them." Her dark gaze searched my face.

"I didn't kill anybody. They made bad choices, and they paid." I took my hand off her car door and let her get in.

"They're still dead. No court can hear their testimony." She started the engine and turned to me. "Believe me when I say I want to help your uncle as much as do you do. Keep thinking. I'm listening."

"There might be something in the police file. You know it's missing?"

Rainey nodded, closing her eyes.

"Sheriff Joey—I mean ex-Sheriff Joey's got it." My anger

flamed up at the very thought. "If I can figure out where he's hiding it—"

"I'm willing to listen to any *legal* ideas you have to help your uncle." Rainey took her eyes off me and started her car.

I snapped my fingers. "My uncle Jesse said to tell you hi."

Rainey said nothing. She didn't even look at me. But I thought I saw her cheeks darken before she grabbed the car door and shut it. She took off fast enough to spin her tires.

Interesting and definitely not my business. Staring out at the silhouettes of the pine trees in the moonlight, I lit a cigarette. Movement on the porch caught my eye. I turned, thinking Wade had come out after all. The soft glow coming from the living room windows made my daddy's ghost look even more transparent than he already was. He stood there, hands in the pockets of his jeans, watching me. Then he smiled, hopped off the edge of the porch, and disappeared around the side of the house. I ran to see where he'd gone and saw him pass through the chain-link fence, walking toward the dark woods. He glanced over his shoulder and blew me a kiss. He kept on walking.

Tears stung my eyes, and all the things I never got to say to him flooded my mind. I held it in and let him go. There was time. My ability to see ghosts cursed me, stigmatized me, made my life a kind of hell. But it also blessed me. Because of it, I got a second chance to have a relationship with my daddy.

I went back in the house. Wade sat at the kitchen table,

reading and smoking and not talking. My aching body demanded I go to bed, but once I got there I couldn't sleep. I kept thinking about the way the right path had been in front of me all along, and I refused to see it. I was what I was. No pretending or wishing would ever change it. Time to be a big girl and face it, if for no other reason than to protect the people I loved.

My phone buzzed, signaling I had a text message. I turned on one of Memaw's glass bedside lamps, making the crystals jingle together, and picked up my phone. It said I had a message from Dean.

I handled things wrong. Can I come over so we can talk?

I thought it over. *There's really no need.*

I turned off the cellphone before he could answer and clicked off the lamp. The dark and the quiet did nothing to slow my mind. Thoughts sped through it like a runaway train. Several minutes passed. I flicked the lamp back on, got Mysti Whitebyrd's card out, and stared at it. I turned my cellphone back on and started dialing.

Keep reading for an excerpt of the next Peri Jean Mace Ghost Thriller.

REST STOP (EXCERPT)

PERI JEAN MACE GHOST THRILLERS #4

I reached for my iced latte, an hour old and mostly water, and fumbled it. It tipped toward the immaculate floorboard of Mysti Whitebyrd's Toyota Camry. She grabbed the paper cup before it could capsize and pushed it into my hand.

"Nervous, Peri Jean?" She turned off the radio, a relief since the Tyler-based station spat more static than music two hours north of its origin.

Nervous didn't cover it. I spent the eight years after my divorce developing my ability to do odd jobs into a lucrative business only to lose it all in the course of twenty-four hours. Venturing into uncharted career territory using my ability to communicate with the spirit world scared the life out me.

"Maybe you should let Brad do this." The few séances I'd done for Mysti's witch-for-hire business did little to make me feel prepared to contract for an actual missing persons investigator.

"Hell, no. My brother, much as I love him, doesn't have the talent to do this job." Mysti pulled her wild, sun-bleached brown hair into a butterfly clip and examined herself in the visor mirror. "He's careless, and he complains all the time. Griffin Reed insists on complete professionalism from his contractors."

What if I don't measure up? I still had hope I could use my curse to make money. Griffin Reed could dash those hopes all to hell. What then? Slinging fried chicken at a gas station?

"Stop worrying. You hear me?" She took her gaze off my face and read the road signs. "Our turnoff's coming up." She pointed at a green sign reading "Nazareth" with an arrow pointing right.

I turned onto a cracked and buckled state highway and immediately saw another sign for Nazareth. This one told me it was two miles away. I sped up to fifty-five, the posted speed limit, and took in my surroundings.

On both sides of the road, cleared pastures full of yellow, dead grass stretched far as I could see. Clusters of Black Angus cows clustered around watering tanks, waving their skinny tails against the horseflies. The land was empty. There wasn't even a convenience store. No man's land.

"Life is about taking chances. Sometimes we jump out of choice. Sometimes it's out of necessity." Mysti glanced at a slip of paper sitting in her lap. "Your part-time bartending gig, working for those bikers, can't pay much."

It didn't. Last month, after I paid for gas to drive out there and back, it paid the light bill and the propane bill. I imagined I'd have the high-speed Internet or the satellite TV cut off before too much longer.

"I'm guessing you don't have too many other options." Mysti squeezed my shoulder, maybe to let me know she meant no harm.

"You're right. The best offer I've gotten came from Benny Longstreet as his personal assistant." I grimaced, reliving the rage I felt when he asked me to come work for him, offered with a lewd wink. I knew what he wanted my assistance doing. *Not in this lifetime, donkey boy.* I'd rather eat boiled raccoon asshole, but I knew I needed paying work. Mysti's help in turning my ability to communicate with the spirit world into money was my last chance. No matter how much sense it made, I still felt like a charlatan. I never imagined it would come to this.

"See the white billboard up there?" Mysti tapped me and pointed. "Pull off in front of it. Griff wanted us to see it before we came into town."

The flaking white billboard winked in the distance. I squinted to read the faded black writing covering it but was still too far away. Sensing movement in my peripheral vision, I took my eyes off the road. Out here in North Texas farm country, hitting an animal might mean hitting a horse, a cow, or a deer. The impact could very well kill us.

At first, my mind rejected what I saw. Then a ringing buzzed in my ears. It spread until my whole head hummed with it. My stomach tried to climb out of my body via my throat. I grunted. What I saw was too weird for words.

A family of four stood on the side of the road. Mother, father, and two kids. Each member of the family wore a bloodstained burlap bag over his head. The bags had no eyeholes and were tied at the neck. The smallest member of the burlap bag head family wore a cute white dress with sunflowers on it. The dress bore dirt stains with blood dripping from its ruffled hem. She raised her hand to wave at me. Somewhere in another part of my brain a child's voice screamed in agony and fear. Sweat popped out all over me as I took in her horror and pain.

Mysti half turned to me. "Peri Jean, girl, it's right up here." She took one look at the expression on my face and leaned forward so she could see out the driver's side window. She turned back to me, lines etched into her forehead and her mouth open in horror. She saw it too. Mysti started to speak but something else caught her attention. Her eyes got even wider.

"Watch out," she screamed.

I jerked my attention back to the road and yanked the wheel. The bumper of Mysti's brand new Toyota Camry barely missed a dude riding his tractor in the middle of the fucking road. I jerked the wheel hard, hitting the gravel shoulder and fishtailing. We slid to a stop less than a foot from a barbed wire fence. I sat there gasping, heart jackhammering in my chest.

The farmer stopped his tractor in the middle of the road. He shook his fist and yelled, "The hell you doing? Slow down!"

I ignored him, closed my eyes, and took a deep breath. The calm crowded out the fear still racing through me. I opened my eyes again. In front of us was the billboard where Mysti wanted us to stop.

"See?" I turned to her. "Here we are."

My friend had her hand pressed to her chest, her eyes still wide and spooked. She shook her head at my attempt to lighten the situation.

I turned my attention to the billboard.

My daughter went missing March 28, 1980. Her name is Susan Lynn Franklin. Susie was born December 18, 1962, has blond hair and blue eyes, 5'2" and weighs 98 lbs. The State Police said she's a runaway, but I don't believe that. If you have any information, please contact Margaret (Meg) Franklin at the following address or phone number.

"This is who your PI friend wants us to look for?" I nudged Mysti.

"You know what I know," Mysti said. "Griffin Reed has his quirks, and not telling about a case until he can talk to me face to face is one of them."

Not for the first time, I took note of the way Mysti said "Griffin Reed." It made me think their relationship consisted of more than professional interest. I held back a smirk and read over the sign again. This girl, Susie Franklin, had been missing for over thirty-five years. Why try to find her after all that time? In spite of my new job jitters, I felt a little spark of curiosity.

The farmer turned his tractor around and parked it across the road from us. *Oh, boy. He wants to chew us out.* I didn't take being chewed out graciously.

The guy got off his tractor and hitched up his plain black pants, probably Dickie's. He waited for an eighteen-wheeler to pass. The wind from it ruffled his thick white hair. He crossed the road, the shine from his black work shoes catching the dull sun. I unbuckled my seatbelt and got out of the car, waiting until he got close enough to hear before I spoke.

"I sure am sorry. I thought I saw"—I paused and searched my mind for an appropriate substitute—"an animal about to dart out on the road. Been driving for a couple of hours, and I'm tired." Truth was, I was always tired these days. It plagued me like a cold I couldn't quite shake. If this old feller copped an attitude, I might give him something to remember me by. We stared at each other a few minutes. I tried to keep my expression humble and contrite. Really, I did.

"It's all right. Anywhere near that curve is always a risk." He squinted his eyes and stared at me, cocking his head to one side and glancing right at the spot where I saw the burlap head family. "You're white as a sheet, girl. You sure you're all right?"

"I'm fine. Shook up is all." I rubbed my hand over my cheek and found it covered with a clammy layer of sweat.

"Where you coming from?" He asked the question the way a country person does, completely sure of his right to know.

"South of here. Tyler."

He nodded. "You headed into Nazareth? Or going all the way to Sandal?"

"Nazareth." Mysti joined us.

The man took in Mysti's handkerchief style skirt of many colors and her fringed shawl. He raised his eyebrows and glanced down at the leather Jesus shoes she wore. He smiled.

"Heard Meggy Franklin hired some folks to find out what happened to her Susie. Y'all them?"

"Sure are. I'm Mysti Whitebyrd, and this is my associate, Peri Jean Mace." Mysti put on a big, toothy smile, but I saw the uncertainty in her brown colored eyes. She held out her hand to the old man. He took it, gave it a token squeeze, and dropped it like it might contaminate him.

"Lewis DeVoss." He glanced at Mysti and frowned before turning his gaze on me, the weight of it drifting down to my torn-up jeans and worn-out cowboy boots. He nodded, almost to himself. "Own this whole stretch o' land, both sides of the road."

"Lotta land." I didn't know what else to say. "Cows? Or crops too?"

"Mostly the cows," DeVoss said. "Some hay."

"How'd you know we were here to work the Susie Franklin case?" Mysti asked.

"Nazareth ain't got more'n eight hundred souls calling it home. We're all related or we've known each other so long we might as well be. Not much stays secret 'round these parts." He wiped at his nose. "Besides, I felt bad for poor Meggy Franklin. She's good folks."

I grew up in a small town. Maybe not as small as Nazareth, but I knew all about the way secrets don't stay secrets. This open landscape and the big sky hanging over it seemed like it wouldn't harbor secrets too happily. Feeling the old man's hard gaze on me, I glanced back at him and recoiled at the intensity of his stare.

"Give you ladies a piece o' advice, you don't mind." He

waited for us to invite him to continue, like country folks do, his arms crossed over his chest.

"Please," I said.

"Don't stay here in Nazareth too long. And don't go in no abandoned buildings. We got a dangerous element 'round here. Outsiders got a way of disappearing." His speech made, he turned to go.

"Thanks, Mr. DeVoss," I called after him, throwing a glance at Mysti. She needed to thank him too, in case we had to talk to him again. I found her frozen, her hands hanging limply at her sides, the way city people get when something scares them. DeVoss half-turned and gave me a little wave and smile. The smile never touched his eyes.

Mysti turned back to the car, but I stepped close and grabbed her arm and shook my head. Keeping my voice low, I said, "Don't let him know he spooked you. Wait for him to leave." I elbowed her. "Try not to look so damn scared."

I might as well have told her to hold her breath and count to six thousand. Everything about Mysti, from her posture to the expression on her face, screamed fear. *Can't win 'em all.*

We stood there in front of the old billboard like it held the answers to the world and watched Lewis DeVoss amble to his tractor. The old man took his time climbing up and turning the thing on. He turned back for one last wave. Then he was gone, and I strolled toward the car. Mysti tried hard not to run, and she almost made it, only jogging the last couple of steps.

"He's just unhappy a couple of outsiders are poking around," I told her.

"I know." She kept her gaze fastened on the road, jaw working. Having seen her like this a few other times, I knew to keep my mouth shut.

I got the car back on the road and drove slowly, hoping not to run into Lewis DeVoss again. We passed an overgrown rest stop with a chain across the driveway. A closed sign and a no trespassing sign hung from the chain. The hair stood up on the back of my neck. The old man's words came back to me. *Don't go in no abandoned buildings. Outsiders got a way of disappearing.*

I was glad to see the green city limits sign for Nazareth, Texas. The population listed on the sign said seven hundred fifty-seven. DeVoss had been close to right.

"This road goes straight through town." Mysti regained some of her composure. She set the cellphone on her lap and tapped on its screen. "The motel's after we pass through."

We drove through downtown Nazareth. Not much to see. The weather-beaten, faded buildings housed a few antique shops, a dollar store, and a couple of diners. Nobody walked the streets, other than a stray dog so skinny his ribs and hip bones showed. I slowed to let him pass in front of us and was struck by the feeling of being watched. I twisted in my seat, casting my gaze about, until a car came up behind us and I had to start moving again.

"This is a creepy damn place," Mysti muttered, almost to herself. "Wonder how Griff is faring here."

Again I heard the lilt in her voice when she spoke his

name. Despite my unease, I smiled. The motel, a single row of about ten rooms set a few hundred yards off the road, came up, and I pulled into the driveway. This place didn't look much better than the rest of Nazareth. The bricks needed a good pressure washing, and the asphalt parking lot was buckled and cracked. The rooms would either be so nasty they made our skin crawl or rundown but clean. I prayed for the latter and pulled into a parking place.

Here we go, I thought. I had to do the best I could and stuff my worries down deep. I hoped it was enough to impress Griffin Reed.

———

I stood in front of the car and smoked while Mysti checked us in. She emerged from the motel office holding an actual brass key. I dug my wallet out of my bag and opened it.

"No, I told you expenses are on me." Mysti walked down the single row of rooms until she came to number eight. She used the key to open the door, and the smell of old carpet rolled out to greet us.

"I'll get our bags." Maybe Mysti would leave the door open to let the room air out. I lugged our two suitcases into the room and found Mysti kissing—and I mean really kissing—a tall, wiry guy with short, slicked-down black hair and one of those sexy stubble beards. His slim cut slacks and suit jacket clashed comically with Mysti's hippie wear. I tried to back quietly out of the room, but the guy, whom I assumed was Griffin Reed, saw me and pulled away from Mysti.

"You're Peri Jean?" He held out one long-fingered hand. His fingernails had been buffed to a shine.

"Nice to you meet you, Griffin." I returned his hard handshake. He grinned. "Sorry to walk in on you guys." And I was. I missed having someone to kiss. Especially the way Mysti kissed Griffin.

"No worries, and call me Griff. My father was Griffin." He grabbed Mysti's suitcase from me and set it on the bed nearest the door. His knowing the right one amused me more than it should have, and I had to bite my cheek not to smile on my way to putting my suitcase on the bed nearest the bathroom. "Not too many places to eat in Nazareth, but I'll take y'all to an early supper. Give you ten minutes to freshen up. Meet me in the parking lot. We'll ride together." Griff gave me another smile and left the room, closing the door quietly behind him.

"I'm sorry I didn't tell you we were a thing." Mysti opened her suitcase and grabbed a little plastic zippered bag. "I was sort of afraid you wouldn't want to come, and I wanted you to do this with me so you could see how satisfying it is to make money with your gift."

You mean my curse? I already knew not to say those words to Mysti. They pushed her hot button.

"Why on earth would I not want to meet your boyfriend?" I saw an ashtray sitting on the particle board dresser and took out my cigarettes and showed them to Mysti. She nodded and went into the bathroom and turned on the light. I lit up and followed her, pulling myself up to sit on the long sink vanity.

"Because you're lonely, whether you want to admit it or not." She glanced up from applying her lip gloss and raised her eyebrows. "Plus, he's not really my boyfriend. Commitment issues, I think."

"Too bad. He's cute." I winked at her.

"He really is." She giggled and finished putting on her makeup. "Griff'll want to work after supper. We might be interviewing people. Make yourself presentable."

I touched up my makeup and brushed my chin-length hair, staring hard at the black for strands of gray, but didn't change out of my worn-in jeans and beat-up cowboy boots. I bet I'd fit in better than Griff and Mysti did.

We found Griff standing next to a new gray SUV, smoking a cigarillo. He stubbed it out and hurried to open the door for Mysti. Without asking where we wanted to go, he drove us to a diner called Family Home Cooking. The sign out front promised all we could eat fried catfish. We had to circle the full lot several times before someone pulled out, and we snagged their spot.

Griff opened the door for Mysti and went around the SUV's back and pulled out a black canvas messenger bag. We walked into the restaurant, a large, open room lined with booths. Tables created an obstacle course through the middle of the room. Every head in the restaurant turned to stare at us.

Most of Family Home Cooking's patrons wore about the same thing I did. Mysti and Griff stood out like a pair of chess pieces on a checkerboard. A young woman wearing a tight, white T-shirt with Family Home Cooking emblazoned on the front hurried over to us.

"Folks, there's a booth about to open up over in that corner." She raised one arm to point, and her shirt pulled up, exposing a fish-belly white roll of fat hanging over her jeans. She left the T-shirt the way it was and went on about her business, leaving us to stand like vultures while the elderly couple occupying the booth she pointed out slowly stood and gathered their belongings and finally sauntered off, the woman staring hard at us as they passed. We slid into the booth even though the other couple's ketchup-smeared plates and half-empty tea glasses still sat on it.

"What y'all want to drink?" A middle-aged woman appeared next to the booth and took out an order pad.

"Do you have beer?" Griff didn't sound or look too hopeful.

"Nowhere in Nazareth has beer. Hall County's dry as a bone." She delivered the speech in a bored monotone. "We got iced-tea, sweet or unsweet and all kinds of Coke."

"Water?" I didn't trust the tea, and soft drinks were too sweet for me.

She scribbled on her notepad without answering.

Mysti and Griff ordered unsweet tea.

"Catfish buffet's all there is. Go over to the steam counter and tell 'em what you want. Price is \$11.99 per person." She turned to walk away.

"Ma'am?" Griff called after her. She turned back, her mouth still set in the same grim line. "Can we get the table cleaned off?"

She heaved out the kind of sigh only the truly put

upon know how to deliver. "I'll have it done by the time you get back with your plates."

Turned out, she didn't and had to rush over and remove the plates and glasses while we stood there holding our food. Griff had to ask her not to take away the drinks she'd brought for us. We ate our food in silence. When we finished, Griff ordered coffee and pulled a laptop and a few files out of his messenger bag.

"As you probably guessed from the billboard, we're here to look into the disappearance of Susan Franklin." He pushed a button to power up his laptop and pushed it against the wall so it faced outward. He tapped a few buttons and a grainy newspaper photo of a smiling girl looked out at us.

"Why after so many years?" I stared at the face, knowing she was probably dead, probably a horrible death.

"Let's let this young lady serve our coffee, and I'll tell you a little story."

The girl with the muffin top set out a thermal carafe of coffee. Then she dug in her apron and set down the bill. Rather than leaving, she stood, staring at us expectantly, until Griff picked up the bill, dug in his wallet, and handed her some bills with a smile. "Keep the change."

The girl's small mouth dropped open, and she drew in a deep breath. "Thanks a lot, mister." She made a big show of dragging the little sugar holder to the middle of the table and giving us a toothy smile before she walked off. Griff said nothing until she was out of earshot.

"Susie was a senior at Nazareth High. Good student,

track runner. She dropped out of high school midway through the fall semester of her senior year." Griff poured coffee into thick off-white mugs. "We have an appointment to speak with her mother in a few minutes. I'm going to let her tell you why Susie quit school."

After the ordeal at the billboard outside Nazareth, Griff's insistence on not telling us the whole story grated on me. "Why don't you just tell us?"

"Good question. What happened to Susan Franklin was fairly well-documented in the news media. It was a huge scandal." He stopped to take a sip of his coffee. "But I've never heard her mother tell her version of events. Since neither you nor Mysti have heard any of Susie's story, I'm hoping one of you will hear anything I skim over because it sounds familiar. The small details are what breaks cases like this wide open."

I was tired of being in the dark, but I nodded. I'd get paid either way.

"Now let's get down to what I really want the two of you to know. I found out about Susie Franklin while looking into another missing person's case." Griff pulled a sheet of paper from his file and slid it across the table to Mysti and me. A picture of a smiling girl took up most of the sheet. Underneath her picture were the words "$150,000 reward for any information on the whereabouts of Kaitlyn Summers who went missing September 16, 2011."

There's the real money and the reason he's willing to hire not one, but two, paranormal princesses.

"I called the number on the flyer." Griff leaned forward, chest pressing into the hard edge of the table, intent on his story and earnest about telling it. "Talked to Kaitlyn's father. Nice guy. He said the last time he talked to Kaitlyn, she had turned off the main road because she saw a sign for a rest stop. She apparently needed a restroom."

I shivered at the mention of the rest stop. Surely Kaitlyn didn't stop at the one Mysti and I passed earlier. It looked too run down and the vegetation too overgrown to have been open in 2011. *Stay out of abandoned buildings.*

Griff took in my shiver. "She lost signal not long afterward, and he never spoke to her again."

"Law enforcement find anything?" My ex was the new sheriff of the county where I lived. I learned during our time together that law enforcement got involved in everything.

"Not even her car. Her cellphone last pinged off a tower near here." Griff stopped talking as a family of four passed our booth. "Thing is, when I started looking into Summers's disappearance, I learned something funny. Somewhere between forty and fifty people have gone missing in the last thirty years, within a twenty-mile radius of where we're sitting." He tapped the table for emphasis.

Outsiders have a way of disappearing. The skin on my back crawled.

"Something's going on here, has been going on for a while. If I can, I intend to find out what it is." Griff glanced between Mysti and me. "The reward'll be nice, but this'll help a lot of families find closure."

"And get your name on the map." I smiled to let him know I didn't think ill of him for it.

"You bet." He pointed one long finger at me. "Get you ladies on the map, too. Maybe lead to some business."

He and Mysti high-fived. Watching them made me feel good. Even if Griff wouldn't commit, they seemed to have a good deal going. Another thing I learned from my abortive relationship with Dean Turgeau was the importance of recognizing when things worked and ending them right away if they didn't.

"Do you think whatever's doing this is something paranormal?" It sounded more like human evil to me, like we might be sitting in a serial killer's favorite hunting spot.

"I just don't know." Griff caressed his stubble beard and shook his head. "Mysti told me you're a powerful medium. I hoped, if nothing else, you'd be able to contact Susie's spirit."

The burlap head family popped back into my mind, and I quickly told Griff about seeing them. He shuffled through his papers and showed me a newspaper report about a family moving cross-country in the days before cellphones who vanished somewhere between the Louisiana border and Dallas.

"This them?" He tapped a photo of a family smiling in front of an old RV.

"I didn't see their faces." I picked up the paper and scanned through it, noticing a PI hired by the family found a truck stop waitress north of Tyler who remembered them coming into the place where she worked. She said the little girl's dress had sunflowers on it. I handed the paper back to Griff. It trembled along with my hand.

The middle-aged waitress marched over to our table

and loomed over us like a schoolmarm who'd caught a bunch of kids smoking behind the wood shop.

"We close in ten minutes." She bit out the words as though she'd have rather screamed them and marched away.

"We need to get to Margaret Franklin's anyway," Griff told us. Mysti and I helped him pack up his things and got out before Miss Meanypants returned.

End of Sample

Rest Stop is available to purchase from your favorite bookseller.
ISBN: 978-1-947462-09-0

Visit Catie's website:
www.catierhodes.com

Find Catie on Facebook:
http://www.facebook.com/catierhodesauthor

Follow Catie on Book Bub.
https://www.bookbub.com/authors/catie-rhodes

Join Catie's email list:
http://smarturl.it/lrdenewsletter

ABOUT THE AUTHOR

Catie Rhodes writes southern-fried urban fantasy with a strong dose of horror and a side dish of humor.

She is the author of the Peri Jean Mace Ghost Thrillers. Her short stories have appeared in *Tales From The Mist, Let's Scare Cancer to Death, and Allegories of the Tarot.*

Catie was born and raised behind the pine curtain in East Texas. She comes from a family of world champion liars.

Their tall tales molded Catie into a purveyor of her own brand of lies and legends. One day, she found the courage to start writing down her stories. It changed her life forever.

Catie Rhodes lives steps from the Sam Houston National Forest with her long-suffering husband and her armpit terrorist of a little dog.

Find Catie online:
www.catierhodes.com